THE PURPLE HAZE

Book 1: The Western Lands and All That Really Matters

ANDREW EINSPRUCH

Cover design by Maria Spada of Maria Spada Design.

Editing by Vanessa of Red Dot Scribble.

Proofreading by Abigail of Bothersome Words.

Layout by Andrew Einspruch of Wild Pure Heart.

ISBN: 978-0-9806272-2-0

DEDICATION

To Billie and Tamsin

Everything of greatest value that I've learned, I've learned from you.

THE PROPOSAL

"**P**lease, please, marry my son," implored the chipmunk.

Princess Eloise Hydra Gumball III, Future Ruler and Heir to the Western Lands and All That Really Matters, sat on the Listening Throne in the ornate Receiving Room of Castle de Brague and took two precise sips of her haggleberry tea, trying not to let her surprise show. She straightened, still holding the cup and saucer. "I... I... Truly, Seer Maybelle? Jerome?"

Seer Maybelle de Chipmunk's delicate whiskers drooped, and Eloise worried she'd been too harsh. "Yes, Princess," she said. "Jerome."

"Goodness." Eloise sipped again, buying a moment. "I haven't really thought about marriage much, but if I may say so, I rather thought I'd end up with a prince of some description. You know, someone more in the direction of a human, perhaps? But, please. I'm happy to hear you out."

The chipmunk clasped her dainty paws in front of her and began an obviously well-rehearsed plea. "My son, Jerome Abernatheen de Chipmunk, is a good boy, as you well know. And believe me, I am aware of his flaws as only a mother can be." She extended her claws to enumerate. "He's forgetful. He's awkward in small groups. He's awkward in large groups. He's prone to wafting off into the La La Realms. His dress sense veers unpredictably and inexplicably from one garish color to another. He knows far, far too much about the musical plays of Lyndia Thrind. He has a penchant for babbling about nothing when stressed. Then there's the whole unfortunate thing with jesters."

Eloise nodded. Twice. "One cannot characterize that description as unfair, Seer Maybelle."

"But Princess Eloise, I've searched the future with every tool I have, methods common and obscure, profound and profane, some passed down from my grandmothers a hundred generations removed. I have stared into the flame of the Burning Fungus, scanned dregs of haggle-berry tea, and listened to the sounds of the Oracle Bellbirds. I've drawn the Twigs of Fate from the Bag of Kismet and sought wisdom in the gurgling mud of the Elder's Swamp. It embarrasses me to tell you, because it took a week to get the stench out of my fur, but I've even taken counsel with Gordon the Noisome, whose twitching earlobes have a strangely accurate predictive quality."

Gordon the Noisome? Wow. Seer Maybelle was serious about this. Standing close enough to Gordon to see his earlobes twitch was a sacrifice no one should have to make.

"Everywhere I look, Princess, I see that my son's destiny is to be by your side. I'm, I'm..." Seer Maybelle's voice slid down to a whisper. "I'm sorry, but I believe you must wed."

Eloise took another sip of her tea, then set down the cup. The saucer clinked on the marble side table, which matched the marble walls of the Receiving Room. Eloise carefully moved the cup and saucer so they were in the exact middle of the table on a serviette whose edges were equidistant from the table's. She placed the spoon on the saucer so it lined up with the serviette and the table. She would rather have put it across the top of the cup, but that would be taking it too far, given that Seer Maybelle was with her.

Until three years before, when Court began demanding so much of her time, Jerome had been her best friend. For a decade, they'd been inseparable, whether exploding whifflenut pies in Cookery and Cuisine class (which she enjoyed despite the mess), plotting paint dart campaigns in Weapons and Stratagems (also fun despite potential mess), ridiculing each other's poetry in Arts and Elocution, or creating the most elaborate contraptions in Engineering and Constructions. Inseparable, until court life had done the inevitable—separated them.

Eloise understood Jerome like few did. He was a klutz. A clever klutz. A verbose klutz. A well-read, musically literate, historically curious klutz. But definitely a klutz. She loved him, klutziness and all, but like a brother and nothing else. Even ignoring matters of species, marrying him was out of the question. That's just not what she felt for him.

The problem was Seer Maybelle de Chipmunk.

Seer de Chipmunk was the Western Lands' visionary. There was never, ever any escaping what the matronly chipmunk foretold. But if Eloise had learned anything in Oracles and Insights (other than that Jerome showed not the slightest hint of divinatory talent, despite his family line), it was that there was *always* another interpretation, another angle.

Seer Maybelle shifted from foot to foot. It was difficult for her to stand like this for so long, but pride and Protocol demanded it. With a quiet rasp, she cleared her throat, preparing to sell, somehow, what was ridiculously unsellable. Her son, short, nervous, and—there was no escaping it—a chipmunk, was completely unsuited to the willowy, athletic, 16-year-old, dark-haired and darker-eyed human. Seer Maybelle opened her mouth, but Eloise held up a finger and stopped her.

"I have an idea."

"Yes, Princess Eloise?"

"I shall name Jerome Abernatheen de Chipmunk my champion."

Seer Maybelle stood gape-mouthed, then closed her eyes and scanned the Unseen. When she opened them again, she graced Princess Eloise with a radiant chipmunk smile. She nodded, amazed that such insight could come, once again, from someone so young.

Mrs de Chipmunk left the Receiving Room lighter of heart than she'd felt in weeks.

Eloise draped the Attention Cape over the back of the Listening Throne and wondered how in the name of Çalaht she would ever convince her parents to allow her decision.

2

NOT A MUSHROOM

"**Y**ou want me to be your mushroom?"

Jerome stood in his best Court suit, ridiculous green and blue pantaloons with a shirt that garishly mirrored the pattern of the pants. His tail fiddled with his ruffled collar.

"No, not *champignon*. Champion." Princess Eloise sat on the Speaking Throne in the warm brightness of the Declaiming Room.

"Because it sounded like you wanted me to be your mushroom."

"I most clearly said 'champion.' I'm talking about naming you my champion. It has nothing to do with mushrooms, and you know it." The wordplay was an old joke between them, and they'd thought it was funny when they were five. That he was trying to use it now showed how unhappy he was with what was coming.

"It sounded a lot like..."

"Jerome."

There it was. The Tone. He always thought of it as "the Tone," ever since he first heard it when they were standing outside the headmistress' door, about to be punished for rappelling upside-down on the Skills Course instead of polishing practice blades in the vault at the Bureau of Bladed Weapons. Jerome had tried to convince Eloise to bolt with him and avoid the upbraiding they were about to get. But she'd used the Tone, telling him to stay and face it.

And so he had. Jerome was no match for the Tone.

Eloise stood up, stretching to her full height. "I shall ask it again. Jerome Abernatheen de Chipmunk. Would it be acceptable to you if I should name you my champion tomorrow at Court?"

He'd known the request was coming. Well, it was a "request" in format, but it wasn't like he could say, "Thanks, awfully, but no thanks. I'd be rubbish at that." His mother had warned him of how Princess Eloise interpreted her prognostication. His obvious, flagrant, and whole-hearted unsuitability seemed not to matter.

"Ellipsoid, I—"

"In the Declaiming Room, it is best you not use nicknames. You should refer to me formally."

With that, Jerome was sunk. When she went all formal, there was no changing her mind.

"Please pardon my familiarity, Princess Eloise. Can we please cover what you'd expect of me, should I have the honor to serve as your champion?"

"Come on, Jerome. It hasn't been that long since we covered this in Protocols and Procedures."

"But, Princess Eloise, champions are always massive blokes or buff gals with..." He mimed a huge, bulging bicep. "They're highly trained warriors. At best, I am a highly trained worrier. Champions have a talent for weapons and tactics. You are more likely to save my bushy tail than the other way around."

Eloise crooked a finger. "Please follow me, Jerome Abernatheen de Chipmunk." She sailed toward the open doorway, careful to avoid stepping on any tile cracks.

Keeping an appropriate distance behind her (which felt strange, since for so many years he'd ridden on her shoulder), Jerome followed her out of the Declaiming Room, through the Hall of Authority and out across the Culpability Courtyard, once used for floggings, but now devoted to hockey sacking games. When they went left at the Arched Arch, he knew exactly where she was headed—the Salon des Champions (which they'd always called the Mush Room).

It was cooler in there than he remembered. And unusually empty. Adorning its walls were hundreds of paired paintings. Each depicted a champion, the Western Lands' bravest of the brave, next to the royal they served. There were generations worth, heading back to Townshend Bellicose Shinglehefter, the first champion, and Agnes Delion Frostbite Gumball, the first monarch of the Western Lands and All That Really Matters to take the Gumball name.

⚜

"Oh, nuts," Jerome thought. He'd have to get a portrait made. He hated how he looked on canvas.

As they walked, Eloise pointed to images of several champions who strayed from the predominant pattern of muscle and weaponry. Some were lithe, others bookish. More than a few were non-human (mainly tigers and horses).

Eloise stopped in front of a seemingly random frame. "Being champion is about character as much as strength. Ability, as much as agility. Take Shauna Haliburton Splinter here. She lost an eye and a kidney in a freak kumquat harvesting accident, but served Queen Joan Mendacity Penultimate Gumball for a dozen years."

They moved along the wall. "Or Gitride de Loamy. Notice anything about his legs?"

"They're missing."

"Technically, I think they're strapped behind him, being boneless. But yes. Not much happening in the leg department. Yet he saved Queen Yvonne Octave Barbell Gumball IV's life over and over during his two months of service, relying solely on his skill in hand-to-hand combat."

They walked past another three dozen perfect specimens of championhood, then stopped again. "Or how about Melveeta the Elusive here?" This painting was a landscape, not a portrait like the others. Jerome shrugged, and Eloise pointed to a faint human-shaped shadow emerging from the darkness behind a tree. "Melveeta served her sister, my several-times-great-great-grandmother, Queen Gwendolyn the Irritable. She held the role for decades, and one rarely saw her. Melveeta was said to have a strong magic for insulating herself against danger. We're not even 100 percent sure what she looked like, or what became of her. But several-times-great-great-grandmother Gwendolyn's diary notes are full of praise for her champion's efficiency, cunning, strategy, and loyalty." Eloise pointed to a light source in the foreground that seemed to come from outside the frame. "This brightness represents the queen, somehow. You'd think if Gwendolyn was so irritable, they'd have portrayed her with a darkness."

"The portraits are painted while the royal is alive," said Jerome. "Perhaps the artist did not think that approach conducive to longevity."

"Hmmm. She was a tough one, for sure." They both turned to the portrait of Gwendolyn Cowpatch Excelsior Gumball. There was little family resemblance to Eloise, except maybe in the eyes. Gwendolyn was squat and spreading, swathed in royal blues and weighed down by finery. She sat on the throne that was now in the Receiving Room, an unnamed greyhound to her left, and an unnamed manx to her right. On her lap was a glowing green stone or jewel, which was supposed to be the long-lost, and almost certainly fictional, Star of Whatever.

Standing side-by-side, Eloise and Jerome stared at the painting, drawn into Gwendolyn's world.

"Back When," Jerome murmured.

"Yes. She reigned at the end of Back When."

"I often wonder what it was like."

"Back when there was strong magic? Me too. I wonder if I would have had it."

"Who knows? Not everyone did."

"No, they didn't." Eloise took a step closer, and looked at the light part of the painting. "Do you think magic was hard to use Back When?"

"Maybe. But it was common enough, so maybe not."

"I wonder how having it everywhere affected the way people lived. Day-to-day, I mean. We read about it in Histories and Hearsay, but that's just words. After so many years, what Back When was really like is just gone."

"We still have weak magic around. My mother's prognostications. Your throwing."

Eloise shrugged. "It seems so pale in comparison. A yawn to what used to be a roar."

"Oh, very poetic." Jerome turned toward her. He stood on his two back legs, straightened, and cleared his throat. "Princess Eloise—"

"We're out of the Declaiming Room, Jerrific. You can relax."

Jerome remained upright and formal. "Princess Eloise, if I may speak plainly..."

"No, Jerome. I don't think so," said the princess. "Look. You will accompany me on official business. You will stand during formal occasions as my protector. You'll speak for me if I am insulted. You'll give advice. You shouldn't have to fight or anything, because almost certainly Guard Lorch Lacksneck will be around." She reached out and gave him a gentle squeeze on the shoulder. "You'll do what you're good at: think and talk. Preferably, but not inevitably, in that order."

"But, El—"

"Please, Jerome. Your mother saw it. And I'm asking you, because you are my friend and I can't think of anyone I'd rather have."

Jerome felt the flush in his cheeks. "Of course, Princess Eloise. When you put it that way, it would be an honor to serve. I most humbly accept." He bowed formally, with just enough paw waggling for her to know there was an irony to it. "Just don't call me your mushroom."

3

MORE SPANGLY BITS

Princess Johanna Umgotteswillen Gumball, Eloise's twin sister, younger by 17 minutes, humphed at her reflection. "More spangly bits." She turned to Nesther de Duck, her handmaid. "I think this dress needs more spangly bits."

"Yes, Princess," said Nesther. "If I may say so, perhaps the dress could stay as it is, but we accessorize with the gold brooch your father gave you. The one with the two hummingbirds. Or maybe the silver toad ear cuff that your uncle gave you."

Johanna pulled taut the front of her dress to examine her neck. You could barely see any scarring from the Thorning Ceremony three years before. "Let's try the brooch. I'll save the ear cuff for Uncle Doncaster's visit at the end of the week."

"Yes, Princess. Do we know yet why he's coming?"

"No. Two is being somewhat obtuse about it."

Nesther pursed her bill as far as it would go, which was not far, and said, "Yes, Princess." She did not like it when Johanna referred to the monarch that way. "The queen" was her preference, and "my mother" was fine. But anything else struck her as a trifle unseemly, and "Two" skated far too close to disrespect.

The duck waddled over to the jewelry box, pecked open the lock, and fished the brooch from the tangle of necklaces, bangles, and gilded finery within. Tidiness in her chamber had never been Johanna's strong suit. She seemed to save it all for her garden. The girl could grow a crocus to make poets weep.

Nesther de Duck hailed from a line of mallards who'd served at Court for more years than she had feathers. She had been assigned to Johanna when the princess turned 14 and had gone through the Thorning Ceremony with her sister. Nesther had been the one to remove the ceremonial thorns from the young maiden's neck, and to rub in the Wisdom Salve. She often wondered if perhaps she had not used enough Wisdom Salve that day. Maybe a smidge more might have prevented some of the bitterness that became so pronounced as Johanna's unhappiness took root.

Nesther truly loved the willful, clever teen. Loved her despite herself. Loved her through the tantrums and raging, the petty needling and grand jealousies.

There was no grander jealousy than the one Johanna harbored toward Eloise. Being second born was rarely easy, and was even less so when the second born happened to be a twin. Usually there was a gap of a year or two at least, to help ease the genuine unfairnesses that Protocol bestowed on the first born. Some second borns dealt with it by becoming confidants. Some were even named champions. But supporting her sister as confidant or champion would never be Johanna's way. The twins had not been close for years. Come to think of it, not since the Thorning Ceremony, when Eloise was presented as Future Ruler and Heir to the Western Lands and All That Really Matters, and Johanna had been presented as "her sister"—not even "second born."

The tears that night had not just been from the thorns.

Nesther brought the brooch to Johanna, who took it with a distracted nod (as close to a "thank you" as the duck ever received), pinned it to her dress, and considered its effect in the mirror. "Not quite right."

"Scarf?"

"Good idea."

"Perhaps the turquoise one with the lichen and conch pattern?"

"Let's try it."

It would have been faster for Nesther to fly to the wardrobe, but that would have breached Protocol. Johanna's tolerance for Protocol breaches was notoriously low. She armed and armored herself with Protocol, clasping to her breast the very source of everything Johanna felt was wrong in her life. Princess Johanna knew the *Livre de Protocol* and the dozen volumes of Protocol Commentaries better than anyone. She wielded this knowledge like a weapon—sometimes like a mace, sometimes like a razordisc, sometimes like a tiny vial of tinctured haggleberry—depending on which approach provided her the most benefit.

So Nesther walked across the room, slipped the scarf into a linen bag, and dragged it back, being careful not to snag it on anything. Johanna spent the time running a thick porcupine-needle comb through her tangle of hair. The comb hurt, but it was the only thing that had any chance of making it through Johanna's tight curls, one of the few obvious traits she shared with her twin.

Another nod, and Johanna reached for the bag. She wrapped the scarf around her shoulders, pinned it with the brooch, and considered her reflection again. The brooch caught the light, adding the flair Johanna had sought. Nesther saw a frown settle on Johanna's face. So It was a "yes" then.

"That should be all until after dinner, Nesther."

"Yes, Princess. Please convey my best to the queen and king."

"Of course," said Johanna.

But Nesther de Duck knew she wouldn't. That was one part of Protocol Johanna always seemed to let slip.

✌ 4 ✌

A STONE AND A STONER

To say that Queen Eloise Hydra Gumball II and her husband King Chafed were beloved in the Western Lands and All That Really Matters was a bit like saying that olives were beloved by Eastern Landers. It was true, but it did not tell the whole, fanatical story.

Eastern Landers prided themselves on having more olive species than any other land, more ways to turn raw olives into something you could actually eat, and more dishes where olives took the main stage than any other foodstuff that grew on that side of the Adequate Wall of the Realms. Eastern Landers once used olives as currency, and they still crowned their royalty with olive laurels, traded olive saplings on the black market, and were more likely to talk about the olive harvest than about a hockey sacking championship. Prayers about olives featured prominently at Çalahtic devotional houses each week.

Eastie kids learned to count by putting pitted olives onto their finger-tips, then eating them off one at a time. Decorated jars of olives were presented to women who'd given birth, children who came of age, newlyweds and retirees. When Eastern Landers died, their bodies were washed in olive brine then buried with a mouth full of olives, thus ensuring their safe passage to the afterworld, where they might stand with Çalaht, who, through the olives, would recognize where they were from and consider their soul's fates favorably. Eastern Lander beauties, both male and female, prized being olive-skinned. The people of the Eastern Lands were so olive-obsessed that they didn't even care that their olive compulsions made them the butt of jokes cracked by people in the three-and-a-half realms. They wore their oliveness with blind pride.

And yet, Western Landers loved Queen Eloise Hydra Gumball II and King Chafed even more than that, if perhaps with a tad more dignity. Were it not against Protocol, banners proclaiming the near-saintliness of the royal couple would have flown from every flagpole, washing line, parapet, and awning. Were it not also against Protocol and royal edict, every female child born would be named "Eloise" and every boy "Chafed." (Only the Queen could pass on her name, as she had done with her daughter, and it was a royal privilege she enforced with her full royal powers.) Praise, both to their faces and behind their backs, flowed like the River Thurmond during the wet season. People made pilgrimages to Castle de Brague almost as frequently as they made them to the Sclerotic Wold in The South, the birthplace of Çalaht.

The thing was, such adulation was substantially earned. When Queen Eloise II (affectionately called "Two") ascended the throne, crisis ruled the Western Lands and All That Really Matters. The Queen's mother —Eloise Hydra Gumball I (known with distaste as "One")—had chosen disastrously when it came time to pick a mate, selecting as king a man of stunning beauty, but one who was so venal, closed-minded, and petty that polite society and less-polite Court never spoke of him by name, simply referring to him as "One's Grand Mistake." And yet, One loved him, at least for a while, even if he was incapable of recipro-cating. With time, their discord became whispered common knowl-edge, then overt public enmity. One's stewardship of the realm dwindled, collateral damage to her marital acrimony. Matters of state simply went all driverless-carriage, decisions left unmade as One and One's Grand Mistake spent their time clawing out each other's hearts, both in private and, especially, in public.

Two was the only brightness that sparked from the calamitous union. However, no one knew how bright her light was until she stood in the Declaiming Room wearing the crown as Queen (much too young, most had said). Decisions began to be made, and competently. Two unexpectedly picked out Chafed Motley de Chëëëkflïïint from a roomful of suitors, despite his being from the Half Kingdom north of the Adequate Wall (it had been centuries since a Gumball had wed someone from there). She saw in him what others had missed—a hand worth holding and a mind worth listening to. Chafed happily took on the Queen's name, becoming King Chafed Motley Gumball née de Chëëëkflïïint, and helped Two restore surety to the land.

So yes, they were beloved.

Mostly.

Unsurprisingly, there were some in the queendom who did not hold the queen and king in such high regard.

Which was why dinnertime was always so awkward.

One of the not-so-enthusiastic was Princess Johanna. On a good day, they were Mother and Father. On a not-so-good day, she referred to them as Two and Two-minus, or simply Them (collectively) or One of Them (individually).

The family sat in the private Salon de Gustation, dressed formally, as always, for dinner. As servers offered the opening course (black soybean and hoisin lettuce wraps), it soon became clear that this particular mealtime would head toward a "Them" day. It happened when the Queen said, "The Ceremonies of the Stone of the Ancestors will be this weekend."

Eloise froze, her face blank, her mind racing at the implications.

"Boy, these look scrummy," said King Chafed. He stuffed a lettuce wrap in his mouth, chewed briefly, and swallowed. "Come on, everyone. Dig in."

Johanna set down her fork before it touched any food and glared at her mother. "No."

Queen Eloise let that one slide. "It's why your Uncle Doncaster is visiting. I'd have thought you would have worked that out yourself, given we're so close to your seventeenth birthdays."

"I can't," said Eloise, stricken. "I can't. Mother, don't. Please."

"And why not?" The queen dipped her lettuce wrap into a shallow bowl of tamari and ate it.

"It's unsanitary," said Eloise.

"It's loathsome," added Johanna. "And degrading."

"I can't say I disagree." Queen Eloise skewered another lettuce wrap from her plate. "But it is in the *Livre de Protocol*, plain as day. And the commonness of it appeals to the people. I've decided we may as well get it over with. Your father agrees, don't you dear?"

Chafed, mouth full again, coughed like he'd choked, and gave an "of-course-dear" nod.

Johanna glowered. "No."

Eloise felt fear coagulating in her guts. "Mother, no. Please, you... You know me. I can't."

There was no question the Ceremonies of the Stone of the Ancestors were utterly disgusting from start to finish. The ceremonies had two parts: the Placing of the Stone and the Receiving of the Stone. These were two ends of a symbolic ritual that centered on the Stone of the Ancestors, a polished lapis lazuli the size of a black muscat grape. The Stone of the Ancestors had been passed down through centuries, and could be reliably traced back dozens of generations to Agnes Delion Frostbite Gumball, who created the Ceremonies of the Stone of the Ancestors.

The Placing of the Stone was simple enough. A designated stoner put the Stone of the Ancestors into the mouth of the heir. There it had to stay for three hours. Anyone—literally anyone, from the lowliest ragpicker or wool disperser to the highest noble—was allowed to ask the heir to show them the stone. The heir had to poke out his or her tongue and show it. If the stone happened to fall, it was considered a good omen for the asker. They had permission to pick it up off the ground, kiss it for luck, and hand it back to the stoner, who held it up for all to see, kissed it as well, then put it back in the heir's mouth. At that point, three minutes were added to the tabulated time, and the process was repeated. Ask, show, maybe drop—if so, pick up, kiss, show, kiss, replace. Inevitably, both the heir and the stoner caught some sort of usually non-fatal illness, and if the heir had a bad run or a particularly maladroit tongue, the process could take most of a day.

As repugnant as that all was, it was not the worst part.

Once the three hours plus the aggregated additional time had passed, the stoner rang the Gong of the Stone of the Ancestors. That meant it was time for everyone (save the heir) to sing the "Hymn of the Ceremonies of the Stone of the Ancestors." Then the heir protruded her tongue one last time to show that the Stone of the Ancestors was still there, and then swallowed it.

At this point, there were usually great cheers from the throng gathered in the Hall of Bald Opulence, as there wasn't much longer to go.

The next part of the ceremony was pretty dull—a recitation of names from the Gumball genealogy. Drinks were served, but no snacks. The Stone of the Ancestors sat inside the heir until exactly one hour had passed. At that point, the Gong of the Stone of the Ancestors was rung again, and it was time for the Receiving of the Stone. The stoner ceremoniously offered the heir a flagon, containing an unpleasant combination of emetic herbs, mainly mustard and puke weed, with four teaspoons of salt to ensure the heir's stomach got the message. Inevitably, it did—sometimes as an energetic projection, sometimes as a subdued retch. Either way, the Stone of the Ancestors was brought forth, and it was up to the stoner to directly confirm its reappearance, fishing it out, cleaning it, kissing it one last time, giving it to the heir for one last kiss, and then—at last—holding it aloft and proclaiming the successful Receiving of the Stone. This triggered another round of cheers, followed by a lavish feast, at which the heir sat in the place of honor, even if she did not much feel like eating.

The Ceremonies of the Stone of the Ancestors were wildly popular—partly because of their simplicity, partly because it meant free food (not just at Court, but for everyone in the queendom), partly because it was a fairly rare ritual, which made it novel, and partly because the very baseness of the process helped everyone involved remember that the royals were just people too. The ceremonies were also ripe with symbolism. The Stone of the Ancestors represented a connection to the land and to the lineage. It was a symbol of the heir's willingness to swallow hard problems, endure discomfort for the greater good of the people, and be willing, when called upon, to output tangible results.

But yes, the whole thing was repulsive. Which was why Eloise was heading toward panic, and Johanna was balking. Eloise could almost ignore the thought that so many ancestors before her—including her mother—had had this thing inside them. Almost. What really riled her innards was the very thought of all that dirt getting stuck to the stone from being dropped over and over, and all that slobber from all those people, and who knew if they'd washed recently or not, or if they ever brushed their teeth, and she'd have the stone in her mouth and would have to hold it there, and there'd be all that contact with untold manner of agues. The more her mind dove into the details, the more overwhelmed she felt.

The sound of arguing cut through her thoughts.

"I can promise you I will never be the stoner," said Johanna, voice rising.

"I can promise you that you undoubtedly will be the stoner," replied her mother, less calm now. "This is Protocol that won't be skirted—and certainly not by you."

Eloise looked at her sister, and not for the first time thought, "Why can't you just deal with it?" At least Johanna didn't have to swallow the thing. And it's not like this was some massive surprise. The two had talked about it when they'd first come across it in Protocols and Procedures more than a decade earlier. They'd thought it a sick joke, or an antiquated anachronism. But then, they had thought the same of the Thorning Ceremony.

"Does this truly warrant such complaint?" Chafed gestured with his fork at Johanna. "It's not that big an ask. Just be the stoner and be done with it."

"Oh? It's not a big ask? You're not the one armed with a vomit bucket and a spoon looking for a stupid rock," said Johanna. "If I wasn't her *beloved* twin, 'her sister,' the joy of being the stoner would fall to someone who'd think it an honor."

"True," said the Queen. "But as you're second born and a twin, the honor absolutely goes to you."

"Please, Mother," said Eloise. "Don't make her do it if she doesn't want to."

Johanna turned on her. "Don't you want me to be part of the ceremony? Is this another way I'm not good enough for you?"

The sudden change of direction took Eloise by surprise. "Oh, for the love of Çalaht, you know that's not what I meant."

"Sounds like it. Sounds like you don't think I'm up to the task of poking around in your digestive expulsions."

The queen set down her fork and stood. Everyone stopped what they were doing and stood as well.

The room clattered into silence.

CHAPTER 137 SUB-SECTION (F) 3

Slowly, Queen Eloise walked around the table, pulling a folded fan from a pocket and rapping it on her open left palm once for every step. She stopped behind her daughters' chairs. They had to turn their backs to the table so they could face her. The queen stood a quarter length taller than the twins, but seemed to loom much taller.

"Kneel," she commanded, her voice fiercer for being a whisper.

Both girls dropped to their knees, eyes locked on their mother's feet.

The queen placed the folded fan under Eloise's chin, lifting her face upward. She locked eyes on her daughter. "Princess Eloise, I have more than a passing familiarity with your..." She paused, looking for the right word. "Your habits." Eloise felt the burn of blood rushing to her cheeks. This was not a topic they normally addressed so directly. "You are the heir, and the Ceremonies of the Stone of the Ancestors are part of that. You will simply adjust yourself accordingly. Understood?"

"I..." started Eloise, but at a small, firm gesture from the queen, the protest died in her throat. She lowered her eyes. "Understood."

The queen shifted her attention to her other daughter. "Princess Johanna, the matter of the stoner is made exquisitely clear in chapter

137 sub-section (f) 3 of the *Livre de Protocol*. So are the consequences of a second born declining that particular duty. Would you care to enlighten us on that part of the text?"

"Fine," muttered Johanna. "I'll do it."

"Thank you, Princess Johanna, but I still need to make sure you understand the full import of that part of the Protocol. So, once again, please relate the consequences of declining to be the stoner. Do not make me ask a third time."

"Mother—" started Johanna.

"Mother? The time for 'mother' passed quite a while ago."

Eloise flinched, even though the comment was not directed at her. "My queen, please don't." Eloise did not meet the queen's gaze. "Please don't force her."

"Enough from you," the queen snapped. "Your sister brings this on herself. Go ahead, Princess Johanna. I'm waiting. Here, I'll give you the start of the passage, although I'm sure I don't need to. 'The second born is given...'"

Johanna straightened her back and dared to look directly at her mother. "Chapter 137 sub-section (f) 3 reads, 'The second born is given a choice of 14 days in the stocks on the public square or five days in the Exposure Pit.' That's the most relevant bit."

"Correct. And?"

Color drained from Johanna's face, but her voice held steady. "I won't quote because the wording is obtuse and flowery, but Protocol calls for the loss of the second born's choice of finger. I'll mention that the Commentaries hold this to be more in the nature of a threat than actual, enacted punishment. There's not been a finger-severing punishment like that for 186 years."

"And what happened 186 years ago?"

Johanna stayed silent, refusing to answer.

"Princess Eloise? Do you know?" asked the queen.

Eloise swallowed. "A second born refused to be the stoner."

"Obviously. That's what we're talking about. Be specific. Do any of the Protocol commentaries give shading or nuance to that part of the text?"

"I said I would do it." Johanna had trouble keeping the snarl from her voice. "I said I would be the stoner."

"I asked a question. Is there nuance provided by the commentaries? Either of you should feel free to answer."

"There is a single comment," answered Johanna. "It comes from Lyndal Halfmast Oberon Gumball."

"Princess Eloise, who was that?"

"Lyndal Halfmast Oberon Gumball was the second born, who 186 years ago spent five days in the Exposure Pit and chose, from among her fingers, to have her left pinky severed."

"Princess Johanna, what was her sole comment?"

"She said, and I quote, 'This dost suck. But such is Protocol.'"

"Apt. 'Such is Protocol.'"

"I said I'd bloody do it."

"Don't speak that way. Not to me, not to anyone. Besides, it's not up to me. It is up to your sister." The queen pointed at the floor with her fan.

That it was up to Eloise was only true as a formality. Johanna blanched at being forced to go the next step. She swiveled on her bent knees so she faced Eloise, then touched her head to the flagstones. She recited words precisely as Protocol dictated, ignoring the bile rising to her mouth. "Princess Eloise Hydra Gumball III, Future Ruler and Heir to the Western Lands and All That Really Matters, I, Johanna Umgotteswillen Gumball, second born, would be honored to serve as your stoner at the coming Ceremonies of the Stone of the Ancestors, if it would please you to have me."

Eloise hated having to play her part in this. Her sister's forced compliance hardly made her want to give the answer she knew she must. But Eloise knew better than to deviate from the scripted reply. "Of course, Princess Johanna Umgotteswillen Gumball. It would be an honor to have you by my side and helping me at the Ceremonies of the Stone of the Ancestors."

"Good," said the queen. "Now we're all on the same scroll." With that she pocketed her fan, strode back to her chair, and sat. Everyone else stood still for an incredibly long three minutes, watching as she ate another lettuce roll. Finally, she flicked her hand irritably in permission.

Eloise and Chafed sat. The servants thawed from a frieze of fear and began serving the main course—a bulgar salad flavored with edamame and quince. Johanna, however, remained standing. "With the Queen's permission, I would like to be excused from the meal."

For a few moments, it was as if the queen had not heard. But then she turned off the ice and flashed her daughter a smile like everything was fine. "Stay, Johanna. Chef has made her best chilled chili and double-chocolate torte for dessert."

"Please, my queen, I am not feeling well."

"Sit. Stay."

Johanna took her seat and ate slowly, precisely, minimally, never taking her eyes off her plate. She didn't say another word.

✤ 6 ✤

THE COMFORT OF NUMBERS

Eloise pelted around the perimeter of the Culpability Courtyard for the twelfth time, breathing hard and trying not to think about the coming weekend. As always, she counted off the pillars as she went past—211, 212, 213, 214, 215. Her mind drifted over the numbers, feeling their comfort. The number 211 was, of course, a prime. Then 212 had a nice palindromic symmetry. Next, 213 had that lovely, simple rearranging of the usual order of one, two and three. She'd always thought 214 was a good one, because the one doubled to two, and the two doubled to four. And 215? The digits added to eight, which in numerology represented wealth and influence. The space between the pillars was just right for her to relish each number as she ticked off her daily run.

Approaching 216, she had to make a decision. It was the last pillar on this loop, so she had to work out if she had two more circuits in her, or if she should just head to the Flinging Field for the rest of her training. A thirteenth lap was an odd number, and 14 felt like a stretch today, given her pace. So she sped up for the last 26 strides, touched the final pillar, counted 216, and slowed to a warm-down jog as she turned toward the Flinging Field.

She trotted past the Equine Green, where Hector de Pferd commanded his herd of ceremonial Horse Guards in a close order drill. The Horse Guards (not to be confused with the Guard Horses) were chosen for their appearance and grace and were there to impress guests to the castle. Hector was a Friesian who personified horse cliché: pitch-black tail, raven mane, and coat dark as midnight. Statuesque, lustrous, and perpetually no-nonsense, he glided through life like a ballet dancer in slow motion, accompanied by a chorus of angel song and a delicate wind that forever caressed his perfect hair with light kisses of motion.

Hector was the son of Ferdinand de Pferd, the proud, royally appointed leader of the Queen's Stables, and Hector fully expected to follow in his father's hoofsteps one day.

Eloise and Hector weren't exactly buddies, but they got on well enough. They'd known each other growing up, and he was Eloise's Equine Designate. That is, when she came of age and a horse was attached to her retinue, it would be Hector. Until then, Eloise did not like to ask him to do anything, because she did not want to impose. She'd done nothing as gauche as try to ride him, even though Protocol specifically said it was her right to do so, as she'd need to be comfortable on his back for ceremonial purposes. Still, carrying a human around seemed below the stallion's station, and Eloise was happy to put off what would surely embarrass both of them.

She wondered if Jerome would have to ride Hector as well, now that he would be champion. Jerome and Hector had never gotten along very well. Hector thought Jerome frivolous. Jerome thought Hector's supreme flawlessness made him pompous. He took it upon himself to needle the horse, if he could do so safely. She'd have to broker an accord between them if this was going to work.

Eloise waved to Hector and his equine squad as she jogged past, calling out, "Looking spectacular, as always." As one, the squad stopped, turned to face her, bowed formally, and said, "Princess!" in unison.

She hadn't meant to interrupt them, but she'd addressed them directly, and Protocol was clear about these things. "Thank you. And apologies for interrupting."

"Princess!" they said again. When she was past, they resumed their drills.

The Flinging Field was an open paddock designed for practicing anything that required objects flying—cannonball tossing, javelin chucking, razordisc gliding, knife hurling, and Eloise's favorite, the hammer throw. Double-checking that there was nothing particularly dangerous going on (just a couple of soldiers practicing archery tag), Eloise loped to the far end of the field, where the practice hammers sat on a rack. They weren't as smooth or well cared for as her competition one, but they were fine for training.

Eloise jogged to where the rack stood and then stopped. Lorch Lacksneck, a former soldier and current castle guard in his early twenties, was in the hammer-throwing circle, just leaning into a wind-up. He was dressed only in breeks, and Eloise thought how his build suited this particular sport—muscled, massive, agile. He had surprising grace for a man whose body looked built more for hauling anvils than playing left flutter on a hockey sacking team. And yet, he did both.

She scrutinized his throwing form as he spun his turns, managing the complicated heel-and-toe foot movement. Unusually, he took a sixth full turn (most throwers only spun four or five times), then let loose a staggering toss. The ball and chain veered away from the middle, but stayed within the allowed zone, well past the "70 Lengths" sign. Eloise applauded with genuine appreciation. "Well done, Guard Lacksneck. A biscuit of a throw!"

Lorch swirled around, startled. "Princess!" He flushed and snatched his tunic from the ground. "Apologies for my state of dress, Princess Eloise. But thank you for your kind words." His voice grew muffled as he scrabbled the tunic over his head.

Now it was Eloise's turn to blush. She'd not meant to cause him embarrassment, and realized that she had not made her presence known far enough ahead of her arrival.

"No, my apologies, Guard Lacksneck. It is my fault for too hasty an approach."

"Princess, it is never your fault. Such is Protocol."

"Such is Protocol," nodded Eloise in resigned agreement, although she knew it was her responsibility, even if technically it was not her fault. She tried to smooth over the awkwardness by pretending to consider which hammer to pick from the rack. Lorch bowed away from the throwing circle, yielding the next throw to her.

In contrast to Lorch, Eloise definitely did not look like a hammer thrower. She had the fine, light build of a sprinter, and the grace of a hockey sacking changer. And yet, she was drawn to throwing things more than anything else. Unusually for someone of her size, she picked a heavier 7 1/4-weight hammer, not the four-weight normally thrown by women. In fact, in the past two Court Tourneys, she'd competed against the men, and had placed twelfth and ninth, respectively.

Eloise settled into her starting position at the edge of the circle with her back to the release area and her feet shoulder-width apart. She lightly swung the ball on the rope with one hand from her left side, across her front, to the right and up. Next, she grasped the handle with the other hand, then spun three loops in a low-to-high arc over her head, gaining speed and momentum. When the sphere once again came around to the front, it was time for the turns.

She spun her whole body, keeping hips, arms, chest, and face in line. One, two, three, four turns—every muscle straining against the hammer's heaviness. Her movements were controlled and predictable. On the fifth and the last turn, Eloise let the hammer fly, punctuating her throw with an involuntary yell. The hammer arced away from her, crossed the 65-lengths line, and landed at around 68.

"Astounding, Princess," said Lorch. "That you can do that never ceases to amaze."

"Thank you, Guard Lacksneck. That is most kind." Eloise stepped out of the circle so Lorch could have another turn.

It was the hammer toss that had made Eloise realize that yes, probably, she had some kind of weak magic for throwing. The discovery that she could hurl heavier things farther than she should have been able to came to her at the same time as the realization that she had surprising accuracy, whether flinging a javelin, flipping a razordisc, or skipping a pebble. Strangely (or rather, strangely until she figured it out), her accuracy absolutely cratered if she threw something at her sister (or her mother, at whom she'd once surreptitiously tried to throw a grape). This inability to throw something so it hit a family member fit the can't-use-magic-against-blood "rule" of weak magic.

So yes, there was likely a weak magic happening there, but nothing to hire a herald about. She could throw. So what? It was hardly a useful weak magic, compared to, say, having a knack for predicting frosts, longwalking, or finding dropped sewing needles. And it was not something she'd talk to her family about. Too embarrassing.

Mainly, Eloise just ignored the whole topic and went about her business.

So did everyone else.

"Princess Eloise, I'll yield the circle to you. I can come back later when you are done. I don't want to impede you."

"That's very kind, Guard Lacksneck, but if it is all the same to you, I'm happy to trade turns. Makes it a little less of a solitary sport."

"Yes, Princess. I'd be honored."

"And don't hold back just to make me feel better. It wouldn't, and I'll know."

"I would never dream of it, Princess."

"Good. You're up."

✿ 7 ✿

THE CONVERSATION OF BEES

A t that moment, Johanna was also thinking about weak magic —weak magic and haggleberries. Specifically, weak magic, haggleberries, the toxicity of raw haggleberry skins, and the whole can't-use-magic-against-blood thing.

Because right then, after her dressing down at dinner the night before, she wouldn't mind testing the boundaries of that prohibition.

OK, not really, she admitted. But the too-familiar rage once again simmered in her, and she had recognized it for what it was. As such, she'd removed herself from all interactions by secluding herself in her garden among tendrils and dirt—but not before venting some of her rage at the undeserving Nesther de Duck. "Poor Nesther," thought Johanna. "Wrong place, wrong time."

Dressed in sturdy breeks and a fine linen top patterned after a croft-woman's tunic, Johanna used tongs to carefully place mulch at the base of the one haggleberry bush that grew in her walled garden. It was, in fact, the one haggleberry bush that grew within 200 strong lengths of the castle, that part of the queendom being too far north and far too wet to grow them. And yet, here it was, all spiked leaves and small yellow blossoms, enjoying the sun and the conversation of bees.

Johanna loved this little plant for so many reasons. She loved the way the saffron flowers yielded a deep indigo fruit. She loved the wildly varying uses of the berries, from poison to paint tint to restorative. She loved the way the plant protected itself, with leaves that grew sharper and more bladed as the berries ripened, such that by the time they were ripe, you risked shredding your hands to harvest them.

The haggleberry plant was notoriously temperamental, and it was this little bush that first gave Johanna the thought that there might be some sort of weak magic flowing in her.

If they could bring themselves to talk about it, everyone would agree that magic still existed in weak forms, but it was nowhere close to evenly distributed. This unevenness made it taboo in polite society. One could have weak magic for just about anything, but it was extremely specific. You could have a weak magic for finding truffles, or a weak magic for knowing the exact number of lengths from the front door to the rear door of any building at a glance. Seer Maybelle's prognostication surely had a well-developed weak magic involved, but you were just as likely to get a weak magic for knowing exactly how long it would take a gutter to fill a rain barrel when a storm broke.

Some forms of weak magic were obvious. If your child could walk five times as fast and five times as far as you, you had a longwalker on your hands. But if your child was really, really good at remembering your market list and not much else, well, was that just a knack or was it a form of weak magic?

In other words, the line between a weak magic and a strong talent was a very thin one.

When Johanna was three, she found a sad, wrinkled little haggleberry in a gallipot at Eldridge the Apothecary's. She did what any child might do—she put it in her mouth.

She would never forget the feeling of the old herbman's gnarled fingers pinching her cheek to open her mouth, nor the panicked scrabbling for the berry inside her cheek. Fortunately, most of the toxins on the haggleberry's skin had faded with age, and Eldridge retrieved it before

Johanna swallowed, saving her, at a minimum, a life of digestive distress. But Johanna, already known for implacable furies, was livid he'd taken what she felt was now hers. She yelled, "My berry! My berry! My berry!" so loud and so long the glass beakers in the apothecary shook.

Eldridge had tried to explain. "This is medicine, young princess. Medicine. Not food."

"My berry! My berry! My berry!"

Thinking the best way to settle the matter was to make sure she never saw it again, the apothecary held it in front of her and asked, "Young princess, do you know what is inside this berry?"

His quiet question stalled her fury. Johanna shook her head.

"Inside this berry is a seed."

"A seed," she repeated.

"And what do you do with seeds?"

"Plant them?"

"Correct."

"Plant the seed! Plant the seed! Plant the seed!"

Eldridge offered the girl his hand and led her to a neglected corner of a disused walled garden at the far end of the castle grounds. He offered her a shovel that was as tall as her and watched as Johanna dug a hole that was much too deep in soil that was much too meagre. He let her carefully place the ancient berry in the hole, and made sure she covered it with a mound of stones, not dirt. He even let her splash a cup of water from a rain cistern on it for effect.

And that, he thought, was that. The fickle plant would never emerge from such unfavorable conditions. Besides, he was sure the girl would have forgotten about it by morning.

Except, she didn't.

To her nanny's irritation, Johanna insisted she visit the garden every day, watering the rocks and whispering encouragement to the hidden seed. Astoundingly, four months later, a shoot appeared.

It wasn't until several years later, in Botanicals and Herb Lore, that Johanna realized just how unlikely it was that her beloved haggleberry bush could survive in this climate, and that it had grown at all in the stony bed. And yet, it did. It was a few more years until she wondered why that might be the case.

By then, she had already claimed the secluded walled patch of land as her own. And no one—not even the queen—would pass its wrought-iron gate, save a few trusted members of the United Flower Pollinators Guild who came on a predictable schedule.

The garden was hers.

Johanna added a riot of plants over the years. Some were there so she could snack, some for their beauty, and some for the shape of its leaf or the color of its blossom. With time, the garden's soil became imbued with her love, her heart, and, she came to suspect, her weak magic.

When she was eleven, she decided she had to test the weak magic theory.

The test was simple: she snuck some puke weed she'd grown into Cookery and Cuisine one day and added it to a biscuit mix, along with enough stevia to mask the bitter with sweet. Hustling the finished plate away from class, she gave a biscuit to a kitchen maid, who immediately retched. So did the guard who got the second biscuit. But when her sister had one, she asked if she could have a second, and her parents complimented Johanna on her cooking.

Johanna finished a circle of mulch around the haggleberry bush, placed the tongs in the holder on the wall, and walked over to the patch of sleetpeas she'd planted three weeks before. Their shoots were just starting to show signs of curiosity. She pulled a ball of twine from her pocket and tied lengths of it to hooks in the wall, so the sleetpea runners' would have something to query as they grew.

Johanna had not yet shaken off the previous night's argument. The stoner thing was just the latest indignity shoveled onto the dung heap of insults that was her life. It was a symptom, not a cause. The cause was Protocol. Protocol and Court. That, and the fact that she was not heir. There was little to do about any of it.

As Johanna thought about the years to come, she wondered just what Protocol and possibility would allow to cross her path. Her sister's life was mapped out, full of grasping the long end of every stick. Meanwhile, Johanna would always get the short end. Eloise would become queen of a massive, prosperous realm. And Johanna? Well, as much as spinsterhood might suit her temperament, it was unlikely to be allowed. At some point in the future she'd be flogged off to a minor noble who possessed a strategic political asset. With any luck, they would be malleable and would practice decent hygiene.

And be human. Being human would help.

The thought of travel to some unknown place in a similarly unknown future cheered her slightly. At least it would be a break from all the cloying strictures, petty processes, and random unfairnesses that marked her days. She wondered if there was some way she could get away from the castle, even if for just a few days. She needed a break. From everything.

Johanna patted the ground near the sleetpeas, brushed dirt from her hands, and went to check the goldbeet plants by the south wall.

8

THE HALF KINGDOM

The royal carriage lurched into another rut, tossing its occupant rudely against the far door. Doncaster Worsted Halva de Chëëëkflïïïnt, King of the Half Kingdom, muttered another in a countless string of minor profanities, and checked to see if his travel hookah had cracked when it fell (fortunately, it hadn't) or spilled an ember (it had, but he found it before the coal started anything interesting).

Doncaster hated this journey to the seat of the Western Lands (he refused to acknowledge the second part of the name) for so, so many reasons, but mainly because of this road, which took him from his own Castle Blotch at Stained Rock across many strong lengths to the border between the Half Kingdom and the Western Lands, at the Adequate Wall of the Realms. The state of the road on his side of the wall was such that it was impossible to travel without one's behind begging for mercy.

They'd already repaired the carriage's axle twice, two spare wheels had been called to duty, and there'd been a maddening half-day's delay that involved clearing a fallen ironwood tree. Thanks to the Purple Haze, what used to be a quick day-and-a-half's sail plus a day's easy ride was now at least two weeks of bumping along by carriage. No amount of the craftsmanship relished on his imported vehicles seemed to make a difference. This was one of the main roads in the land, yet there was not enough in the Half Kingdom treasury to keep it in decent repair. Nor did the will of those charged with doing so seem to extend to the ends of their shovels.

Such was the Half Kingdom and its people.

It did not help that the carriage listed heavily to the left because of the weight imbalance of his two jesters, one being three times the size of the other.

The Half Kingdom was once a whole kingdom, called the Northern Lands. But that was before the Purple Haze.

Exactly 232 years before, everyone woke up on a Tuesday to find a massive, dense, lavender-tinged fog settled across the rough mid-point of the realm. The edge of it was within a guava's throw of the royal seat, Castle Blotch, at Stained Rock. The fog formed a perfectly straight line, like it had been drawn by a spiteful, maddened, mist-loving cartographer. Half the Northern Lands was simply no longer there, shrouded forever in mystery. Anything that crossed into the Purple Haze never crossed back. No bird, lizard, or worm ever emerged from it. If a human ventured in, they were consumed by its overwhelming silence, and immediately disappeared forever.

Experimentation could not determine the cause, but it established limits. Stones hurled in were swallowed into its silence. Court seers could not See into it. Children reported that if they put an arm into the nearest parts of the fog, they felt a tingling, but adults did not. If someone walked into the fog with a rope tied around them, it remained taut until shortly after ceased to be visible. Then there would be a few jerking tugs before the rope would drop to the ground. When hauled back, the rope would return broken off, its person gone. Explorers sent to go around the Purple Haze reported that it had no end, that it stretched out into the seas. Seafarers confirmed it had no discernible finish, and was just as dangerous at sea as on land, as it could swallow whole ships.

Eventually, the people and their rulers (Doncaster and Chafed's ances-tors) accepted the strange, unyielding boundary that had robbed them of relatives, subjects, and half the kingdom's land. The land they had lost was the kingdom's most verdant and productive. The realm's valu-able ports and long coastline had also disappeared, and with them, the bustle of trade. The Northern Lands were now landlocked, and all travel and commerce had to pass through the Adequate Wall. As everyone in all the realms began calling the Northern Lands the "Half Kingdom," the pride and motivation of the people shrank. This was partly due to the lingering trauma of personal loss, and partly because if something so strange and devastating could happen once, who knew when something similarly bad, or even worse, might happen again?

The Half Kingdom slowly adapted to the Purple Haze's presence, even embraced it in odd ways. For example, it became part of the judicial system. Felons committing grievous enough crimes were sentenced to fogging—being forced to walk into the fog—and were never again a burden on society. It was unclear if this was actually a punishment. For all anyone knew, the Purple Haze might have transformed the missing half of the realm into an amazing paradise, in which case the worst of the worst were being sent into a life of ease and decadence. But no one knew for sure, and so the threat of fogging successfully deterred crime.

Doncaster's carriage slammed into a pothole, and his teeth clacked against the travel hookah's stem.

As the present ruler of the Half Kingdom, Doncaster Worsted Halva de Chëëëkflïïïnt saw the Purple Haze as an embarrassment more than anything else. He considered the fog some sort of personal failing by his ancestors, whether or not that was fair. Çalaht must have been unhappy about *something* to have smitten the land and its people thus. Doncaster ruled over the Half Kingdom with surly frustration. It rankled him that with no ports and few productive farms, the available base for tributes, levies, imposts, and taxes was disastrous. Daily, he wondered why he was cursed to be the eldest child, saddled with the responsibility of presiding over the place.

Had he been a little more personable, Doncaster might have found a wife (or husband, he wasn't choosy) from the royalty of the other four realms, giving him a chance to be king of something more worthwhile. He'd been among the pool of suitors when the definitely worthwhile Queen Eloise II (he never even thought of her as "Two") chose her mate almost two decades before. For a while, Doncaster had thought himself in the running for her hand, maybe even leading the pack. But then, Queen Eloise had stood in her Declaiming Room and, in front of Court and following proper Protocol, offered marriage to his brother. Chafed. His idiot brother! Somehow that nong had caught her fancy. Days later they were married, removing the Western Lands from Doncaster's reach.

For a year or two, Doncaster harbored a vague hope that something might go astray with the union and he'd get another chance with the queen. Then she got all family-wayish and popped out two pipsqueaks. That's when Doncaster realized it was really over. Even if the marriage did break up, the brats were there to take on the crown. The news of their births hit him hard, and he locked himself away with his hookah for a week.

If he was truthful, Doncaster more or less liked the younger of the two. Johanna treated him like he was worth being with, which was nice. She brought out whatever uncle-ness he had in him. She laughed at his jokes, rode on his shoulders, appreciated the plush toy rutabaga he gave her, and called him "Uncle D" because "Doncaster" was too hard for her to say when she first learned to speak.

Eloise III, however, agreed with him like a stomach ulcer—some combination of being heir, being named "Eloise," and not wanting to give him the time of day when he visited. He found her a prim, humorless little Miss Such-and-Such. Whether it was fair or not, whether it was just resentment or something more than that, he could do without the older one. And from the way she treated him, the feeling was mutual.

So, yes, the Western Lands were off the table in the making-his-kingdom-suck-less department.

That left the Eastern Lands, The South, and the Central Ranges—none particularly palatable options. The Eastern Lands were dominated by swamps and cliffs, and anything in between had olive trees on it. All that olive fanaticism irked him. The South was graced with wide swathes of tundra and wolds, and everyone (especially the Southies) knew the people there were all manic, divisive, cantankerous religious fanatics. The Central Ranges were commonly referred to as the Central Carbuncle, thanks to a preponderance of active and close-to-active volcanoes, and its ashen people, many of whom were equines of one sort or another, had temperaments to match.

Yes, there was a reason the Western Lands had "and All That Really Matters" in the name.

So, no, not a lot of choices for him.

Now that he thought about it, there was only one, really.

He *had* to take over the Western Lands.

Somehow.

Doncaster thought about it, taking another puff from the hookah. One perk of travel was that he could enjoy a bit of prattleweed without raising eyebrows, given how strict the laws against it were in his Half Kingdom. They were his laws, and they were his to bend, but it was easier to do so away from those who might wonder at the contradiction. The prattleweed helped keep the journey tolerable, but it made him feel like having a chat, a conversation, a chin wag.

The carriage rounded a torturous bend, bringing the Adequate Wall into view. Doncaster muttered, "Finally, we're getting somewhere, someplace, along." He slid open the window and called up to the smarter of his jesters. "Turpy. Come down here. I've had an idea, a thought, a cogitation. And for the love of Çalaht, tell your brother to stop humming that song, that ditty, that melody. If I dream about groats again, I'm going to have him dragged by his nose hairs and fogged."

Turpentine Snotearrow McCcoonnch eased his jester's scepter into his belt, seated his fool's hat onto his shaved head, and handed the reins to his brother, Gouache Snotearrow McCcoonnch, silencing the humming with a hard look. He gripped the ladder tightly so he would not be flung off at the next rut and opened the hatch into the cabin.

Turpy had been whispering thoughts into Doncaster's ear while the king slept for months. As the jester descended into the carriage, he muttered to himself, "Finally, we're getting somewhere."

❧ 9 ❧

CHAMPION SELECT

Eloise had never seen Jerome sweat so much. Rivulets poured off his fur, soaking the traditional gray champion's tunic he'd been fitted with that morning. "Calm down, Jerissimo," she said, digging a hankie out of her court bag.

"I'm just fine, Wheezy. Just fine. Truly." He dragged a sleeve across his brow, leaving a wet patch on the royal ornate coat of arms (a weasel on a bushel of onions and a one-eyed otter holding a fire poker). He then noticed the hankie, took it distractedly, and dabbed at the sweat dripping from his tail. "I've been studying up since yesterday. Did you know that of the several hundred champions documented in the Bibliotheca de Records and Regrets, 87 percent met their deaths within seven months of their naming? That's why there are so many more of them than there have been rulers and heirs. Champions seem to be a somewhat consumable commodity."

"You are hardly a commodity, Jerome," she said. "Besides, you are dealing with a skewed sample. Given the way things are these days, I imagine we'll be doing a lot less traversing the realms, conquering, and settling of armed disputes than they used to."

"I am also the smallest Champion. By far. By a factor of seven, at least."

"Possibly. I don't think there has ever been anyone smaller than an ocelot before. And an ocelot your age would easily be 20 times your size. Not that it matters." She took back the hankie, pinching its one dry corner between thumb and forefinger so she could avoid touching any chipmunk sweat. Eloise discreetly handed the sodden cloth to her handmaid, Odmilla de Platypus, who supplied a couple of fresh ones in return. "You're not trying to back out, are you?"

"No. No, no. Of course not. Hah! The very idea is..." A soft knock at the door interrupted his protestations, and Maybelle de Chipmunk peeked into the room.

"Seer Maybelle. Please come in and tell your son he's not going to die in the next seven months."

Maybelle, dressed in a celebratory version of the simple robes of her office, closed the door behind her and softened her focus.

Eloise gasped. "No! Don't do that," she shouted, waving her hands to interrupt.

"Mother! No!" echoed Jerome.

The Seer opened her eyes. She smiled and gave a small sigh of relief. "Princess Eloise, as heir, you are well within your right to ask such a question. Protocol is very clear on that. Your mother. Your father. You. It's a short list, fortunately."

"I'm so sorry. Jerome and I were just talking. I would never ask you to divine anything about anyone's death, and certainly not your son's."

"I'm glad you didn't mean it," said Maybelle. "Besides, the Unseen's answers can be very strange when asked questions at the edges. It's not something you would have covered in Oracles and Insights, but I've seen it over and over. Highly specific questions can whirl around and produce the vaguest, most maddeningly obtuse of replies. Similarly, extremely broad questions can yield incredibly specific results, and trust me, you'd better follow them."

"I'll keep that in mind. But I hope not to have to call on you professionally any time soon."

There was another knock. "Princess Eloise?" boomed a voice from the hall.

"Yes, Guard Lacksneck?"

"Permission to come into the room, Princess."

Jerome shook his head. "He's always so formal. Annoys me," he whispered.

She half-nodded agreement. "Please, Guard Lacksneck. Come in."

Lorch Lacksneck opened the door swiftly, took a silent step into the room, and stood at full attention. "Princess Eloise Hydra Gumball III, they'll be ready for you and Champion Select Abernatheen de Chipmunk at the top of the hour. About 15 minutes."

"Thank you, Guard Lacksneck."

"You're welcome, Princess Eloise." He pivoted, spun with snap and precision, and marched from the room.

Eloise turned to Jerome. "Almost time. An hour from now, it will all be over."

"No! It will just be starting. Çalaht dangling from a doorknob, I still don't think this is a good idea. It's not too late to name someone else. What about Lorch? He's probably peeved that you didn't pick him." Jerome's speech sped up with every word, and his eyes lost their sharpness. "He's got the right profile. Can cleave a boulder in half just by looking at it, can probably recite the Gumball ancestry from heart, and I bet he can bake a mean batch of apple biscuits. I can't bake anything! You know, I was walking down the Thurmond Road once, a couple of years ago, when a group of badly dressed, ill-mannered badgers jumped in front of me. It took everything I had not to squeal like a little—"

Maybelle gently gripped her son's elbow, caught him in her gaze, and said sharply, "Jerome, breathe in." Reflexively, her son did as he was told. "Hold it," she said. "Now let it out slowly." Jerome let his breath out with a whoosh. "Again. Breathe in. Slower and deeper this time. You're safe," cooed Seer Maybelle. She moved her paw to her son's shoulder, squeezing gently. "Everything's OK. You'll be fine." She glanced at Eloise. "Panic attack."

"Yes. I've seen this before. Can I help?"

"Not just now. I interrupt the panic with a grasp of the elbow," said Seer Maybelle. "And I've made it so he feels calm when I squeeze his shoulder." She raised her index claw and moved it left and right in front of his face. Jerome followed it with his eyes. "OK. He's pretty much back."

"Is he right, Seer Maybelle? Is this a mistake?"

"I think he'll be fine. The Unseen seem to agree. Mostly, this is fear of the unknown."

"I realize it isn't an open and shut choice to make him champion. But..." Eloise shrugged. "I trust him."

Jerome swallowed and again wiped his brow. "He's still standing right here, you know. And he can most certainly hear both of you. And no, he's not sure he will be fine."

Maybelle let go of his shoulder, then pulled Jerome into a hug. "My beautiful, brave son," she said. Then she held him at arms' length. "I have something for you, in honor of your naming as champion." She reached into a hidden pocket inside her loose sleeve and held out a clear glass vial. It was the size of a cat's incisor, about as round, and was attached to a magnificently knotted hemp lanyard.

Jerome gently took it from her. "Thanks, Mother. Am I supposed to put something in here?"

"Look closer."

He hopped up onto the windowsill to find better light. Dangling the vial from its lanyard, he stared at the glass. Eloise leaned in next to him, peering. "Look there," he pointed. "It's not empty,"

"What is that? A scrap of gray thread, maybe? A bristle from a brush?"

He tapped the vial with a claw. "I think it's a hair."

"Correct," said Seer Maybelle. "It is an ear hair. Specifically, one from Gordon the Noisome himself. Last time I saw him, he plucked it from his right ear—the more intuitive of the two—and gave it to me as a mark of respect."

"Mother, I can't take this from you. You need this for your work. The Unseen don't seem to have much use for me. Never have."

"I want you to have it," she said. "As champion, there will be times when you will need to provide guidance to Princess Eloise. Whether Gordon's ear hair helps with that or not, I think it is important to remember that wisdom can sometimes be found in the oddest of places."

Jerome handed it to his mother. She fastened it around his neck, and whispered the formal words, "Honor to the Champion."

"Honor to the Champion," repeated Eloise.

He bowed politely to them both. "Thank you, Mother. I'll treasure it."

"Good. However, I suggest you treasure it inside the vial, and not out. I wrapped it in a cotton bundle at first, but the hair's stench was excruciating. I'm sure a mere whiff would send even Guard Lacksneck running for a bucket. Truly, Gordon's gift of fetor is at least as great as his gift of prognostication through earlobe twitching."

She turned to Eloise. "Princess, if I may. I have something for you as well."

"Why, that's very kind, Seer Maybelle."

The chipmunk again reached into the sleeve pocket and pulled out a silver ring. "For you."

Eloise took it. The outside was engraved in beautiful knot work, but it was the inside the caught her attention. Three words: "Tenacious. Sagacious. Bodacious."

"I acquired the ring some time ago. You can see from the engraving that it is from the Central Ranges. The words came to me in a brief vision about a month ago, and I had them inscribed. I got a strong sense they were for you. Of course, these are qualities a good ruler should have, but I think there's more to your having it than that. I'm just not sure what."

"Thank you, Seer Maybelle. It is beautiful. Exquisite silver work." She slipped it onto her right middle finger—a perfect fit—and took the chipmunk's paws in her hands to thank her. But before she could say anything else, Maybelle's chin jutted into the air, her eyes rolled back, and her fur sprang out straight with a sudden crackle of energy. The chipmunk's paws locked onto Eloise's fingers, and she oscillated her head back and forth, emitting a low growl.

"Seer Maybelle? Jerome, is she all right?"

"Don't let go of her! I've seen this before, but not for years. Whatever is coming, it's for you. Your touch triggered it."

Seer Maybelle's head continued its strange back and forth, her tail mirroring the motion. Then the growl cut off suddenly, replaced by rapid breathing. And then a voice—otherworldly, straining, hollow, gossamer thin. "Day and night merged. The hum thrums through the bones. That which was once in hand but was lost, can be found again, still in hand, unreached by the clawing of the doomed."

The chipmunk's head dropped, and the wisps of power dissipated from her fur. Eloise caught her when she slumped forward.

"It will take her a while to recover now," said Jerome. He gently felt her wrist for a pulse. "Her heart feels strong, so I don't think we need the apothecary or a healer. I'll lay her down somewhere. She'll need a pot of haggleberry tea when she wakes. And salty food, like crackerbread."

Eloise looked at the eight-hour candle marking the time. "It's almost the top of the hour. We're supposed to go in for the Naming. Perhaps we should postpone the ceremony."

Jerome shook his head. "No. Mother would hate that."

"Princess, if'n I may?" It was Odmilla. Her rural Southie drawl was not particularly helped by the build of her rubbery platypus snout, but her assured manner was instantly comforting. Odmilla opened her arms, indicating that she would take the unconscious chipmunk.

"You are, as always, a lifesaver, Odmilla." Eloise gently handed Maybelle to her handmaid. "Feel free to tend her in my room."

"I'll ask Chef for the haggleberry tea and the salty vittles, then I'll stay with Seer Maybelle until your return, Princess."

"Thank you so much, Mistress Odmilla," said Jerome, bowing.

Odmilla nodded back. "It is an honor and my pleasure, Champion Select Abernatheen de Chipmunk. And may I say, honor to the Champion."

A peal of trumpets sounded, playing "The Champion's Clarion." It was muffled until Lorch Lacksneck opened the door again, ready to lead the way. Jerome leaned over his unconscious mother and pecked her on the cheek. "This one's for you, Ma," he whispered. "I'll make you proud." He looked up at Odmilla, nodded another thank you, then turned to Eloise. "Let's do this thing."

"Yes, Champion Select Abernatheen de Chipmunk."

As they followed Lorch Lacksneck toward the Throne Hall, Eloise had just enough time to wonder what the Seer's words meant, then left them in her mind's back cooking pot to stew.

10

THE NAMING

In some castles, a throne hall tries to be the grandest place in the realm—explosions of gilt, tapestry, paintings, and velvet. Not so in the Western Lands and All That Really Matters. Tradition (but not Protocol) insisted that the Throne Hall be a working room, kept barely adorned so the rulers focused on their decisions, and subjects found it less intimidating to approach with matters of concern. Sometimes the Throne Hall was gussied up with finery for medium-sized parties or to receive honored guests, but a Naming ceremony for a champion hardly warranted that kind of fuss.

Still, someone had put in an effort. A canopy of white canvas stretched above the dais, bunting the color of wisteria blossom was pinned to its front, and a few streamers in champion's gray hung on the walls. It was just enough to say, "This is special" and "Know your place" at the same time. Queen Eloise sat on her rosewood throne in the middle. To her left was King Chafed on a mahogany throne he had brought with him from the Half Kingdom, then Johanna on the oak one that used to be the Queen's. Johanna looked her usual bored self, but not particularly disaffected. To the right of the Queen was the Heir's Throne, ash with simple kingwood inlays.

Princess Eloise left Jerome at the entrance to the room with a last glance. She could see that his nerves were roiling again, and his forced smile had too much twitch. But things were in motion, so all she could do was trust. She stepped into the hall as the last phrase of "The Champion's Clarion" trumpeted through the room, and headed toward her family, stepping carefully in the middle of the stones that tessellated the polished floor.

When the queen sat at court and held her day-to-day working sessions, the Throne Hall was usually only a quarter to a third full, depending on the weather and the matters at hand. Eloise figured the combination of a sunny day and the Naming ceremony was why it was closer to capacity, with easily eight score people. That and, she had to admit, the unusual nature of her choice of champion.

As happened at Court, it had taken all of five minutes for everyone to know Jerome had become Champion Select, and five minutes and three seconds for the feverish, whispered commentary to begin. A chipmunk? As champion? How will he hold the Champion's Sword, much less swing it? Yes, he's her friend, but he doesn't exactly have a commanding presence. Is he a placeholder? Sometimes that happens. Maybe this is a strategy, and she will choose someone much more suited once he gets squashed in the line of duty.

And on and on and on.

Eloise heard snippets, but knew wagging tongues were wont to wag, and there was nothing to be done. They didn't know Jerome the way she did, nor did they know what Seer Maybelle had foreseen.

Eloise had expected a fight with her parents, but they spared few words. "Whatever makes you happy," shrugged her father. Her mother asked a few questions about the practicalities, suggested that a size-appropriate replica of the Champion's Sword could be managed, and kissed her on the forehead. "Jerome is Jerome. You know what you're getting," she said. "There's value in that."

Even Johanna simply looked at her, muttered, "Odd," and let it be.

Eloise stepped up onto the dais, curtsied to her mother, and took her seat. Then Queen Eloise stood and everyone rose, chairs scraping the floor. The sole exception was the Court scrivener, who sat, quill poised over scroll, ready to note every detail of the proceedings, which he would transcribe into the official record.

"My friends!" she began.

"Our queen!" came the familiar response.

"Please be at rest." With a rustle of clothing and a softer scraping of chairs, everyone sat.

Queen Eloise looked from one side of the room to the other, pensive. When she finally spoke, her contralto lilted. "Too often, the duties we perform in this room are workaday. Scroll signings. Resolving heated arguments that ten years later are reduced to the embarrassed memories of petty squabbles. Admonishments. Judgments. Communications. The reckoning of ledgers, both business and personal. All of it important, but clearly not of great interest, or you'd all be here every day." There was a titter of agreement from the crowd.

"But a naming of a champion. Now, there's something." The Queen stepped behind Princess Eloise's throne and rested her hands on her daughter's shoulders. "I welcome that you are here. I welcome your enthusiasm, and I even welcome your curiosity. For it is, indeed, a curious choice. There's no avoiding the fact that our Champion Select is uncommon for this calling. Uncommon for his size and uncommon for his species." Again, there was murmured agreement, and heads turned to look at Jerome standing in the shadow of the doorway. Those closest could see the nervous tremble of his whiskers.

The queen continued, walking around the thrones to the front of the dais "Yes, Jerome Abernatheen de Chipmunk is uncommon for this calling. But, I put it to you, not for the reasons you think. He is uncommon for his wit and for his heart. He is uncommon for the keenness of his mind and the tenacity of his curiosity. He is uncommon for the speed of his tongue and the sharpness of his insight. So, yes, he is uncommon. But it is an uncommonness to treasure."

At that moment a cloud moved, and the sun, fortuitously positioned, cast a perfect shaft of light on the doorway. Jerome squinted into the sudden brilliance. A smile was frozen on his face, and he wondered vaguely why all the sounds he heard resembled a muffled wash from a distant ocean.

"Let it be known that the heir has the Throne's full support in her choice of champion. And I am glad I can count on your full support as well." There were a few grunts of half agreement. The queen frowned. "I'm sorry. Is it not correct that I can count on your full support?" Now the room filled with a more enthusiastic rumble. She raised her hand for silence. "I thought so." Suddenly, she opened her arms wide, and called out the formal words everyone was waiting for. "Honor to the Champion!"

"Honor to the Champion!" came the reply.

The queen leaned down and whispered in Eloise's ear, "I think they're warmed up. All yours."

"Thank you, Mother. That was lovely."

"All true."

Eloise stood as her mother sat, and once again everyone, save the queen, rose. Eloise moved to the center of the dais. As heir, she'd spoken to crowds in the Throne Hall many times, especially since her Thorning Ceremony, so she was familiar with the butterflies jigging in her guts. She had learned to accept them as a sign she cared about what she was doing. This time, the butterflies were in full balletic flight. This was the most important, most visible thing she had ever done. The Naming of the Champion was every heir's first decision that directly affected Court and, by extension, the realm. She knew that despite her mother's endorsement, her choice would be scrutinized from every angle. A bad result wouldn't sink her, but it could easily taint public perception.

But she'd chosen Jerome. Decision made. She prayed to Çalaht that he'd grow into the role.

"My friends!" she started.

"Our heir!" came a less familiar response.

"Please be at rest." Once again, everyone sat. "Thank you for being here today. I had intended to say a few words before the formalities, but the need is no more, thanks to the eloquence of our queen. And you have been waiting so patiently. Let us simply start." She turned to where Jerome stood illuminated in the doorway and launched into the script laid out in the *Livre de Protocol*. "I welcome to the Throne Hall the Champion Select."

"Welcome, Champion Select," echoed the crowd.

All eyes sought Jerome. He stood, unmoving, a strange, distant look on his face.

11

A MARVEL OF FAKE PROTOCOL

Jerome wondered where the closest sea was, and what tides would be required to produce the rushing sound of water he was hearing. He did not know a lot about tides and had only been to the coast a few times.

Somehow—incredibly, strangely—it seemed like the ocean in his ears spoke to him. Called to him. But he didn't speak the language of water, so couldn't discern what words of beauty and wisdom the waves whispered.

Eloise felt the silence hang. The first 15 seconds were full of anticipation. Jerome had an innate flair, so she wouldn't put a dramatic pause past him. But the pause stretched a further ten, then 15 seconds. She could feel the crowd's mood shift to a mix of confusion and amusement. Eloise tried a subtle head nod, indicating that he should approach, but Jerome stood frozen.

It was Lorch Lacksneck who broke the silence. From behind Jerome in the doorway, he said, "Pardon me, Princess. I missed my moment."

Eloise had no idea what he meant. "Not to worry, Guard Lacksneck. If you please."

Lorch stepped past the chipmunk, spun 180 degrees with a ceremonial sweep of his cape, knelt, and popped the back of his open hand on the ground. He leaned toward Jerome's face and in a stage whisper said, "If the Champion Select will allow." The "thawp" of his hand on the stones and the force of his voice were just enough to reach the edges of Jerome's trip to the La La Realms. His fuzzy look remained, but a flicker of recognition crossed the chipmunk's face. Lorch's massive back blocked the room's view, and he waggled his fingers slightly. In a voice only Jerome could hear, he said, "It'll be all right. Step onto my hand and keep your balance."

Jerome walked onto the middle of Lorch's palm, his mind still far, far away.

With another spin, Lorch stood upright and faced the throne across the room. "Princess Eloise Hydra Gumball III, it is my honor to carry forth to you the Champion Select. Welcome, Champion Select!"

The confusion of the moment was swept aside as Eloise and the rest of the room automatically responded, "Welcome, Champion Select!" Lorch hefted Jerome aloft for all to see, and paraded majestically toward the dais. It looked practiced, professional and, most importantly, planned and purposeful. He arrived at the dais, knelt, let Jerome wobble off his hand, then stood back up, booming, "I, Lorch Lacksneck, son of Lydia and Lorien Lacksneck of Clan Lacksneck from Lower Glenth, the twelfth in my family to serve as a guard within these hallowed walls, present the Champion Select for your consideration!"

It was a marvel of fake Protocol, and Eloise could scarcely control her smile. "Thank you, Guard Lacksneck, son of Lydia and Lorien Lacksneck. Our veneration of Clan Lacksneck of Lower Glenth and its loyal guards blossoms anew each day."

Lorch bowed deeply, spun with another flourish, and paraded back to the other side of the room, his commanding presence drawing all eyes with him. With everyone's attention on the retreating guard, Eloise had a moment with Jerome. He looked a thousand strong lengths away.

"Jer, you OK?"

"Do you happen to know how far away the closest ocean-like body of water is?"

"What? The closest ocean? The Gööödeling Sea, around 280 strong lengths north-northeast. Jerome, I need you here. Here in the Throne Hall."

"The Throne Hall? There's no sea in the Throne Hall," he said.

"You're right. No sea." Eloise felt a dull panic. "Listen, Jerome, I need you to focus. We've got a naming to get through. Can you do that? The naming?" She snapped her fingers sharply in front of his face.

And with that, Jerome's gaze cleared, and Eloise could see her friend was back. "Oh, goodness. Holy Çalaht on a stick!" He looked around, frantic. "What have I done? Do you think anyone noticed anything? How did I get here from the doorway?"

"Don't worry about all that right now, but you might put Lorch on your Yuletide card list this year. You ready to do this?"

Jerome nodded, and Eloise turned back to the room as Lorch reached the far wall. She resumed the arcane script. "As is our way and the way of those who came before us, it is my privilege as Heir to call upon one of us to grace our court as Champion. Do I have your permission to name a Champion?"

"Yes, you have our permission," came the ceremonial reply.

"Who among you will step forth as Champion?"

A small bell rang, signaling the start of 60 seconds of silence. During that time, Eloise scanned the room, as if looking for someone. When the bell rang again, Jerome said his line. "My Princess, I volunteer!"

"A volunteer!" Fake astonishment rang through the Throne Hall.

"State your name, volunteer," continued Eloise.

"I would prefer to be faceless and nameless in service to the House of Gumball. However, since you asked, I am Jerome Abernatheen de Chipmunk."

"Who are your mother and father?"

"My mother is Seer Maybelle de Chipmunk née de Sciuridae. My father is now passed, but he was Edgar Flawrence de Chipmunk."

"Are you true, dedicated, and determined?"

"I am, Princess."

"Will you be brave, humble, and selfless?"

"I will, Princess."

"Then let it be done."

Normally, Eloise would have given her champion the emerald and navy Gumball sash she'd worn since her Thorning Ceremony. Sometimes alterations had to be made when a champion was much larger than the heir, but it was unusual for the sash to be much too big. Odmilla had solved the problem, snipping a section from the sash and stitching a version that would fit Jerome.

Eloise handed the small sash to her mother. The queen kissed it, then dipped her fingers into a dish of oils that sat on a low table in front. "These are the oils of cananga, yellow swede, haggleberry, and ebony. Together they represent insight, for that is what we wish for the champion." She traced the queen's insignia onto the sash and gave it back to Eloise.

Taking the sash, Eloise offered it next to her father. Chafed kissed it and put his finger into a different dish of oils. "These are the oils of cedar, applewood, ragwort, and olibanum. Together, they represent gallantry, for that is what we wish for the champion." He drew the king's insignia in oil on the sash.

Eloise handed it to Johanna. One might have expected Johanna's participation to be begrudging, but she was on display to a full house. Her performance was note-perfect and clear for all to hear, if delivered with a faintly ironic tone, perceptible only to those who knew her well. She kissed the sash, then dipped a pinky into her oil dish. "These are the oils of pantswood, guillotine fruit, vetiver, and sedgeland willow. Together, they represent resourcefulness, for that is what we wish for the champion." She sketched the Gumball insignia with her pinky on the sash and returned it to her sister.

Finally, Eloise kissed the sash and reached for her own saucer of oil. "These are the oils of spikewood, dandelion, neem, and hedgehog cactus. Together, they represent humility, for that is what we wish for the champion." She put her finger in the oil and wrote her name on the cloth. "I offer this sash to the champion as a token of our esteem." Jerome ducked his head slightly, and Eloise placed the oiled sash so he wore it over his right shoulder.

Next was the Champion's Sword. The usual ones were at least ten times Jerome's body weight, but the Court bladesmith fashioned a small basket-hilted broadsword, modeled, as all Champion's Swords were, on the one carried by the first champion, Townshend Bellicose Shinglehefter. It was supposed to be ceremonial only and was decorated with the Gumball crest on both scabbard and hilt, but too often in the past, the Champion's Sword had been pressed into battle, so the bladesmiths always made sure they were as useful as they were beautiful.

Eloise took the small weapon from a cushion and held it in front of her. "The Champion's Sword, etched with a prayer seeking blessing from the divine Çalaht." At that point, Queen Eloise's own champion, Sylvia Cloisterfeld, a tremendously athletic woman of middle-years, stepped out from a hidden corner at the edge of the dais. She took the sword from Eloise and drew it from its scabbard, saying, "May this sword never be called on to express the purpose of its making, but should it be needed, may it be swift and sure in the hands of the Champion. Honor to the Champion!"

"Honor to the Champion!"

Sylvia Cloisterfeld returned the blade to its scabbard, knelt, and presented it to Jerome, saying, "From one champion to the next, may you continue our traditions of service and loyalty."

Jerome bowed to her. "Thank you, Champion Cloisterfeld. May I be worthy of your traditions."

She bowed back. "Congratulations, Champion Abernatheen de Chipmunk."

Next came token gifts presented by ambassadors from the other realms. The Eastern Lands representative gave Jerome a simple, clear container with three olives in it. They were perfect, jet-black specimens in a purified brine as clear as water, save hints of decorative gold dust swirling in the jar.

The consul from the Central Ranges gave Jerome a small pocket-sized knife—a single piece of obsidian fashioned into both handle and razor-sharp blade.

The ambassador from the Half Kingdom offered a hinged case with an antique coin, a corroded specimen that was the only coin ever minted in the realms with a chipmunk on the obverse side.

The envoy from The South shook Jerome's paw and said, "Perhaps I've lived here in the Western Lands and All That Really Matters a few too many years, but I have grown accustomed to the ways here, and as such, I present you with a gift that I hope represents a shift in the winds from The South, and a hope for a more tolerant future between the species than is currently the case in my queendom."

The envoy produced a small, embroidered, felt-lined pouch with a tenth of a weak weight of prattleweed. It was just enough for a minor devotional in The South, small enough to get you a stern look in the Western Lands, but large enough to get you tossed in the clink if it was found on you in the Half Kingdom. It might not have looked it, but it was a sensational gift, and the crowd buzzed when they saw it.

In The South, the possession of religious herbage by non-humans was strictly forbidden, and considered much worse than speaking the

Queen's tongue in public, which was also positively verboten to non-humans. Had the envoy handed a chipmunk, or any non-human, this tiny parcel at home, he'd have been arrested. Such were the ways of The South. Eloise thought it a marvelous, forward-looking gesture, and hoped the man was never made to account for it on his home turf.

With the gifting done, Eloise relaxed slightly, as there was not much more to go. Jerome just had to drink of the water drawn from the source of the River Thurmond. "Bring forth the Champion's Cannikin," she called.

The River Thurmond touched each of the realms as it meandered across the land. The Champion's Cannikin was a small, glorified bucket, filled to the brim. The Champion Select had to drink the whole thing without spilling a drop, as a way of showing a unity with the realms. Jerome knew it would be a lot for him to drink, so he'd been practicing with a goblet that held about the same amount, and was confident it wouldn't be a problem.

What he hadn't reckoned on was Stoofy.

12

STOOFY

Stoofy Trebuchet McNniister was the Court jester, an affable, mostly deaf, elderly man long past using barbed humor to point out royal foibles. His jokes, and it was generous to label them as such, had stopped being funny several decades before. But jester was a role for life, and Stoofy was a fixture at Court, where he was much more likely to doze off, drooling on his cushions, than offer anything approximating entertainment.

Jerome was petrified of him.

Not Stoofy, per se. Jerome was afraid of all jesters. Always. Flat-out phobic. As a pup, he'd hidden from them. As he grew older, his irrational fear intensified, such that he avoided dignitaries at Court who brought their jesters with them. When he was younger, an outlined drawing of one was enough to send his mouth dry, and a full-on painting of one could leave him panting.

It was the one bit of the Naming ceremony that neither Jerome nor Eloise properly reckoned on—old Stoofy shuffling amiably forward, focused on the small bucket of water to make sure it didn't splash. As soon as Jerome heard the tinkling bells jouncing at the ends of his multi-colored hat, his pulse quickened. As the ill-fitting clothing and the curled-toed shoes shambled closer, he hyperventilated. "Steady on," he thought to himself. "No need for panic."

When Stoofy came within three paces, Jerome's tail fluffed and he let slip an involuntary, nervous chatter.

Stoofy looked up from the cannikin, his age-slowed mind confused. He'd never had a Champion Select chatter at him at a Naming. He wasn't sure what to do with that. Usually they took the goblet and drank the water. Was it something he'd done? He knew how important it was that everything went to Protocol. A fug of doubt spread through his already foggy thoughts.

Stoofy looked down at Jerome and realized his mistake. He needed to get lower and closer so the Champion Select could reach the thing he was holding. "Sorry, little fellah," he mumbled, lowering himself onto his arthritic knees and holding the cannikin forward for the chipmunk to take. For a man his age and health, it was a delicate balancing act.

As the jester leaned in, Jerome's lizard-brain instincts took over, launching him into survival mode. His arms flailed, and a pained squeal tore from his soul. With one particularly wild movement, a claw sliced the back of Stoofy's hand, and the jester instinctively pulled it back. The Champion's Cannikin tumbled forward, dumping its symbolic contents all over Jerome. The splash only made his terror worse. He ran two complete circles around Stoofy, then in and out of the legs of those sitting on the thrones.

Not a good look for a new champion.

"Jerome! Stop!" commanded Eloise. Her use of the Tone penetrated his mind and he froze, huddled behind the queen's legs.

The room was silent. It was a performance never before seen at Court, and no one knew just how to react. The queen and king sat stock still, betraying no emotion. Only Johanna moved, shaking her head slowly.

A few seconds later, Jerome calmed enough to realize what he'd done. "Oh, Çalaht certifying sandwiches," he blasphemed quietly.

A sole cough echoed in the hall.

There was only one thing to do: keep going.

Jerome straightened to his full height and walked, dripping wet, out from behind the queen's left ankle. He turned to her, bowed, and said, "Apologies, Your Majesty, for the water I may have left beneath your throne." He then sloshed forward to stand in front of Eloise. "Apologies, Princess Eloise. It is possible I might have behaved with a mild lack of decorum."

"Not to worry, Champion Select Abernatheen de Chipmunk." She turned to Stoofy. "Jester Stoofy Trebuchet McNniister, I would be grateful if you could please refill the Champion's Cannikin."

Stoofy cupped a hand to his ear. "What?" His voice was overly loud, thanks to his deafness.

Eloise cleared her throat and raised her voice. "Jester Stoofy Trebuchet McNniister, I would be grateful if you could please refill the Champion's Cannikin."

"Sorry. Can't hear much these days," he shouted. "What was that you said, little girl?"

Eloise blushed at "little girl," even though she knew he meant nothing by it. She tried again, arms wildly miming her intention as she spoke. "Jester Stoofy Trebuchet McNniister, I would be grateful if you could please refill the Champion's Cannikin."

"Oh!" he yelled through his deafness. "More water in the wee bucket thingo. Got it!"

As the stunned silence lingered, the old man groaned to his feet, keeping a wary eye on Jerome. He wiped the back of his hand, beaded with blood, on his diamond-patterned pantaloons, leaving a small red smear on the already dirty white. Stoofy reached for the cannikin that had rolled off the dais, couldn't quite get it, creaked back to his knees, managed to grasp the bucket, pushed himself back upright, then shuffled to the end of the dais, where a crystal decanter held the remaining River Thurmond water.

The jester poured all that was left into the cannikin, but it was barely a quarter full. He looked into the decanter to see if there was any more, then shook it to get another couple of drops. Turning, he warily approached Jerome again. Unwilling to suffer another scratch, he bent arthritically back down, leaving the cannikin on the ground a safe distance away, then backed up like he was stepping away from a rabid lion.

Jerome, painfully upright, marched forward toward the cannikin. He bowed to Stoofy, bowed to Eloise, bowed to the crowd, bowed to the queen and king, then grabbed the ceremonial bucket and gulped down the small amount of water, letting out an exaggerated, "Ahhhh!" when he finished. Setting it down, he bowed to the cannikin, bowed to the crowd, bowed to Stoofy, bowed to the queen and king, bowed to Eloise, and moved to his spot, turning to face the crowd with as much flourish as his soaked clothing allowed. He waited for Eloise to continue.

Eloise did just that, picking up the script where she'd left off with as much enthusiasm as she could manage. "Friends, family, and indeed, foes, if there be any, it is with pride and respect I call out the one who will serve by my side. I hereby name Jerome Abernatheen de Chipmunk my Champion. Honor to the Champion!" she called.

"Honor to the Champion!" said everyone perfunctorily. The luster of the moment was well and truly gone.

With that, the deed, such as it was, was done.

The queen wrapped everything up with a few closing words, and within moments, the royal family headed for the exit.

"Not exactly an auspicious start," muttered Chafed to Queen Eloise as they stepped from the dais.

"No. 'Complete disaster' probably covers it," she whispered. Before leaving the room, she paused at the scribe's table and pointed to the record scroll. "The record needn't be too painfully honest for today."

"Yes, my queen," the scribe replied. "Consider it done."

❧ 13 ❧

BLESSINGS OF THE DAY

The day after the Naming Ceremony, Jerome arrived early so he could be at Eloise's beck and call as needed. Each heir and champion found their own rhythm and relationship, but it took time. Given the less than perfect start, he thought he'd better try to sort things out sooner rather than later.

But when he reached her room, the door was closed and there were no sounds within. He didn't want to disturb her, but he also didn't want to be wandering the castle halls when she emerged. So he settled for standing at attention outside the door, like a common sentry.

Johanna emerged from her room across the hall wearing her gardening clothes. "Blessings of the day to you, Princess Johanna," he said automatically.

She turned and saw who spoke. A huge grin spread across her face, and she walked across the hall toward him. Jerome knew exactly what Johanna was capable of and wished he'd held his words. But she bent down and chucked him gently on the shoulder. "Blessings of the day to you, too, Champion Abernatheen de Chipmunk. And if I may say so, yesterday was stellar. I swear, it was amazing. Thank you."

Jerome squinted at her. "I beg your pardon?"

"Oh, there's no getting around that it was a terrible, embarrassing debacle. Eloise must have at least the teensiest of second thoughts about her choice. But I couldn't wait to get out of the Throne Room, because I could barely hold my laughter in. I cackled at the memory all night." Johanna straightened, smiling. "When you scratched him, I thought poor old Stoofy would turn in his Jesters' Guild card right then and there. I know it's not part of your role as champion, but, goodness, that was absolutely top entertainment." She slowly flicked open her fingers at him and made a soft splooshing sound. Jerome flinched reflexively, but Johanna didn't seem to mean it maliciously. "Priceless. Gotta go. See you at breakfast." She chuckled her way up the hall and around the corner. The last words he heard seemed to be something about plucking a lemon from the orchard of possibility. But he couldn't be sure.

Jerome was completely mortified, and had been since it happened. His mother had already heard the details and made appropriately mother-like, saying it surely wasn't as bad as he thought, and that people would forget soon enough. Still, he was grateful that Çalaht had seen fit to arrange it that she would not be there for his humiliation.

Johanna was right about Eloise's decision. Jerome didn't think he'd survive a month of this championing thing, much less the average of seven. The likelihood of him lasting until she was crowned, much less longer, seemed desperately remote.

Eloise's door opened and Odmilla stepped out, balancing an armload of laundry. "Oh, Champion Abernatheen de Chipmunk. Blessings o' the day to you."

"Blessings of the day to you, too, Mistress de Platypus."

"How fares your mother this fine morning?"

"She is very well, and asked me to again thank you for your kind attention. She said I should give you this, if I should see you." Jerome reached into the pouch slung from his belt and drew out a packet of folded paper. "Spiced haggleberry tea. You mentioned to her that you were partial to it. This blend includes cardamom, cinnamon, cloves, ginger, and a hint of pepper."

Odmilla lit up like a night watch lamp. "Precisely as we Southies like it. Please thank your mother for me. I can't wait. Now if you'll pardon me, Champion Abernatheen de Chipmunk, I have the Princess's washing to attend to. Blessings o' the day," she trilled as she walked off.

"Blessings of the day," he repeated.

ELOISE SAT AT HER VANITY DRESSED IN CLOTHES SUITABLE FOR STUDY and looked in the mirror. Odmilla had styled her hair in a Southie braid, which was as good a way as any to exert control over her curls when the humidity was up like this. But Eloise was feeling a bit down, and fiddling with her appearance was an attempt to lift her spirits. It rarely worked, but was worth a try. She picked out three stick pins with enamel flying red jays on the ends, and stared into the mirror, trying to fit them into the solid rope of her braid in a way that would not reflect badly on Odmilla.

She heard her handmaid speaking to Jerome outside the chamber door and sighed. Yesterday had truly been an unmitigated fiasco. Her parents hadn't even tried to sugarcoat it. Her father told her she would need to repair the people's faith in her ability to make decisions of import. Her mother said, simply, "Welcome to Court," and then, "You'll need to figure something out."

Cold, but Eloise reckoned she deserved it. She knew choosing Jerome was a risk, but thought she'd be starting in the plus column, not the minus.

She got the red jay pins to sit in a neat formation and grabbed a hand mirror to double-check the back. Surely the Jerome situation was salvageable. She'd come up with something. Or maybe they would come up with something together. The thing she knew for certain was she mustn't let Jerome sense any doubt from her. If he did, he'd crumple.

Eloise set down the mirror, stood up straight for one last look at her outfit, and headed out the door. "Ah, Jerome. Blessings of the day. I thought I heard you out here. Have you eaten?"

"Blessings of the day, Princess. And yes, thank you, I had porridge before I came."

"Well, in the future, you don't need to. It's been a while since Protocols and Procedures, but you might remember that meals are part of the deal."

"Oh. Right, there's the Champion's Table in the corner of the Dining Hall. Of course. I can sit with Sylvia Cloisterfeld. It will be an honor to compare myself to her every day."

"Stop it. So, can I persuade you to have another mouthful or two of food?"

"Perhaps, Princess. Princess, I..."

"You know they'll make a chamber available to you. Somewhere close to here, in case I need you. I don't mind where you stay. If you want to keep living with your mother, or split your time between the two places, that's OK. But you might find it a lot less back and forth if you know you have a place here at the castle."

"Princess..."

"Has Seer Maybelle recovered? Did she say anything about what happened to her?"

"She is almost fully recovered this morning and is in good spirits. Odmilla was spectacular with her. She didn't really have anything to add to the vision, as she did not remember having it, just the recovery afterwards."

"I'm glad she's well."

"That's kind. Princess, before we..."

"Is this about yesterday's ceremony?"

"Yes. I..."

"I have a strategy," said Eloise.

"Oh?"

Eloise smiled at him. "We're going to tough it out. Pretend it went a bit, um, smoother than it did."

"Are you..."

"We're in this together, Jerome. It will be fine. Now, if you don't mind, I'm starving and would like to get to breakfast. Shall we?"

And that was all the discussion she would allow.

❧ 14 ❧

A KING ARRIVES

The welcoming line for King Doncaster of the Half Kingdom was 200 people strong. Queen, king, family, servants, envoys, and trade representatives all stood in four deep rows carefully arranged by rank. Hector de Pferd and his Horse Guards stood at careful attention by the far end of the assembly so that the arriving monarch would see them first in their lustrous perfection. They were the best the Western Lands and All That Really Matters offered, and offer it up they did.

Eloise stood beneath the indigo umbrella that Odmilla held against an enthusiastic rain as she and her family watched Doncaster Worsted Halva de Chëëëkflïïïnt's royal coach scritch down the last hundred lengths of the sweeping drive that led to Castle de Brague. The magnificent carriage that had left the seat of the Half Kingdom now looked like something you'd buy at a dodgy used dray shop. The repairs to the axle kept it functional, but there was a teeth-aching metallic scrape to one of the wobbly wheels, which made all four storm-drenched members of Doncaster's royal stables skittish as they dragged the wreck forward.

Eloise looked down at Jerome, who stood at attention, eyes fixed forward, sheltering in the shadow of her leg. "Don't say anything about the carriage," she whispered. "Uncle Doncaster will be touchy about it. Besides, he'll pick up a new one while he's here." Jerome looked up, nodded, then resumed his forward gaze.

Eloise squinted through the rain and saw two sodden figures on the carriage dressed in a motley of black and gray, the larger one driving. "Oh, bloody Çalaht. That creepy jester Turpy and his brother are with him."

"Turpy's the one who smells like anise and donkey sweat?"

"That's the one."

"I'd forgotten he had a brother."

"Yeah, Gouache is a jester too," said Eloise. "Please don't lose it."

"No, your early warning jester alert will help," muttered Jerome. "I'll keep my distance."

"So will I, if I can."

Johanna peered from below the bright yellow umbrella that Nesther de Duck held above her. To get adequate height, both Nesther and Odmilla stood on portable stands placed behind the twins. "Please, Eloise," said Johanna. "They might hear you. You don't want them to think us rude."

"You're right. Of course we don't."

As the carriage limped toward its destination, the trumpeters let fly with a rain-soaked rendition of "Hey! Look! A Visitor!"—a plodding piece written with a musical pace that allowed even the most fundament-sore travelers ample time to collect themselves and emerge from their transport with dignity. It was always played at occasions like these. But Doncaster ignored it. The moment the carriage wheezed to a stop, he burst through the door, not waiting for the First Footman to open it—a mild breach of Protocol that was easy enough to overlook, given that he was a king. The pelting rain beat down the fog of prattleweed smoke that coughed out behind him, so no one caught the whiff of it.

Flustered at the unexpectedly early emergence, the trumpeters spluttered out an ungainly end to the piece. At a quick nod from their maestro, each grabbed a bombard, the official instrument of the Half Kingdom. The bombard was a double-reeded relative of the oboe, but lacked the warmth and smoothness of its cousin. Listening to a group of them made you yearn for the joyful pleasure of being slammed in the head by a dozen bagpipes. Every entrance of a royal from the Half Kingdom was met with bombards belching out an aneurysm-inducing rendition of "Çalaht Save Our Currently Reigning (Fill in the Appropriate King or Queen) and Let's Hope (Fill in the Appropriate Gender Pronoun) Lasts a Bit Longer Than The Last One," the centuries-old anthem of that realm.

Mercifully, it was a short song, which kept the diplomatic skirmishes set off by its instrumentation to a minimum.

Johanna ignored the din and seemed happy for once. "Uncle Doncaster looks well." The king wore a jet-black travel cloak over midnight-blue pants and tunic. His travel crown had a simple thin band of silver, with the de Chëëëkflïïïnt family crest (an antelope with bagels hanging from each of its points and a gecko holding an origami limpet) stamped in the front. Impervious to the rain, he strode like the ruler he was toward Queen Eloise II, arms outstretched to accept her embrace.

The queen gave him the customary Western Lands and All That Really Matters kisses (right cheek, left cheek, forehead), then stepped back, holding his arms above the elbows. Taking the required formal tone, but with a genuine smile, she said, "Welcome, King Doncaster Worsted Halva de Chëëëkflïïïnt. The lofty strains of 'Çalaht Save Our Currently Reigning (Fill in the Appropriate King or Queen) and Let's Hope (Fill in the Appropriate Gender Pronoun) Lasts a Bit Longer Than The Last One' played on your native bombard stirs the soul almost as much as the presence of the person it presages. It is my pleasure to officially welcome you to the Western Lands and All That Really Matters. May your stay here be healthful and prosperous."

"Healthful and prosperous," echoed the queen's retinue as one.

"Thank you, Queen Eloise," he replied with equal formality. "I bring greetings from the people of the Half Kingdom. May our lands always live side by side in peace and harmony." He did not give her a Western Lands kiss back, but instead, took her hand and put her palm on his forehead in the Half Kingdom way.

"Peace and harmony," repeated everyone.

Doncaster turned to his brother. "G'afternoon, brother mine," said Doncaster. "How good to see you again, and in such radiant luster."

"Radiant luster," everyone said.

"G'afternoon, my brother," replied Chafed. "May Çalaht smile upon you and your people with her gap-toothed benevolence."

"Gap-toothed benevolence."

The jester Turpy ran up, unfurling a soot-colored umbrella. He then had to keep up as Doncaster walked down the reception line. The already unpleasant rain doubled down, pelting the welcoming dignitaries. None of them dared seek shelter, as breaking short a Welcoming was considered an ill omen for the visit.

Making his way down the line of dignitaries, office holders and advisors, Doncaster finally made it to where Johanna stood, and kissed her right cheek, left cheek, and forehead. "Johanna Umgotteswillen Gumball. How is my favorite niece?" He smiled. "And look!" He gently chucked her chin and turned her head to the side. "You're wearing my ear cuff. May I say, it suits you perfectly, splendidly, beautifully."

"Thank you, King Doncaster."

"Oh, please. Call me 'Uncle D' like you did when you were young." He leaned in conspiratorially. "Even if it goes against Protocol just a little."

"Yes, uh, Uncle D."

"That's better." He bowed formally at her, winked, then turned to Eloise.

His smiled stayed the same, but the spark of warmth evaporated. "Princess Eloise." No kisses. No palm to forehead.

"King Doncaster," she replied with a small curtsy. "Welcome back to our home."

"Yes, your home, house, domicile. Indeed. Well, it warms me to be here, and all that." A movement at Eloise's feet caught his eye. "And who have we here?"

"King Doncaster, it prides me to introduce to you Jerome Abernatheen de Chipmunk, my champion."

Doncaster's eyebrows shot up, and he frowned down at Jerome. "You named a rat as your champion? Really?"

Jerome straightened and looked Doncaster in the eye as best he could. "Sir, we chipmunks are rodents, but not rats."

Doncaster shrugged at Jerome. "Rodent. Rat. Whatever." He looked back at Eloise, a genuine curiosity relighting the spark in his eye. "How's that working out for you?"

"Fine, King Doncaster. Just fine."

"I'm sure it is." He reached out to chuck her on the chin as he had her sister, but she stepped back to avoid his hand. Doncaster clucked disapprovingly. "Well, let's hope that the young lady, lass, damsel who will most likely one day rule this queendom has not plucked a lemon from the orchard of possibility." He looked down at Jerome again. "Good luck, little rat. If history is our guide, you'll need it."

HAGGLEBERRY TEA AND A
STOLEN NOSE

Welcoming formalities concluded, the bombard players splished toward the front doors, playing "Halfway to Halfway from Halfway," another Half Kingdom favorite. Everyone followed them into the Entrance Vestibule, shrugged soaked overcoats into the arms of waiting servants, then proceeded to the Receiving Room, where they were handed steaming, fragrant mugs of haggleberry tea. The room was decorated in various dark hues, reflecting Doncaster's preferences. Branches of polished ebony lined the walls, recalling the antlers of the family crest. They were bedecked with blackbread bagels and gray, limpet-shaped sweet biscuits. Guests plucked the food from the branches as a snack to go with their tea.

Eloise and Jerome stood at the far side of the room, safely away from the press of activity (and, for Jerome's sake, away from the cadaverous mien of Turpy and the hulk of Gouache). Eloise blew across the lip of her cup, trying to get the tea to a sipping temperature. Jerome stood on a table at her elbow and sniffed his cup. He sighed, took a small taste, and made a face.

"What?" asked Eloise.

"Nothing."

"Go ahead."

"Well, it's the haggleberry tea. It's been brewed about ten degrees too hot and left to steep like an old sock in a laundry cauldron. That brings out the bitterness and emphasizes the chalky undertone that's normally easily masked by the fruity highlights when brewed properly."

"When did you become a tea snob?"

"Snob? Really?" He set down the cup next to him and nudged it away with his foot. "May I speak frankly, Princess Eloise Hydra Gumball III?"

Amused, Eloise said, "You may, el Champo. You're the expert."

"I am far from an expert. I like to think I'm a well-rounded aficionado. But snob? Please. There's nothing wrong with caring about things that are important to you. The difference between properly made haggleberry tea and *that*?" Jerome pointed with the toe of his boot. "It's the difference between being able to drink with pleasure and wanting to hoick it against the wall."

Eloise took a sip and shrugged. "Tastes OK to me."

"Well, there you go. Look around." He waved his tail, implicating everyone in the room. "Pretty much all of them would agree with you. But they—and, if I may say so, Princess, you—are ignorant of the palate of flavors the humble haggleberry can command when properly prepared and cleansed of its toxins. If you wish to wallow in ignorance, by all means, be part of that philistine throng. But if you'd like me to share some of the marvels properly brewed tea can bring, it would be my pleasure. I can tell you, for example, that despite the butchery of its brewing, that batch of haggleberries is unusually high quality, brought in from The South, and grown not last season, but the season before. The berries were watered by the River Thurmond, because it was a drier year, and the usual rains were not enough. That gives them an oaky bass note. They were harvested using a blade, not plucked, because the bruising that happens when you pluck them leaps out in the flavor, and that's missing here."

"Who picked them?"

"A 14-year-old lass named Gerte from the de Haggland family."

"You can tell that from the taste?" Eloise sipped again. "Impressive."

"No, I saw a package in a shop. She was on the label."

A twitter of laughter from the center of the room drew their attention. Johanna chatted animatedly with her parents and Doncaster. Eloise was grateful Protocol did not demand she be over there.

"They seem very comfortable together," observed Jerome. "But he practically frosted your eyebrows when he spoke to you. Why would one not get along with one's beloved uncle?"

"One can remember exactly when one's uncle first got up one's nose. And one's uncle has been firmly lodged there for most of one's life."

"What happened to one for one to feel so strongly?"

"One's first memory—I can't keep that up. My first memory of him must be from when I was about two, maybe two-and-a-half? He was doing that 'I'm going to take your nose' trick you do to kids, where you pretend to take their nose, then make your thumb look like the stolen nose by poking it between your index and middle fingers."

"We didn't do that in my household. Maybe it's hard to get a claw to look like a chipmunk nose."

"Well, I was sitting on his knee in the Mush Room, where he'd been trying to play with me and Johanna. I remember Johanna was playing with a plush toy rutabaga he gave her. She adored that stuffed vegetable. Kept it with her for years. I'm pretty sure he gave me a toy broccoli."

Jerome's whiskers twitched. "Just what every young girl wants—a toy broccoli."

"For sure. Anyway, when he 'took' my nose and 'showed' it to me, I thought it was real. I screamed like part of my body had been torn off, which is exactly what I thought had happened. I bolted from the room shrieking, desperately trying to find my mother. I howled my way into the Declaiming Room, where she was giving a speech of some sort, and flung myself at her, inconsolable. Doncaster came in after me, and when I saw him, I ran around the room, hands clapped over my ears, convinced they were next. It took both of my parents and three nannies a good 15 minutes to calm me enough to convince me that my face was OK."

"I'd love to read the scribe's notes from that day," said Jerome.

"I'm sure they're somewhere in the Bibliotheca de Records and Regrets. Anyway, when I'd regained enough composure, I stamped my foot and demanded Uncle Doncaster return my nose, which he did by showing me the thumb between his fingers again, pressing my face, and then opening his hand to show he no longer had it. I also insisted he promise never to take it without permission again. Which, to his credit, he did. But I think I've been wary of him ever since, and over time, he's been about as friendly as you saw earlier."

"You know he didn't take your nose, right?"

"Of course."

"So, maybe you can let that one go."

Eloise looked at Jerome, head tilted, considering. "Point taken, Champion Abernatheen de Chipmunk. Point taken." She set down her cup. "I'd love for you to enlighten me about the wonders of haggleberry tea. But not just now." Then she turned away, glided to the center of the room, and slid into the conversation her sister was having with her uncle and parents.

❧ 16 ❧

JESTERS' GESTURES

The lavish welcome dinner for Doncaster traipsed lightly past a lot of normal Protocol, since it was so soon after the earlier formal reception. Still, the hall was packed, and the throng enjoyed Chef's finest truffle-stuffed mushrooms, a curry featuring cauliflower, parsnip, and cashews, and for dessert, six forms of caramel served as mystery tasters (Eloise particularly liked the one that hinted at lime). Jerome sat in his attendant's spot behind her, resolutely looking at anything that wasn't Turpy or Gouache, who lurked seven chairs away, behind Doncaster, as his servants.

As pots of haggleberry chai were wheeled in, thoughts turned to entertainment. Queen Eloise waved for the lutenist to take her place on the platform at the center of the room. She played a stirring acoustic version of "I Would Walk 500 Strong Lengths," a melancholic rendition of "Born in the Western Lands and All That Really Matters" (surprising, since it was usually more anthemic), and finally brought smiles with a slightly ribald "Stuck in the Middle with Ewww."

When the applause subsided, Chafed leaned forward so he could see Doncaster on the other side of his wife. "What about you, brother?"

Doncaster's full attention was on his caramels. "What about me?"

"You brought your jesters. Would they care to entertain?"

Doncaster put down his spoon. "Trust me. I advise against it."

The queen jostled her brother-in-law with an elbow. "Come now. As I recall, they did not take the stage last time they were here, either. Surely your jesters have some amusement to spare in them. Why else would you have them with you?"

"Oh, *I* find them amusing enough. But are they 'entertaining' to others? Well, that's patchy. But, if you insist..." Doncaster swiveled in his chair to look at them. Turpy leaned back against the stone wall, his eyes narrow, calculating. Gouache sat next to him on a stool, his bulky posture pulled in on itself, clearly saying, "Not me." Doncaster pointed at Turpy. "Go. But keep it above the waistline. We're guests." He turned back to the king and queen and, with an exaggerated flourish, said, "I give you one of my jesters, Turpy."

The jester looked straight at his monarch, but did not move, eyes challenging.

Doncaster looked back at him for a moment, annoyed, then realized what the problem was. "My apologies. My introduction was inadequate. May I present to you, His Jesterness, Turpentine Snotearrow McCcoonnch." Doncaster drizzled sarcasm over each word. It was like the honorific "His Jesterness" was a concession, won from the king when Doncaster lost a bet.

Having been "properly" introduced, Turpy pushed himself from the wall to walk toward the stage.

"Wait, wait, wait. Snotearrow McCcoonnch?" said Chafed. "Snotearrow McCcoonnch! I've known you, what, 15 years? All this time, and it only just occurs now to ask if you are related to Alstaria Snotearrow McCcoonnch. Are you?"

Turpy did not bother to hide his sigh. "Yes, sire. She was our mother."

Chafed beamed. "She was a genius! I loved her work, especially the Late Middle Period, when she devoted herself to painting on black velvet. I know for a fact we have at least six Snotearrow McCcoonnchs here in Castle de Brague, don't we, dear?" The queen nodded, not sharing his fervor. "I don't know which is my favorite," Chafed burbled. "The one with the cats wearing period garb playing hockey sacking? Or the one with the cats wearing period garb playing cards? Or maybe the one where the cat in period garb is looking down from the ceiling. Oh! Such delightful whimsy! And you, my good man. How did you end up a jester? And working for my esteemed brother, no less."

"Just my good fortune, sire, I'm sure." Turpy's words were remarkably clear, given his clenched teeth.

"Do you also paint? Does talent follow talent in your family?"

Doncaster butted in. "Any facility with paintbrush or charcoal that once flourished among the Snotearrow McCcoonnchs well and truly went to the grave with Alstaria. Turpy—wait, sorry—His Jest-er-ness Turpentine has proven that time and time again. Haven't you, Turpy?"

"His Highness has been kind enough to look at some of my work and give his learned opinion," said Turpy. "It is, as he said himself, 'Unfit to be hung in a store selling second-hand chamber pot cleaning utensils.' So, by the gap-toothed smile of our blessed, long-thumbed Çalaht, I am a jester."

"I see," said Chafed. "Well, there you go."

That line of enquiry having stumbled to an end, Turpy sloped to the platform, stepped up, crossed his arms, and slowly turned a full circle, assessing the crowd. He was cadaverously thin, as if his closest confidants were intestinal parasites. His black and gray harlequin was expensive—Doncaster would have made sure of that—but it hung like a dishcloth, worn with an air that made it clear his mind was elsewhere, presumably scheming. He picked up the megaphone.

Jesters normally told jokes, sang songs, or sang jokey songs. Turpy was more of a joker, but they were jokes in form only. He started with, "Being in Her Majesty's presence is a complete joy, like what one feels when a putrefying abscess finally bursts," and went downhill from there. Turpy skewered, jabbed, inveighed, and taunted his audience with insults and invective—every word a bitter fruit born of a poisoned tree. When he sang, which he did exactly once, it was like listening to barbs being ripped from the flesh, if slightly less musical.

No topic was off-limits, least of all the royalties of the four and a half realms, their politics, and their courts. There were barbs about Queen Eloise's supposedly bloodthirsty enforcement of the ban against people naming their children after her, a joke about the Central Ranges khan that centered on him being known as "Khan't Be Bothered," some could-be-interpreted-as-off-color remarks regarding bits of the Southie queen falling off and being replaced with religious relics, an incredibly long string of groan-worthy olive puns at the expense of all Eastern Landers, delivered at an auctioneer's pace, and even a series of swipes at his own king, skewering his dress sense, his incompetent manage-ment of state affairs, his inability to land a suitable spouse, his odor, his lack of facility with numbers, musical tunes, or pickles, and a joke that only Doncaster got involving a galah, a pot of treacle, and a wand of burning sage. It was all extremely clever. Clever and served with enough truth that one could not help smirking, despite the pain it inflicted. But only Doncaster seemed to truly savor it, his lone belly laughs punching out after each joke.

Eloise glanced back at Jerome, who shook his head.

Then Turpy said, "That, nobles and ignobles, kings and king hits, queens and quacks, is your taxation levies at work." He then dropped the megaphone and sloped off stage. Apparently, he was done.

The room sat in silence, save a slow clap and a few "bravos" from Doncaster.

The queen turned to her brother-in-law and said, "Now that was a performance. I daresay we'll not hear anything like that within these walls for years to come."

Doncaster ignored the faint praise. He turned, pointed at Gouache and, like he was waiting for a punch in the nose, said, "Go ahead." Gouache glanced at Turpy, who nodded assent, then heaved up from the stool and slouched toward the platform.

Gouache was Turpy's younger brother by 22 months. Triple his brother's size, he was muscled like a former warrior gone soft and three decades past his prime, and he wore the look of a sullen dullard in the "before" picture of an advertisement for nervines. Everything about him screamed, "Please don't be mean to me again." As he reached the platform, Doncaster stood to announce him, but unlike his introduction for Turpy, his tone was long-suffering. "May I present my other jester, Gouache Snotearrow McCcoonnch."

Gouache stepped up on the stage, sighed one more time, then picked up the megaphone and stared at his feet for a while.

And then the light in him came on.

"Ladeeeeeeees and gentlemen—and all points in between!" The transformation to crowd-engaging performer was startling, and his mild jest got appreciative chuckles. "I'd like to sing a favorite for you. 'Three Bags of Groats for My Sweetheart.'" He turned to the lutenist. "If you please? In A minor." The lutenist, surprised, grabbed her instrument and plucked an arpeggiated chord. Gouache, head tilted slightly, let the last note hang, like he was savoring every lingering harmonic, and then he sang.

"There's a lady who knows all that glitters is groats..."

His voice, a countertenor, was startlingly high for a man his size. It was pure sweetness, and he caressed each word. When he got to the end where the singer convinces his sweetheart to trade the overflowing groat bags for true love's first kiss, he held the last word, like he was cuddling a baby dove.

The room exploded in applause.

Gouache smiled shyly, and quipped, "I'll be selling groats afterward, if anyone requires three bags." Again, appreciative laughs. "And now— 'Jester Went A-Courtin.'"

"Jester went a-courtin, and he was snide. Mhmm.

"Jest went a-courtin, and he was snide. A word and a pistil were his pride. Mhmm. Mhmm. Mhmm."

He picked out one lady near the stage and focused his performance on her. Gouache's interpretation of the song infused the lyrics of a jester's clumsy attempt to woo a noble's daughter into a self-deprecating confessional. It was met with even more applause than the first song.

Gouache bowed, and said to the woman, "You're the accoucheur of my *cri de coeur*, a force majeure to this poor raconteur, a de rigueur saboteur, a cocklebur in my underfur. Were I not a jester, I would come a-courtin. But, alas, I shall content myself with a kiss on the cheek." And with that, he boldly leaned over, demanding a kiss, which the maiden gave, to hoots from the crowd.

"And finally, 'The Baleful Sorrows of Jedd the Sea Urchin.'" It wasn't a tune anyone knew, and it was odd for someone to sing a song about a sea urchin's unrequited love for someone named Larissa the Anemone. But by the end, there was not a dry eye in the hall.

And with that, Gouache waved, bowed to the crowd, bowed to the royal table, and finally to King Doncaster who, unlike everyone else, seemed unimpressed.

The transformation when Gouache stepped off the stage was as sudden and complete as before. Eloise joined in the enthusiastic applause but watched, puzzled, as the jester resumed his hulking, sullen manner, folding in on himself like a tissue crocus left out in the spring rains.

Eloise looked at Jerome and furrowed her brow. He shrugged back. "At least it was entertaining," he whispered.

17

THE CEREMONIES OF THE STONE

Eloise nodded to the wheat monger, who bowed to her twice and walked away, pleased to have received a good omen. With a sigh, Johanna once again put the Stone of the Ancestors on her sister's tongue and another three minutes were added to the total.

Eloise moved the stone to the side of her cheek, as much embarrassed as annoyed. "Bloody stone. Bloody ancestors. Why couldn't they have used a smaller one? Or at least one less slippery."

Jerome made another tick on the parchment in front of him. "That makes 347 requests to see the stone so far. 72 drops. So roughly one in five people got to kiss the Stone of the Ancestors."

"I'm going to vomit," lisped Eloise around the stone.

"Don't!" the other two shouted.

Eloise sipped water and waved to indicate that the nausea had passed. It was exhausting and confronting. All those potential sicknesses practically coating the stone. Part of her wanted to run screaming from the room. She was controlling it, but only just.

"Seriously, do you have issues with your tongue?" asked Johanna. "I'm sure you're on track for the longest Placing of the Stone ever." She'd kept her anger at having to be the Stoner more or less in check, but it burbled along.

"It only feels like it," mumbled Jerome as he calculated in the margins. He looked up to see the two girls staring at him. "Really, she's not on track for anything yet. Princess Eloise has only added 216 minutes to the clock, which is, what, a bit over three and a half hours? Maybe that might qualify for the top 20 percent. But there have been Placings of the Stone that lasted as long as three days, and one that lasted an entire two months."

"Really?" slurred Eloise. "Two months?"

"Came across it while I was researching the Ceremonies. Orina Flechette Bufferdale Gumball, about 170 years ago. Apparently, she was born such that the muscles of her tongue couldn't curl. The thing just wouldn't stay on. For that one, they brought folks in from all over the countryside so they didn't run out of people to ask to see the stone, since you can only ask once."

"Çalaht spare us that," said Johanna.

"Never heard of her," said Eloise.

"She died, so never ruled. Contracted some sort of ague toward the end of the seventh week of the Placing of the Stone and was pushing up daffodils three days after the Ceremonies finally finished."

Eloise looked around the Hall of Bald Opulence, shuddering to think about the variety of agues lurking there. The room overflowed, and the line of people waiting for their turn with the princess and her stoner seemed endless.

Plus, she'd done so much counting. The "yuuuuuuuuuck!" of her habits clawed at her, and she counted to keep them in check. She'd counted the people in line. She counted shoes on the wall, the number of tables, the number of people at the tables, and stones in the walls. It was all that kept her in the seat.

Johanna looked at her sister and shook her head slowly. "Let's see what we can do about keeping that bloody stone on your tongue better. I don't want to be doing this another three hours, much less three days." She turned a sweet smile on the next person in line and beckoned forward what might have been mistaken for a large bundle of rags.

The squat croftwoman shuffled up the steps of the dais and took her place in front of Eloise. "Princess Eloise Hydra Gumball III," she began. "I am Hoarfrost de Blotter." A puzzled look took over her face, followed by a sudden flush that shot from neck to forehead. She shoved her hand into her left pocket and pulled out a small ball of yarn and an oversized yam, which she tucked under her arm. Her hand went back into her pocket and she peered in, making sure there was nothing else there. Shoving the yarn and yam back in, she fished around in her right pocket, half her lower lip tucked between her teeth in concentration. The woman pulled out a dozen acorns, one of which bounced away from her. Finally, she exhaled and smiled, having found the thing she'd been looking for—a shred of paperbark with smudged, half-legible notes for the ritual words she was supposed to say to the princess.

The woman stared at the bark, looked up at Eloise, ducked a small curtsy as an apology, cleared her throat, looked down, squinted, looked up again at Eloise, looked down, turned the paperbark right-side up, cocked her head and mouthed the words in rehearsal, frowned, then shoved the paperbark into her left pocket. She decided that starting over was the way to go. "Princess Eloise Hydra Gumball III. I'm Hoarfrost de Blotter." She froze, eyes suddenly frantic, and shoved both hands into her pockets, desperate to find the paperbark again.

Eloise gestured to stop her. "It's OK," she said, words muddied by the stone. "You'll be fine. Just wing it."

"Beggin' yer pardon, mu'um. That's most kind of yer. I'm a wee bit skittsy to be here in yer presence. And yours," she added, bouncing her head toward Johanna. "And the queen and king just over there. Me daughter and I have traveled a week to be here. Çalaht on a dung heap, who'd have thought I'd be standing next to the likes of you fine ladies. Oh! Pardon my language mu'um."

"It's OK, Goodwoman de Blotter," said Johanna. "Now, feel free to continue when you're ready."

The croftwoman cleared her throat and started once more. "Princess Eloise Hydra Gumball III. I'm, uh, I'm..." She trailed off, having gone vague again.

"Hoarfrost de Blotter," prompted Jerome in a stage whisper.

"Oh, Çalaht on a sackbut, I forgot me own name. I'm Hoarfrost de Blotter, and, and..."

Eloise pointed to the bulge in her cheek as a hint.

"And I would ask if you could please show me the Stone of the Ancestors."

Johanna exhaled an audible sigh of relief when the croftwoman finally got her sentence out. Eloise nodded, smiled, and extended her tongue so the stone was visible, only to have it drop into her lap.

Hoarfrost de Blotter squealed with delight. "It fell! The Stone of the Ancestors fell! It's a good omen fer me, fer sure."

Johanna retrieved the stone from Eloise's lap and presented it to the croftwoman. Hoarfrost promptly bobbled the stone, which went skittering toward the escaped acorn. Without warning, she jostled over to where they lay, which caused Lorch Lacksneck to stiffen, ready to tackle her in case she was some sort of assassin. The woman snatched up both the stone and the acorn, wiped them on her dress, cupped them in her hands and, scrunching up her face, gave them a massive kiss. Mission accomplished, she shuffled back to her spot in front of Eloise and extended her hands to Johanna. Johanna cupped hers beneath and, when the woman opened her hands, caught both the stone and its acorn neighbor, Johanna gave the woman a pleasant enough smile, returned the acorn, and kissed the stone. Eloise opened her mouth and her sister put it back in it, reciting, "Herewith I return the Stone of the Ancestors." Then she added under her breath, "Again."

Hoarfrost de Blotter oscillated her bobbing thanks from Eloise to Johanna to Jerome to Lorch and back to Eloise. Then she made her way off the dais, bubbling, "I got me a good omen."

With the woman gone, Johanna shook her head at Eloise. "You dropped that one on purpose, didn't you?"

Eloise shrugged, trying to hide the part of her that felt revulsion. "She seemed like someone who needed a good omen. What's another three minutes on the clock?"

"Or another shot at catching the ague," Johanna added. She waved forward the next in line, a young mother holding a dribble-nosed son. "Next, please."

Morning became afternoon, headed into evening, and dragged on into night. The throng in the Hall of Bald Opulence remained strong, but the mood shifted as hours passed. The first few dozen times that Eloise dropped the stone, people seemed happy to have others receive good omens. As the day, then night, wore on, and the prospect of getting to the feast seemed to move farther away, each new drop caused a sigh of disappointment. Plentiful snacks ensured that no one went hungry, and while people were free to come and go, only those present when the time ran down to zero could wait for the Receiving of the Stone and the subsequent feast. So they stuck around, but the mood soured.

Coming so soon after the disaster of the Naming ceremony, it was almost inevitable that there might be whispers about the princess's fitness for her role as heir.

By midnight, Eloise felt like her every muscle twitch and nostril flare was being scrutinized by a room that got less hospitable by the quarter-hour. She had no choice but to stick this out. There was no end to the line of people wanting to see the stone, which was fine. That's what they were there for. But everyone was tired, and well and truly ready for the Placing of the Stone to be over. Johanna kept her snark level relatively low, but recognized that they were all tired. Jerome seemed indefatigable, happily ticking off numbers on his tally, and quipping to keep the mood up as much as possible.

Around 1:30 in the morning, Doncaster wandered over from across the room, where'd he been camped for the day with his brother and the queen. He sauntered onto the dais, his midnight blue velvet cape billowing once, perfectly. Doncaster reached for Johanna's hand and gave it a brief, formal kiss. "You're doing an excellent job as the Stoner. The line has moved smoothly all day, and the repeated replacing of the stone has been efficient and economical, both excellent qualities. Well done, niece."

Johanna blushed at the flattery. "Thank you, Uncle D."

He turned to Eloise. "Can't you do this?" He stuck out his tongue, curling both sides upward to form a kind of tube. "You could hold it in better that way."

"No. My tongue doesn't do that," she said. "Not everyone's does, apparently."

"Could be worse," he smirked. "Could have been the Ceremony of the Liver Cactus, like they do in The South, the loons. Anyway, while I'm here..." He trailed off, and looked at Johanna. "Do you mind?"

"Of course. Go right ahead."

Doncaster bowed formally to her, then fixed his eyes on Eloise, unblinking. "Princess Eloise Hydra Gumball III. I am Doncaster Worsted Halva de Chëëëkflïïint, Monarch of the Half Kingdom, formerly known as the Northern Lands." He spoke each word with clipped precision, like he was dictating them to a headstone engraver. "And I would ask if you could please show me the Stone of the Ancestors."

Eloise met his gaze. There was no way she would drop the stone. Not this time. Not for him. Staring straight back at him, she slowly, carefully, extended her tongue, balancing the slick stone perfectly for the requisite time, and then took it back into her mouth.

Doncaster nodded again, quirking a half smile. He reached over and patted the cheek where the stone nestled. "There you go, niece. That's not so hard, is it?" Then the smile left his eyes, if not his mouth, and he leaned forward so that only Eloise could hear. "Now, let's get this ridiculous ceremony over with, shall we? And for the love of Çalaht, show the people you deserve to be sitting there."

Eloise felt the slap of his words, and blood rose in her cheeks. She turned from his gaze, mortified. Not waiting for a reply, Doncaster turned, gave Johanna a friendly wink, and hopped off the dais, his velvet cape again billowing exactly once. He strode back to his seat, sat down, and fixed Eloise with his gaze. From the corner of her eye, Eloise saw Turpy lean in and whisper something. Doncaster nodded, and the two of them stared at her, unblinking.

Something went cold and determined inside Eloise. Exhausted and feeling like a deadly ague was setting up residence in her body, she drew a breath and straightened. Eloise turned and faced the four eyes locked on her from across the room. Without breaking their gaze, she motioned to Johanna to bring on the next person.

For the next three hours and 22 minutes, her showing of the Stone of the Ancestors was flawless. She was a stone-showing, tongue balancing mechanical device. She even stopped counting, not needing to distract her habits. Not a good omen was to be had anywhere. Ask, show, ask, show, ask, show. Jerome's quill scratched marks one after the other as the minutes ticked downward uninterrupted. Eloise continued to stare at her uncle and his servant. Sometimes both looked back at her, sometimes it was only one or the other. But she focused on them to keep the resolve in her gut.

When the time ran out toward dawn, an exhausted applause rose from the room. Johanna rang the Gong of the Ancestors, everyone stood, and she lifted her voice to lead the "Hymn of the Ceremonies of the Stone of the Ancestors." Her voice echoed through the hall, rousing the tired gathering. The song had several verses, which allowed those who'd fallen asleep to be wakened, and messengers sent to fetch those who might have snuck away but wanted to slip in unnoticed so they could be there when the stone was swallowed.

Twenty-three verses later, the room was revived and refilled. Eloise showed the stone one last time, then gulped it, trying not to think of all the agues going down into her stomach. The crowd clapped, tired but grateful that this stage of the proceedings had been reached. The court scribe droned the Gumball lineage, starting with Agnes Delion Frostbite Gumball, as the hour of waiting began.

Eloise realized she must have dozed when Jerome's tug at her sleeve startled her into wakefulness. "Two more minutes," he whispered, between Lucian Lanyard Halitosis Gumball and Lyallia Kostbar Chilblain Gumball. Johanna rang the Gong of the Ancestors just on Maab Anchusa Tarboosh Gumball. The hour had passed.

Johanna reached over to a small table, handed Eloise a large bowl, and hefted a black glass flagon full of the emetic. "Time for the Receiving of the Stone," she called.

Eloise hardly needed the encouragement inside the flask. Already her guts were calling on her to expel the intruder, and the smallest sip of the vile liquid convinced the rest of her body to go along with the plan. With surprising force and speed, the stone shot into the bowl, bounced off the inside, and clattered to the floor. This had the small benefit of saving Johanna the need to poke around for it, but required a few extra towels.

Johanna picked it up, cleaned it, kissed it, gave it to Eloise to kiss, then, in her last act as Stoner, Johanna pinched the stone between finger and thumb and, holding it aloft, said, "Let us welcome the return of the Stone of the Ancestors, and all the ties it has to those who came before us."

"Welcome, Stone of the Ancestors," replied the room.

"Let the feasting begin!"

A relieved cheer rose, and the people moved into the dining hall, for once ahead of the royal family, not after. Plates, tongs, and forks clattered, and Eloise felt grateful she'd never have to ever do anything so deliberately vile again.

Her family gave her hugs, then left her to recover before joining the throng. "Don't feel obligated to eat," her mother said as she left. Eloise could only roll her eyes in a not-going-to-be-a-problem way.

Jerome looked at her, concerned. "You OK, Ellery?"

"Yeah. I think so. Thanks for your help."

"That must be what champions are for," he said. "Now, I'm guessing you're on a fast path to a nasty illness if we're not careful. Stay here, and I'll get Odmilla to make you an echinacea, ginger, and haggleberry infusion."

18

KING AND CARROTAGE

The afternoon was garrulously bright, so Doncaster returned to his chambers. He sat looking from the third-story window at the town surrounding the castle and the fields beyond, slowly stroking the gray streak in his beard, his thoughts a million strong lengths away. Gouache sat on a stool in the corner, embroidering delicate gray roses onto the black patches of his jester's harlequin, quietly humming "Three Bags of Groats for My Sweetheart."

Turpy opened a hemp bag and fished out another half thimble of prattleweed. He'd been encouraging Doncaster to enjoy more than usual. They were, after all, away from home and the watching eyes of those who might point out the hypocrisy of the king's enjoyment. Plus, Turpy needed the king amenable. Turpy just needed to time it right, so the king did not show up to the evening's official dinner over-prattled.

Turpy put the prattleweed in the top bowl of the hookah, replaced the mesh cover, snagged a coal from the fireplace with tongs, and set it on the screen to heat the dried leaves and twigs (but not the seeds, which were way too potent). Turpy sat the hookah on the table, handing Doncaster the hose. The king absently put the mouth tip to his lips.

The long puff of prattleweed smoke produced a sigh and a smile, one of the first since he'd arrived at Castle de Brague.

"You seem pensive, Sire."

Doncaster looked at Turpy, blinking his way back into the room. "Pensive," he repeated. "An excellent word, young Turpentine. Pensive indeed. Thoughtful, preoccupied, contemplative."

"Would it help to talk about it?"

"Talk. Discourse. Converse. Confabulate. Yes, young Turpentine, let us jaw together."

"Yes, Sire."

"You know what the problem with being a king is?"

Turpy could guess, but shook his head.

"Lack of options. One's options are limited. Bounded. Constrained. Circumscribed."

"You are king, Sire. Surely not."

"But there you'd be wrong. The Half Kingdom, being half a kingdom, doesn't have the resources, the wherewithal, nor the gumption to rise from the ennui that has stricken it for 200-plus years."

"Well, Sire. I'm sure something will turn up. May I make a suggestion, Sire?"

"Yes. For sure. Indubitably."

"A walk, Sire."

"You suggest a stroll, a saunter, a perambulation. Excellent idea. Clear the cobwebs. Where do you suggest?"

"Have you seen Princess Johanna's garden? I understand it is lovely."

"No one has seen Princess Johanna's garden. It is off-limits. Gesperrt. Verboten. Not to be breached."

"Then you, Sire, should be the first."

Doncaster puffed again. And again. Then he stood, grabbed a cloak, and headed for the door, muttering, "Closed. Restricted. Barred. Unenterable."

Turpy followed him out the door, leaving Gouache to his needlework.

❧

JOHANNA WAS PLANTING LEEK SEEDLINGS WHEN THE GATE TO HER garden rattled. She didn't bother to look up. "Go away. It's locked for a reason."

"Princess Johanna?"

"Uncle D!" She patted down the dirt, stood, and hurried to the wrought-iron gate. "What a surprise! Are you lost?"

"Indeed not!" he said. "Could I come in?"

"Uh, no. Sorry. People don't."

"I can't have a look?"

"You want to see my garden? Why?"

"I understand it is pretty."

"Who told you that?"

Doncaster looked around and pointed at his jester. "Him. His sense of these things is rather good."

"Uncle D, I'm sorry, but—"

Doncaster threw open his arms, and in his most majestic, prattle-infused voice, said, "Princess Johanna Umgotteswillen Gumball, I would ask you to do me the kindness of sharing the beauty, the wonder, the verdancy of your garden."

"Oh. Goodness." Johanna blushed. "Uh, sure, I guess. When you say it that way." She fished a key from her tunic pocket, and the gate soon swung open. Doncaster crossed under the stone archway and swept past her. Turpy tried to follow, but Johanna put up a hand. "Not you.

Sorry." Then she locked the gate and turned her back to find Doncaster already among the foliage.

Turpy watched the two of them go, his upper lip twitching at the slight.

Johanna watched Doncaster stride the pebbled paths up and down from one end to the other, then around the perimeter, like he was scoping a battlefield. He then stepped to the exact middle and pointed down at a plant. "This one," he said to Johanna.

"What about it?"

"Tell me everything about it."

"The carrot?"

"Ah! It's a carrot. I would not have known. Yes, yes, tell me everything about the carrot. Why, for example, is it not orange?"

"That is the carrot top."

"The carrot has a top, an upper bit, an apex?"

"Are you teasing me? Do you really want a discourse on carrots? Did you not take Botanicals and Herblore? Or Cookery and Cuisine?"

"The odds are very good that I did. But they are also very good that I did not attend, or if I did attend, be present, participate, that my attention was likely elsewhere. Go ahead. Elucidate, explicate, and expound upon the carrot."

"Right." Johanna straightened, still wary that he was tricking her some-how, but went with it. "The carrot, *daucus carota*, subspecies *sativus*, is a root vegetable that grows easily in both cold and temperate climes across the realms. It is known for its edible taproot, which as you previously observed is commonly orange, but in this case—" Johanna bent to grasp the base of the carrot's foliage, and with an exaggerated flourish, pulled it from the ground and held it up for him to see. "Ta dah!"

Doncaster gasped. "It's purple!"

"Indeed."

"Then it is not a carrot."

"Au contraire. It is a purple carrot."

"It cannot be. Carrots must be orange." It was the prattleweed, but Johanna was not to know that.

"Uncle D. You cannot decree these non-carrots. The purple ones are my favorites." She handed it to him. "A gift."

"I am honored, Princess."

"But wait! There's more." Johanna's tone was still somewhat mocking, but she was pleased at his seemingly genuine interest. She walked to different beds and pulled a series of carrots, presenting them one at a time. "Red. White. Black. Yellow. And the one you know and love, orange."

"A rainbow of carrotage." Doncaster examined them closely, then turned to her, serious. "I would taste them."

She pointed him to a basin and table at the south wall, near an alcove where she stored seeds in carefully labeled wax-sealed clay pots. The basin looked like it had been scavenged from a disused bathing room, as it featured the Gumball Crest and unused spouts for both hot and cold water. Johanna poured a pail of rainwater into the stoppered basin, and with a boar hair brush (boars, badgers, and camels being the main members of the Brushmakers Guild), scrubbed off the dirt.

"Start with the orange one, since that is what you know best," said Johanna. "Let that set a standard for the others to follow."

King Doncaster held up the orange carrot, greens still attached, and took a delicate bite from the middle. He chewed, contemplating, then declared, "It tastes like a carrot."

"As you would expect." She poured him a mug of water. "You should cleanse your palate."

Doncaster swished, and at a nod from Johanna, spat into the azalea patch beside him. "Next?"

One by one, Doncaster tasted the carrots, praising each. "A bit woodier, but sweet." Or "smooth and silky." Or "surprisingly nutty." Johanna was impressed with his acuity and discernment.

When he had tasted them all, Doncaster took her hand and gave it an overly formal kiss. "Perhaps the best discussion about carrots I have ever enjoyed. Thank you, Princess Johanna."

"Shall I have Chef prepare a carrot salad for the feast tonight?"

"A riot of carrot. Indeed." Then he waved, swirled, and headed for the exit, clanging into the locked gate, his grand exit stalled. Johanna ran over, unlocked it, and let out the garden's first visitor in a decade.

Turpy was waiting for the king. He dropped into an exaggerated bow that included a lot of waving of his jester's tricorn hat. Doncaster ignored it, but Johanna watched, curious. Turpy flashed her what was either a smile or a sneer, then followed his monarch back to his chambers.

19

INVITATION

Eloise sipped the shaved fennel in lemon broth, the second dish at Doncaster's second formal dinner. The anise flavor was an interesting contrast to the tart broth, and showed that Chef was trying to impress. The six-carrot salad had also been a surprise, since she assumed the ingredients could only have come from Johanna's garden. Again, someone's attempt to impress. But this time Eloise wasn't sure whose.

She turned to Jerome at full attention in his spot behind her. "You should try this when you get a chance. It's the biscuit."

Jerome nodded, eyes locked straight ahead, once again controlling his panic with two jesters a few lengths away. "Yes, Princess."

"Hang in there. They won't be here forever."

"Yes, Princess."

The Hall of Bald Opulence was bedecked with black and gray in tribute to the Half Kingdom. It was tricky to make it look festive rather than funereal, but someone in the housekeeping staff had the idea to use lots of mirrors and candles, and the multitude of flickering reflections did the trick.

Since the visit of a King was a "Big Deal," as Protocol put it, the place was jammed as full as the previous night, and the smell of perfume and reasonably washed bodies was almost as pungent as Chef's food, if less appealing. Eloise had been pushed along the main table to sit between the Head Exchequer, who expounded on the lyrical beauty of ledgers, and the Head Nature Adept, whose conversation centered on igneous rocks.

Johanna's laughter tittered over from where she sat chatting with Uncle Doncaster. They seemed to be particularly interested in the carrot salad, which only half made sense. Eloise didn't begrudge her sister's ability to get along with the king, but it was just odd, since her relationship with pretty much everyone else had the texture of sandpaper. Still, it kept the pressure off Eloise to interact with him.

After a main of chickpea cakes topped with mashed avocado, a side of marinated artichoke hearts, and a dessert of pumpkin eclairs, the Queen invited the lutenist to perform. To honor the guest, all three pieces came from the Half Kingdom: "The Haberdasher's Reel," "Three Score Arguments Doth Not a Lawyer Make," and "Betty, You'd Better Bring a Boffin." All well known; all well received.

The queen looked around at Doncaster's jesters, and then her brother-in-law. How to get the beautiful singing without the acerbic monolog? "I think, Doncaster, that I'm still enjoying Turpy's—sorry, His Jesterness Turpentine Snotearrow McCcoonnch's jokes from yesterday," she said, nodding at Turpy. She lifted a hand toward Gouache, who hulked sullenly behind his king. "But perhaps His Jesterness Gouache Snotearrow McCcoonnch would like to sing again?"

Doncaster tried to wave her off. "First, Gouache does not rate the honorific. No 'Jesterness' for him. Second, I can promise you, good queen, that it will not be as enthralling as yesterday."

"Well, perhaps we can give it a chance."

Doncaster shrugged. "As you wish." He turned to Gouache and pointed to the platform in the middle of the room. Gouache checked with his brother, then dragged himself forward reluctantly. As he had the day before, he stepped up on the stage, sighed, picked up the megaphone, and stared at his feet.

And then the light in him came on.

The exact same light.

"Ladeeeeeeees and gentlemen—and all points in between!" The transformation to crowd-engaging performer was less startling, since everyone had seen it before. The mild jest was not so funny the second time. Gouache was oblivious to the lack of response. "I'd like to sing a favorite for you. 'Three Bags of Groats for My Sweetheart.' He turned to the lutenist, who was ready this time. "If you please? In A minor." The lutenist plucked the chord. Gouache, head tilted slightly, let the last note hang, exactly as long as he had previously, and then sang.

"There's a lady who knows all that glitters is groats..."

His voice was just as sweet, his attention to the song's emotion just as complete. But there was something odd in how he replicated the performance so exactly. He held the last word, "groats," like he was cuddling a baby dove—the exact same baby dove.

The room applauded politely.

Gouache, right on cue quipped, "I'll be selling groats afterward, if anyone requires three bags. And now—'Jester Went A-Courtin.'"

Eloise didn't mind hearing the song again. But the excitement that held the crowd the day before was gone. Gouache even picked the same lady near the stage to be the focus of his performance. Eloise glanced at Jerome, who shook his head, as puzzled as everyone else. It was not so much a performance as a mimicry of a performance.

When he finished, Gouache again said to the woman, "You're the accoucheur of my cri de coeur, a force majeure to this poor raconteur, a de rigueur saboteur, a cocklebur in my underfur. Were I not a jester, I would come a-courtin. But, alas, I shall content myself with a kiss on the cheek." He leaned in for the kiss, which the maiden perfunctorily provided.

"And finally, 'The Baleful Sorrows of Jedd the Sea Urchin.'" It was still a strange song, and his delivery was just as heartfelt, except everyone knew how it would end, so the effect was blunted.

The song done, Gouache waved, bowed to the crowd, bowed to the royal table and King Doncaster, then stepped off the stage, immediately caving in on himself.

"Odd," Eloise muttered to herself. "Very odd." To her left and right, the Head Exchequer and Head Nature Adept nodded agreement.

King Doncaster stood. "Good Queen Eloise. Dear brother King Chafed. May I please speak?"

"Of course, King Doncaster." The queen's voice held amused curiosity. She assumed what would follow would explain what they'd just witnessed.

But no. Doncaster's thoughts were elsewhere. "Today, I had a most fascinating tour of one of your castle's most secret delights, dear Princess Johanna's garden."

"Truly?" said Chafed. He glanced at Johanna, who shrugged.

"Your hospitality here in Castle de Brague has been formidable. In return, I would like to extend a small invitation," he said. "I should like to request Princess Johanna be my guest at Castle Blotch and consult with my staff about possible improvements to the gardens. Her talent is without question. And my gardens show a great need." He looked directly at his hosts. "Queen Eloise and King Chafed, could you please allow the princess to travel with me to my home?"

The hall fell silent. Eloise saw Johanna's jaw drop, as surprised by the offer as everyone else. Inviting her in this way wasn't exactly improper. But Protocol would suggest a handwritten proposal delivered by a valet on a silver platter, first to Johanna herself, and then onward to her parents for private consideration. Johanna's face flushed with embarrassment, no doubt due to the public way the invitation was offered.

"Well," said the queen. "That comes as a surprise. How generous of you to think Princess Johanna worthy of such an honor." She was stalling. "Perhaps..."

"No need to decide now. I leave the day after tomorrow, as you know," he said. "It is simply my hope you will open your hearts to this possibility, and what will surely be a very helpful, very short visit. And perhaps, not too much of a burden on Princess Johanna herself."

With that, he sat back down, winked at Johanna, and went back to his pumpkin eclair.

Behind him, Turpy actually smiled. It was the least mirthful smile Eloise had ever seen.

20

SHOULD SHE STAY OR SHOULD SHE GO?

"It was impertinent," sniped the queen. Her teacup chinked down onto its saucer, and she absently picked up a shortbread from a side table and started dunking. "And calculated. Why else would he do it in the Hall of Bald Opulence like that, instead of following Protocol?" The shortbread disintegrated under the stress of repeated immersion.

The impromptu family meeting assembled in the misnamed Salle de la Famille—it was much less salle and much more antechamber—at the front of the king and queen's quarters. When they were young, this was where Eloise and Johanna had slept and played, always attended by Láäàne or Löööïïïss, their tag-teaming otter nannies, who Eloise now suspected were trained and armed as formidably as guards. Chafed paced from unlit fireplace to window, sloshing tea. Eloise sat on a chair where their cradle had once been, taking careful double-sips of the peppermint and ginger brew that also teased a taste of vanilla. She wondered if a second pair of shortbread biscuits might be pushing it. Johanna, seated where their toy blocks were once stacked, held her face in a careful blank, teacup immobile on her lap.

"Well, we know Doncaster isn't a big fan of strict Protocol," said Chafed, finding a napkin to dry his hand then topping up his cup, only to have the sloshing resume. "He proved that when he gifted us pudding bowls for our wedding. Beautiful, finely crafted, gilt-edged pudding bowls. But c'mon. Pudding bowls?"

"Politically, it is a plus, I suppose," said the queen, leaving the matter of pudding bowls aside. "High-level engagement, royal cooperation— all that blah-blah."

"That blah-blah matters," said Chafed.

"I know, I know," said the queen. She sipped, realized her cup held a mush of disintegrated shortbread, and set it aside. Eloise stood and poured her a fresh cup, snagging two spare shortbreads while she was at it. "Blah-blah inter-realm cooperation. Blah-blah fostering closer ties. Blah-blah building bridges. Blah-blah cementing connections."

"Blah-blah giving our daughter a chance to represent the Western Lands in a way she's unlikely to enjoy a second time." Chafed glanced at Johanna, hoping he hadn't offended. Johanna looked down at her cup, accepting the truth of it.

"I guess," the queen agreed, taking the cup from Eloise and resuming her shortbread dunking, this time managing to nibble a bit before it disintegrated. "There are whole swathes of Protocol she could practice, which might be useful to her. Plus, how many times has she spent the night farther than five strong lengths from the castle? Not more than a handful. It's... There's just something about it that abrades. It seems so un-Doncaster-like."

"He isn't known for his gardens, is he? But then, maybe he's trying to turn over a new leaf."

A king joke. Chafed was known for his king jokes. As king, they were his prerogative. But that didn't make them funny.

"And it is safe enough, I suppose," said the queen, ignoring her husband. "He'd guard her well, and that lout of a jester would scare off anyone. Plus, Johanna can fend for herself well enough if needed.

Which, thank Çalaht, it isn't these days." The queen finally looked at Johanna. "I've been working under the assumption you wish to go. Do you?"

"Yes, my queen."

A formal response. Eloise was surprised. Coming from Johanna, it was a threat. Those three words conveyed not only that she wished to undergo the journey, but also that if she was prevented from doing so, she would cause such ongoing unpleasantness at Court that life would be an endless misery for anyone unlucky enough to cross her path. She would pull out all stops, consequences be damned. Chafed bobbled his cup, taken aback at the effrontery.

Eloise set her undunked shortbread on her saucer and waited to see what kind of explosion might come from her mother, provoked so directly.

To her credit, Queen Eloise's only visible response was a nostril flare. It was as if she hadn't heard all the subtext lumbering behind Johanna's statement. She put down her cup and stood. Eloise and Johanna immediately did the same, and Chafed straightened. The queen walked to Johanna, took her hands, and said, "Then you shall travel, my daughter. Please let me know if you need anything for your journey." She kissed her on the cheek.

21

A CAPE

Eloise offered to help Johanna pack, but Nesther de Duck had things under control. Johanna was kitted out with travel bags and a trunk containing a combination of practicality and frippery. Only one valise got Johanna's personal attention. It held small cotton bags closed with drawstrings. Each bag had a particular type of seed, and Johanna wrote symbols on them, a code that told her what was what, but kept it a secret from others. "Just in case they fall into the wrong hands." They may well have been state secrets. And perhaps, to her, they were.

Eloise found herself feeling sad. And then annoyed that she was sad. And then frustrated at herself for feeling annoyed.

True, the two of them hadn't gotten along all that well for years. But her twin had been the one constant in Eloise's life since birth. Eloise was already poking around the feeling of Johanna being gone like a tongue at the spot where a milk tooth once was. It would take some getting used to, even if it was just a few weeks. Eloise didn't want her to go without saying something, but she wasn't sure what.

She caught up with Johanna at the tailor's, where she found her sister in brisk debate with the formidable Seamstress Linttrap. "What I'm trying to say is that the cape needs to be functional," said Johanna, "not flouncy."

"But Princess, you like flouncy," argued Seamstress Linttrap, an echidna who, if she really liked you, would use one of her own quills for your needlework. "Besides, a traveling cape is never strictly functional. It is also a reflection on your parents. On your queendom. On *me*!"

"Yes, Seamstress, but—"

"Princess, a black cape makes you look like you are leading a funeral procession," declared Seamstress Linttrap. "Will there be dead bodies going with you?"

"No, Seamstress, but—"

"Priests quoting the more turgid, dismal passages from the *Scrolls of Çalaht?*"

"No, Seamstress, but—"

"People in floods of tears, keening, gnashing their teeth, and generally making those around them wish they, too, were no longer among the living?"

"Certainly not, Seamstress. But—"

"Then. Black. Will. Not. Do." And with that, she snapped shut her sewing kit and folded her arms. In all of Court, there were only a handful of people unfazed by Johanna. Seamstress Linttrap was one of them. Johanna and the echidna stared at each other, wordlessly livid.

"Excuse me," ventured Eloise.

"What?" they both snapped.

"A suggestion?"

Johanna and Seamstress Linttrap continued their stare-down. The echidna spoke, not breaking eye contact. "Be fast with it. I won't be working on this all night, and I'm most certainly not going to miss the Farewell Ceremonies because a certain princess's sense of style veers recklessly toward the terminally unacceptable." Johanna opened her mouth to protest, but Seamstress Linttrap cut her off with a raised claw.

"Dark jungle green," said Eloise

"Continue," said the seamstress.

"A deep green can be made to look close to black, while still cleaving to the set of hues that Protocol enjoins. At night, it would be indistinguishable from black. During the day, it would simply be luxurious."

"Acceptable," Seamstress Linttrap said immediately.

"Acceptable," agreed Johanna.

And then it was as if there had never been any tension. "Very good," said the echidna. "I have your measurements, so be off with you." She turned to her helper, a cowering civet holding spools of colored thread. "Get moving, Adelmeyer. We have pigments to mix." The last thing the twins saw as they left the room was Seamstress Linttrap plucking a fresh quill from her back.

"She scares me," said Eloise after the door closed.

"Over the years, we've reached an accord of sorts."

"Do you have a few minutes?"

"Çalaht in a dirndl, certainly not. There are three days' worth of preparation being squeezed into…"

"Perhaps a cup of haggleberry tea? As a farewell?"

"Oh." Johanna stopped and looked at her sister. "Really?"

Eloise nodded. "Really," she whispered.

"But you—"

"Really."

"I suppose," said Johanna. "Tea sounds lovely."

22

SO...

Johanna set down the tea tray on a white, wrought-iron table beneath an ancient alder tree and took her seat. For years, Eloise had thought of the spot as "theirs," since they'd spent hours playing or reading in its shade in warmer months. But Eloise hadn't gone near it in three years, ceding it to Johanna in the aftermath of the Thorning Ceremony and the ensuing breakdown between them. They'd gone from being close to Johanna barely communicating with her, and even refusing to use their private sign language. She wasn't sure if Johanna had picked this place to give her a home field advantage or as a way of saying, "Come be in my space."

Eloise set down a second tray next to the first. Hers had a selection of Chef's cakes, including two slices of brownie pumpkin pie still warm from the oven, four rectangles of fudge, and two avocado key lime squares.

Johanna poured the haggleberry tea into cups while Eloise divided the sweets evenly onto two dessert plates.

They sipped tea in silence.

"So," said Eloise.

"So," said Johanna.

Another sip.

"So..." started Eloise.

"So?" asked Johanna.

Eloise had instigated this sit-down, but hadn't thought through what she might say. For another moment, she said nothing, slicing the brownie pumpkin pie with her fork and trying it. "Goodness," she said. "That's exquisite. Have some."

Johanna nodded agreement. "Yes, that's excellent."

A breath of wind rustled the leaves above them.

"Are you looking forward to the journey?" asked Eloise.

"Yes. Yes, I am. A lot."

More tea sipping.

"So," said Eloise.

"So," said Johanna.

"I—" They said it at the same time.

"You go first," said Eloise.

"No, you go ahead. I didn't mean to interrupt. Say what you want to say."

Eloise took another sip of tea, then set the cup on its saucer. "I know we haven't exactly been getting along all that great."

Johanna, hands wrapped around her cup like it was a mug, shrugged a noncommittal response, but didn't contradict her.

"The past few years have been..."

"They have been what they've been," said Johanna. "There's no need to dwell."

That was bit rich. Eloise thought that if anyone dwelt on the past, it was her sister. "Right." She drew a breath. "I guess I wanted to say it will be odd not to have you here in the castle, and at Court."

Johanna nodded. "It will be odd not to be here."

"I'll miss you." There. She'd said it.

Johanna paused. "Really? Because..."

"Really."

"I see." Johanna put down her cup. "To be honest, I hadn't thought I'd miss anything. Now, I realize that's not true. The closer I get, the more I look around and see things I won't have, and that I'll miss." She pointed at her dessert plate. "I'll miss Chef's culinary miracles. I can't imagine Uncle Doncaster's cook is anywhere near as good. I'll miss my garden, of course, but I think it will be OK without me for the few weeks I'm gone." She rotated her cup on its saucer, and Eloise had to restrain herself from doing the same. "And, despite everything that's gone on, I will miss you as well. I know it isn't like it used to be. But can you remember the last time we didn't see each other at least once in a day?"

"No."

"I can. It was when we were six. You caught an ague and had a fever. Mother got it in her head she should keep me away from you so I wouldn't get it too."

"I remember that. I remember you arguing with her."

"I don't remember arguing. I remember yelling. I forced them to make me a bed just outside the door, so we could talk. I remember saying goodnight through it."

"I remember that, too. She wouldn't even let you crack open the door. I also remember you ended up getting the ague anyway, at which point, they tucked you into the bed next to me."

"We recovered together."

"Yes," remembered Eloise. "We recovered together.

Johanna took a bite of the avocado key lime square. "How does Chef know she can put avocado in something like this and have it work?"

"It's what she knows," said Eloise.

"True." Johanna dabbed her mouth with a napkin. "I have to say it: I'm really looking forward to getting away from the castle and Court. I can't wait.

"I bet."

"But it's temporary. A diversion. A welcomed diversion, but a diversion. A few weeks from now, I'll be back here."

"Yes."

Johanna tilted her head to the side a little. "So, maybe, when I get back we can try to recover together again."

"I'd like that," said Eloise. She reached out to give her sister's arm a squeeze, but hesitated, not wanting to push it. She ended up leaving her hand awkwardly on the table halfway between them, fingers curled under.

Johanna looked at Eloise and then her hand. She reached over and gave the back of it a gentle pat. "I think I'd like that, too."

❧ 23 ❧

GIFT

Eloise was seated to the king's left for the Farewell Ceremonies, with a trade representative for the Half Kingdom on her other side, a foppish dandy named Theoplonkilis. Eloise was unsure if this was his given name or surname. Because the farewell suddenly encompassed Johanna as well as Doncaster, the decorations included splashes of green and gold along with the black and gray. This dinner celebration somehow outshone the stellar feasts from the previous two nights.

Behind her, poor Jerome was almost hyperventilating, being so close to two jesters. Eloise tried to give him an out, but he insisted on performing his duty. She hoped that would not involve fainting or high-pitched squeals.

Doncaster nudged her elbow with his. "Are you annoyed with me, Princess Eloise?" he asked.

"No, King Doncaster. Should I be?"

"Well…" He picked up a spring roll and swished it in a saucer of ginger peanut sauce. "I didn't invite you to Castle Blotch."

"True." Eloise speared two spring rolls with her fork, and swirled them once clockwise, then once counter-clockwise. "I'm sure you have your reasons. I'm fine with that."

"I'm relieved," he said, relief distinctly absent from his voice. "It's just that, if I may be so bold, you have—habits. I don't think they suit travel."

"That might be true." Eloise carefully cut her spring rolls into four parts each, and ate the first quarter (top left), then the last (bottom right). "May I ask a question, Sire?"

"Princess Eloise, you may ask me anything. Whether I answer, however, remains to be seen." He jostled her arm again to show he was kidding. He wasn't.

Eloise looked behind them toward Gouache. "Your jester's performance last night. And the night before. It was—singular."

"It is always singular. Young Gouache Snotearrow McCcoonnch knows exactly three songs and three jokes, though they barely rise to the level of a king joke once you've heard them for the thousandth time. Or the second time, even." Doncaster glanced at his jester. "From time to time, I have commanded, inveighed, appealed to Çalaht, decreed, asked, badgered, and begged for him to learn a new song or witticism."

"It does not strike me as a big ask."

"And there you'd be wrong. He can lodge one in that brain of his for a little while. An hour. Maybe a day if it has the lyric complexity of a nursery rhyme. And then it is gone. Like spun sugar in a monsoon."

"Odd."

"Odd is generous. Çalaht barbecuing on a brazier, he is as thick as the Adequate Wall of the Realms. He is as dense as the Gööödeling Sea is deep. He is as bright as the darkest alcoves of the Caves of Määännääsäs."

"Why do you keep him as a jester?"

Doncaster chuckled. "Have you seen him? He's built like half a hockey sacking team. And he can follow an order. Plus, they..." Doncaster flicked his hand, indicating the two brothers. "They're sort of a package deal. The value of the one tips the scales for the other."

Eloise forked the second and seventh quarters of her spring rolls. "Then he is lucky to have found a place with you."

"Perhaps."

Over polenta arepas topped with black bean sauce, Doncaster talked shop with Theoplonkilis. They discussed the difficulties of importing raw haggleberries, and wondered if something could be done about the tariff levied by the Southie Queen, Onomatopoeia Handrail Lúüù-derming, on Half Kingdom wart creams, one of the northern realm's better exports. Theoplonkilis simpered that a state visit to The South might help nudge her toward more favorable terms, and Doncaster grudgingly said he'd consider it. Disinterested, Eloise's mind wandered, homing in on whether Jerome was adequately stifling his squeaks each time one of the two jesters moved.

She noted there was no official entertainment that night, probably to avoid any awkwardness around not having Doncaster's jesters perform again. Just before dessert, the queen rose and the Hall of Bald Opulence stood in automatic response. "My friends!" she called.

"Our queen!"

"Please be at rest." Everyone sat, and Queen Eloise waved for servants to distribute dessert while she spoke. "Protocol is quite specific about how one treats visiting royalty, and I'd like to publicly thank everyone at Court for your hard work and attention. I believe we have discharged our duty to King Doncaster with flair and aplomb."

"Hear, hear" filled the hall, fists rapping on the tables. In response, Doncaster stood and bowed elaborately to the queen and then the room. A lone voice yelled, "Good on ya, Donc!"—an egregious breach, but one that was met with a mock scowl.

"If our guest can forgive that, then perhaps he'll also indulge my breaking Protocol just a little here at the Farewell Ceremonies. Tomorrow you depart for Stained Rock and Castle Blotch with precious cargo—our daughter. I wish you and your party safe travels, and I charge you with her safekeeping."

Doncaster raised his right hand, like he was taking an oath. "Charge accepted, good queen."

"I hope she shares some of the mysteries of her gardening with you and your people. Çalaht knows, she hasn't shared them with us." Her tone was openly affectionate, so what might have been a jab was more a josh. Queen Eloise turned to her daughter. "Princess Johanna, we await your return in a few weeks, and hope you come back wiser. We wish you boring travels."

"Boring travels," repeated the room.

It was Johanna's turn. She had guessed that she'd be put on the spot, so she was prepared. Johanna lifted a small basket from the floor near her feet. "Mother, my queen. Father. Sister. I have for you a small token to remember me by during the few weeks of my absence." She gave each of them a transparent sphere with a flattened bottom so it could sit without rolling. Inside, suspended in a viscous clear liquid, was a flower of stunning beauty—one of her incredible crocuses.

The queen kissed her on the cheek, then held hers up for all to see. A rain patter of table rapping from the hall echoed approval.

Eloise hugged Johanna when she handed her the gift and whispered, "Such a beautiful thing, and for so short a journey. Thank you." When she pulled back, she thought it might be possible that there was a tear in Johanna's eye.

"I hope you enjoy it," said Johanna. "I chose this one for you in part for the light purple edging at the tips of the petals. I thought you might find that pretty."

"It's beautiful. Again, thank you."

The queen held up a hand to regain everyone's attention. "And now, let's proceed with the official Farewell Ceremonies so we can enjoy our dessert."

✣ 24 ✣

LEAVE-TAKING

"**L**ook at that," whispered Eloise, seeing Doncaster's new coach. "Lurid Eddie strikes again." She and Jerome stood outside, ready for the leave-taking.

Lurid Eddie was a towering figure in carriage sales. His garishly painted, overly ornate vehicles were spruiked by handbills posted (usually legally) everywhere. Each had a caricature of Lurid Eddie with an arrow through his head or a razordisc poking out of his skull, and they screamed, "Oy ye, oy ye, oy ye! Lurid Eddie Commands You to Have a Bargain", or "Lurid Eddie Wants You! (To Have a New Carriage!)", or "At these prices, you'd have to question both our mental stability and our business acumen! Lurid Eddie's!"

"The thing is," said Jerome, "he has good prices, and excellent workmanship. But his decorations can rot your teeth from across a paddock. I see Doncaster's new carriage is no exception."

"Maybe it was the only one Lurid Eddie had on hand that suited the client's requirements," Eloise speculated. "It takes time to create such art."

King Doncaster's carriage was a triumph of florid jocularity, resplendent in bright colors (dominated by lemon yellow), curved lines, frivolous trimming, and asymmetrical touches. Elaborately rendered cherubim peered out from carved sea shells. Wood nymphs and satyrs frolicked partly clad among acanthus leaves. Every inch of the exterior was crammed with imagery, visual puns, and ostentation. It was like a drunk Mythologies and Legends professor had babbled directions to an apprentice Court cake decorator, screaming, "Too much is too little! Do more!" The result—a transportation device of such gaudy magnitude that everyone would know the king was coming from two realms away.

"Hideous," murmured Jerome.

"A visual torture," agreed Eloise.

"I think it's cute," said Johanna, who'd come up behind them. "And I can't wait to ride in it. Now give me a hug. Not you—her!" Jerome stepped back, tail flicking, abashed. Eloise gave Johanna a hug, saying, "Be safe and boring travels." She gave Johanna the traditional Western Lands kiss, pecking lightly to make sure she did not smear Johanna's make-up, and then Johanna returned it.

"Of course I'll be safe. Uncle D will make sure of that. And you've seen that galoot he travels with. No one would mess with him." Johanna fiddled with the side hem of her new cape, which Seamstress Linttrap had finished in record time. The deep green set off Johanna's eyes perfectly, the hood could conceal her curls, the reinforced lining was peppered with secret pockets, and if Johanna twirled, it caught the air and spun like a magician's trick.

Eloise looked around. "Where's Nesther de Duck?"

"I'm going to rough it! Be independent. No handmaid. How bad can it get in just a few weeks?"

Eloise couldn't imagine it, not for Johanna. "Good luck with that. I hope you broke it to her gently."

Johanna shrugged. "She's a tough old duck. She'll live."

They watched porters cinch down the last of the travel gear in the mid-morning sun, as Queen Eloise, King Chafed, and King Doncaster emerged from a side door. Chafed still had half a piece of toast in his hand and was brushing crumbs from his trousers. Protocol required much less formality for leavings compared to arrivals. The Protocol Commentaries said this was because the mood should not be one of sadness, but of joyful anticipation of the next welcoming. Eloise wasn't sure the person who wrote that explanation had much experience with goodbyes.

The queen gave Doncaster the Western Lands kiss, then Chafed did the same. Doncaster reciprocated, then it was all repeated with Johanna. As Eloise Western Lands-kissed Doncaster, she said what Protocol directed: "May the road be smooth, the weather pleasant, may Çalaht light your path with her gap-toothed smile, and may you not be accosted by wild, marauding, bloodthirsty, ravenous bandicoots." Clearly, this was a saying from another era, as bandicoots were now rarely brigands. But Protocol was slow to change. Then she added, more familiarly, "Boring travels, Uncle Doncaster."

"Thank you, Princess Eloise."

A formal reply. Oh well, it was worth a try.

Doncaster and Johanna climbed in, Gouache heaved himself up to his spot on top, severely testing the new carriage's left-side springs, and then Turpy swung into the driver's seat. And with that, they were off, clopping down the Castle Road toward the North Gate.

When they were out of sight, everyone relaxed, but they stayed in place until the canine guards could no longer hear them. When the lead dog gave the all clear, the small group trailed away.

"C'mon, Champorista," Eloise said. "Time to lace up my running shoes. Those laps around the Culpability Courtyard won't run themselves."

"Yes, Princess Eloisimocity. I look forward to watching you."

25

VISIONS OF JOHANNA

The rest of the day passed uneventfully, although Eloise managed to slice off a wooden manikin's head with a razordisc from 150 lengths—a personal best, both for distance and damage done.

After dinner, she was surprised and pleased to see both Jerome and Seer Maybelle in the Salle de la Famille. "It has been a long week," said Queen Eloise. "I thought it might be nice to relax with a nice cup of Chef's haggleberry chai."

Eloise took her cup, breathed in the mix of haggleberry, chai masala, ginger, and sugar, then sipped. "Çalaht on a bulbous brioche, this is heaven."

Everyone settled next to the fire, which had been lit more for the dance of its light than for evening warmth. The queen, king, and Seer Maybelle did most of the talking, covering nothing and doing so in amused detail. They guessed Doncaster and Johanna would by now be settling into their rooms at the First Night Inn (formerly the First Knight Inn). They would soon be tasting the inn's famous cold broccoli and three bean soup, served with warm mulled cherry cider.

Jerome was still uncomfortable in the queen and king's presence, so kept quiet. Eloise also suspected that he thought making chai from haggleberries was a breach of haggleberry propriety, but he kept that pretty much to himself. Only a slight grimace with every sip gave him away.

Under the pleasant drone of conversation, nestled into an overstuffed armchair, Eloise found herself heavy-lidded and slipping into a doze.

She dreamed, as she often did, of throwing—impossibly long throws that sailed forever. This time, she was flipping waffles like razordiscs across the Gööödeling Sea, watching them skip, skip, skip, skip across the water. It didn't matter that the closest she'd ever been to the sea in the last half-decade was the background image in a painting that hung in the Salon des Champions. One after the other, the waffles skimmed across an improbably glassy azure surface.

It was the word "cone" that woke her, squeaked at a high pitch by Seer Maybelle. Eloise opened her eyes, momentarily disoriented, and found chaos. Chafed yelled, "What? What is this? Is she sick? What is she saying?" The queen, crowding toward Seer Maybelle, reached to steady her, but Jerome shouted, "Don't touch her! You must not make contact, or it will be ruined!"

Not "cone." Something else.

Seer Maybelle's fur stood straight, crackling with power like it had a few days before, and her eyes were rolled back. She did not oscillate like the last time, but stood rigid. Instead of a low growl, her voice was a banshee's wail, a keen of despair.

"Crone." She said the word like Çalaht's own heart was being ripped through her throat.

"Why did she..." started Eloise.

The queen put up a hand for quiet and knelt in front of her Court Seer. Eloise saw that Seer Maybelle holding something round and transparent. A crystal ball? No, not her style. Plus, there was something inside it.

A crocus.

It was one of the preserved crocuses that Johanna had given them the night before. It must have triggered the whatever-this-was.

Seer Maybelle clutched the crocus to her chest, cradling it, holding it like a precious evil, repeating, "Crone! Crone! Crone! Crone!"

"Paper and quill," the queen snapped at Chafed. "Get every word." He dove for a desk in the corner and began writing.

"I see Johanna," moaned Seer Maybelle. "I see her from behind, but it is her. She is old. Old, old, old. Her hair. Oh, her beautiful hair. Her hair is a whitened ghost, her curls are tired and slack, their black a long-lost dream." Tears streamed down the fur of her cheeks. "I dare not look at her face. These visions of Johanna—they are all so cruel. Cruel, cruel, cruel."

Jerome moved next to the queen. "Mother. Where is she? Say what you see."

"She sits on a throne. By herself. Room empty. The chair next to hers never filled, kept ready for a future that will never happen."

Maybelle held forward the preserved crocus, forever frozen in time. It caught the firelight and seemed to move slightly in its transparent prison. "It started with this. This!" She opened her paw, and the transparent orb dropped to the carpet, wobbling until it came to a stop at Eloise's foot. "This journey is her doom. That is my warning. That is *her* warning."

Then Maybelle de Chipmunk, Court Seer and prized seeker of hidden knowledge, collapsed unconscious into the burning fireplace.

❧ 26 ❧

LATE INTO THE NIGHT

T here was no hint of sleep in the Hall of Authority as the on-duty horologist cuckoo called out, "3:00 AM." The hall was often used as a meeting place when matters were urgent. The queen and king called their closest advisors from their beds to consider Seer Maybelle's vision. The assembled group included the First Advisor, the Other Places Advocate (a sort of foreign minister and diplomatic advisor), the Head of Half Kingdom Studies from the university, the Knowledge Navigator from the Library of Stuff We Really Need to Keep Around But Aren't Sure Where, and the Venerated Prelate Herself, a tapir whose in-depth understanding of the *Scrolls of Çalaht* was always handy.

Seer Maybelle had been hauled from the flames and rolled in a towel to put out her fur. Odmilla was fetched to tend her, smearing her burns with a salve of lavender oil and aloe vera. As soon as the chipmunk was out of her daze, Odmilla fed her salt potatoes, crackerbread, and a strong haggleberry tea that Jerome prepared, then bundled her into bed in a guest room. By midnight, she'd reported to the queen that, "Seer Maybelle is in no state to provide insight into her vision."

Eloise sat along the side wall, quietly following the debate. Her straight-backed wooden chair, its four feet centered exactly in the middle of four of the floor's square tiling stones, was much less comfortable than the overstuffed armchair she'd enjoyed earlier, but more conducive to staying awake.

"What's clear," the First Advisor said, "is that we cannot ignore the Court Seer's statement."

"I agree," said the Venerated Prelate Herself. "But how do we react? And what, specifically, are we reacting to?"

The queen scratched notes on a spare scroll. "Read her words again, please."

Chafed did. When he'd finished, he said, "It's the word 'warning' that surprises me the most. That seems so direct. Seer Maybelle's pronouncements are usually much more bendable or obtuse."

"I agree. So let's summarize what we think we know," the queen said. "First, Princess Johanna is in some sort of danger."

The Knowledge Navigator interrupted her. "Is she? Is becoming a crone not one of the natural stages of a woman's life? All women should be lucky to live so long. Crone is an honor."

"One might agree, Knowledge Navigator," said the Venerated Prelate Herself, curling her prehensile snout, "were it not for the words 'before her time.' I think that indicates a threat. Or undesirable outcome, at a minimum. Whether danger is the right word..."

"This is dithering," said the Other Places Advocate. "What do we know? This journey is ill-advised. Seer Maybelle said it started with the crocus. Preparing the preserved crocuses happened after Johanna got permission to go on this journey. That was a way to leave a memory of her behind, and was the first step on this trip. What is clear is that this journey must not be allowed to unfold."

"I agree," said the queen. "Our options?"

"That's tricky," said the Other Places Advocate. "Imagine sending a diplomatic representative to catch up with King Doncaster and say, 'So sorry. Princess Johanna can't continue with you because she will turn into a crone.' I wouldn't want to be the one to deliver that kind of message. King Doncaster will not take such things mildly."

"Could the Guards help us somehow?" asked the queen.

"A military response against my brother?" said Chafed. "Not if you ever want so much as another pudding bowl from the Half Kingdom. Doncaster holds a grudge like a professional wrestler holds a head. Send a band of soldiers anywhere near him, and that'd be it for a decade."

"I have to concur," said the Head of Half Kingdom Studies. "Rulers from the north are thin-skinned on their best days. Reason and logic often take a break when it comes to their thinking."

"Hey!" objected Chafed.

"With due respect, King Chafed, it is true."

"It is," said the queen. "Sorry, love. It is."

The conversation washed back and forth, with ideas considered and discarded.

Eloise knew what she had to suggest, but hated the thought. She hated the dirt, the distance, the stepping away from the order of her world. But this was her sister they were talking about. She knew Seer Maybelle's visions were not to be denied, even if they had to be interpreted.

But there was more to it than that (and she hated that her thoughts were going in this direction). Between the naming of her champion and the Ceremonies of the Stone of the Ancestors, the past few days had been a complete washout in the worthy-to-be-the-heir department. Maybe successfully undertaking the retrieval of Johanna could put a point or two in the plus column.

Eloise stood from her straight-backed chair, making sure she did not step where two stones met, and interrupted. "Excuse me. I believe I have an answer."

Everyone stopped. The queen looked around, clearly having forgotten Eloise was even there. "Yes?"

"I'll go."

A beat of silence, then they all spoke at once—disagreeing and objecting. But Eloise cut across them. "They have, what, a day's head start? I can travel without a carriage, which means I can go faster and meet up with them with roughly a day's journey. Me showing up won't have the weight of a diplomatic mission or the threat of a military response. I can find them, have a private moment with Johanna, convey Seer Maybelle's vision, convince her of its importance if need be, and then we can fashion a way for her to gracefully excuse herself. Johanna understands Seer Maybelle. She respects her as Court Seer. I think she'd listen to me."

There were more arguments, but Eloise knew how it would end. She excused herself so she could sleep a few hours before leaving on a journey that appealed to her as much as eating a handful of raw haggle-berries with a side of dirt from an unwashed plate using a spoon that had been licked by everyone in Court.

But still, she would go.

❧ 27 ❧

RETINUE

Eloise woke to knocking at her door. Bleary-eyed, she opened it to find Odmilla trying to keep Jerome from knocking again.

"I'm sorry, Princess. I tried to stop him."

"So," Jerome said, dodging into the room around the maidservant. He wore a jaunty, gray traveling version of his champion's outfit, and carried a backpack. "What time do we depart, Eloquence?"

"Oh, right," Eloise yawned. "Champion. You assume you're coming with me."

"Of course I'm going with you. Isn't that what champions are for?"

"Right. I guess." Eloise leaned against the doorframe and rubbed sleep from her eyes. This must be what it was like having a champion. Someone to be there and go with her. Someone who assumed his place was by her side. This was going to take some getting used to.

"I leave as soon as everything is set. I just have to work out what constitutes 'everything' in this case. Perhaps you can give me a few minutes to wake and prepare?"

"Of course. Let me know if you need me." Jerome closed the door behind him.

Eloise wasn't sure how the news had spread (except that at Court, news always spread), but by the time she made it to breakfast in the Salon de Degustation, everyone in the castle seemed to know she was going on a mission of some sort, and that it involved Johanna. Those who felt comfortable enough to talk to her asked if she was OK to make a journey of this type. It got on her nerves, but she swallowed that back, along with the dread she felt about making the trip.

Yes, dread was the word. Absolute, complete, unadulterated, paralyzing dread.

She pushed it out of her mind. There would be plenty of time for it once she was underway. Plenty of time to feel the itch of missing comforts, the many small rituals that got her from one end of the day to the other without everyone thinking her a freak.

Sitting by herself at a table near the back, she spread jam on her bagel, carefully sculpting a small circular mound and making sure the jam did not extend over the side. Two bites in, Odmilla arrived looking concerned. "Perhaps you would like to attend a matter in the Culpability Courtyard. Soonish would be splendid." It was as direct a suggestion as Odmilla ever made.

She could hear the argument before she could see it. Hector, Jerome, and someone else. A man's voice. Lorch? She rounded the corner. Yes, Lorch. And from the look of it, things were plenty heated.

"Listen, Pretty Boy. This is a serious undertaking," said Jerome, leaning into his argument with the stallion. "It isn't some trot around a parade ground."

"Do not insult me, you pittance of a portion of a rat." Hector tilted his head down so he could look squarely at Jerome with one eye. "How do you plan to get there? Hire an eagle?"

"Both of you need to—" tried Lorch.

"I'm a rodent, not a rat, you glorified donkey. And I'm Champion. So it is up to me to set this thing up. I'm choosing, and I don't choose you, Sir Prancealot."

"If you two could just—"

"That's speciesist. I will not be insulted by an undersized squirrel wannabe." Hector stamped the ground for emphasis, coming suspiciously close to Jerome.

But the chipmunk, dander fully up, barely flinched despite the real possibility of being crushed. "How about you just head back to the stables and let one of your gelding buddies braid your mane. I have an excursion to prepare for. And it does not include you."

Lorch tried again. "I daresay we might make better—"

Both of them turned on Lorch, yelling "Can it!"

Looking back at Jerome, Hector snorted so hard the chipmunk's hat flew off. He drew up to his full 16.2 hands of Friesian height, saying, "How dare you, you impertinent bite-sized scoundrel. Am I not Equine Designate?"

"Yes. And we hear about it all the time, Your Equatorial Greatness."

"Then it is my duty to be her servant. And I will not be denied the chance to fulfill my duty."

"Blessings of the day to you all." Eloise had joined them without their noticing. The arguing annoyed her, which, for the moment, pushed aside her fear about the journey. Her mild greeting and use of The Tone brought them to a fumbling, embarrassed halt. "I see eloquent, reasoned discussion is alive and well here in the Culpability Courtyard."

All three had the good grace to look abashed.

"Guard Lorch Lacksneck of Lower Glenth. Could you please summarize the state of this debate?"

"Princess, I—" started Hector, but Eloise simply put up a finger without looking, as she had seen her mother do a thousand times when addressing squabbles between her and her sister. "Guard Lacksneck has the floor."

Lorch ahemmed, uncomfortable with the assigned role of Designated Summarizer. "Champion Abernatheen de Chipmunk and Equine Designate de Pferd could not reach a meeting of minds regarding the composition of the accompanying party for your journey."

"And the assumption built into that statement is…?"

Lorch frowned, puzzled.

She looked at the other two. "Anyone? Equine Designate de Pferd?"

"That there will be an accompanying party," he said. "But—"

"Correct. So let's start by testing that assumption. Who is the only essential person to this matter?"

Jerome raised a paw, asking permission to speak. At Eloise's nod, he said, "You, Princess."

"Again, correct. Is it possible for me to travel on my own and achieve a satisfactory outcome?"

Hector lifted a hoof, and when recognized, said, "Possible, but not probable."

"Why not?"

Lorch raised a hand. "Speed, Princess. Travel on foot is much slower compared to the speed of King Doncaster's royal carriage."

"I would agree," she said. "Now that we've established a civil tone, let us speak freely and work this out. Each of you may make a case for your own participation, or that of someone else. You first." She pointed at Jerome.

Jerome had added his Champion's Sword to his gear and looked ready for anything. Perhaps not a posse of jesters, but pretty much anything else. "Well, Princess, I am Champion. Protocol insists. Such is Protocol."

"Such is Protocol," echoed the others.

"And yet, Protocol alone is not enough justification," she said. "Make a case for coming with me, if you care to."

"Çalaht sprouting feathers, El. We talked about this, and we need to get going." Eloise just looked at him, so he tried again. "Princess Eloise, I believe I should accompany you as your Champion, so I may do as you requested of me: accompany you on official business, stand as your protector, speak if you are insulted, and give advice."

"This is not official business, but I accept," she said with a small bow. "Thank you." She turned to Lorch. "Guard Lacksneck?"

Lorch wore the usual ceremonial outfit that guards wore at Court. His black hair was cut to a regulation stubble, and his tanned face looked like it would be as tough as an elephant's hide by the time he was 25, a testament to plenty of days in the sun. "I would prefer an entire guard of guards, were it up to me," he said. "It would be safer. But that is at odds with the nature of the mission. So, instead, I offer my humble services as what Champion Abernatheen de Chipmunk has been referring to somewhat uncouthly as 'the muscle.'"

"I accept," said Eloise. "I doubt muscle will be needed for such a quick outing, but I appreciate your offer to help ensure it isn't."

"And I will be riding one of the Guard Horses."

"Agreed." She bowed to him. She looked at Hector. "Equine Designate de Pferd?"

Hector had unconsciously positioned himself at the perfect angle for the morning sun to catch and enhance the sheen of his coat. His magnificent musculature was relaxed. Each strand of his mane was so richly lustrous and vivacious that it was probably eligible for its own life insurance policy. Yet he seemed uncertain. "Princess, you've been most polite and deferential to the Horse Guards and, in particular, me. You've long well been in your right to call us, and especially me, into service. But you have not. We've not discussed it, but I assume you were waiting for your coming of age. Again, that is most honorable. But as Equine Designate, Protocol places upon me certain, shall we say—"

Jerome's impatience boiled out. "Çalaht banging a gong, just say it!"

Hector whirled at him. "I mean to say that I am both duty-bound and embarrassed. There. I've said it. Happy? Are you?" He turned back to Eloise. "The relationship between rider and ridden is surprisingly intimate. On my back, you cannot so much as twitch, scratch, or brush away a fleck of dust without me knowing it. I can sense your soreness, your moods, and many of your thoughts. And that communication goes both ways. You will know my proclivities, when my thoughts stray, if I hunger or thirst, even what I think of your humming. All without words."

Eloise looked at Lorch, who nodded confirmation.

"Princess, to put it bluntly, we don't know each other that well. Perhaps that fault is mine. I could have insisted. But that is my embarrassment. And as I said before, I am duty-bound. More than that, I choose to be duty-bound. I respect you. I admire you. And if I may be so bold, I like you. Even if I was not Equine Designate, I would vie to be the one honored to provide you transport, whether by carriage or on my back. As such, I ask to be a member of your retinue on this mission of such great import."

"Oh, Hector. I had no idea." Eloise cleared a small lump of emotion from her throat. "Equine Designate de Pferd, I accept your generous offer."

"So that's us," said Jerome.

"Yes, that is us," agreed Eloise.

"Plus the Guard Horse," added Lorch.

"Yes, the Guard Horse. So, now that's settled, what do we really need for a journey of, say, three or four days through friendly territory?"

✺ 28 ✺

ODMILLA'S GIFT

In her room, Eloise's horse panniers were packed and ready to go. She'd allowed Odmilla to take charge of the process and was fascinated at the choices she'd made. The platypus balanced competing requirements of practicality, weight, space, and Protocol. There were two changes of travel clothes and one fancy cotton outfit just in case, plus items for grooming and eating, and a few food treats. Any cooking gear would be carried by Lorch, and food would be sourced along the way. Eloise marveled at how much Odmilla could fit into such a small space.

Along with a miniature copy of the *Livre de Protocol*, Odmilla had included a small edition of the *Scrolls of Çalaht*. Eloise protested. "But Odmilla. I'm not that devout. Nor are you, for that matter."

"True enough, Princess. But traveling with a book like that can save your life."

The book stayed.

Odmilla also insisted that she pack her glassed crocus from Johanna. "There is something about it. You should have it with you." She wrapped it carefully in felt and placed it inside the folded fancy outfit.

Eloise was dressed in simple gray travel breeks, a dark green tunic with the Gumball crest embroidered in indigo thread, and a dark indigo cape that even the quickest glance revealed was another of Seamstress Linttrap's sewing miracles. She sat in front of the mirror on her vanity, watching Odmilla wrestle her hair, as she did most days. She had combed it out to subdue the curls, and was now knotting it into a journeyman's braid, threaded with a lavender-colored ribbon imported from The South. The braid was a good choice for keeping maintenance to a minimum while still looking elegant.

"I wish you could come with me," said Eloise.

Odmilla laughed. "Oh, Princess. Can you imagine?"

Eloise looked at her. "What? Why are you laughing?"

"Princess, what do we know about me?"

"That you are my maid servant. That would make you a perfect companion."

"True, Princess. Though I meant about my kind. What do we know of my species?"

"Your species? I've never thought much about it. But, you must be a marsupial. Platypuses are marsupials."

"Yes. But more, we platypuses are water-dwelling marsupials. We are most definitely not cut out for a life on the road." She laughed again to herself. "Can you imagine?"

"There must be platypuses who travel. Surely."

"There are. If you are rich enough or important enough or royal enough, then they will build a water carriage for you, and you can roam the breadth and width and length of the realms. But for one such as me? That will never happen. Now, please hold still while I finish your hair.

When Odmilla was done, Eloise wore a braid so tight it could smooth the wrinkles off a Çalahtist fanatic's attitude. It would hold for the duration of the trip, meaning her hair would be one less thing to worry about.

There would be enough other worries.

Eloise stood, smoothed down her cape, and prepared to face what she feared would be the worst few days of her life. She reached to hug Odmilla, but the maid servant stopped her.

"I have something for you, Princess." She reached into a pouch belted at her waist and drew out a small, hemp, drawstring bag. "Princess, I have known you for several years, have I not?"

"Of course. Since the Thorning Ceremony."

"So, it would be fair to say I, perhaps more than anyone else, understand your discomforts. Your habits. Your, with respect, peculiarities. Pardon my frankness, Princess."

Eloise's cheeks burned. Of course Odmilla must realize her freakish quirks. How could she not, living so close to her? But until now, it had always passed unspoken. Eloise felt mortified that Odmilla had felt the need to bring it up.

"I see I may have offended. But with permission, I would continue."

Eloise nodded, but kept her head aside, avoiding eye contact.

"I have been considering your situation and thinking what might help. I have chosen this for you."

Eloise opened the hemp bag. Inside was a magnificent set of Çalahtist prayer beads. The intricately carved spheres of differing sizes and woods were spaced in the traditional groupings: 1, 1, 2, 3, 5, 8, 13, 21, 34, and, unusually for a set of prayer beads, 55. Clearly ancient. Clearly loved. Their silken smoothness was a delight to the touch.

"Magnificent," she said. "But, Odmilla, are you suggesting I pray a lot? Çalaht knows that is not the Gumball way, and I am no exception. And again, from what I know, you are the same."

"Correct, Princess. But consider, please. What is their purpose beyond prayer?"

"Keeping track of prayer."

"Which is another way to say..."

"Counting."

"Princess Eloise. If you feel the urge of your habits, I suggest that you distract yourself with counting. It is what you do."

Eloise ran them through her fingers, starting, as one always did, with the two single beads, then moving higher. It felt somewhat grounding. Perhaps they might help. Perhaps. Eloise bowed formally. "Thank you, Mistress Odmilla. I will treasure them."

"Please do more than that. Please use them."

And with no further words, Odmilla tucked the prayer beads into the bag and hid it in one of the cape's pockets.

❦ 29 ❦

BORING TRAVELS TO YOU

Since it was not an official farewell, there was no fanfare for Eloise's departure. She and Jerome stepped through the same side door as they had the day before. Lorch awaited them, mounted on the Guard Horse, panniers in place. He rode bareback and bridleless, as everyone did.

Then Eloise saw Hector, gasped, and felt embarrassment stamp red all over her face. "What is that?"

"It is a saddle," said Jerome.

"I know it's a saddle," snapped Eloise. "Why is he wearing it?"

"El—"

"Don't 'El' me. You knew about this?"

"Uh, I did. Yes." Jerome flicked his tail nervously.

Hector walked over, looking uncomfortable. The saddle and her panniers sat on him like a hair shirt. "Actually, Princess, it was my idea."

"What am I? Four years old? Are we going to tie a few streamers to your tail as well?"

"Princess—"

"This is demeaning. It is demeaning to me and it is most certainly demeaning to you. Not to mention your fellow Horse Guards. They must be cackling with laughter back at the stables. Hold on. Let me run back inside and get some bows. Çalaht kissing a prickly pear, I can't believe this. As if having to go get my stupid sister because of an idiotic and vague vision wasn't bad enough."

The baldness of the statement hung in the air.

Hector tried to tiptoe into the awkwardness. "This was not my first choice, Princess. But—"

The queen and king emerged from the side door, and discussion slammed to a halt. Eloise bent down to hide her face and became very occupied with retying her bootlace.

"G'midday to you all," said the queen. "I trust preparations are satisfactory?"

"Splendid, Mother. Thank you."

The queen caught her tone. "Is there a problem?"

"No, Mother. Everything is perfect, thank you." Eloise finished knotting tight her boot and stood, her face a careful blank, but a telltale red still rouged her cheeks.

The Queen looked at her, then to Lorch, then Jerome, and finally Hector. "Oh. I see." She went to Hector and inspected the saddle. "It looks comfortable enough."

"Yes, Mother. I'm sure it will be fine."

"Eloise, let me ask you a question. How many hours, say in the last ten years, have you spent on the back of a horse?"

"That is not the point."

"I think you'll find it is. How many hours? Feel free to round up."

"Out of respect, I have kept it low. Forty-five. Maybe 55 if you count children's parties, which I don't."

The queen turned to Lorch. "Guard Lacksneck, how about you?"

"That is difficult, my queen," said Lorch. He sat motionless on his horse's back, once again forced to take part in an argument not of his making.

"Give it a shot. Feel free to round down."

He was quiet for a few moments. "I have been on six significant campaigns. We ride roughly 14 hours a day, but there were days where we didn't ride. So call it—"

"Can we skip to a result?"

"I don't think it would be any less than 20,000, Queen Eloise."

"Ah. Thank you, Guard Lacksneck." She came back to Eloise. "There you have it. This is not so much about you as about numbers."

"I beg your pardon? Numbers?"

"Yes. You require speed. You have to catch up with someone who has more than a day's head start on you. It is harder to ride at speed than slowly. If you had Guard Lacksneck's 20,000 hours, then you would not need the riding aid. But you are riding Equine Designate de Pferd as a less-experienced rider. It will exhaust him keeping you up there. And you will exhaust yourself doing the same. This..." She pointed at the saddle. "This is not a slap in the face. It is an essential tool for the success of your undertaking."

Eloise was unconvinced, but it was no longer in her hands. She bowed to Hector. "Thank you, Equine Designate de Pferd, for your consideration and thoughtfulness."

Hector nodded. "Princess."

Then she bowed to her mother. "And thank you, Queen Eloise, for the lucid clarification."

"No need to get snippy with me."

King Chafed stepped forward to head off a confrontation. "Shall we get you going?" he said.

"Yes, Father. That seems a good idea."

He took Eloise by the elbow and walked her a few steps away.

She let him embrace her, and he whispered, "You can do this. Otherwise, she'd not let you go. It is only a couple of days. Plus, you're in good company." He slipped a small hemp envelope into her hand. "Look at that later. Just pop it somewhere for now. I didn't want your mother to see it." He released her, and she slipped the folded paper into her cape. "Boring travels to you." He smiled.

"Thank you, Father."

He walked to Jerome and shook his paw. "Çalahtspeed to you, and boring travels."

As the king continued on to the others, Queen Eloise stepped over to her daughter. She'd dropped the frostiness of a few moments before. "Thank you for doing this. You know, that wasn't an idiotic and vague vision. And your sister, like you, is far from stupid."

Eloise sighed. "You heard. Sorry. I was angry."

"But sometimes anger speaks truth that politeness prefers to hide, as it did in this case—just not the truth you wished to express." She took Eloise's hands. "I appreciate your doing this. I know how hard it was—and is—for you to face this task. But you were right. You are the best option of those before us." She pulled her into a surprisingly warm hug. Eloise hugged her back, just as warmly, her eyes surprising her by watering. The queen let go and put a small hemp envelope into her hand. "Slip that in your cape for now. Just something for later. I didn't want your father to see it."

Eloise palmed it into the pocket along with the one from Chafed.

"Boring travels to you," said the queen fondly.

"Thank you, Mother. I'll see you in a few days."

"And Eloise..."

"Yes, Mother?"

"Make sure you return with your sister, not without."

❧ 30 ❧

THROUGH THE BILIOUS GATE

I t was close to impossible for Eloise to leave Brague, the city around the castle, unnoticed, but it was worth attracting as little attention as possible. So they headed toward the Bilious Gate, so named because up until a century or so before, if you wanted to spew bile at the monarchy, you were free to do so, so long as you stood just outside that particular gate. If you did not engage in treason or slander, it was open slather, and so long as you finished and came in before the gate closed at dusk, you could go home.

The practice fell into disuse as rulers tired of encouraging a platform of disloyalty and complaint. In Eloise's time, the only remnant of the gate's previous use was the Festival of Invective. This happened once a year. Anyone with a grievance stood at the Bilious Gate, and at a signal, held open their Bag of Bellyaching—usually an empty cotton sack with a drawstring—and shouted their grievances into it. These bags would then be tied closed, piled onto a cart, and delivered with great pomp to the castle gates. The queen would emerge and set fire to the cart and contents, thus symbolically resolving all the grievances. Everyone treated it as the joke it had become, but it was in the list of celebrations enumerated by the *Livre de Protocol*, and no one could be bothered to go through the process of removing it.

The Bilious Gate also served as a minor exit and entrance, as most traffic went through the more monolithic William Gates, named after a merchant from a lost era who had made a mint selling framed glass panes.

Eloise and Jerome rode Hector, Jerome sitting in front of Eloise on a small extension of the saddle, forward of the horn. Lorch followed on the Guard Horse. It might have been possible for Eloise to draw into her cloak and bring less notice to herself, but it was pointless to try. Hector's overwhelming beauty meant it was like traveling with a herald who constantly screamed, "Make way! Royalty approaches!" So Eloise sat tall, proclaiming herself to all who looked.

As they threaded through side streets toward the Bilious Gate, people bowed and smiled, wishing Eloise and her family good health and long life. One wag, possibly inebriated, even yelled out, "Tell Two I love her!" Jerome stiffened, ready to take up the queen's honor, but Eloise called back, "I shall extend your fond regards," leaving him to ribbing from his equally altered companions.

Several observers raised an eyebrow at Eloise's saddle, but held their whispered commentary until she was out of earshot.

Brague being old and unplanned, the trip to the lesser-used gate took a solid two hours. Finally, the simple wooden archway stood 50 lengths ahead. As Hector paced toward it, Eloise felt fear reassert itself in her guts. She knew she shouldn't, but she turned to Jerome and, as nonchalantly as she could, said, "A quick tea before we truly get underway?"

Jerome, always tempted with tea, looked eager to say yes, but Hector got in first. "Princess, it will already be a challenge to reach the First Night Inn (formerly the First Knight Inn) before midnight. I suggest we do not add to that burden."

So they continued forward, and Eloise forced a smile at the two gate attendants who waved them through the opened archway. The horses lifted to a trot, and they were on the road.

❦ 31 ❦

THE ROAD IS HIT

They set out at a quick pace, alternating between a canter and a fast trot for the first three hours, covering 30-odd strong lengths on a well-maintained road. The five of them barely spoke, focusing on distance while not making a spectacle of themselves by galloping.

Eloise was immersed in a flood of feelings and thoughts. She'd been out of the castle walls before, but never like this. Never in charge of anything, responsible for an outcome, and in the company of those there to facilitate and protect her. And then there was the countryside itself. For the first time, she was not seeing it through a carriage window. Riding, it seemed much more immediate. Almost overwhelmingly so.

But realistically, the bulk of her attention was bound up in the mechanics of staying on Hector's back. It was soon obvious how inexperienced a rider she was. She could feel Hector constantly shifting beneath her to compensate for her lapses in balance. She could only imagine how much worse it would have been if she'd been bareback. Still, she'd braced herself for the strangeness of riding, and was handling it.

What she hadn't braced herself for was Hector's sweat. Given their pace and the warm day, he was soon lathered, and it was just as soon soaking into the calves of her riding breeks. She would never have said it out loud, but thank Çalaht for the saddle, protected her knees, thighs, and seat. Even so, she had to control the rising revulsion she felt as the horse's dampness slowly wicked its way up her legs. To put her mind elsewhere, she concentrated on the one-two, one-two beat of his trot, the one-two-three, one-two-three of his canter, and the random bobbing of Jerome's head.

They took their first break at a copse of trees that featured a drinking pool carved into stone, which was fed by a cascading trickle of water.

Eloise let Jerome dismount first, then hopped off herself. Her legs, strong as they were, were unused to the constant press of that particular set of muscles in that specific arrangement, and they immediately gave way in a most embarrassing manner.

"Princess!" Jerome had instinctively scampered away, narrowly avoiding the crush of her elbow, but he was immediately by her side, worried. Lorch was there a moment later.

She sat up and brushed off the dirt. "I'm OK. Really, I'm OK. I wasn't expecting my legs to do that." She didn't mind falling in front of Jerome. He'd seen plenty of silly stuff from her over the years. But Lorch? And worse, the perfect Hector? That was painful. She retreated to formality. "Apologies, Equine Designate de Pferd, Guard Lacksneck, for my clumsiness. That won't happen again."

"Princess Eloise, I—" started Hector.

But Eloise waved him off. "Perhaps we can pretend I didn't just land like a sack of potatoes?"

"Yes, Princess."

Lorch helped her wobble to a bench shaded by an elm, Jerome following. "Princess, riding like this takes getting used to. A day or two from now, it will be different."

"One wonders if I'll get used to it by the time we're returning. I'd hate for Johanna to see me sprawled in the dirt like that."

"It's OK, Elorimus," said Jerome. "If it's any consolation, I can barely feel my claws. They've been clasping the saddle extension so long and so tight they're numb. I kept feeling like I'd fly off at any moment. Did I mention this is the first time I've been on the back of a horse?"

"No, you didn't," she said. "That might have been worth mentioning."

"I thought it a mere detail, but I'm thinking I might have underestimated the implications."

"Me, too."

Lorch handed Eloise a mug of water. She wasn't game to ask if it was water from the castle—which she could be confident had been properly run through a clay and coal filter—or if he'd just held the mug under the trickle at the drinking stone. Having made a fool of herself already, she didn't want to push it. She sipped the cool water, grateful for its relief and ignoring the many, many ways it might be tainted.

Hector and the Guard Horse drank from the pool, then paced slowly to stay warm. After ten minutes, Eloise eased to her feet, and limped over to the Guard Horse. "Pardon me, but in our rush to get away, we were not properly introduced. My name is Eloise, and I thank you for your help with this task."

The horse was a bay, with a dark brown body and black mane, and almost as perfectly muscled as Hector, but more travel worn. He nodded, but said nothing.

Lorch came over. "He does not speak, Princess."

"No?"

"No. It is the way of the Guard Horses. It is a choice they make to help them focus on their duty and their work."

"I had no idea. What is his name?"

"I don't know."

Jerome came over, nibbling an almond. "You don't know your horse's name?"

"He does not have one."

"What?"

"Like their choice not to speak, their dedication to the Guard Horses is such that they do not wish a specific identity."

Jerome was genuinely puzzled. "Names are useful. They help distinguish. If you were to call to him, how would you do so?"

"I refer to him as 'the Nameless One.' They all answer to that."

Jerome looked at the Guard Horse. "So if he says, 'Nameless One, soup's on,' you're good with that?"

The Guard Horse looked at him, not deigning to answer.

"OK," Jerome said, wandering away. "Whatever haggles your berries."

Lorch watched the chipmunk go, then added, "This Guard Horse is a fine companion. We have traveled together on all of my campaigns."

"To where?" asked Eloise.

"All over. Last year we traveled to the rainforests of Inner Splutter, and from there we went to the arid hills of Tooth Dunes and the sandy drylands of Cactus Bends.

"So, you've been to two deserts on a horse with no name. How was it?"

"After sloshing through Inner Splutter? It was good to get out of the rain."

A quarter hour later, Jerome came back. "Elympia, we still have some time ahead of us. Are you ready?"

She ached her way onto Hector's back and settled in for more hours of jouncing.

They took a shorter, second break another three hours down the road. This time, Eloise managed a more elegant dismount.

Once again nibbling his almond, Jerome sauntered over to Lorch and the Guard Horse, who stood together under a birch, sharing slices of apple. "I've been thinking about this name thing, and I think you're wrong," said Jerome.

"Oh?" Lorch offered him some apple, but Jerome waved it away.

"You said they all answer to 'Nameless One,' correct?"

"Yes."

"Well, that is a de facto name."

"But he has no name."

"Sure he does. I mean, if I said the Guard Horses all answer to 'John' or 'Lorraine' or 'Splork,' then in essence, that would be their name. Your Guard Horses are all named 'Nameless One.'"

The Guard Horse snorted. Lorch looked at him and then back to Jerome. "But he has no name."

"You don't seem to be listening. What I'm saying is that the no-name thing is a convenient fiction. They are, for all intents and purposes, named..."

Eloise held up a hand. "Jerome. Stop. This trip is already trying enough without you arguing the semantics of nomenclature."

"Princess Eloise, I submit to you that there is a grave breach of—"

"Jerome." The Tone stopped him in his tracks.

The chipmunk sighed. "Yes, Princess. Shall we depart?"

"I'm ready if everyone else is."

And so they rode on as the sun slunk its way into dusk.

❦ 32 ❦

FIRST NIGHT INN (FORMERLY THE FIRST KNIGHT INN)

T he First Night Inn (formerly the First Knight Inn) was a predictable, if longish, day's ride from Brague. A favorite of merchants and farmers alike, the First Night Inn (formerly the First Knight Inn) was known for its crowds, its fermented morel and fenugreek soup, which was almost as popular as its famous cold broccoli and three bean soup, and the apple cider (both tipsy inducing and non-tipsy inducing varieties) that was a fine choice if you were not in the mood for the warm mulled cherry cider. It was also known for the certainty that any guest could reliably hear the latest gossip about Court goings-on, or be the source thereof if word about something needed to get out.

Eloise had stayed there with her family a half dozen times over the years. Its accommodation was far from royal, but whenever her mother felt a need to "get in among the people," this was the place she'd visit.

When Eloise's party finally clopped into the inn's courtyard, it was almost midnight. They'd made good time, but the price was exhaustion. Before they could even dismount, a string bean of a woman wearing a beehive hairdo, a load of possibly expensive jewelry, and a practiced smile emerged from the kitchen holding a shaded oil lantern that cast shadows across her deep, owlish eyes. "G'evening to you all. Not much time until I should have had to say, 'G'midnight.' But here you are, and either way, welcome to the First Night Inn (formerly the First Knight Inn). I am Halcyon Spleenfluke. You are in need of a room?"

"G'evening to you, Mistress Spleenfluke," said Eloise. "Apologies for our late arrival. It is good to see you again."

Even in the dim light, Eloise could see the change in the innkeeper. She strode closer, held the lamp up at Hector, and gasped. Then she held the lamp up at Eloise and gasped again, falling into an obsequious curtsy. "Well, spackle closed dear Çalaht's tooth gap, if we've not been blessed a second night in a row with unexpected royalty. Princess Eloise, it is an honor to welcome you back to the First Night Inn (formerly the First Knight Inn). We delighted in the company of your sister and uncle last night, and lo, Çalaht's blessed bunions, here you are this evening."

"Thank you so much, Mistress Spleenfluke. You are too kind. It is a pleasure to be back after so many years."

"Please, please, let me show you to a room."

"I guess we'll be needing three rooms in the inn, and two places in the stable."

"No, Princess." It was Lorch and Jerome, somehow saying the words in unison. They looked at each other, surprised. "Princess, I—" Again, unison. Lorch bowed to Jerome, indicating that he should go first.

"Princess Eloise, I neither need nor want my own room," said Jerome. "My place is to be close to you."

"Princess, I will sleep outside your door," said Lorch. "This will not be under discussion."

"Which means that I will cover your window," said Jerome.

"You would stay in my room?"

"Come on, El—"

Hector snorted a soft "people are listening" warning.

"I mean, begging your pardon, Princess Eloise, but it would not be that different to the sleepovers we used to have. It is not like I've never seen princessly foundation garments before."

"Jerome!"

"And Lorch here is a guard. If you don't let him guard something he'll probably plotz."

Hector piped in next. "The Nameless One and I will not be confined to stables, Princess. We shall have a meal of oats brought to us in that paddock there." He gestured to a side yard with a thick grassy cover. "And we will remain ready to depart as quickly as needed.

Eloise had not even thought about sleeping arrangements, but she could tell argument would not change the outcome. "Fine," she said. "Mistress Spleenfluke, a modest, out-of-the-way room would be wonderful."

"The room your sister had last night has been freshened. I hope you will find it adequate."

Eloise was surprised just how much opulence was tucked away in the room at the top of the First Night Inn (formerly the First Knight Inn). Either her mother had insisted on more modest accommodation, or the inn had spruced itself up since her last visit. But the chintz and glitz was lost on her. "I might just rest my eyes for a moment before din—"

And she was asleep, dreaming of throwing bowls across a vast pot of cold broccoli and three bean soup.

❦ 33 ❦

ITCHIER

Dawn cracked well before it was polite to do so, and Eloise felt her joints do the same. "Anyone see who pummeled me during the night? Every muscle I have hurts, along with a few that might belong to someone else."

"Whoever it was, I think they used me to hammer you with," said Jerome, standing on the windowsill and surveying the courtyard. Typically, he only reclaimed the use of language after a morning haggleberry tea. But he'd pushed against his own inclinations and years of habit to be dressed and articulate, if not exactly bright, at first light. "I'm hoping to move as little as possible for the next three months."

Eloise ducked behind a dressing screen painted with cranes playing cards, which was either an homage to Alstaria Snotearrow McCcoonnch or a blatant theft of her style. Either way, the screen gave her enough privacy to wash off road residue before dressing. She put on her travel outfit with a suppressed "yuck" at the thought of the dried sweat that must be collected in it. At least its smell was passable, having aired overnight.

Breakfast at the First Night Inn (formerly the First Knight Inn) was as good as anything served at Castle de Brague. The pumpkin gingerbread slurry was like manna from Çalaht. The raw buckwheat porridge topped with fruit was something Chef could take notes on. And the sweet potato breakfast casserole? There were not enough superlatives in any of the languages Eloise knew to cover it.

That it was all ready and beautifully presented before the sun formed much of an opinion on the day seemed a miracle. Having missed dinner the night before, Eloise ate like a soldier on a 60-day march, and Jerome kept pace spoonful for spoonful.

"You know," said Eloise as she scooped up more breakfast casserole, "I've long suspected Chef has a weak magic for the combination of unexpected things, or at least one for the use of seasonings. I wonder if the cook here does as well, or if that's just what it means to be good in the kitchen."

"We'll never know, I guess," shrugged Jerome. "I might manage more of that slurry, if you'd pass it over here, please."

Having chowed down enough for four, they found Lorch, Hector, and the Nameless One in the courtyard gathered around a map spread across the lid of a pickle barrel. The guard and horses were loaded up and ready to go. "Blessings of the day," smiled Eloise. "You've broken fast?"

"Yes, thank you, Princess," said Lorch. "Did you have the apple pie porridge? It was magnificent."

"No. Perhaps next time. Mental note made." Eloise looked at the map. "This looks different to mine." She fished her own map out of her bag, spread it next to Lorch's, and helped Jerome up so he could see them both. "I'd assumed we'd take the main road to Itchy. But your map does not have Scabrous."

"It does, Princess. That village is here." He pointed to a dot.

"Itchier?"

"Yes, Princess. This map is newer than yours."

Eloise shook her head. "It appears the long rivalry between the villages continues."

Itchy and Itchier were on different routes from the First Night Inn (formerly the First Knight Inn) toward the Half Kingdom, and they'd been battling for traffic as long as anyone could remember. Itchy was originally called Pleasantville. The road to it was better maintained and more suited to carriage traffic, and the Chamber of Commerce kept it planted with seasonal flowers. Their rival town, Itchier, was originally called Dangly Dale, and the road to it was more steeply curved and less maintained, but had the advantage of being a few hours quicker if you were willing to put up with the conditions.

Decades before, the Dangly Dale Commerce Council felt they needed to attract more traffic their way, but did not have much budget. Court records showed that many options were canvassed, including sabotaging the Pleasantville road, paying heralds to spread falsehoods about the road's condition, and even hiring bandits to harass Pleasantville-bound travelers. But those sorts of options were unfeasibly costly, not to mention shady and illegal. Eventually, the Dangly Dale Commerce Council hit on an idea so blindingly simple and cheap that when put to a vote, it was unanimously accepted.

They would change the town's name.

So Dangly Dale became Pleasanterville.

To everyone's surprise, it made a difference. A measurable amount of traffic diverted from Pleasantville toward Pleasanterville, benefiting its shops, inns, and eateries.

The Pleasantville Chamber of Commerce, feeling nettled in the hip pocket, could hardly sit idly by. So they, too, chose a name change to try to reclaim traffic. Pleasantville became Beaumont, emphasizing the beauty of the place and the one thing Pleasanterville could not claim— a mountain.

Pleasanterville retaliated by becoming Prettier Flats.

This started years of tit-for-tat name changing, as each village tried to capture the hearts and minds of travelers, confusing everyone and creating a cottage industry in map reworking. Beaumont became Floral Heights, leading Prettier Flats to become More Flowered Glen. Floral Heights changed to Funtown, causing More Flowered Glen to become Funnerton. Funtown became Spectacular, leading Funnerton to switch to Staggeringly Awesome. Spectacular became No Place Better, so Staggeringly Awesome changed to Except For Here.

And so on, and so on.

Eventually, the Chamber of Commerce of the place originally known as Pleasantville, but currently called Don't Let Those Cretins Tell You Their Town is Better got jack of the whole thing and tried reverse psychology. They decided to go for a negative, figuring that the other town would never follow suit. So Don't Let Those Cretins Tell You Their Town is Better swapped their name to Lice Mounds, just to put an end to it all. But the Commerce Council of If You Go There You'll Have Nightmares And Your Toes Will Fall Off could not stop their momentum, and became Lousierburg.

Which is why the village of Scabrous on Eloise's map was Itchier on Lorch's.

Both roads ultimately led on to the same place, a quaint little village called For The Love of Çalaht Cut It Out You Two.

Lorch traced the route toward Itchy. "Given how I'm guessing you are feeling, I was suggesting to Hector that we take the better road. I think we can take this route and still make up time, catching them in For The Love of Çalaht Cut It Out You Two around evening tea time.

"Well and good, Guard Lacksneck," said Hector. "And there is nothing particularly wrong with that choice." He used his nose to indicate the alternate route. "However, if the princess can handle the more difficult terrain of the road to Itchier, we'll pick up several hours by the time we reach For The Love of Çalaht Cut It Out You Two. That would give you time to speak with Princess Johanna earlier in the day, Princess.

And if something unexpected comes up, we'll have more time to respond."

Jerome tapped the map with a toe. "What do you say, El? You up for Itchier?"

"Itchier it is."

"Very good," said Lorch.

Eloise patted her travel cloak, feeling for her coin purse. "Does anyone know where Mistress Spleenfluke is?"

"No need," answered Lorch. "I took the liberty of settling up with the innkeeper while you and Champion Abernatheen de Chipmunk ate."

"Oh, I see. Thank you." Eloise was grateful not to have to show her ignorance of dealing with such a mundane task as paying for accommodation. She'd rehearsed a conversation with Mistress Spleenfluke in her head, unsure what Protocol would allow or demand. She made to untie her purse, but Lorch stopped her. "Our beloved queen provisioned me adequately to cover the requirements of these few days of travel. But thank you for the offer of reimbursement, Princess."

"I see. Well, that was thoughtful of her." Eloise limped stiffly toward Hector, but Lorch zipped ahead of her. "Princess, if I may be so bold. May I show you some stretches that might help ease some of your riding discomfort?"

"Please, Lorch, anything like that would be most welcomed. Jerome, you'll join us?"

"My belly is full of breakfast, but I think I'd better." With a small belch, he followed Lorch's lead, stretching his paws heavenward.

❧ 34 ❧

MARBLE STATUE SCALE

The road to Itchier was definitely devoid of Chamber of Commerce-provided seasonal flowers and was replete with bends and switchbacks. The going seemed slow, so the speed advantage that accrued from taking this route was deceptive.

The weather continued to cooperate, and Eloise lost herself in listening to horse steps as they came in and out of unison due to the different lengths of stride and the variations in speed. A noise off the side of the road—a falling branch—startled Eloise back to alertness. She stiffened, ready for any problems, and accidentally jabbed Hector in the sides with her heels.

"Oof," grunted the stallion.

"Oh, Çalaht praising persnickety platitudes. Sorry Hector," said Eloise.

"It's OK, Princess."

"Is my riding really that bad?"

"You're staying up there, Princess. That is something." Hector walked a few more steps. "It's just that for a while there, you finally relaxed into your riding seat."

"'Finally?' So all of yesterday..."

"I'd rather not say, Princess."

Jerome butted in. "Come on, Your Equitationality. How can you expect the princess to improve if you are evasive?"

"Yes, Hector. I need your candor. And no need for names, Jerome."

"Apologies, Princess. And apologies to you, Equine Designate de Pferd. But let's try this. On a scale of, say, a marble statue to a centaur, with Lorch's riding being somewhere well to the right of the mid-point, where would Princess Eloise's riding from yesterday fall?"

Hector bent his neck a little to look at Jerome, then turned back to the road. "I am uncomfortable with the underlying characterization of your scale. But Princess Eloise asked for candor. Unfortunately, Princess, you were far at the marble statue end of that scale. And your riding seat, Champion Abernatheen de Chipmunk, was distinctly similar. But you are smaller, so it was less noticeable."

Embarrassment crept into Eloise's face. "Goodness, Hector. Why did you not say something?"

"May I speak plainly?"

"Yes. Please do."

"Yesterday, you had put in little time on the back of an equine. Today, you have a full day's more experience. Yesterday, your riding was tolerable, and needed to be tolerated so we could make our distance. Today, this path requires us to be more careful, so the pace is slower. And before—just before that branch broke, when your thoughts were elsewhere—you settled into a rhythm of not trying. It was a distinct notch or two to the right of a marble statue. I didn't want to say anything because I did not want to interfere with it."

"I see," said Eloise.

Hector stopped and turned his head to fix one eye squarely on her. "Princess, I cannot promise you will be a great rider. But I can promise you will, with enough time, slide toward the right-hand side of Champion Abernatheen de Chipmunk's scale. And you, Champion Abernatheen de Chipmunk..."

"Yes, Equine Designate de Pferd?"

"Perhaps you could do me the kindness of not digging your claws into my neck for purchase. Feel free to grip the saddle as hard as you need."

"Oh. Sorry."

"Not to worry."

Hector started moving again, and when they reached a flat stretch in the road, he picked up his pace to a trot, then a canter.

As the sun topped the sky, they noticed signage prolifically, if not horrifically, demarcating the way to Itchier. They trotted down Mount Try Our Lovely Scones and across the Children Eat Free fields onto Delicious Apple Turnover Way. Beyond a sign that said "Itchier Welcomes Careful Carriage Drivers," they turned left onto Cleanest Facilities Anywhere Street, and at its intersection with Finest Haggleberry Cuppa Crescent, they found an inn named I Still Think "Dangly Dale" Was Just Fine. The lunch specialty was a fried black-eyed pea tempeh with a side of potatoes sliced into strips and deep fried in oil until crisp on the outside. Hector and the Nameless One left the other three at the inn to go find suitable grass to crop.

As the dishes were served, Eloise realized that Lorch had barely spoken since they'd left the First Night Inn (formerly the First Knight Inn). "You seem lost in thought, Guard Lacksneck."

"It's just that there was something odd back at the First Night Inn (formerly the First Knight Inn)."

"Yes? What sort of odd?"

"As I was having breakfast, and then later when I was clearing the bill with the innkeeper, I asked about Princess Johanna and King Doncaster. I wanted to scout, if I could, their travel intentions, just in case they were not the obvious return to the Half Kingdom."

"And?"

"It was, as I said, odd." Lorch tried to find the right words. "I got different stories. Pretty much everyone agreed they were headed north toward the Half Kingdom, but a stable hand and a kitchen maid both separately said that the destination was southward."

"Odd," said Eloise.

"Odd, but explainable. It is not like a stable hand and a kitchen maid would have a direct line to the king's plans."

"Agreed." Eloise went back to eating her fried potato strips. "Let us not doubt ourselves. We'll see them this afternoon, I'm sure."

❧ 35 ❧

PAMPLEMOUSSES

Around mid-afternoon, they crested a small mountain above For The Love of Çalaht Cut It Out You Two. And there was Doncaster's carriage. It acted as a beacon down into town.

"Oh! A local festival," said Jerome with genuine pleasure. "Can you tell the occasion? Is there a theme?"

Lorch discreetly pointed out locals. "Young lads wearing hollowed-out grapefruits as helmets. Young maidens wearing decorative grapefruit wedges on their hats. Couples exchanging nets of grapefruits apparently as tokens of affection."

"Oh! Oh! It's the Celebration des Pamplemousses! This is fantastic," chortled Jerome. "They will have grapefruits everywhere—in shop windows, at the Miss or Mister Pamplemousses Pageant, in the Pamplemousses Parade, and at the Grapefruit Gala. Grapefruit fritters. Grapefruit and sarsaparilla cordial. Grapefruit tossing. Grapefruit juggling. Grapefruit stacking. Largest grapefruit. Sweetest grapefruit. Sourest grapefruit. Funniest-shaped grapefruit. Best grapefruit decorating. Speed grapefruit classifying. Feats of strength involving weights (and even strong weights) of grapefruits. There will even be a grapefruit poked onto the spire of the local Çalahtist devotional house, which the house minder will pretend to rail against, then take bets on how long it will take to decay—all proceeds going to the good works they do in Çalaht's name."

"That all seems so..." Hector searched for a word. "Quaint."

"It's the best, especially if you're a fan of celebrating sour citrus fruits," said Jerome. "And I don't mind saying I am. Look! They're selling grapefruit punch over there!"

"Then today's our lucky day. I shall try to contain my enthusiasm."

"I think it's charming," said Eloise.

"Do not be a cynic, Hectorino," chided Jerome. "Open yourself to local color."

"Champion Abernatheen de Chipmunk, do not refer to me either directly or indirectly as 'Hectorino.' Is that clear?"

"Ooh, touchy. My apologies, Your Hectorness."

"Do. Not. Mock. Me."

Eloise could sense something was coming, but she wasn't sure what. "Don't push it, Jerome."

"Come on, Eloise. Pretty Boy here really needs to lighten up."

Eloise wasn't sure how he did it, but Hector gave a small, sudden shake that barely jiggled a hair of hers, but sent the chipmunk flying. With incredible accuracy, Jerome bounced off a stacked pyramid of grapefruit, toppling them, rebounded off the back of a man wearing grapefruit earrings who was built to play defensive girder, and splashed into the bowl of grapefruit punch.

The stall holder fished him out, held him up like a soaked rag doll, and said, "You will pay for that swim, my good sir." Then he dropped Jerome back in the ruined punch.

"Hector, for the love of Çalaht. This has gone too far." Eloise jumped off his back and went to the punch bowl. "Jerome! Jerome! Are you OK?"

Jerome pulled himself up to the edge of the punch bowl, his face a mix of anger and embarrassment. "I'm fine, thank you. Just fine."

"Enjoy your local color, chipmunk." Hector turned and walked in the other direction.

"Hector, stop!" snapped Eloise.

"I would rather not, Princess." Hector kept walking.

"Lorch, please help Jerome."

"Yes, Princess."

Eloise rushed to catch up with Hector. "Equine Designate de Pferd."

The horse stopped. "Yes, Princess?"

"You could have hurt him."

"You saw. He is fine."

"This will not do. Equine Designate de Pferd. I recognize that Champion Abernatheen de Chipmunk can be a right royal pain in the backside. But you can't do that. You just can't. I need you to refrain from acts that might damage my champion. I need everyone on the same team."

"Yes, Princess."

"Thank you."

"Shall we find where Princess Johanna is staying?"

"We should get Jerome."

"I would rather not, just at the moment. Guard Lacksneck will handle it capably, I'm sure."

Perhaps it was better to keep them apart for the moment.

"Do you promise better restraint?"

"Yes, Princess."

Obedience, but no contrition.

"Fine. Let's go find my sister."

36

THE LEGS NOT ARMS

Lorch and Jerome caught up with Eloise and Hector outside an inn called the Legs Not Arms. Jerome did not look chastened by either the drying stickiness of grapefruit punch or the indignity of unexpected flight. He stood stiffly, careful not to look at Hector.

"Jerome."

"Yes, Princess."

"I'm thinking there's something you should say."

"What, that he shouldn't have pitched me into the punch? I'm happy to say that."

"I warned you. But you kept going. Now say it."

Jerome blanked his face. "Equine Designate de Pferd, my apologies. I will endeavor from now on to interact more appropriately and professionally."

Hector remained silent.

"Hector?" said Eloise.

"Apology accepted, Champion Abernatheen de Chipmunk," said Hector. "And for my part, I shall attempt in the future to refrain from throwing you into punch."

"I would appreciate it," said Jerome.

"Thank you, both of you." Eloise hoped this civility would last, but wouldn't wager on it.

The Legs Not Arms was a half-timbered five-story building a block off the town's main square. It was easy to see why Doncaster's carriage was parked to the side. He'd definitely want to overnight in a place that was this clean, classy, and beautiful. If the reception area spoke to the rest of the building, then it would be filled with dark wood paneling, oak furniture, silver ornaments, and artwork that testified to both taste and purse.

Eloise walked in a few paces behind Jerome. Lorch remained in the doorway, where he could survey the room and control in and out traffic if he needed to.

"Welcome to the Legs Not Arms," said a plummy basso from the direction of the reception desk. Eloise looked, but could not see the person speaking, her eyes still adjusting to the darkened interior. "How may we be of service." It was a statement, Eloise noted, not a question. She still couldn't find the speaker. "Adjust your gaze downward 60 degrees, if you please."

Eloise did, and saw the most resplendent centipede she'd ever met. He wore a finely embroidered cotton outfit that was more coat than robe, and silver rings on each of his legs, which gave a small metallic clack to his movements. His head was red, his body segments ebony, and the hairs on his head were pomaded to a cliff-sheer pompadour. He sat, presumably in honor of the local fest, on a most deliciously fragrant grapefruit. Near him on the desk, a tented card politely informed the reader in exquisite calligraphy that there were, unfortunately and with deepest regrets, "No vacancies."

How that low voice could come from such a small body was inexplicable, but when the centipede spoke again, there was the same velvet rumble. "I am Elgin Lëëëäääfääännïïïhïïïlääätööör, proprietor. How can I be of service, Mistress? Or perhaps I should say..." His eyes flicked from Jerome to Lorch to Hector and the Nameless One, visible through the blue-hued glass of the window. "How may I be of service, Princess." Again, a statement, not a question.

"Pleased to meet you, Master Lëëëäääfääännïïïhïïïlääätööör. I am Princess Eloise Hydra Gumball III."

"One surmised."

"One does not want to assume. And may I say, the Lëëëäääfäään-nïïïhïïïlääätööör inns are renowned. I had no idea we had such august accommodation so close to Castle de Brague."

"You flatter, Princess. Our presence here is humble compared to other places run by my family. But may I compliment you on your pronunciation of 'Lëëëäääfääännïïïhïïïlääätööör.' Few in the Western Lands and All That Really Matters can do justice to it."

"Now you flatter, Master Lëëëäääfääännïïïhïïïlääätööör. You must know our father hails from the Half Kingdom, so northern names are second nature."

The centipede nodded. "You are here to see your uncle."

"My sister, actually."

"Ah. It has been a pleasure to entertain your sister. She has been most vivacious. Loquacious even."

"Loquacious? Really? Traveling must suit her. At home one would hardly call her chatty. Would you be so kind as to tell me where I might find her?"

"The lovely Princess Johanna has been bitten with a similar affliction as my much beloved wife—botanical curiosity. They are in the side garden, conversing. About bulbs, I believe. I'll have someone show you the way."

"That would be most kind. Might I ask something else?"

"Of course, Princess, but I fear the answer will be 'no.'"

Eloise pointed to the card on the desk. "So that represents truth, and not a negotiating tactic?"

"This time, I'm afraid, we really are beyond capacity. You can thank the grapefruit. It seems a popular fruit—we've been booked for months. I can send the concierge to one of my competitors to see if they have something for you. It won't be as nice, of course, but it might do for a night."

"Thank you. I would appreciate that very much."

37

WHO WOULD MARRY ME?

Eloise left Jerome and Lorch at reception, figuring she'd better talk to her sister alone. A grasshopper in a bellhop uniform, complete with bellboy hat, led the way to the side garden. Eloise smelled its perfume well before she reached it. Stepping into the garden's embrace was like slipping into a fecund, ripe bath of foliage and flowers. Heavenly.

Johanna was talking to a centipede who was the mirror of the proprietor. Her body segments were bright red, and her head and tail ebony. Their only commonalities were their bright yellow legs and the clacking silver adornments. Her garment was also more robe than coat, embroidered with leaves and vines, and was fastened around her midpoint with a fine silver chain.

As soon as Johanna saw Eloise, her face fell. "Oh, Çalaht criticizing culottes, really?" She knew exactly what it meant to see her sister, even if she did not yet have the details. She shook off the surprise and retreated to Protocol. "Excuse my lapse. Mistress Blúúümenfresser, may I please present to you Princess Eloise Hydra Gumball III, Future Ruler and Heir to the Western Lands and All That Really Matters.

Eloise, may I present Mistress Siñgfried Blúüümenfresser, co-proprietor of this fine establishment, creator of this luscious garden, and an exquisite conversationalist."

"Pleased to make your acquaintance, Madam Blúüümenfresser. You are not a Lëëëäääfääännïïïhïïïläääätööör?"

"Oh, do call me Siggy. I am, indeed, a Lëëëäääfääännïïïhïïïläääätööör by marriage. But I'm Southie-born. The thought of spelling that name over and over for the rest of my life sent shivers down my antennae, so I kept my name. As it turns out, when one is married, one gets to spell one's spouse's name anyway. But on the whole, I think I'm ahead on the transaction."

Eloise smiled. "I shall keep that in mind, Madam Bl—. Siggy. However, as you know, we keep our names, and 'Gumball' has a distinct lack of umlauts and accents. I should be safe."

"So you should, so you should," said Siggy. "I'm guessing the two of you need to catch up. This should be plenty private for you once I'm away."

"Siggy," said Johanna, more comfortable with the first name than Eloise. "Would it be too much for me to offer to carry you somewhere?"

"That's most kind, Jo," said the centipede. "But I'll be out of your way in a jiffy. Perhaps we can all take dinner together? Can I invite the two of you and the king to join me and my husband?"

"We'd have to consult with our uncle," said Johanna. "But I'd love to. Eloise?"

"Sounds lovely."

"I'll assume a 'yes' unless I hear otherwise. See you at seven." And with that, Siñgfried Blúüümenfresser moved to a small, metal tube set at the base of a plant. It looked like part of the watering system until she flipped up its hatch, slid in, and closed it behind her.

"Interesting," said Johanna, stepping closer to examine the centipede's exit mechanism.

"Jo?" said Eloise. "You don't let anyone call you Jo."

"And I still don't," replied Johanna. "Don't take this the wrong way, but I really don't want to see you here."

"I know."

"Whatever you're about to say, I'm going to say 'no' to, right?"

"Probably that's where you'd want to start."

Johanna turned so she faced her sister. "Let's get this over with. I suppose you're here to fetch me?"

"'Fetch' is not the word I'd use. But circumstances have arisen, and a return might be best."

"Circumstances? Is someone ill? Are Mother and Father OK?"

"No, yes—they're fine. Here's the deal." Eloise conveyed Seer Maybelle's vision, her falling into the fire, the fevered discussion about the vision's meaning, the unclear path forward, and the distinct, unavoidable conclusion that Johanna's continuing on this trip would bring dire consequences for her.

"That's ridiculous," said Johanna. "Completely ludicrous."

"Is it? It's Seer Maybelle we're talking about here."

Johanna snorted, but said nothing as she thought about it all. Finally, she said, "They buy into this vision, and realize that it's Uncle D we're talking about here, so they can't send a diplomat. Or military. Or a common messenger. I get all that. So they send you, figuring you have enough weight to convince me and are less likely to spark an inter-realm conflict." She shook her head. "You have to hand it to Mother. She knows how to play this game. I'm just surprised."

"Surprised at what?"

"That you agreed to do it. You're completely, utterly, and unfathomably unsuited to this kind of travel. I'm surprised you're not in the corner hugging your knees."

Eloise felt slapped by the words. "Actually, it was my suggestion."

"Truth?"

"Truth."

Johanna nodded at that, silently acknowledging the cost it must exact on her sister. "You know it is rare for these visions to be directly predictive."

"Yes," agreed Eloise.

"So, convince me."

"It's Seer Maybelle. That's what I have."

Johanna sighed, then sighed again. She knelt to smell a particular flower with deep brown petals, then smiled with appreciation. "You should smell it," she said, examining the plant carefully. "It's a chocolate cosmos flower. They're rare. I'd read about them, but I'd never seen one before. And here it is." She allowed herself a second, longer smell. "There's a distinct vanilla-ish odor. Remarkable. This alone is something I can treasure." Johanna stood, brushing a few specks of dirt from her hands. "You know, I just wanted a break. I just wanted a chance to do something a little different. Apparently, that's too much for everyone."

"I'm sorry. I really am."

"I suppose I have to go back with you." Johanna used a knuckle to wipe the corner of her eye. "We don't want me a crone before my time. Who would marry me then? Not that that's such an issue."

"Who are you marrying?" Doncaster swept into the garden, black cape swishing the tops of the plants. His glance froze on Eloise. He, too, gauged exactly what it meant to see her. "Oh, Princess Eloise. You've come to deprive me of my gardening advice, haven't you?"

"G'afternoon, King Doncaster," replied Eloise, avoiding the accusation.

He struck a dramatic, mocking pose. "Say it isn't so, niece."

"How has your journey been so far, Uncle?"

He dropped the playfulness. "Princess Eloise. Do you or do you not intend to remove your fair sister from my company?"

"Yes, King Doncaster. Johanna needs be returning with me."

"'Needs be'? What are you, from the last century? Has someone died?"

"No, King Doncaster."

"Then what could possibly be so overwhelmingly urgent that it can't wait a few days for her return? Do say, Princess Eloise."

Eloise had no idea what to say to that. She hadn't considered that Doncaster might object—an obvious oversight, in retrospect. "King Doncaster, I—"

"She isn't at liberty to say, Uncle D," said Johanna. "But you know it must be a doozie if they're calling me back." She walked over to him and pecked him on the cheek. "I've had a stupendous time so far. The soup at the First Night Inn (formerly the First Knight Inn). The way you haggled at the market in Itchy for that lovely scarf. Surely, you can forgive me for running off? Can we do it another time?"

Doncaster seemed mollified. "You'll come visit whenever this what-ever-it-is resolves?"

"Of course. Now, did you hear Madame Blúüümenfresser has invited us all to dine with her and Master Lëëëäääfääännïïïhïïïlääätööör?"

"Well," said Doncaster. "We can't miss out on that. You'll leave in the morning then?"

At Eloise's nod, Johanna said, "Yes. After breakfast." She turned to Eloise. "You'll need to see to your evening accommodation, if you haven't done so already. And I assume you've organized transport for me?"

"Of course." She hadn't.

"Then I'll see you here for dinner." Without waiting for a reply, she took Doncaster's elbow and steered him out of the garden.

Eloise took a moment to smell the chocolate cosmos, noted its odd vanilla odor, then found her way back to reception.

❧ 38 ❧

MOST MIDDLING

Lgin Lëëëäääfääänniïïhiïïlääätööör disparagingly called the
accommodation he'd found for Eloise 'average,' but the
Middling Inn was proudly so. Located in an average side
street in a nondescript part of town, and built literally in the middle of
the road, the sign on the Middling Inn proudly proclaimed it was,
"The most middling inn in the realm."

"Looks OK to me," said Eloise.

"Good enough," said Jerome.

Eloise settled in to a room that was perfectly adequate, and before she
knew it, it was time for dinner. She left Hector and the Nameless One
negotiating at a local stable for a suitable third horse and walked back
to the Legs Not Arms with Jerome and Lorch.

"Welcome, welcome, welcome," trilled Sñïgfried Blúüùmenfresser as
they arrived. She sat on a cushion carried by a silent lemur dressed in a
distinctive gold and maroon livery. "Come in, come in, come in." She
waved at Lorch and Jerome. "You two as well. I have a table for you as
well."

Eloise raised her eyebrows at that. Very progressive, especially for a place like this.

The dining room delivered on the reception area's promises of restrained elegance. Dark wood sideboards camouflaged themselves against a similar deep paneling along the walls. Candlelight glinted from half a dozen beveled mirrors, which refracted the light into rainbows at deliberate, interesting angles.

Doncaster and Johanna sat at the table, already deep in animated conversation with Elgin Lëëëäääfääännîîïhïîlääätöôör, along with, to Eloise's surprise, Theoplonkilis, the Half Kingdom trade delegate with the wart cream problem. He must have tagged along with his king. A servant drew out Eloise's chair, and she slid into the last seat at the far end of the table, next to Siggy, whose cushion was placed opposite her husband's at the head of the table.

As Eloise reached for her serviette, she heard Jerome gasp. He and Lorch were led to a table at the back of the room where two people already sat.

Turpy and Gouache.

Jerome was about to spend the evening parked a length and a half away from two jesters. Eloise saw him grit his teeth, avert his eyes, and climb onto his raised chair. He was in for a very long night. "Hang in there, Jerome," she muttered to herself.

At a tingle of Siggy's bell, servers—one per diner—paraded in with trays of covered dishes. They set down the plates and, with a simultaneous flourish, revealed the first course: innumerable and varied fresh leaves palatable to both centipedes and humans, prepared and served in a way that was clever, surprising, and delicious. This was followed by a tomato salad made from five different varieties, and topped with a macadamia drizzle, alongside cucumber noodles with a spicy basil and lime dressing. Dessert was a dish Eloise had never had: a peach tart spiced with cardamon, made on a pecan and ginger crust.

Johanna threw herself into the conversation in a way Eloise had not seen for years. "I would never have thought to combine the fresh basil and fresh lime leaves like that," she burbled. "They came from your garden?"

"Yes, they did," said Siggy.

"Excellent. Outstanding. Fantastic. You have the most wonderful results."

"I'll pass on your compliments to our cook and gardener," said Elgin.

The discussion careened all over the place, and Johanna seemed determined enjoy every morsel of pleasure the evening offered. They talked of travel. "The weather's been so good, and I can't believe how incredibly comfortable Lurid Eddie's carriage is," said Johanna. "Luxurious, sumptuous, lavish. Mother and father will have to get one just like it." They spoke of shopping. "Uncle D, you have an unfair advantage when it comes to merchants. It's practically impossible to get them to give you a fair price when they know they're dealing with the king." On and on she burbled. It truly had been a long time since Eloise had seen her sister so animated, but she couldn't begrudge Johanna's last blush of enjoyment from this particular freedom. If nothing else, it meant all Eloise had to do was nod, smile, agree now and then, and try not to think about how many other mouths her spoon had been in previously.

Every now and again, Eloise looked over at Lorch, Jerome, and the jesters at the other end of the room. Not a word was spoken. They didn't even make eye contact. Jerome stared fixedly at his plate, and Eloise knew he was exerting every weak weight of will he had to not run squealing from the hall. Gouache punctuated his loud eating with louder sighs. Lorch appeared to eat without giving the food any attention. Turpy left his food untouched, focusing unblinking eyes on the main table where Eloise and the others sat. The staring was unnerving.

Finally, late in the evening, Doncaster stood and offered a final toast, raising his teacup. "To our royally gracious hosts, and this pleasant, enjoyable, agreeable evening. Bravo."

"Bravo," echoed the others.

Less than a quarter hour later, Eloise, Lorch, and Jerome walked home. The evening air was crisp and refreshing, and she was in good spirits when her head hit the not-firm, not-soft Middling Inn pillow.

All was set for an early departure back to Brague.

❦ 39 ❦

GONE LIKE A BIRTHDAY CAKE

Eloise had slept fairly well on a bed that was almost firm enough, and had about the right number of blankets covering sheets that were clean enough not to disturb her, although her unbothered sleep was aided by the exhaustion of the day's ride and her late night as a dinner guest. Now, ignoring muscles just as sore as the day before, if not a smidgen more, she enjoyed the Middling Breakfast Special, made up of a very reasonable porridge with adequate toast, a perfectly serviceable selection of jams and raw fruits, and a drinkable (in her opinion, not Jerome's) cup of haggle-berry tea. The Middling Inn deserved its good enough reputation.

Outside the inn, Eloise, Jerome, and Lorch found Hector and the Nameless One ready to go, idly chewing the bark off a stand of willow trees while they waited. With them was a gold and blonde palomino Andalusian stallion Eloise did not recognize. He had the thickest, longest mane and tail she'd ever seen. When they saw her, all three snapped to attention. Hector took a step forward. "Blessings of the day to you, Princess. I trust you are well and ready for the return journey?"

"Blessings of the day to you as well. And yes. Home beckons."

"May I introduce Alejandro Diego Ferdinando Felipe Esteban Iglesias Desoto de Lugo, who has kindly agreed to help us with Princess Johanna."

"Pleased to meet you, Alejandro Diego Ferdinando Felipe Esteban Iglesias Desoto de Lugo. I am Eloise Hydra Gumball III."

The horse bowed extravagantly. "It is my honor, Señorita Princesa, to be of service. You can call me Al."

"With such a beautiful and extravagant name, do you hail from the Eastern Lands?"

"Yes, Señorita Princesa."

It occurred to Eloise that she was not sure if Johanna knew how to ride a horse. Did she need a carriage? Oh well, they would find out. If she needed a carriage or a saddle, then they would deal with it.

They trotted down the main street of For the Love of Çalaht Cut It Out You Two, where preparations for the Pamplemousses Parade progressed purposefully. Eloise heard Jerome sigh.

"What?" she asked.

"Nothing." He sighed again.

"Go ahead."

"It's just that we will miss the pageantry and pomp of the Pample-mousses Parade."

"Apologies. Presumably it's a palpably powerful performance."

"Precisely." Jerome fingered a small brass grapefruit hanging from an inexpensive chain. It hadn't even occurred to Eloise that it might be fun to have a souvenir. Oh well, too late now. There was not enough time before they left.

Eloise sensed something wrong even before they arrived at the Legs Not Arms. Something was missing.

The glaring decorative monstrosity that was Doncaster's carriage—it wasn't parked to the side like it had been the day before.

Jerome looked at Eloise, puzzled. "I distinctly heard you confirm we'd meet up after breakfast. It was the last thing you two said."

But they were gone. King, princess, jesters, and hideously bedecked carriage were absolutely not there. Verschwunden like a birthday cake at a gathering of gourmands. Elgin Lëëëäääfääännïïïhïïïlääätööör confirmed their absence. "Yes, they made an early start. Asked for a packed breakfast and a picnic lunch and off they went, all cheery good-byes when the sun was barely hinting at the day."

"Strange," said Eloise. "Did they say where they were going?" This wasn't right. Not at all.

"Why, yes," replied the centipede. "Both King Doncaster and Princess Johanna seemed keen on seeing the Whacking Great Hole."

"Really. Isn't the Whacking Great Hole at least a half day's ride from here?" asked Eloise.

"Depends on how exuberantly you travel and which way you go," said Elgin. "It's not close, but it is also not an arduous day trip. They purchased two copies of the map showing the way there and the local environs, and two copies of 'Your Guide to Seeing the Whacking Great Hole Without Dying.' You know, 'Once, twice, thrice,' and all that."

The Whacking Great Hole was exactly what it sounded like—a huge, circular hole in the ground roughly 75 lengths across and an unknown number of lengths down, as no one who'd tried to measure it had made it to the bottom and returned alive. It was certainly farther than you could see if you looked over the edge holding a lit torch. And if you threw the torch into the hole, it fell and shrank until it was swallowed by soundless blackness. It was, for all practical purposes, bottomless. Some said it actually *was* bottomless, although that struck Eloise as unlikely.

Some said the Whacking Great Hole was created when Çalaht slammed the end of her staff into the ground, but that didn't hold logically, because wouldn't she have ended up at the bottom, craning her gap-toothed expression skyward, trying to figure out how to get back up? Some said it was a long-forgotten act (or misdeed) of strong magic, which was at least vaguely plausible, but highly unlikely given what was known about magic Back When. Some said it was made when a giant fiery rock fell from the heavens and smashed into the earth. But that was just stupid.

Eloise could get it to make a kind of sense in her mind that Johanna and Doncaster might want to see it. The "once, twice, thrice" Elgin mentioned referred to an old saying: "Everyone should visit the Whacking Great Hole at least once for good memories, and twice for good fortune, but thrice is a curse." It wasn't the catchiest of old sayings.

"This really is odd," said Eloise, once she'd explained the situation to the horses. "Johanna and I had a clear understanding. Breakfast, then home. This concerns me."

"So, what do we do?" asked Jerome.

"I say we go catch up with them. Find out what's going on."

"Agreed," said Lorch.

"Who knows," said Jerome. "We might even get ourselves some good memories."

❧ 40 ❧

WHACKING GREAT HOLE

Lorch purchased a copy of "Your Guide to Seeing the Whacking Great Hole Without Dying," and the local map, even though Alejandro knew the area well.

"Señorita Princesa, there are several ways to get to the Whacking Great Hole, which is not surprising, given how popular it is," said Al. "Because King Doncaster and Princesa Johanna have several hours' head start, I suggest we take the quickest route, rather than the one they likely would have used. Our way will not be a pretty road, nor is it easy. But I—" He paused dramatically, drawing up to full height. "I, Alejandro Diego Ferdinando Felipe Esteban Iglesias Desoto de Lugo, shall lead the way."

Jerome and Hector shared an eye-roll, but managed to not say anything.

Their route was less road and more trail. Loose stones made the steep slopes tricky, both up and down. Half the time, Eloise felt like she was about to slide off the front of Hector and topple onto Al, and the other half she feared slipping backward and taking out Lorch and the Nameless One. Her riding seat lost any smoothness she might have gained over the previous two days, and she worried that she'd cause

186

Hector to misstep, causing both of them to end up in the ravine they skirted. Eloise listened to the four-beat clop of the walking horses, but found herself less able to lose her mind in it. As Hector's sweat once again seeped into her riding breeks, the "yuck" in her grew.

What was Johanna thinking? A quick visit to the Whacking Great Hole? Not exactly a stupid idea, but why not organize it with her? Or at least tell her. Leave a note, maybe? For that matter, why not invite Eloise along? Was her company that odious? Maybe Johanna didn't know how long it would take to do the side trip. But then, a packed breakfast and a picnic lunch suggested she knew it would be more than an hour or two. It made little sense, which sat badly with her. Of all the people Eloise knew, Johanna made more sense than anyone.

At last, the steep hills gave way to an open flat, and an hour later they stood in front of a tiny wooden booth that said "Whacking Great Hole Greater Park Area Tourist Complex." Copies of "Your Guide to Seeing the Whacking Great Hole Without Dying" lined the wall, and were priced at three times what they'd paid at the Legs Not Arms. Among the guide books sat a bored-looking skink wearing a ranger's cap and a khaki tunic. A button pinned to the tunic read, "Hi, My Name is _____. Welcome to the Whacking Great Hole, the Hugest Hole in the Realm. Please Don't Die While You Are Here."

The skink stifled a yawn, and said, for what was clearly the ten thousandth time, "Hi, My name is _____. Welcome to the Whacking Great Hole, the hugest hole in the realm. Please don't die while you are here. How may I help you?"

"We'd like to see the Whacking Great Hole," said Eloise.

"You're in the right place," said the skink. "That way. Two coins each, please."

Eloise was surprised. "It costs to see the Whacking Great Hole?"

"No, ma'am, it does not," said _____. "It costs to maintain this booth. It costs to tell people not to die here. It costs to maintain the refreshments stand inside. It costs to pick up the bits of crud that people leave behind, both accidentally and because they can't be bothered to take their trash to one of the many convenient receptacles located around the Whacking Great Hole Greater Park Area. It costs to empty those many conveniently located receptacles. It costs to tell families and friends that their loved ones have unfortunately perished while visiting the Whacking Great Hole, the Hugest Hole in the Realm. But seeing the hole—that's free. Two coins each, please."

"Oh, OK. Twelve coins then, for six of us," said Eloise.

"No, Señorita Princesa," said Al, shaking his white blanket of a mane emphatically. "I shall not be joining you to see the Whacking Great Hole."

"No? Why not?"

"I have seen the Whacking Great Hole. It is, indeed, a huge hole, and well worth your looking at it. I have done so. Twice now. I have my good memories and my good fortune. I—" He paused dramatically. "I, Alejandro Diego Ferdinando Felipe Esteban Iglesias Desoto de Lugo, do not need a curse."

"Isn't that just an old saying?" asked Jerome. "And not a very good one, at that. Come on. We might need your help in there."

"No, my bushy-tailed amigo," said Al. "Some fates are not worth tempting. I shall remain here and enjoy the company of the lovely _____."

"I can hardly wait," muttered _____.

Lorch paid ten coins from a decidedly lighter purse, and they left Alejandro trying to jolly the skink into conversation.

The path to the Whacking Great Hole was clearly marked and well worn. Carriages were parked in neat rows beyond the skink's shack, but there was no sign of Lurid Eddie. "You'd think we'd see *something*," said Eloise.

"I agree, Princess. This does not make sense."

After a strong length or two of walking, they saw people up ahead of them. There it was. The Whacking Great Hole, with a convenient, if likely overpriced, refreshment stand to the side.

A vendor sold pads of blank paper so that the tourists could sketch themselves in front of the hole—something to share with their family and friends who were not there with them. The sketches tended to be more flattering and exciting than the mundane reality of standing near a large hole in the ground, but then, that was the point.

They split up to see what they could find, agreeing to meet where they'd left Alejandro in an hour. Hector went one way, Lorch and the Nameless One another, and Eloise and Jerome headed for the hole, stopping a safe distance from the edge.

"Well," said Jerome. "It's a hole."

"Yes," agreed Eloise. "It certainly is large. You have to give it that."

"Yes. There is no getting around the fact that this is a big hole. Huge."

"Hugest, apparently."

"It could use a safety rail."

"Yeah. Maybe a warning sign or two."

"But a safety rail, or even a piece of string in the way, would not go astray."

The pad vendor came over to them, another skink wearing a button that read, "Hi, My Name is Vendor. Welcome to the Whacking Great Hole, the Hugest Hole in the Realm. Please Don't Die While You Are Here." He coughed to get their attention. "Buy a blank pad? Sketch yourself in front of the hole? You just have to be careful not to do it too close. They get shirty when people die here. Still, it happens all the time. Don't know why they get all tied up in knots about it."

"No thank you," said Eloise. "We'll just look."

The skink would not be put off. "Come on, Mistress. Sketching your-self is all the rage. We had a king and a princess here doing just that not more than a few hours ago. A fine way to make your friends jealous, for sure. And that way, if you do die here, there'll be a last memory of you for them to have—so long as you don't take the pad with you when you cark it. And so long as you've put a name and address on there so it can be delivered. We have a stack behind the shed with no name or address. Can't do much with those. Except maybe rip out the used pages and sell the pads again. You know, I hadn't thought about that until just now. Hmm."

"Wait, wait, wait," Jerome broke in. "Did you say a king and princess?"

"I sure did. Sold them each a pad myself. Buy a pad, and you can be like the king. Or the princess."

"King Doncaster and Princess Johanna?"

"That's them."

"Did you hear what they were planning on doing after seeing the Whacking Great Hole?"

"Of course," said Vendor. "Because the king of the Half Kingdom tells me everything. We're close as."

"So, no, then?" asked Eloise.

Vendor shrugged, then wiggled the pads. Once. Then again. There was an awkward pause.

Then Eloise pieced it together. "You know, Jerome, I *am* in a sketching mood. Master..." She squinted at his button. "Master Vendor, how much are the pads?"

"A coin, Mistress," he said. "Half a coin if you can wait a couple of minutes and don't mind a few pages missing."

"A new one will do," she said.

"Each."

Eloise shook her head. "Then we'll take two of the half-coin ones." She fished a coin from her purse.

Vendor took it, smiling. "Actually, the king did not speak to me, but I was standing nearby when he and the princess finished their sketches. She said something about needing to get back, and he said something about of course, and then she said something about how her sister was likely very annoyed, and then he said something about that being her way and that there was nothing that could be done about that, and then she said something about how deep the hole is, and he said something about yes it is, and then she said something about they really ought to be going, and he said something about, well, of course, but would she like an overpriced refreshment first, and then she said something about a drink that had carrot in it, and then he said something about blech he'd rather drink grass, then she said something about certain grasses being nutritious, and at that point I think I may have stopped listening, because I, too, would rather drink grass than carrots. But then, I'm a skink."

Another awkward silence.

"Was that the entire pad's worth of information?" asked Eloise.

The skink half-nodded. "As much as I'd love to sell you another pad, I'm an honest pad salesman, and that's all I have in the way of information."

"Then, thank you, Master Vendor. I appreciate it very much."

"My pleasure, Mistress." He saw her and Jerome turn to leave. "Hey, aren't you going to sketch yourself? That's what the pads will be for, once I fetch them for you."

"Thank you, but if you can catch up and give it to me, my companion and I have some friends to find."

They found Alejandro laughing uproariously with _____. "Ah, my friends have returned from their once or twice but not thrice in a lifetime experience of the Whacking Great Hole. It has been a pleasure, _____. I hope to return someday soon to again enjoy such marvelous company."

The skink actually blushed. "Don't be a stranger, Al Baby. And I'm glad your friends didn't die in there."

Alejandro reached down and gave the skink a delicate kiss on the forefoot. "Adios, my flat-tailed amigo."

Hector, Lorch, and the Nameless One arrived moments later, each with a sketch pad. Only Hector had taken the time to sketch himself in front of the Whacking Great Hole. Jerome looked at the drawing. "That's amazing. You've emphasized your presence here, made yourself look great, and we can still see the hole in the background. The potential for jealousy in the viewer is huge, just like the hole. How did you do that without an opposable thumb?"

Hector seemed genuinely pleased at the praise. "I didn't have much time. Otherwise, I would have done more shading on the details. And I hold the charcoal in my mouth. Who needs opposable thumbs?"

"Let's stick to the matter at hand," said Eloise. "Jerome and I have good news." Jerome related what they'd heard, even imitating Vendor's rambling speech.

"That is not what I heard," said Hector. "I spoke to the skink at the refreshment stand. You should see the prices they are charging for a cup of tea and a biscuit. Outrageous! Anyway, she said she overheard something about an urgent trip to The South. Something about a wart cream crisis."

Lorch frowned. "Most confusing. I spoke to a pad vendor on the far side of the hole. I was told they were rushing to make it back to For the Love of Çalaht, Cut It Out You Two to get rooms at the inn for tonight." He turned to the Nameless One. "You?"

The Nameless One nodded once at Eloise, once at Hector, and once at Lorch. "All three," interpreted the guard.

"I have something concrete," said Alejandro. "_____ said the yellow carriage definitely left heading down that road." He pointed toward a road heading east. "Unfortunately, this is not of great use. That road leads to connecting roads that go back to For the Love of Çalaht Cut

It Out You Two, toward The South, and also toward the eastern section of the Adequate Wall of the Realms, and onwards to my homeland or to the Half Kingdom."

"Not back to Brague?" asked Jerome.

"If you are clever, you can go to Brague from that direction as well."

"So, we have no idea where they're going." Eloise pushed down her rising unease.

"No, Señorita Princesa. We do not."

"This is a worry, Princess," said Lorch.

"Yes. Yes it is."

They stood silently, letting the confusion and uncertainty settle. Jerome fished his almond from a pocket and took a bite. The crunch was deafening.

"I say we return to For the Love of Çalaht Cut It Out You Two," said Eloise. "I can't believe Johanna would deliberately disappear without saying something to me. My guess is they've had an outing, they'll meet us back at the Legs Not Arms, and we can depart for home tomorrow." It's what she hoped was going on, anyway. Trepidation brushed the back of her neck, but she ignored it, letting annoyance at her sister's behavior take precedence.

"Agreed," said Jerome. "They can't be more than three, maybe four hours ahead of us."

They mounted up and headed back, this time taking the road most favored by carriages, in case they might find the king and princess along the way.

❧ 41 ☙
THE LAUGHTER OF HORSES

"You did not find them at the Whacking Great Hole?" Elgin Lëëëäääfääänniiïhiiïlääätööör was genuinely surprised. "Interesting. Still, to answer your question, Princess Eloise, no they have not come back. Nor have they, as far as I can tell, returned to our fair village. Apparently, the Grapefruit Gala has proven insufficient lure to them." It was unclear if this was sarcasm.

"Oh, the Grapefruit Gala," said Jerome. He tugged on Eloise's sleeve. "We haven't missed it. Perhaps..."

"Jerome." The Tone.

"Sorry."

They had come straight to the Legs Not Arms, hoping to catch Johanna and Doncaster at dinner. Eloise was disinclined to make a big deal of the Whacking Great Hole side trip if they could get on their way home the next day. But apparently, whatever Vendor had overheard did not eventuate. Elgin had invited Eloise, Lorch, and Jerome to enjoy a complimentary haggleberry tea and biscuits from a sideboard, to help them revive from their long day's riding. Lorch politely declined, but from the look on Jerome's face, someone at the Legs Not Arms knew their way around a cuppa.

Lorch stepped from the doorway into the reception area. "Excuse me, Master Lëëëäääf—, Master Lëëëäääfääännï—, er, good sir. Would it be possible for us to briefly examine the rooms they were in? Perhaps there is a clue there that will shed light on this confusion. Have the rooms been tidied?"

The centipede looked offended. "Of course they have, young Guard. Please. The Celebration des Pamplemousses portends people pulling portmanteaus perambulating persistently toward our portico. Those rooms already have new occupants in them."

"Oh. I see. Even so, might we examine them, Master Lëëë—"

"No." His low voice gave it extra finality.

"No problem. We understand," said Eloise. "Master Elgin Lëëëäääfääännïïïhïïïläääätööör, is it possible you might have a room for the night?"

"Actually, Princess, we've had a last-minute cancellation. The room is not our best, but likely you'll find it comfortable."

"Oh, excellent. I'll take—"

Lorch's politely cleared throat stopped her. His eyes darted down to where he kept his purse, then to where she likely kept hers.

"I see," said Eloise. "Master Lëëëäääfääännïïïhïïïläääätööör, might I ask how much the room is for the night?"

The centipede looked somewhat disapproving, but he slid a piece of paper toward her. Eloise picked it up, turned it over, and saw a number written in the most beautiful handwriting she'd ever seen. "400 coins," she read.

Jerome's surprised spit of tea almost hit the wall across the room, and the coughing fit that followed lasted a full two minutes. Eventually he gasped an embarrassed apology and excused himself to catch his breath outside. His sporadic coughing could still be heard through the window when Eloise said, "Lorch, by way of comparison, how much was our accommodation at the Middling Inn last night?"

"Twenty-seven coins for all of us, including meals."

"That's normal?"

"Average, Princess, yes."

"Our price includes a complimentary selection of jams if you upgrade to the breakfast option," offered Elgin.

"I'm sure they're lovely, too," said Eloise. "I think I might confer with my colleagues to see if we have a consensus on what our plans are. If you'll excuse me, please."

Eloise and Lorch joined the others outside. The horses and Jerome were guffawing, gasping for air. "May I ask what's funny?" Even the Nameless One was emitting the strange spasmed neigh that passed as a horse laugh.

Alejandro was the first one able to speak. "Señorita Princesa, the—" Then laughter overtook him again.

"The price, Princess," managed Hector. "Jerome told us the price."

"I take it you think it's high? Even if it comes with selected jams if one orders breakfast?"

The horses burst into renewed guffaws.

"Right. Got it. Pull it together, you lot. We need to work out what we're doing," said Eloise.

"Princess Eloise," said Lorch. "I still think I need to look for clues in their rooms."

"But why? The rooms are no longer as they were when they left. You've seen how this place is run. What self-respecting mote of dust would allow itself to remain? Plus, how would any of us get in there? They have security tarsiers everywhere, watching everything. It's creepy."

"We need something to go on, Princess."

"I understand, but..."

"I can get in," said Jerome. "I'll scale the wall, climb in the window, unlock the door from the inside, and Lorch here can just waltz in—assuming he can get up there."

"I'll get in," said Lorch.

Eloise remained unconvinced. "What about the occupants?"

"They won't be there."

"How can you know possibly that?"

"Pamplemousses, El," said Jerome. "Whoever they are, they'll be stomping the dance floor at the Grapefruit Gala. As we should be, I'll add. But instead, we'll be perpetrating a felony break-and-enter."

Eloise blanched. "No. No crimes. What if you're apprehended? What if I'm arrested as an accessory?" The thought of sitting in a vermin-infested dungeon for who knew how long made her bile rise. (Not that there was anything wrong with vermin. Vermin represented a proportionately appropriate percentage of the realm's nobility.) "I can't countenance this."

"Yet, Princess, what is our alternative?" asked Lorch. "Return without Princess Johanna? Pick a direction at random? We need something to go on."

"Señorita Princesa, do you dance?" Alejandro's question was a jarring non sequitur. They all looked at him.

"Reasonably, if I may say so."

"Then will you accompany me to the Grapefruit Gala? I—" He paused for effect. "I, Alejandro Diego Ferdinando Felipe Esteban Iglesias Desoto de Lugo, shall be your alibi. We shall stomp at the dance, far away from the felonious criminal activity. At worst, you will have to rescue these miscreants from detention, should they be caught."

"Really? The Grapefruit Gala?" protested Jerome. "How about I help her with the alibi, and you work with Lorch?"

"Because I, my stripe-backed amigo, do not have such dexterous claws as you, and cannot scale sheer walls."

They argued details in hushed voices and ended up with a plan. Eloise would politely decline the 400-coin option, then she, Hector, and Al would seek a reasonable room at the Middling Inn. Hector would remain there, keeping watch, while Eloise and Al attended the Grapefruit Gala. The Nameless One would act as the lookout for Lorch and Jerome, who would break, enter, spy, and rummage, hoping to uncover something—anything—that would guide their next steps.

❧ 42 ❧

GRAPEFRUIT GALA

E loise was grateful for the just-in-case dress Odmilla had packed. She removed the day's grime in the Middling Inn's lukewarm bath and was glad that any loosening to the journeyman's braid could be patched with a few hairpins.

The Grapefruit Gala was deliberately quaint to the point of kitsch. The banquet was served in hollowed-out grapefruit rinds, the grapefruit punch was potent, and the music, mainly jigs and reels rather than the minuets and gavottes that Eloise preferred, was played energetically by Grapefruit Knife and the Pips.

The big surprise was Alejandro. Eloise thought the alibi idea might not work if no one noticed her attendance. But there was not much chance of that with Alejandro around. He was the biggest attendee with the biggest presence, had the most flamboyant hair, having teased his white Andalusian mane to a massive volume, and wielded hoof-stamping, rollicking dance moves that had men and women alike lining up to fill his dance card. Eloise did her best to keep up, and the others moved aside to give them room to let fly.

It was a citrus-y hoot. Eloise couldn't remember having had that much fun in a long, stuffy, Protocol-controlled time.

And of course, the presence of Princess Eloise Hydra Gumball III, Future Ruler and Heir to the Western Lands and All That Really Matters, was in itself remarkable. Eloise should not have thought otherwise. She was first approached by the Master of Ceremonies, and, when she confirmed who she was, was practically dragged to the main table. "We tried to convince His Highness King Doncaster to stay for the Gala," bubbled the man. "But he apparently has pressing business elsewhere, which one can only imagine the importance of." Eloise wondered if that was ruse, truth, or a standard line to fob him off. She realized she'd heard her mother say the same thing often enough. But before she could ask details of that business, she was presented to the main table, introduced to various dignitaries and local celebrities, and placed in the chair of honor.

Right next to Theoplonkilis.

Eloise couldn't believe it. The man was everywhere. But perhaps this was good fortune. Maybe he'd know of his monarch's whereabouts.

Theoplonkilis was atwitter with grapefruit giddiness. Surely a man of his travels would have grown bored with regional festivities, but he was a kindred spirit to Jerome, delighted with the slightest grapefruity reference. The grapefruit-shaped napkins, the grapefruit-scented candles, the grapefruit appetizers, the grapefruit-clad lads and lasses—all an endless source of joyous commentary.

What was not a source of commentary, however, was the whereabouts of his monarch. "Oh, His Highness hardly tells me anything. What he does tell me, you could write on your pinky nail and still have room for the lyrics to 'Three Bags of Groats for my Sweetheart.'" Theoplonkilis had no sense of road weariness to him at all. His ample coat was tailored and fresh, what little hair he had was trimmed and shaped, and his cravat, amazingly, had grapefruits printed on it in honor of the festivities. "I like to think I've made some headway in persuading His Highness to visit The South to intercede in what I think is deteriorating into a wart cream crisis. But it is hard to tell."

"Would he have taken Princess Johanna? Did you see her at all?" It was impossible for Eloise not to worry.

"Sorry, I've got nothing for you. Have you tried the glazed grapefruit with truffle sauce? Çalaht sucking sago, it is dee-vine." He put a mound on her plate and then attacked his own like a prisoner digging out of a dungeon with a spoon.

Eloise took a mouthful. The dish was an explosion of flavors she would never have expected to work together, and yet, they did. She decided then that the humble grapefruit was, indeed, something to celebrate.

After that course, the servers placed a dish between her and Theoplonkilis bearing grapefruit-flavored chocolates fashioned to look like a peeled grapefruit, its sections splayed open like a flower. Eloise lifted the plate and offered one to the trade envoy. "Master Theoplonkilis, may I ask you a possibly difficult question?"

"Of course, Princess," he said, plucking four of the chocolatey sections and putting them on his dessert plate. "Ask away!"

"What is the deal with King Doncaster and his jesters? The arrangement strikes me as..." Eloise searched for the word as she placed a section of the dessert on her own plate. "Odd. Just odd.

"Far be it from me to ever say a word against His Highness and the two strange companions he has engaged. I would never be the one to cast shade upon my fellow human."

"Of course not," agreed Eloise. But there was a twinkle of invitation in his eyes, so she kept going. "Not you, Master Theoplonkilis. But if someone else might say something, what might they say?"

Theoplonkilis chortled. "Why, Princess, they could only speculate."

"What might they speculate?"

"They might speculate that there's a lot going on there. A meshing of ambition and need."

"Which is the ambitious, and which is the needy?"

"It varies on the day. And, one speculates, it varies based on the amount of certain substances that have been enjoyed."

"Substances?"

"We can leave that one there. But suffice it to say, the king seems to genuinely enjoy His Jesterness's company, when the mood is right."

"'His Jesterness.' That, too, is odd. I really don't understand him."

"Your puzzlement is not unique in the realms." He picked up a chocolate section and eyed it in the candlelight. "He has the joviality of a barnacle. But I have a guess. A theory, if you will."

"Oh?"

"It's this. It is hard to be the son of a wizard."

"His father was a wizard?"

"I'm being figurative, my dear. My guess is that His Jesterness Master Turpentine Snotearrow McCcoonnch lives in a shadow."

"I'm not sure I follow."

"Alstaria Snotearrow McCcoonnch was a wizard with a paintbrush. Your father certainly seems to think so. Sadly, not so with her finances. And as His Highness said the other day, the pool of talent really did stop with her, leaving her elder son and his less-than-brilliant younger brother with bugger all. Extreme bugger all. His Jesterness feels hard done by. He has ambitions that extend far beyond anything he has any rightful hope of achieving. His Highness feeds those ambitions just enough to keep it interesting or amusing or toxic, or all of the above. I think Turpentine demeans himself as jester to orbit the sun that is our king, to bask in his glow and hide in his shadow. But I also think he seeks to influence the sun, to nudge it as it crosses the sky, so it shines in a manner, or at least at an angle, of his fashioning. I might be mixing my imagery here. Blame the grapefruit cabernet. But you get the idea. There is the odd bit of evidence that the angle of shining sun might shift from time to time."

"I see."

"I thought you might. My guess is that this living in a shadow is perhaps something you yourself might have some familiarity with, no?"

"Really? I don't think so."

"Please don't take offense, Princess. Your mother is the most important person in the most important realm. How could you not help but feel her shade cast over your life? Like I said, it's tough being the son of a wizard."

With that, Theoplonkilis diverted his attention to non-royal topics, leaving Eloise to ponder shadows and mothers, wizards and artists, and kings and queens.

43

BAKED IN A BISCUIT

Eloise and Alejandro made it back to the Middling Inn just after midnight and found the others huddled around a table in a corner of the guest stables, deep in conference.

Jerome saw them approach first. "They're back. And goodness. You're glowing. You must tell me everything. Every grapefruit-filled detail. But not now. You should see what Lorch found."

"First, how did you go with getting in?"

"Oh, that was a disaster," said Jerome. "I climbed up with no problems, but the bloody windows were bolted from the inside."

"What did you do?" asked Eloise.

"Whist," said Lorch.

"The card game?"

"Yes, Princess Eloise. Tarsiers have a proclivity toward Whist, so when I 'happened' to meet a lovely young fellow—about your age, actually— who happened to be the Second Apprentice to the Deputy Head of Observation at the Legs Not Arms during his dinner break at the nearby public inn, I found him amenable to a game."

"You gambled your way in?" Eloise had no idea that Lorch had it in him.

Lorch's embarrassment crept up his neck. "Well, Princess. That might not be an unfair characterization of the evening's activity. What started as a half-coin ante had progressed to more interesting stakes by the last hand. I told him I'd never seen the top floor of such a fine establishment as the Legs Not Arms, and wagered to have him give me an inspection while the occupants were out."

"Goodness. What was the opposite side of the wager?"

Now his embarrassment conquered his face. "I would rather not say, Princess."

"Oh, now you have to," chided Eloise "Fess up. It can't be that bad."

Lorch looked like he'd rather down a handful of raw haggleberries with an arsenic chaser. "You, Princess."

"What? What do you mean?" Eloise looked at the others. Jerome, Hector, and the Nameless One appeared to be trying not to laugh.

"If I lost the bet, the Second Apprentice to the Deputy Head of Observation would get dinner with you, and..." The rest of the sentence trailed off in a mumble. Beside him, the mirth was escaping.

"And?"

"And we would pay for it, and..." Again, the rest of what he said collapsed into a mumble.

"Sorry, Guard Lacksneck," said Eloise. "The last part of your statement was not clearly enunciated." The Tone.

"Apologies, Princess," Lorch said, then cleared his throat a couple of times in delay. "If I'd lost, the Second Apprentice to the Deputy Head of Observation would get dinner with you, which we would pay for, and a kiss."

"What!" Eloise's eyebrows shot up. "You wanted me to kiss a tarsier? You wanted me to kiss a tarsier!"

Now the three gigglers could hold it in no more, and Lorch, impossibly, reddened further as their hoots spilled out.

"The terms of the kiss were very clearly defined, Princess—oh, Çalaht, please don't make me say it."

"Continue, Guard Lacksneck."

"If you insist, Princess. Cheek, not lips, a prohibition against the use of hands or paws, the duration defined as 'that which might be considered a peck,' but left otherwise vague so there was room for the wagerer's imagination to romanticize a little. It would be attended by me and one other tarsier of the Second Apprentice to the Deputy Head of Observation's choosing, such that there would be a corroborating witness and thereby lending veracity to his later retelling." Lorch delivered the information standing at full attention with as little emotion as he could, a soldier giving his superior a report.

"I'm... I'm scandalized." Now it was Eloise's turn to battle embarrassment. "You've gambled with my reputation and virtue. What if... No, that's unthinkable. But what if you'd lost?"

"Oh, there wasn't much chance of that, Princess," said Lorch, still clipped.

"Is the Second Apprentice to the Deputy Head of Observation so unlucky? Are tarsiers that bad at Whist?"

"No, Princess."

"What then? How could you be sure?"

"The deck was marked."

"What!"

"And stacked."

"Why, Lorch!"

"The Second Apprentice to the Deputy Head of Observation, as nice as chap as you'd ever meet, never had a chance, Princess."

"Oh." Eloise fell silent.

Then Alejandro let out the loudest horse laugh Eloise had ever heard. Uncontrolled, unabashed, pure laughter. "Oh, Señorita Princesa," he practically cried. "Oh, Señorita Princesa. This is priceless!"

Eloise could not help but join in the laughter. After the stress of the past few days, the release was welcome. Plus, it gave her something to do other than feel a pang of shyness about the idea of having to kiss someone, even if it was a tarsier's cheek.

Eventually, Lorch managed to say, "I apologize, Princess Eloise. For my dishonesty, and for the effrontery of using you in my, um, negotiations. But I knew I had to wager something undeniably tempting. Otherwise the Second Apprentice to the Deputy Head of Observation would never have put up his side of the wager. Or stuck to it."

"Well, having been given the full picture, your actions are understandable," said Eloise. "Even if there is now, right here in For the Love of Çalaht Cut It Out You Two, a tarsier who can dine out on his story of how he was almost kissed on the cheek by the heir."

They let that sit for a while. Then Eloise said, "Lorch, Jerome said you found something?"

"Two things, actually, Princess," said Lorch. "But first, did you notice anything about Princess Johanna's manner last night?"

"She was certainly in a good mood. While unusual, that's not unheard of, or, given the circumstances, uncalled for."

"Did you not notice how she was speaking?"

"What do you mean?"

"Well, for example, how did she describe the basil and lime leaf salad?"

"I believe she said it was excellent."

"Begging your pardon, Princess Eloise, but I must differ. She said 'excellent, outstanding, fantastic.' And, if I may ask, how did she describe riding in the king's carriage?"

"Luxurious?"

"Close. It was 'luxurious, sumptuous, lavish.' Princess, the employ of synonyms. Does that not indicate something to you?"

Eloise furrowed her brow. "No, Lorch. I'm sorry, it doesn't."

Lorch's face took on his uncomfortable-when-faced-with-truths-he'd-rather-not-speak look. "I suspected something at dinner last night, but a crumb I found in her room confirmed my fears." He pulled a folded white handkerchief from a pouch at his waist. Placing it on a table, he carefully unfolded it, revealing a small black speck of almost nothing set in a crumb of some sort.

"I see. You literally meant a crumb, not metaphorically. A poppy seed?" said Eloise.

"This, Princess, is a prattleweed seed, sometimes called a prattleseed, although not by the people who typically consume them," said Lorch. "The seeds are significantly more potent than the leaves, roots, bark, or stems."

"What does it mean?" asked Eloise. "How much danger is she in?"

"I suspect that your sister has been given prattleweed seed in baked goods. This—" He wiggled his index finger gently. "This appears to be a seed with biscuit around it. A butterscotch almandine, if I'm not mistaken, to mask the seed's slightly bitter aftertaste."

"Prattleweed," said Eloise. "Is she damaged? How much of a problem is this?" The thought of Johanna turning into a slack-jawed, toothless prattleweed user filled her with dread.

"I'm not sure if 'problem' is the right word. Possibly." Lorch set the crumb on the table. "I'd say the most likely problem is suggestibility. Prattleweed, and especially prattleweed seed, heightens a person's openness to ideas and suggestions, especially if they nudge someone in a direction they are already inclined to go. Much more than any other part of the plant. It might explain the unexpected trip to the Whacking Great Hole and her willingness to go along."

It reminded Eloise of Theoplonkilis at the Grapefruit Gala, talking about nudging the sun as it crossed the sky.

Another silence.

"Is Princess Johanna in danger?" asked Jerome quietly.

"Not from the prattleweed or its seeds," said Lorch. "Not yet, anyway. You have to consume a lot for a long time for there to be damage to the body. As for the person or people giving it to her, that I cannot say. If they are giving it to her without her knowledge, surely their intent is at least suspect. Or worse. I certainly don't like that we've discovered this."

Silence.

"You said there were two things you found," said Eloise. "What was the other?"

Lorch brought something else from the pouch. "The biscuit crumb was in Johanna's room. This, however, was on the floor next to the desk in the king's room." It was a bright red fragment of wax about the size and shape of a fifth of a coin. There were letters: "ina Ono."

"Sealing wax," said Jerome. "From a sealed document."

"Yes," said Hector. "And the letters?"

"The Southie queen," said Eloise. "My mother's seal reads 'Regina Eloise' then a bunch of fancy stuff. I suspect this is a fragment of 'Regina Onomatopoeia.' Maybe Theoplonkilis did, indeed, succeed." She explained who Theoplonkilis was and recounted his entreaties to Doncaster to help with the wart cream situation. "Maybe Uncle Doncaster went south after all, and invited Johanna to go with him. That would jibe with what Hector heard from the refreshment stand skink at the Whacking Great Hole. And so did you," she said to the Nameless One, who nodded in confirmation.

Jerome bent to look closely at the wax and crumb. "So, where does this leave us, El?"

"Nowhere I like," she answered.

"Señorita Princesa. Your options are clear. Go home and let your sister enjoy whatever journey she is on, or go after your sister the Princesa, wherever she is, which we do not know."

"Yes," said Eloise. "It looks like I have a decision to make."

❧ 44 ❧

DECIDED

Eloise did not sleep well at all that night. More than anything, she yearned to go home to its comforts and all the familiar scratches to the itches of her habits. The mere thought of striking out into the unknown for who knew how long practically made her gag. This was supposed to have been a quick two-or-so-day trip. She'd steeled herself for that and had more or less handled it. So far. But she wanted her bed and her running path and her Court and its Protocols and her Odmilla and her Chef who knew she liked three pinches of cinnamon sprinkled on her warm cashew milk, not two and not four. She did not want the dirt, disturbance, and uncertainty of chasing down Johanna, who almost certainly did not want to be chased down.

But her mother's last words rang in her head. "Make sure you return with your sister." Not "try to." "Make sure."

And what if Johanna really was in danger? That seemed a very strong possibility. Certainly it seemed likely she was being manipulated. Her behavior and the biscuit crumb added up to something Eloise did not like the look of.

Over the same adequate breakfast as she'd had at the Middling Inn the day before, this time taken in the courtyard where the horses could take part in the discussion, Eloise made her decision. "The probability that Doncaster and Johanna are heading south to a meeting with the Southie queen seems high. I say we head that way and see what other clues we can find. If we don't sniff out their trail in a day or two, we'll reassess. In the meantime, can we be underway in 30 minutes?"

"We can leave in twelve," said Lorch.

"Call it 20. I'll see you then." Eloise left them to gather her things.

Lorch caught up with her as she returned to the inn. "May I have a word, Princess Eloise?"

"Of course."

"I have concerns about continuing to include Alejandro in our party."

"Concerns? He seems upright, capable, affable, and in good health."

"Yes, Princess," said Lorch. "My concerns are more of the purse."

"Oh. Are there issues there?"

"There could be. Your most generous mother the queen provisioned us with an ample amount for a three-day trip for five. Six or seven days if stretched, and if we were careful," Lorch said. "But we are embarking on a trip of unknown duration and distance. We will, by necessity, have to adjust how we deploy our resources, in particular, those of the coin. My concern is that including Alejandro further will be a strain we will regret, and sooner, not later."

"I see. I will speak to him."

But Alejandro was not to be put off. "Oh, Señorita Princesa, I protest. You must imagine my life. I am transportation for hire. This adventure, this grand quest for the Señorita Princesa Johanna, is the most glorious thing to happen in years. I—" He assumed his dramatic pose. "I, Alejandro Diego Ferdinando Felipe Esteban Iglesias Desoto de Lugo, shall defer my already extremely reasonable fees until we return to your castle home, and a reckoning can be arranged."

"You want to come that much?"

"Yes, Señorita Princesa."

"Then Alejandro Diego Ferdinando Felipe Esteban Iglesias Desoto de Lugo, it will be a pleasure and an honor to have you continue with us."

"Thank you, Señorita Princesa."

THEY SET OUT ON A ROUTE THAT WOULD JOIN UP WITH THE Queen's Roadway, the main carriage-friendly road to The South. If Doncaster and Johanna had gone south from the Whacking Great Hole, they would take the Whacking Great Hole Greater Park Area Boulevard—little more than a rutted track—to the Queen's Roadway.

The two roads joined at Scoff. There, both a yam monger and a cooper confirmed that an ugly yellow carriage had sped through town the day before, but hadn't stopped. It seemed they were heading the right way.

Scoff's main inn was the Gobsmacked Jester, a neatish place with a huge, crudely written sign posted next to the door that read, "Do Not Enter This Public Inn Through the Chimney!" Jerome refused to go anywhere near the place.

They ended up having their late lunch at a pretentious eatery called Perfect Consumption. "Do you think that refers to the wasting disease?" asked Jerome as they stepped through the doorway.

A slope-nosed young woman with perfect teeth and a tribal piercing through her eyebrow seated them and handed them each a page of hemp parchment that had the individual food options written on it. "Ooh, fancy," said Jerome snarkily, but Eloise could tell he was genuinely impressed.

"Hi, my name is Elbowbagette. I'll be your serving wench today. Would any of you care to start with a beverage? I can recommend the water. We wildcraft it locally from a natural spring about two strong lengths away, and it has been a long time since it was the source of any illness. I had some last week, and it was superb."

"Uh, sure," said Eloise. "Water for everyone, thanks."

"Very good," said Elbowbagette. "I'll leave you to consider your food choices."

They barely had time to read the whole page before she was back. "Are you ready to order?"

"I'll have the tuber soup," said Lorch.

Jerome looked up for the list of dishes. "May I ask, what is in the tuber soup?"

"Potatoes."

"And?"

"Just potatoes."

"No other tubers? No sweet potato? Cassava? Desert yam?"

"No. The potatoes are grown by a regional sharecropper who plants a select breed of chat potato indigenous to this locality, and particularly suited to the soil's specific acidity and the varied rainfall levels Scoff experiences. Also, part of the proceeds from the sale of the soup go to helping him extricate himself from his sharecropping servitude, so he can be a more self-determined member of our community."

"But no mountain yam? Earthnut? Breadroot?"

"Just potatoes."

"Why not call it potato soup?"

"Because it's tuber soup." Elbowbagette gave him a you-just-don't-get-it look.

"But..."

Eloise cleared her throat to get Jerome to stop. "He'll have the tuber soup," she said. "As will I. Sounds lovely, doesn't it, Jerome?"

"Yes. Potato soup sounds great."

"It's tuber soup," said Elbowbagette, collecting the pieces of parchment and refusing to give him the last word.

❦ 45 ❦

ADEQUATE WALL

T hey took the best part of a week to follow the increasingly cold trail as far as the Adequate Wall. Meager clues kept them going that way, but for a king and princess traveling at what seemed to be a surprising speed, there was scant evidence. A village elder said she'd hosted a lovely dinner for her royal guests, but was not at liberty to discuss anything about it. A candlemaker said he'd sold a box of candles to His Highness. A traveling door-to-door prune merchant who said King Doncaster had chosen not to buy any of his wares. So there were thin hints all along the roadway—just enough to keep them heading toward The South.

The trip took its toll. Eloise's inability to attend to her inner tics in her usual ways caught up with her again.

There was the dirt. It was everywhere—on her skin, her clothes, her hair—and opportunities to wash it off were infrequent and inadequate. She did what she could to avoid picturing it sitting there, but at any chance she had to at least splash her face with water, she did.

Then there was the rough sleeping. They'd already spent three nights roofless under the stars to save coin. Eloise found it fascinating.

For ten minutes.

After that, she tossed and turned on the blankets laid out for her. "I wonder what malevolent insects might decide I'm worth tasting," she kept thinking. "Or taking up residence upon." Like the dirt, she did what she could not to think about what might be crawling on her, but when her thoughts strayed there, the urge to scratch followed.

It was mid-morning the following day when she snapped. "Stop it, Jerome! Just stop it! For the love of Çalaht, stop!"

Jerome turned around to look at her, confused. "What?"

"That idiotic song about groats, that's what! By Çalaht's distended digits, you keep singing little snatches of it. It is driving me spare!"

"I do?"

"Yes, you do. Over and over. Unexpectedly. From nowhere. Unannounced. And then, boom! I have that stupid song in my head as well, where it sits like an ague of the brain, gnawing away at my sanity."

"I'm sorry, I didn't realize."

"Al's over there singing songs about the virtues of Andalusian mares, especially their manes, which was cute a few days ago, but is less so now. But you! That song! I swear, I'm going to make you go ride on Al, so you can inflict yourselves on each other."

"I'm sorry, El. Really, I am."

The others looked at her, saying nothing. Her face flushed with shame. "Hector, please. Let me get off. Just... just let me get off."

Hector walked to a stand of trees and Eloise slid off. "I'll be over there. Give me a few minutes." She walked away from the others for 26 paces (an even number, not a prime but it was two times a prime, so it would do), sat down beneath the canopy of a live oak, and hugged her knees to her chest. It took three long minutes before she was in control enough to take some long, slow breaths. "Get a hold of yourself," she muttered. "Just get a grip." She wiped her eyes with the back of her hand, hoping it was cleaner than her palm.

Thank goodness, they left her alone. She'd hate them to see her like this.

Half an hour later, it was Jerome who approached. "Hey, El."

"Sorry I lost it at you."

"It's OK. I was kind of waiting for something like this."

She sniffed. "You were?"

He nodded. "We've known each other a while. You were keeping it together pretty well—until you weren't. I wasn't all that surprised when it burst out."

"The others must think I'm a freak."

"The others think you're their princess and are worried about you."

They sat there saying nothing for a while.

"What about the beads?" said Jerome.

"What beads?"

"The prayer beads. You told me that Odmilla gave you prayer beads. You didn't say why, but I guessed. Maybe you can use them? Would that help?"

Eloise took another long, deep breath, then reached into her cape pocket for the bag containing the prayer beads. She took them out, wrapped them around her right hand, and replaced the bag.

"Nice set," said Jerome. "They look loved."

Eloise nodded. "I think they were." She stood, straightened to steel herself, then walked back to the horses and Lorch. She found them— silent, waiting, their expressions worried.

"My apologies, Guard Lacksneck, Equine Designate de Pferd, Nameless One, for my outburst. And apologies, Alejandro Diego Ferdinando Felipe Esteban Iglesias Desoto de Lugo. My words were both unkind and untrue. Your singing is a delight and a boon. Thank you for your patience while I collected myself. I'll try not to let it happen again."

"Not a problem, Princess," said Hector.

"Señorita Princesa, I, Alejandro Diego Ferdinando Felipe Esteban Iglesias Desoto de Lugo, did not take offense at all, and am comfortable enough with myself to know my singing is exquisite. No apology necessary."

"Is there anything you need, Princess?" asked Lorch.

"No, thank you. Shall we continue?"

With Odmilla's beads in her right hand, they resumed the journey, and Eloise counted. She started with counting Hector's steps, but soon ran out of beads. So she devised a system that aggregated multiples of 100 hoof clops, with each bead representing either a hundred, a thousand, or ten thousand steps, depending on how she held the bead and where in the prayer sequence it was. It calmed her and gave her mind something to do other than resume worrying and focusing on things that were not helpful.

They reached the Adequate Wall of the Realms around noon on their thirteenth day away from Castle de Brague, and even at a distance, they could see the start and stop of travelers making their way through the gateway to The South.

The Adequate Wall of the realms had, once upon a time, been controversial. Those with any nous saw it for what it was—an unnecessary boondoggle created to appease the egos of the monarchs some centuries past. Unfortunately, those in charge of purse strings, ego-building monuments, and monarch appeasing were without nous. And so, the Adequate Wall was built.

Seen dispassionately, the fact that the Adequate Wall stretched all along the border between each of the realms was a feat of engineering and construction. An achievement, for sure. But the wall could have been really impressive. There could have been more height, more width, more observation towers, more ornamentation, more booby traps, more secret passageways, more gates, more inscriptions above those gates, more soldiers manning the comings and goings through those gates, more anchorage points for boiling cauldrons of oil, more scary spiky things that clearly said Do Not Pass, more amenities, more food stands, more places for the kids to play if you took them on an outing, more paint, more paintings, more touches, tweaks, and grand gestures that could have catapulted the wall into greatness.

And it was originally supposed to be a great wall, not a greatish wall. The original plans had all of those things, from height, width, and ornamentation to scary spiky things and places for the kids.

What happened?

The usual.

The bean counters got involved. And the actuaries, occupational health and safety people, finance ministers, exchequers, purse-string-holders, insurers and claims adjusters, opportunists, sycophants, nanny-staters, not-in-my-patch-of-the-woods rabble rousers, those opposed to walls in principle, the dull and unimaginative, the knee-jerk worriers, plain old jerks, and all manner of social and business parasites. They white-anted the project (not that there's anything wrong with being a white ant), hobbling all attempts to raise it to something splendid.

The result: the Adequate Wall of the Realms.

Which was good enough. It was amazing that it got built at all. It fully deserved the smattering of applause and compliments of "Good job done" that it had received when it was officially opened a couple of hundred years before.

Eloise remembered the first time she'd seen the Adequate Wall. Her reaction was the same as everyone else who saw it for the first time: "Yeah, that'll do, I guess." Not quite the awe that the original designers had intended, but they'd been dead a long time, and their hopes and dreams had been sucked from their souls well before then.

THE TROOP OF GUARDS ON THE WESTERN LANDS SIDE OF THE WALL wore snappy blue outfits emblazoned with the Gumball crest. They were white ants, in positions gained through a patronage system that stretched back to the Wall's building.

A white ant stepped over to where Eloise and the others waited.

"Good, uh..." The white ant turned around and yelled up to the tower. "Yo! Henriette, what time is it?"

"Twenty-seven minutes past the hour of noon," came a cuckoo's voice.

"Our on-duty horologist," said the white ant. "Lovely gal. And sharp as a tack when it comes to time. So, g'afternoon, gentlemen, Mistress. I shall act in my official capacity as border crossing guard on your behalf today. Shall we go through the proceedings as hundreds of years of Adequate Wall traditions dictate?"

"Why, yes," said Eloise. "Please do."

The ant stood formally for a few moments, preparing both himself and them for the process. Then he cleared his throat and said, "You're free to go through."

Jerome looked at him. "That's it? That's hundreds of years of Adequate Wall tradition?"

The ant looked embarrassed, and as if he might cry. "You know, that's what I said when I started this job. Apparently, we have to change with the times."

"What do you mean?" asked Eloise.

"It's very kind of you to enquire, Mistress. It's nice when people take an interest in one's work," said the guard. "We used to have to check for weapons. But we're at peace, so there's not much need for that. And we used to have forms and registers. We filled out a form for every person and every bit of trade that went through. Kept track of it all. It was glorious! So much to do. Those were the days. But then a couple of decades ago, someone in charge of the border guards looked at all these records, and thought, 'Does anyone actually use any of this stuff?' She just stopped doing it and ordered everyone else to do the same." The white ant became wistful. "No more forms or records. We all let everyone and everything through. Sped up the process no end, but it meant that we didn't have much to do anymore."

"So, a few decades ago, someone could have looked up, say, if the Half Kingdom's king had just passed through?" asked Eloise.

"Exactly! And when, and who was with him, and what they carried."

"And now?"

"Now we smile and wave, and think back to better times full of paper-work and bureaucratic overhead, ignorant of what happened during someone else's shift."

"So, *did* the Half Kingdom's king pass through recently?"

He grimaced. "I have no idea."

Eloise felt bad for the white ant and how the purpose he served had dwindled. "I'm sorry for your loss and for the difficult circumstances faced by you and your fellow border guards," she said. "Truly."

"Thank you, Mistress," said the guard. "Now, I shan't detain you any longer." He stood once again at attention. "In the name of Queen Eloise Hydra Gumball II, I wish you safe travels to The South."

As they went through the gate and into the tunnel of the wall, Jerome said, "That will be your name they say someday."

The sadness that overwhelmed her took Eloise by surprise. Sadness, because the only way a guard would say her name like that would be if her mother died, and she survived to see it, which was feeling pretty unlikely at the moment.

She swallowed back the feeling, replying, "There is too much water to pass under the bridge between now and then. You'll pardon me if I leave any curiosity about that to a future me."

"I'm just saying," said Jerome. "No need to be snippy. Or maudlin."

❦ 46 ❦

INTERVIEWED

T he South side of the gate was a whole different matter. It was staffed exclusively by humans—humorless humans wearing hushed tones and dull gray uniforms featuring Çalahtist embroidery and ceremonial weaponry. Everything that crossed into the realm was inspected and registered. Every person (human or otherwise) was interviewed and quickly sketched.

The white ants on the Western Lands side of the wall would have loved it.

Eloise was ushered into a plain, private room where an interviewer, scribe, and sketch artist were flipping to new pages in synchronously numbered notepads. The sketch artist immediately outlined her drawing, and the interviewer launched into the first question. "Name."

If they recognized her name, none of them gave it away, although Eloise thought perhaps the sketch artist's eyebrow twitched once. The interviewer covered purpose and planned duration of her stay in The South. Eloise decided a vague version of the truth would be best, so said she was hoping to meet up with relatives. When they'd finished, they asked her to sign both the interview notes (verbatim) and sketch (credibly accurate), handed her a small blue-covered pamphlet, "Welcome to The South! Enjoy Your Stay!" and indicated that she could leave.

"May I ask a question?"

The interviewer nodded. It was as though words were expensive. Anything that could be done with a nod or gesture, was.

"Is it possible for me to find out if someone traversed the border to your fine realm in the past couple of days?"

"I'm sorry, Mistress," said the interviewer in a monotone. "We are not free to divulge that information."

"Even if that person is a relative with whom I'm hoping to meet up? As per my previously stated purpose?"

"I'm sorry, Mistress," said the interviewer. "As I said, we are not free to divulge that information." He'd spent an additional three words. The added emphasis was palpable.

"Right. Well, thank you for your explanation."

With that, Eloise emerged into the sun of The South, and looked around for her friends.

And that was when she realized that she no longer thought of them as traveling companions, or as Equine Designate, guard, hired transport, or Champion. That realization brought an unexpected smile, and lifted her heart.

But her friends were nowhere to be seen. Their processing must still be going on.

Eloise walked around the arrival area, from a stall that sold a kind of rolled-up sandwich to a person who seemed to know everything about tourist attractions in The South, and whose job it was to disseminate this information. She thought how Jerome would be good at that since he liked to talk and was good at seemingly useless details.

"Excuse me," Eloise said to the tourist information woman. "Would you happen to know if your realm welcomed King Doncaster of the Half Kingdom recently?"

"Sorry, deary," she said. "Haven't heard so, but haven't heard not. I've been away with my daughter who was giving birth to my seventeenth grandchild. Not all hers. This was her third. Would you like to see a sketch? Such a cute baby."

It was another 45 minutes at least before the others emerged, a disproportionate amount of which were spent admiring the tourist information woman's badly drawn likeness of a baby, which looked like every other bad drawing of a baby Eloise had ever seen. When they came out, Jerome was fuming, Hector bristled, and Lorch and the Nameless One both seemed one notch away from outright rage. Only Alejandro looked nonplussed.

Lorch waved to her, indicating she should duck with them into an alley.

"What's the matter?"

"Everything," said Jerome. "This place is a nightmare."

"They seem a bit uptight," said Eloise. "But tolerable."

"Tolerable? Tolerable!" Jerome held up a black-covered pamphlet. "Did they give you one if these?"

"Sure. Mine is blue. 'Welcome to The South! Enjoy Your Stay!' I can't say I agree with their liberal use of exclamation marks, but to each their own."

"You must have gotten the human one. Look! Look at this!"

Jerome's pamphlet was "Non-Humans: Know Your Place: How to Survive and Remain Out of Jail in The South."

"Oh."

"Did they point out Section 18, Clause 47, Sub-Paragraph 23?" Hector asked Jerome. "My interviewer specifically made mention."

"Ah, yes," said Alejandro. "Section 18, Clause 47, Sub-Paragraph 23 is one of their favorites. They refer me to it every time. And I have crossed this border 56 times in the last three years. Fifty-seven, including today."

"Section 18, Clause 47, Sub-Paragraph 23?" asked Eloise. "What does it say?"

"I've got it. They bent down the corner on my copy so I could find it easily," said Jerome. "It says, 'It is the Law of the Realm that under no circumstances shall those of non-human beingness engage in the public use of the Queen's Tongue, the punishment for which is incarceration. Should such use result from a life-threatening situation, the jailed non-human can appeal the punishment to a Magistrate of the Realm, who will have discretionary power to consider mitigating circumstances on a case-by-case basis.'"

"Read Sub-Paragraph 24," said Hector.

"Sub-Paragraph 24 says, and I quote, 'Seriously, non-human. Don't push your luck.'"

"Wait," said Eloise. "They're saying you can't talk in public? That's stupid. What are you supposed to do, use message flags? What about in private?"

"It is why we are in a deserted alley, Señorita Princes. In private, we non-humans may speak freely."

"This is barbaric." Eloise flicked through her pamphlet. "This one is all friendly. No sections, clauses, or sub-paragraphs. Just 'Make sure you visit the Sclerotic Wold' and 'The birthplace of Çalaht awaits your pilgrimage' and 'Try the spiced haggleberry tea.' Alejandro, how seriously do Southies take this?"

"That depends, Princesa. In some places, like there..." He nodded toward the border crossing facilities, "they take it very, very seriously. In others, much less so. The trick is to distinguish the two." Alejandro gave what passed as a shrug for a horse. "It is best to be careful. And so we will be."

Eloise saw that Lorch's face was nearly purple. "Lorch?"

The guard put a hand on the Nameless One. "They took him aside and forced him to tell them his birth name. It was demeaning."

"Why? You've been to The South before. Both of you. Did he have to do that then?"

"No, Princess Eloise," said Lorch, his voice reduced to the clipped official manner he used to hide anger. "But that time, we traveled as part of a unit. Here, we do not proceed as a presentative of the queendom. We do not have the paperwork nor the status of an official delegation. That means we are private subjects of the crown. They do to us what they want."

"I'm sorry. If I had known..." But Eloise stopped. Would knowing have made a difference? To any of them? "But I didn't, and now we are here. Are we in agreement to continue?" Mute nods all around. "Then let us put some strong lengths between us and this officious malarkey."

❧ 47 ☙

FEBRILE SPRINGS

T he weather turned grumpy around dusk as they made their way into Febrile Springs.

Febrile Springs was known for an allegedly curative, natural spring about the same temperature as a human with a decent case of the ague. The sign at the entrance to the town proclaimed, "Welcome to Febrile Springs. Who Knows? Maybe It Will Help."

Through a gathering rain, Lorch guided them past any number of inns to one that, while clean enough, made the Middling Inn look positively posh. "Apologies, Princess," said Lorch. "Resources."

Eloise, wet and exhausted from another full day of riding, gave in to the screams of her muscles and her worries, checked that there were no bedbugs with whom she would have to converse during the night, and then fell into the sheets, missing dinner and any chance to gather information.

Morning zoomed in unannounced, splashing sun everywhere and proclaiming more pleasant weather for the day. Over the inn's porridge, Eloise found out she was the only one who had slept so long. "What tidings do you have?"

"The tidings are odd, Princess," said Lorch. "Last night, while you got some much-deserved rest, we discussed how to proceed. Jerome was the one who suggested we speak to the milk deliverers as people who are likely to be out and about, and observant of changes in their town."

"Plus," said Jerome, "they're horrible gossips. It's like it's in their job description. 'Must be scurrilous.' The ones in Brague probably know more about Court intrigue than your mother."

"Really?"

"Absolutely. More effective than Elgin Lëëëäääfääännïïïhïïïlääätööör's crack squad of Observation tarsiers."

"Anyway, we decided to divide and conquer. I took the rice and soy milk deliverers," said Lorch. "Hector tracked down the hemp and almond milkers. Jerome found cashew and coconut."

"And?"

"There seems to be agreement that Lurid Eddie's masterpiece arrived in town," said Jerome. "All six say they at least glimpsed it. What's odd is that no one agrees whether it left. Almond and hemp both said yes. Rice and soy were no. My cashew started out a no, then changed to yes. Coconut shrugged and said he didn't care, but didn't think so. Like Lorch said, odd."

Continuing southward remained their best option, but before leaving Febrile Springs, Lorch wanted to stock up at the market. "We'll need to be responsible for preparing our own food," he said. "Apologies, Princess, but resources."

"I've been thinking about that." She handed him her purse. "I've kept back a little, but you've much more experience with these things. Please use this for us."

"Thank you, Princess. That will make matters easier."

The Febrile Springs market was in full swing when they arrived. Food and knick-knack stalls overflowed with the mundane and the florid, and their sellers called out their wares. "Oddmints!" shouted one woman, who sold mints that were both strange and unsorted. "All sorts!" yelled an actuary with lists arranged in different ways. "Armaments!" spruiked the jeweler offering bracelets. "Possibilities!" said a woman peddling random cards drawn from her tarot deck, ignoring the prognostic implications of an ever-decreasing set of cards. "Taro!" sang her neighbor operatically to entice customers to her root vegetables. One vendor even sold small vials of the town's allegedly curative water, barking, "Possibly healing water! Who knows? Maybe it will help?"

Eloise let herself get lost in the melange of smells and color, and almost didn't see them. At a stall filled with what at first glance seemed to be mere junk sat an incongruous cluster of fine wood panels the color of caricatured lemons. "Jerome, look."

Jerome stepped closer to examine them. They were carved with nymphs, leaves, satyrs, and cherubs. "Uncanny."

"Yes," said Eloise.

"It's like Lurid Eddie's understudy produced a set of samples, then flogged them off to this poor sap," he said. "Wow, it makes my teeth hurt to look at them."

"What if... What if they aren't samples?" There were easily a dozen pieces, which if put together might have formed a rough carriage shape. Eloise looked around to see how far away the others were. Lorch was haggling over a net of crackerbread. Hector and the Nameless One stood watch by a water trough. Alejandro was speaking very quietly to a donkey, trying to charm the spelt milk deliverer and winnow information under the guise of gossip. None of them would have seen Doncaster's carriage up close the way she and Jerome had, so would not be able to tell if these came from the carriage or not.

The stall-holder was an ancient pug with greasy fur, a persistent, wheezing cough, a linen coat that was more patches than original cloth, teeth that were more memory than fact, and wrinkles on his wrinkles. He seemed to specialize in hoarder's supplies—piles of paper, bundles of toothbrushes, bags of used baling twine segments, stacks of empty containers. The carved panels were propped up on buckets of measuring scoops, and stood out for their quality and newness.

"Foine bit of wood that is," said the pug, waddling arthritically to where Eloise and Jerome stood. He looked around to make sure no one was there to hear him speak. "Purdy. Would look lovely in the home."

"SWEETHEART," blurted Jerome. "They're GORGEOUS! I absolutely LOVE them."

"What?"

"Can't you PICTURE them near the DIVAN? They'd PERFECTLY set off the ARMOIRE." He feigned a swoon. "Please, lovey dimples. Can we get them?"

"Oi sees yer a gentleman of foine, discriminating tastes," said the pug.

Eloise caught on. "Now, now, sugar claws. We have to be careful. Maybe we should know more about them."

"But I WANT them," whined Jerome. He turned to the pug. "You MUST tell us about them. Their PROVENANCE. Their HISTORY. Their ORIGINS."

"Their price," added Eloise.

"Oh, don't listen to HER," Jerome confided to the pug. "SOME things don't matter. Now TELL me about them." Jerome lovingly stroked the frontmost panel.

The old pug tugged at his sleeve, torn between his desire for a sale and, Eloise guessed, an inability to say much about the source of the panels. A silence sat awkwardly while Eloise and Jerome stared at him with eager faces. "Well," he coughed. "There's really not that much to say."

"Don't be SHY, my good fellow," chided Jerome, flicking his tail teasingly. "If we're going to pay TOP COIN for these BEAUTIFUL pieces, I need to know EVERYTHING. That way, when people ask about them at our many SOIRÉES, we can not only say who we bought them from, but we can tell them the whole SORDID story." He chuckled. "Imagine if we had to say, 'Well, there's really not that much to say.' That WON'T do, now will it? That won't bring you much more CUSTOM." Jerome gave a little gasp. "They're not STOLEN are they?" His tone indicated that might be a good thing.

That touched a nerve. "No! Of course not! Oi don't deal in pilferage," protested the pug unconvincingly.

Jerome gave him a disappointed look, "Oh, well. I guess they still might do. DO tell us what you can."

"Oi only gots them two, maybe three days back. They come off a foine-looking carriage. Couple of fellas drove this yellow-hued, foine-looking thing out behind Old Ben's Tulip Bulbery and Carriage Parts Retrieval Service. Oi was having me late evening snooze, so was nestled where they couldn't see me. It was dark, see, but I could tell one of them was big and one of them wasn't. They drove up, there was a bit of banging, and they drove off in an ordinary, beat-up, old black carriage. A very toidy, very toight business. When Oi strode over, only these foine bits of wood remained. Oi thought to meself, 'Rule of Capture.' So Oi captured them."

"That's BRILLIANT," squealed Jerome. "What WERE the men like? Brutes? Ruffians? VAGABONDS? TELL me!"

"Not much to say. Honest. One bloke sang under his breath a bit. A song about goats."

"Groats, perhaps?" asked Eloise.

"Could be. When he wasn't singing, he was complaining about wanting to go home, but the other bloke just ordered him about, ignoring him. Also asked what 'incognition' meant, but got no answer."

"This is SPLENDID!" Jerome turned to Eloise. "What do you SAY, Rice Malt Eyebrows? CAN we get them?"

Eloise scrunched up her nose. "I don't know, Agave Tail. The good gentleman here didn't actually buy them. I'm not sure they're his to sell. What if the big man and the non-big man come looking for them? I wouldn't want them breaking into our brand-spanking new marriage home and messing up the divan or the armoire to get their fine pieces of wood back. Also..." She turned to the pug. "The rule you are thinking of is 'Finders Keepers.' The Rule of Capture would not apply to this circumstance."

"But, Stevia Teeth, I—"

"Princess, is everything all right?" Lorch, having settled on the net of crackerbread, came over, looming like the guard he was.

"P-princess! What do you mean, 'Princess?'" stammered the pug. He looked Lorch up and down, and the unlikely truth blossomed in his head. "Sorry, me stall's closed. We're about to get a horrible rain." And as though he'd practiced a thousand times, which doubtless he had when faced with authorities asking questions, he closed, loaded his cart, and disappeared.

Eloise looked at Jerome. "Rice Malt Eyebrows? Stevia Teeth? Really?"

"Agave Tail?"

"You started it."

"Excuse me, Princess Eloise," said Lorch. "Shall I retrieve him?"

"No, Lorch. Thank you. I believe we have what we're likely to get."

The group assembled at the edge of the market, and Eloise and Jerome told the others what they'd learned.

"This, Señorita Princesa, is fantastic! The spelt milk deliverer was of no help. But this gives us direction."

"How?" Hector still looked marvelous, even after days of travel, but his manner was losing fire. "We now know we need to find an unremarkable black carriage going somewhere that is not home."

"I think we know more than that," said Eloise. "We know to stop looking for yellow. We know they were here as recently as a couple of days ago. We know that Gouache wants to go home, which seems to indicate that they aren't going that way. We can guess he meant 'incognito,' not 'incognition.' So they are trying not to attract attention, which a king traveling would inevitably do. I say we continue southward. Press on and catch up with them."

"I agree, Señorita Princesa. Let this marvelous adventure continue!"

✣ 48 ✣

YE OLDE

I
f Doncaster intended to parlay with Queen Onomatopoeia, then he would head to her castle at the Sclerotic Wold, four days' ride away. This likelihood was confirmed when they met a wheelwright who told them he'd repaired two of Doncaster's carriage's wheels, describing the vehicle disparagingly as "rather ordinary for a king," and mentioning Johanna's travel cape, and then again when a fruit seller they bought oranges from said a woman claiming to be a princess had been there just the other day.

The problem was time, measured in coin. And now, the weather.

The longer the trip took, the tighter Lorch's resources got. "Princess Eloise, we are OK if we truly rein in our outgoings. But I'm afraid that means we'll be sleeping rough. I'm confident we can last the few more days until we catch up with Princess Johanna again, although our strategy for returning to Castle de Brague will need to be considered carefully. But the priority is finding her."

Two days out from the Adequate Wall, the weather started up its comedy routine. It was as if the weather said, "A funny thing happened on the way to the Sclerotic Wold," then cracked every weather-based witticism in its repertoire. Simultaneous rain and sun. A crushing, soaking sleet, followed by wind. They even had a most unlikely snow that was immediately burned off by a most unlikely heat. If it was a comedy routine, the audience wasn't laughing.

During a particularly vicious evening's bucketing, they sought refuge in a place called Ye Olde Public Inn in the village of Colander. It was as fake inside as it sounded. Reproduction heraldic symbols did not quite ring authentic, nor did the cheap-looking goblets, the deliberately cracked crockery, or the foodspears—pointy chopsticks that were never widely used, but appeared in children's stories. If Chef's food had ever been served under this kind of duress, Chef would have grabbed one of the foodspears and done someone harm, before doing the same to herself.

Being the only public inn for strong lengths around, it was packed.

Eloise, Lorch, and Jerome found a small table crammed into the back corner where three seats sat empty near a somnolent and, from the smell of him, recently inebriated older man. The serving wench bustled past, and said, "Go ahead and sit with Léëèstéëèr there. He had an amazing stint of wakefulness a few days back, but seems to be making up for it now. He's typically harmless. You should be good."

So they sat with the normally harmless Léëèstéëèr and his toothless snoring.

The food selection featured "Ye Olde Salad," "Ye Olde Polenta Pie" (hardly an authentic dish from anywhere) and, for dessert, "Ye Olde Custard Pudding." The names made it sound like the food was just stale. Which it wasn't, thank Çalaht. It was warming, filling, and helped Eloise ignore for a few minutes the outdoor sleeping that awaited them.

"Lorch," moaned Eloise. "I don't think I can sleep rough in this rain. I just can't."

"Apologies, Princess Eloise." Lorch seemed miserable about it. "Were there coin enough, you could stay upstairs."

"Yes," whispered Jerome, trying not to be heard above the din. "You could have a ye olde sleep in a ye olde bed, to be awakened in ye olde morn by ye olde sun."

"That sounds ye olde divine," said Eloise. "And better than cowering under ye olde sodden blankets in the lee side of ye olde rock outcropping."

They started in on their ye olde soup of the day—ye olde yam bisque— listening to the pelting rain compete with the noise of sipping.

"There must be something we can do," muttered Eloise.

Jerome slurped another spoonful. "My mother could handle this," he mumbled.

"What? Your mother?"

"Yeah. She'd do a few prognostications and..." He mimed coins dropping into a purse. "Clink, clink, clink."

Eloise looked at Jerome, lost in his soup. "I see," she said. "You're right. It's too bad she is not here." She sat, considering, then stood. "Back in a moment."

✺ 49 ✺

POSITIVE
PROGNOSTICATIONS

Eloise returned to her seat, broke off a piece of ye olde bread and dunked it in her ye olde soup. Lorch excused himself to check on the horses.

Four minutes later, a gruff barrel of a man shoved through the crowded room. He reached their table looking like trouble taking the fast carriage into town. Arms like a blacksmith, tunic like an armorer, odor like a goat perfumer, hair plastered flat to his skull. He leaned across the table and caught Jerome mid-slurp. "So. Is it true?" he snarled.

Jerome looked up at the man. Surprised, he flapped back his ears and pointed to himself, remembering not to say anything.

"Yes, you. Is it true what Dóöòrîîs said?"

Jerome mimed a very credible, "Who is Dóöòrîîs and for the love of Çalaht, what did she say?" although he could not capture the vowel inflections.

The man looked at Eloise, puzzled.

Eloise interpreted. "He merely enquired who Dóöòrîîs might be, and the nature of what she said."

The man pointed at Jerome. "That he's the spawn of a court seer."

Jerome gasped and shot Eloise an are-you-out-of-your-Çalaht-be-blessed-for-all-the-wrong-reasons mind? Followed by a Çalaht-help-me-I'm-going-to-substitute-carob-for-your-chocolate-for-the-rest-of-your-living-days-of-which-I-promise-you-there-won't-be-many-more   look. Eloise understood him perfectly. She returned him a have-you-seen-the-weather-outside-and-if-you-think-I'm-going-to-sleep-rough-in-that Çalaht-forsaken-rain-you-can-think-again look. Jerome missed the specifics, but caught the gist.

"Why yes, good sir," said Eloise to the barrel man. "This is indeed the son of the Court Seer to the Western Lands and All That Really Matters, the direct descendant in both blood and talent. But we are here as private subjects and do not wish to bother you."

"And who be you?" He still looked doubtful.

"My name is El. I am but a humble assistant to this great talent, Jerome the Astounding." Jerome shot her a filthy look, but she ignored him. "Is there a concern?"

Barrel hesitated, then said, "I would have a prognostication."

"No, no, no. Jerome the Absolutely Astounding is much too weary from his travels to your fine hamlet."

With no other option, Jerome played along, yawning and indicating the need to go to bed.

Barrel seemed determined. "I have coin. How much for a prognostication?"

Eloise pretended an exasperated sigh, trying to give the sense that this happens all the time, so she might as well bow to the inevitable. "Five coins."

"Five coins!"

"Apologies, good sir. Did I say 'five?' Sorry, seven."

"But it was just five," protested Barrel. "And how do I know it's worth it?"

"Price goes up for doubters. It'll be nine pretty soon, good sir," said Eloise. "As for value, well, Jerome the Absolutely Incredibly Astounding provides a coin-back guarantee. If your prognostication proves unsatisfactory in any way, he will provide a no-questions-asked refund. The only thing is you have to allow a month to let the prognostication unfold."

"I'll give you five," said Barrel. "And two weeks on the guarantee."

Eloise looked at Jerome, pretending to consult. Jerome shook his head a violent, pleading 'no.'"

"You are in luck, good sir. Jerome the Absolutely Incredibly Unbelievably Astounding has agreed. Is there a private room, so the son of the Court Seer can speak freely without violating Section 18, Clause 47, Sub-Paragraph 23?"

Barrel pointed toward a side room that was the size of a vegetable locker but had a door and an unlit candle.

"Perfect," said Eloise. "Light the candle, then leave us for exactly seven minutes while Jerome the Absolutely Incredibly Unbelievably Magnificently Astounding prepares to channel your prognostication from the realms of the Unseen."

Once the candle was lit, Eloise closed the door, giving her and Jerome a moment's quiet. Jerome took that moment of quiet to hiss at her. "Have you lost ye olde plot? You know better than anyone, save the Court Seer herself, that I don't have it, whatever 'it' is."

"*He* doesn't know that."

"But *I* do! And you gave him a coin-back guarantee."

"We'll be long gone in two weeks."

"Why, Eloise Hydra Gumball III. That is nothing short of devious."

"Why, thank you, Jerome the Absolutely Incredibly Unbelievably Magnificently Stupendously Astounding. That is most kind."

"But seriously. What do I do?"

"What do you mean? You've seen your mother do this all your life. Pretend. Just make stuff up."

"Mother would have a fit."

"Your mother isn't here. Your mother is not about to spend the night chilled to the bone, hoping to avoid a visitation from the ague."

Jerome was quiet. "I don't know what to say."

"That's a first. Look, it doesn't really matter. We'll be gone tomorrow, anyway. Just keep it upbeat. No one wants a negative prognostication. So whatever you do, leave them feeling happy."

"Do I really have to do this?"

"Of course not. All you have to do is make your apologies to..." There was a soft knock on the door. "Him."

Jerome's whiskers sagged. "Fine. Let's get this over with."

Barrel, whose actual name was Cromulent Stump, handed Eloise his five coins and took a seat across the table from Jerome, who sat with his eyes closed. Eloise saw sweat gathering on his fur. "Oh, no," she thought.

Two full minutes of silence crowded the room. When Jerome finally spoke, it was a nervous, high-pitched chatter. "Oh, blessed ones of the Unseen. Those who we cannot see. Those who are invisible to us. The transparent ones. The translucent ones. The glassy and the diaphanous. BE WITH US NOW!" He screeched a cry so loud it stilled the conversation on the other side of the door.

Eloise was pretty sure Seer Maybelle didn't do that.

Jerome opened his eyes, stammering. "Wh-wh-what d-do you w-want?"

Stump looked at Eloise. She smiled, like that was the way it always went, and nodded that he should answer. He coughed, then said, "I want a prognostication. Isn't that why we are here?"

"Um, I guess," said Jerome.

"What Jerome the Absolutely Incredibly Unbelievably Magnificently Mind-Blowingly Stupendously Astounding means to ask you is whether you have some particular line of questioning for the Unseen, or are after a more general prognostication?"

"Both."

"Not for five coins," said Eloise. "You have to choose."

"Then a general one," said Stump.

"F-fine," said Jerome.

Jerome squinted his eyes shut and rocked back and forth, saying, "Cromulent Stump, I see... Cromulent Stump, I see... Cromulent Stump, I see... Cromulent Stump, I see..." This went on for at least five minutes, but felt like two years. Finally, he said, "Cromulent Stump, I got nothing."

"What?" said Stump. "What do you mean nothing?"

"I mean, I don't see—"

"What he means," interrupted Eloise, "is that he has nothing of yours. He needs to be holding an object of importance to you, so he can accurately tune in to the Unseen on your behalf. What might you have?"

Stump looked stumped for a moment, then, looking serious, said, "I think I know what you mean." He removed his nose ring—not something he'd done in quite a while, from the look of it—and offered it to Eloise to give Jerome.

Eloise felt her ye olde soup thinking about revisiting its place of origin, but she kept it down. "No, no, no," said Eloise. "You'll need to give it directly to Jerome the Absolutely Incredibly Unbelievably Magnificently Mind-Blowingly Stupendously Overwhelmingly Astounding. I would contaminate the energy of it."

"Thank you, El the Squeamish." Jerome pointed to a serviette on the table. "Wrap it in that, Cromulent Stump. I, too, must not feel its energy directly."

Jerome grasped the wrapped nose ring in both paws and shook it, listening to it like he was trying to guess the contents of a present. He chanted gobbledygook, sniffed the serviette, then seemed to go into a deep trance. To Eloise, it all seemed overkill, but added to Jerome's increasing sweatiness, at least it looked like he was trying hard. Jerome took on a sing-song delivery. "Rain. Rain. I see rain in your future."

"It's raining right now," said Stump. "So what?"

"Then I have succeeded!" said Jerome.

"What?" Stump looked like he was heading toward angry.

"Please don't interrupt," whispered Eloise. "You'll ruin his concentration."

"And after the rain, after the rain, after the rain—you will experience periods of dryness."

"This is stupid. Give me my coins back. He ain't no seer." Stump stood up, thrusting out his hand for Eloise to replace his coins.

Jerome opened one eye, casting a frantic look at Eloise, and with a slight shrug conveyed that both his psychic and his just-make-it-up wells were dry.

Eloise mouthed a desperate, "Just do something."

"I see—a woman!" screeched Jerome.

That got Stump's attention. "A woman? Is it my mother?"

"She is your heart's mirror. Your one true love. She is to whom you shall be glued."

"So not my mother, then. What's this woman look like?"

"Teeth bucked. Chin tucked. Tunic rucked. Hairs plucked."

"That sounds like my mother," insisted Stump. "I don't want to marry my mother."

"Not your mother. It is another. Not one to smother. Looks like your brother. A union from which you'll never recover. But first you must meet. And I see, I see, I see, I see that a bucket of paint will lead you to this woman of your destiny."

At that, Jerome pretended to faint.

Eloise and Stump looked at each other, unsure. "Well," said Eloise. "That was a most profound prognostication. And so full of specifics. You must be thrilled."

"Thrilled. Right," said Stump, distinctly unthrilled.

Eloise stood and shuffled Stump toward the door. "Remember, find us in two weeks if you're not 100 percent satisfied, and we'll happily return your coins. Çalahtspeed to you, good sir." She practically clunked him in the back as she closed the door behind him.

Jerome, lying on the ground with eyes still closed, whispered, "Is he gone?"

"That, Jerissimo, was perhaps the worst fake prognostication in the history of fake prognostications. 'A bucket of paint?' Really?"

"I told you, I'm no good at this. That's what came to mind. Well, at least that's over with."

There was a timid knock at the door. "Yes?" said Eloise.

The doorway pushed open, and a cross-eyed shih tzu peered in. He found Eloise with one of his eyes. "Excuse me, but is it true that the son of the Court Seer of the Western Lands and All That Really Matters is conducting prognostications?"

"Actually, there's been a slight misunderstanding," started Jerome.

"I have coins."

"Please come in, good sir," said Eloise, ushering the dog into the chair opposite Jerome.

They did the same routine—Jerome calling in the Unseen, and screeching like Çalaht was removing his soul while he was still alive, Eloise asking if the shih tzu wanted a specific or general prognostication, Jerome not getting anything, Eloise asking for an item (the shih tzu gave Jerome his reading glasses, which fortunately did not need wrapping), Jerome saying something that sort of rhymed, and then pretending to faint. For the shih tzu, Jerome's message was, "The trials of life cannot be pipped, their lessons must be sipped, and forewarned you must be tipped, that your dew claw from your leg will be ripped."

The shih tzu looked horrified, and Eloise looked at Jerome, aghast. She mouthed "Happy. Keep it happy."

So Jerome added, "But you'll be happy about it," as he fell into his faint.

The shih tzu left, unsure but open to the possibility of being happy about part of him being ripped away.

And so it went. A man wanting to know which of two women he should wed got an answer involving a garden rake, a bowl of figs, and a gnome statue. A woman after a general reading was told in great detail to go to a nearby village on a specific date and time, carrying a trowel, a towel, and a dowel, while wearing a cowl and a scowl. A slow-speaking slug spent most of his allotted time asking a very complicated question about a dubious real estate matter, to which Jerome responded with an even slower, "Yeeessss."

Jerome really was terrible at this.

Even so, when Lorch returned, Eloise handed him 37 coins (five of them covered in slug slime), a pot with a weight's worth of kiwi fruit preserves, and a wooden comb with a baby lemming carved into it. "Please, Guard Lacksneck, would you be so kind as to see if there might be ye olde accommodation for us tonight?"

Lorch hesitated long enough for Eloise to know the sudden appearance of coins baffled him, but held his usual composure. "Yes, Princess Eloise. It will be my pleasure."

❀ 50 ❀

PAID

Y e Olde Public Inn was as busy for breakfast as it had been for dinner the previous night, probably because the weather still looked like it needed a good cup of haggleberry tea. Eloise did not relish the prospect of spending the day subject to its hungover whims, but they had to push on.

They found the same seats in the crowded room as before—the three next to the gummy, allegedly harmless, and still slumbering Léëèstéëèr. "This guy's going to set some sort of record if he keeps going," said Jerome, sitting next to the stranger.

While they waited for their order of ye olde flapjacks to arrive (and couldn't they at least have called them ye olde griddle cakes?), they were surprised to see Cromulent Stump pushing through the crowds again, the barrel of his being clearing all from his path. "Oh, no," said Jerome. "He's going to want his coins back, I just know it. If you need me, I'll be under the table."

Without even a "g'morning," Stump bellowed, "Where's the spawn of the seer?"

Lorch stood protectively, "Good sir..."

"I would have words with the spawn."

"It's OK, Lorch." Eloise stood. "G'morning, Master Stump. I present to you Jerome the Absolutely Incredibly Unbelievably Magnificently Mind-Blowingly Stupendously Overwhelmingly Unbearably Astounding, at your service."

At that, Jerome poked his eyes above table height. "G'morning to you, Master Stump," he whispered, unsure if that was too much talking in public.

"You!" said Stump, pointing at Jerome.

"Yes?" whispered the chipmunk.

"You are amazing! Look at this!" Stump pointed to his hair. "Paint! And look at this." He waved over a woman almost as big as him, wearing a too-tight tunic, hair like a mountain, and enough piercings in her face to make her a danger to canoodle. "This be Cháäàrléëën. She be the one who accidentally dumped a bucket of paint on me. She's perfect!" Stump took his life in his hands, dodging her piercings to give her a massive kiss. "Jerome the Astounding, you be that exactly."

Jerome was stunned. "Th-that wasn't supposed to happen," he whispered. "I just made that up."

Eloise jumped in. "We're so pleased you are happy. Çalaht's gap-toothed blessing to you both."

Stump stomped away with his inamorata in tow.

"I don't get it," mumbled Jerome. "How is that even possible?"

Eloise shook her head. "Who knows? At least we didn't have to argue with him about his coins."

There was a cough from behind her. It was the shih tzu, accompanied by a husky five times his size. His front right leg was bandaged to the elbow, and there was a small stain of blood where his dew claw might be. "I, too, would like to say a thank you."

"Really?" asked Jerome. "Your dew claw?"

The shih tzu laughed gaily. "Ripped away. Just like you said. I don't think I've ever been in more pain in my life," he trilled. "I caught my leg in a grate I accidentally stepped into. Couldn't get it out for love nor coin. That's when Jáäàxxóòòn here showed up." He nodded at the husky, who Eloise thought might look abashed. "Yanked me free by the scruff, but left my dew claw behind. But I'd never have gotten out on my own. I would have been stuck there forever without him." The shih tzu showed the bandage. "He went with me to get this done, and we've been chatting ever since. So, my thanks, son of the Court Seer of the Western Lands and All That Really Matters. The pain was worth it." With a short bow, they were gone.

Jerome's gob was well and truly smacked. He bowed at their retreating backs, then sat, looking dumbfounded, at the stack of ye olde flapjacks, which had arrived sometime during the shih tzu's speech.

"Princess Eloise," said Lorch. "Perhaps you could do me the kindness of telling me exactly what happened yesterday evening. Just so I can be ready in case a customer is irate, instead of pleased."

As Lorch became increasingly horrified, she sketched Jerome's short career in prognostication, including her less than self-flattering instructions that Jerome "just make stuff up."

"Flukes," muttered Jerome, distractedly nibbling a flapjack. "Flukes."

Dóöòríîîs the serving wench came to collect their plates. "Everything OK here?"

"Yes, thank you," said Eloise. "Delicious."

"Need anything else?"

"No, thank you. We're fine."

"Oh, good," said Dóöòríîîs. "Then you might like to attend to them." She nodded toward a line of people waiting patiently at the door to the vegetable locker. "That is, if the son of the Court Seer is available. And if so, I'd like a prognostication as well." She patted her apron, where coins jingled.

"Of course," said Eloise. "Jerome the Absolutely Incredibly Unbelievably Magnificently Mind-Blowingly Stupendously Overwhelmingly Unbearably Teeth-Achingly Astounding would be delighted.""

It took most of the day to clear the line. An old man wearing a crocheted cap and tailored tunic was first. Jerome told him to expect both a cold on a hot day, and heat on a cold day. Two pre-teen girls were next. They only had enough coins between them for a single reading, but Jerome held the one girl's locket and the other one's hair ribbon, and predicted they would have long and happy lives together, which left them confused (but which became clear years later).

And on and on. Everyone seemed to want a prognostication—from chickens to humans to a lynx, a minx, and a skink with a jinx. Lorch kept order, Hector, the Nameless One and Alejandro rested and kept watch, and Jerome kept babbling nonsense to happy customer after happy customer. Dóöòrĩĩs was last—just before the dinner rush. Jerome, absolutely exhausted, let loose, telling her to look out for a loon, a goon, a full moon, a spoon, a dune, a swoon, a spittoon, a poltroon, a tune, a monsoon and a contrabassoon—and that when they all came together, she'd get a boon.

His pretending for the day done, Jerome strode over to what they now thought of as "their" table, sat down, ordered the strongest haggleberry tea they could brew, and promptly fell asleep.

At that precise moment, the toothless Léëèstéëër snorted once, then again, and woke up. It was as if his sleep state had transferred itself to Jerome.

Léëèstéëër's instincts for waking up in unrecognized and possibly unfriendly places were well-honed. At first, only his eyes moved, blinking twice, then darting left and right to assess if danger was immediate. He quietly tested the air with a few sniffs, presumably checking for smoke, perfume, cooking, or explosives. Only then did he allow his body to move, in this case from a slump against the wall to a more upright posture. "Whuh ammuh?"

"I beg your pardon, good sir?" asked Eloise.

Lééèstéëèr patted his sides and chest, looking for something through his clothing. Whatever it was, it wasn't there. He wriggled to look on his seat. Nope. Then the floor. Success! He brought up a set of carved wooden teeth. Lééèstéëèr used several puffs to blow off dust and dirt, shined them on his sleeve, then shoved them in his mouth and repeated his question. "Where am I?"

"Ye Olde Public Inn," answered Lorch.

Lééèstéëèr looked blank.

"In Colander."

That got a half nod. He rubbed his hand across his face, assessing the amount of beard stubble on his cheeks. "Any idea how long I've been here?"

"We've been here about a full day. It has been at least that long," said Eloise. "Dóöòrîîs..." Lééèstéëèr furrowed his brow, not recognizing the name. "The serving wench?" Noncommittal nod of possible recognition. "She gave us the impression you'd already been here a while. If that helps."

"Thank you for not stabbing me in my sleep," said Lééèstéëèr. "Or poking. It happens more often than you'd think. I almost prefer the stabbing to the poking since I know for sure that something has happened. With poking, it's a maybe-maybe not thing." As he spoke, he looked around the inn like he was looking for clues to help him work out how he'd gotten there. "That must have been a big one."

"Sorry?" said Lorch.

"Just saying that from how badly the cogs are grinding up here," Lééèstéëèr tapped his head indicating his brain, "whatever I was doing before I fell asleep, it must have been impressive. But nothing seems broke, so there you go."

Dóöòrîîs brought over Jerome's tea, setting it down in front of the sleeping chipmunk. "G'evening, Lééèstéëèr. Good to see you awake again."

"Thank you, ma'am."

Dóöòrîîs shook her head. "He never remembers me when he first comes back."

Léëèstéëèr reached over and slid Jerome's cup and saucer so it was in front of him. "Wow," he said. "That's good service. I didn't even have to order it." He sniffed the tea. "Haggleberry. That'll put me right." He downed the steaming hot cup of tea in one long gulp. It was as if his mouth's ability to feel pain had been burned away from previous abuse.

That's when he noticed Jerome. "Yours?" he asked Eloise.

"In a manner of speaking."

"Hold on, hold on, hold on," he said. "Chipmunk, dark-haired girl, beefy bloke. This is ringing a bell."

"Oh?" said Lorch. "What kind of bell, good sir?"

"You got a couple of horses with you? One, uh, yeah, no, yeah, uh... One huge and black. The other a normal sort? A bit fit."

"Again, in a manner of speaking."

Léëèstéëèr sucked in his cheeks in thought, muttering to himself. "What was it I was supposed to say?" He picked up the empty cup, waving it to catch Dóöòrîîs's eye and ask for a refill. Setting it back down, he returned to his mumbling. "Something, something, king, something, something." He looked up at Eloise. "Don't worry, little lady. It'll come back."

"Take your time." Eloise mouthed a silent "King?" at Lorch.

"Chipmunk. Chippy. Bloke. Horse. Horse," muttered Léëèstéëèr, absorbed in the dull ache of remembering through the remnants of what must have been a monumental bender. "He said to watch for a chipmunk who chatters a lot—but then, they all do, if you let them. A chippy with a posh voice and a stuck-up manner. A dull-looking big bloke. A quiet horse who don't say much. And a beaut-looking horse who thinks the sun shines from his..." He trailed off into indistinguishable syllables. When he became audible again, it was, "The coins were for saying something to them. What was it? What was I supposed to say?" Dóöòrĩĩs delivered his boiling refill, which, like the first cup, he slugged down like it was tepid bathwater. The haggleberry must have reconnected some of his brain bits, because the story seemed to settle back into his consciousness. "Oh, that was it. The king was going to see Her Maj Ono, and he had some sort of dark-haired princess with him."

"Good sir, you mentioned coin?"

"Yeah. Gave me a fair bit. Must be how I afforded to end up asleep here."

"Who gave you a fair bit of coin?" asked Eloise.

"Thin bloke. Pale. Walked fast."

"Good sir, Léëèstéëèr. Did you actually see the king? Or this princess?" asked Lorch. "Perhaps the carriage they traveled in?"

"Naw. No carriage. Just a thin bloke distributing coins. Like I said, he told me to look out for a chipmunk, chippy, bloke, horse, horse. He said I could mention a carriage. And something about a cape." Then Léëèstéëèr cracked a massive, false teeth smile. "I bet you're them. Hey, do you reckon I've remembered enough to have discharged any explicit or implied obligation I might have to said thin bloke? Because I've spent all the coins."

Lorch reached into his purse, pulled out a coin, and flicked the edge of it so it spun on its side in front of him. Then he quickly did the same with two more, so the three coins all spun at the same time. Then he flattened his palm over them and slid them in front of Léëèstéëèr. The man reached for them, but Lorch held up his index finger, stopping him. "I would love for you to have these, good sir. We'll need a little more time and cooperation. Plus, I'll need to wake our friend here so he can also enjoy your company. Do we have a deal? Coins for a bit more chat, and a lot more exactness in the remembering?"

"Throw in some ye olde dinner, and I think we have ourselves an accord," said Léëèstéëèr.

In the end, there was not that much more detail to be had. Someone who matched Turpy's description had paid him to watch out for them and lie about having seen King Doncaster and Princess Johanna on their way to the Sclerotic Wold.

They shared a desultory dinner with Léëèstéëèr, then watched him leave three coins richer. Eloise, Jerome, and Lorch joined the horses in the stable, which they hoped was private enough for them to all speak freely.

"It all fits with the other clues we've been following," said Jerome. "All those little hints along the way, but not the usual sturm and drang that attends royal proceedings. Looking back, it was all a bit convenient, wasn't it?"

"I feel like such an idiot." Eloise was picking up bits of lucerne from the ground and laying them out in a cross-grid pattern. Just something to do while the rest of her mind worked elsewhere.

"Princess Eloise," said Hector. "We were all fooled. Fooled by our own hope of a quick resolution. Fooled by the desire to see what we hoped we were seeing. Fooled by what we thought would be a simple task, so we did not allow for much complexity. And fooled by someone who was definitely trying to fool us."

"But how? If there was no carriage, and no horse involved, how did he do it?" asked Jerome. "How did Turpy stay ahead of us? There's no way he could have known who we'd meet or exactly what we'd do. He would have had to seed that misdirection strategically and widely, which would have taken forever on foot, not to mention be extremely expensive."

"The coin is not an issue. He is close to King Doncaster, and seems to wield influence," said Lorch. "Plus, there's prattleweed involved. Add it all up and he has access to a significant purse."

"Do you think Doncaster is in on it?" asked Eloise.

"Princess Eloise, it is not obvious one way or the other," said Lorch. "From what we saw, he might be complicit, and he might not be."

Eloise added lucerne twigs above the cross-hatch, twisting the tops together, creating a pyramid of horse food. "So what do we do? And how reliable is what Léëèstéëèr said? Can we decide based on someone so inclined toward epic benders?"

"Señorita Princesa, may I make a suggestion?"

"Please, Al."

"Let us stay in Colander tonight and get an early start tomorrow morning. With a few days' hard riding, we could make it to the Sclerotic Wold. There, we can see for ourselves whether King Doncaster and Princesa Johanna are there, and thus confirm or contradict what the gentleman in the inn said. If they are, great. You can undertake your task, and we can be on our way back to the Western Lands and All That Really Matters with your sister. If they are not, then we have, at least, eliminated that possibility."

"That strikes me as sound advice. El, I think we should follow it," said Jerome. "Lorch? Hector? Nameless One?" Nods from each of them.

"The likelihood of a dead end doesn't bother you?" asked Eloise. "It bothers me. A lot."

"To be honest, yes, Princess, it does," said Lorch. "But there's enough logic to it that it seems a reasonable choice. No other option outweighs that one."

Eloise shook her head slowly, but said, "Agreed, then. Let's get a ye olde goode night's sleep and set out at ye olde first light."

51

FIVE BALLS AND HOOP

They set out as planned, riding hard toward the Sclerotic Wold. Two hours closer to their destination, Eloise heard Jerome mutter. "What was that?" she asked.

"I said 'longwalker.'" Jerome turned around on the saddle to face her. "It's the only thing I can think of that would explain how Turpy could have been to so many places."

"Clever," said Eloise. "That would work. A longwalker could cover that much ground and stay ahead of us. For that matter, a longwalker could keep an eye on us, going back and forth between where we are and wherever we're headed."

"I hadn't thought of that," said Jerome.

They both fell silent, thinking through possibilities and implications.

Lorch stopped them close to midday. "I think Inevitable Splat has a market," he said. "I'd like to go there and stock up, if possible."

"Oooh, Inevitable Splat at this time of year," said Jerome.

"What about it?" asked Eloise.

"Nothing. Nothing at all."

When they reached Inevitable Splat, it became clear what Jerome was referring to—another local festival. "You have to be kidding me," groaned Eloise when she saw the signs and decorations. "Aloe vera?" But there it was. Aloe vera plants, both real and simulated, everywhere.

"Come on, Elotastic. The Aloe Vera Jamboree is an important regional event. If you meet anyone today, greet them with 'aloe, aloe,' instead of 'hello, hello.' All the men change their name to 'Aloe' for the day, and all the women are 'Vera.' There's aloe arranging, aloe juice, foods shaped like aloe plants, since you can't do a lot of cooking with it, a pageant where they crown a Mister Aloe and a Miss Vera, the All Aloe's Eve Ball and a Burn Fest, where people deliberately burn themselves so they can avail themselves of the soothing qualities of the aloe vera plant. It's exquisite," he cooed.

"No fritters, tossing, juggling, or funniest shapes?" teased Eloise.

Jerome wouldn't bite. "Inevitably, along with feats of strength and size. Prepare to be aloed and verad to an extent previously unimagined. It will be grand!"

"Right. I can't wait."

"You mock, but it will be the highlight of the day."

The Aloe Vera Jamboree wasn't quite the spectacle of the Celebration des Pamplemousses, but it had a folksy, rural charm. One thing it had that the other hadn't was a string of midway booths. These included food stalls, barkers, sideshow oddities, blaring music, and games of skill or chance (it was not always obvious which was which) featuring prizes one could win at the risk of a coin or two. A favorite of the kids were the chaud bags—bundles that contained hot, spicy sweets that necessitated a gulp of aloe juice, along with various inexpensive trinkets. The bags appeared to contain a lot, but as the bookkeepers in the crowd could tell you, the value of the contents did not quite reach the number of coins it took to buy them. Even so, they were the desire of every child.

Lorch despatched the Nameless One to the market. Eloise wondered how he haggled without speaking, but obviously Lorch trusted him to do so. Hector and Alejandro did not want to push through the crowds, so found a side paddock where they could rest in the shade. Jerome, eyes lit up like a child who'd been promised a chaud bag, dragged Eloise into the middle of it all, Lorch trailing along behind. Eloise did not care for the press of all those bodies, but couldn't deny Jerome his pleasure.

⚜

THE MIX OF SIGHTS AND SOUNDS VEERED FROM THE FAMILIAR, LIKE boiled cabbage candies and overly exuberant vendors from the East selling a vast variety of olives, to the bizarre, like a sheep shearer who specialized in haut coiffure and a spider who did the most uncanny imitations of passersby. Eloise allowed herself to get lost in the humor and strangeness of it all, the tangy smell of peppery spices and the gleeful cries of children. Though coins were tight, Eloise contemplated what she might get for the others as a thank you for their perseverance. She wondered if horses might enjoy jalapeño licorice, or maybe a skewer of roasted aloe vera leaves (was that even edible?).

A man's voice broke her reverie. "Aloe, aloe, sweet Vera. Win a chameleon, Mistress? Five coins a try."

"Pardon?" Eloise looked around to see who'd spoken. It was a barker, a slovenly man with gray at his temples, grayer eyebrows, and a tunic that looked like water and soap were its mortal enemies. "What do you mean, 'win a chameleon?'" asked Eloise. She knew things were a bit strange in The South, but winning a chameleon? Was it a metaphor? A colloquialism?

"I mean, Mistress, that you, being the person on that side of the counter, for a mere five coins, can win, not so much the person of a very talented chameleon, but a contract for his time, services, and cooperation," smarmed the barker.

"That's barbaric!" gasped Jerome. Several passersby shushed him.

"Where is this chameleon? And how would one go about winning him?"

The barker pointed to the side of his stall, where a chameleon wearing a fake monocle and an even faker mustache sat, looking resigned. "Him. You can win him. All you have to do is stand behind that line there," he said, pointing to a pole lying on the ground. "Pick five balls from that basket there and toss them through that hoop over there."

"Let me get this straight. Five coins. Five balls. If I get all five balls through that tiny little hoop over there, I can win, essentially, the bondage of this person?"

"Ah, Mistress Vera. You must be from the Western Lands and All That Supposedly Really Matters with talk like that," said the barker. "Not a 'person.' Also, not 'bondage.' Contracted indentured service. He is serving out the obligations of his immediate family, and, to a lesser extent, his ancestors. Aren't you, Cäääsëëëy?" It was clear this was not the first time the barker had to gloss up the status of his prized prize. The chameleon slowly nodded assent, a perfect mix of insolence, boredom, and conquered acquiescence.

"That seems rather a long shot," said Eloise. "Five coins and the chameleon or nothing?"

"No, no, no, Mistress Vera. Plenty of prizes to be won. Get one ball through and you can win an aloe vera leaf bag. Two wins you a stuffed aloe toy. And so on. But the real prize, the big one, is Cäääsëëëy here."

"Why, exactly, would one want such a chameleon?" asked Lorch. He could sense Eloise's indignation rising and tried to paper over it with conversation. "And how does one know he isn't broken?"

"Well, Aloe, me chum. This is a talented chameleon," declaimed the barker to the gathering crowd. "He does the required color changes, of course, but also has full control over them. You want him to look like a rainbow on a sunny day? Simply ask, and he will. He can do it. And he has to do it because it's in his contract. Show them, Cäääsëëëy."

The chameleon, long used to this part of the patter, changed his skin color so he was striped like a child's drawing of a rainbow. This was met with appreciative applause.

The barker warmed to his sales pitch. "He has traveled with me for five harmonious years," said the barker. "He has the jester in him. Songs. Witticisms. Soliloquies. I can't have him demonstrate now, seeing how we're in public. But we have had many a splendid time, haven't we?" Again, a resigned nod from the chameleon. You could tell it had been long enough that he'd no hope of his contract being taken over by a mark.

"If he has been with you for five years, then this game is not winnable," said Eloise flatly. "I don't believe it is possible to put that sized ball through that sized hoop."

"You assume he has been a prize that long, Mistress Vera. That is not the case. It is only recent circumstances that have forced me to take such steps. As for winnability, well, watch." The barker snatched up five balls from the basket, jumped to a spot behind the line, juggled them into a five-ball cascade, then in fast succession flicked them through the hoop, the last one traveling by way of behind his back. "Apparently, it can be done," he smirked.

"Please allow me to see the contract," said Eloise.

Now the barker was taken aback. "Pardon me, Mistress? Do you distrust me?"

"Of course not, Mr Aloe. I do, however, distrust contracts. If I'm going to try to win one, I want to make sure it is one I'd like to actually have."

The growing crowd was amused by the interaction between the self-possessed teenager and the wily barker.

"Well, of course, Mistress. I show that to everyone. Shall I make you a haggleberry tea while I am at it?" That got the laughs he expected. "This is but a game, Mistress. A contract? You and I are not getting married." That jest also landed well.

"Five coins is a lot and I don't find slavery a game. If I am going to try to free your 'prize,' I would see what strings are attached."

"Strings! Slavery! Mistress Vera, you are as misguided as you are pretty." He smiled in a way he clearly thought charming. "But I like you. So I shall indulge." The barker reached under the counter and hauled out a satchel. He made a show of rifling past socks, the remnants of lunches past, and a flattened hat, until he found what he was looking for—a scroll tied with a silver thread. He held it aloft to the expanding crowd's applause and with a flourish exclaimed, "Ta da!" The barker curtsied to Eloise, miming a dress, then handed her the scroll.

Eloise was unused to such disrespect, and her face betrayed both her embarrassment and her irritation. The man's manner vexed her, even though she knew his jokes were part of his patter. Eloise unfurled the scroll, trying not to think of who or what might have touched it before her, nor about the several dozen eyes that scrutinized her as she read it. She could also feel Lorch's unease rising. Still, she read, letting her silence counter some of the barker's wordiness.

Finally, she rolled up the scroll, retying the silver thread, and said to the chameleon, "I am sorry for your troubles, and those of your family." She reached for a pocket in her cape and pulled out the purse where she'd kept back a few coins. There were seven, and she handed five to the man. He mockingly bit one, less to test its veracity and more for humor. Then he majestically pointed to where she should stand, held out the basket of balls, and let her choose five.

Eloise noted that their weights were somewhat dissimilar. Well, that was to be expected. She picked the roundest five she could see. Then, with an underhand throw similar to the barker's style, took a first toss. The ball hit the hoop and bounced off. The second one flew high. The third one went through, which got her a few claps. The fourth and fifth hit the hoop. When she'd finished, the barker called out, "Let's have a round of applause for the young Mistress Vera!" As everyone clapped, he handed her a chintzy aloe leaf bag worth a dozen to a coin.

The wrongness of it all grew in her and blended with the frustrations of the whole journey. She knew she should apologize to the chameleon and leave him to his fate. Their coins were tight, and giving more of them to this man was irksome. But she couldn't walk away. She dug out the remaining two coins then turned to Lorch, wordlessly asking for the rest. She'd learned to read the small movements in his stoic face, so could tell he disliked the idea immensely. But he gave them to her. "Another try!" called the barker. Again, the exaggerated invitation to take five balls. The first went through. So did the second. But the third and fourth did not. Eloise did not even try the fifth; her mission had failed.

Shame filled her, and sheer will kept the tears from flowing. She truly did not understand this land and its ways with non-humans. "Thank you, good sir," she said to the barker. "I'm sorry," she said to the chameleon, and she turned her back on the stall, leaving someone else to lose five coins on the slim chance of taking home a servant.

Fifteen steps along she stopped. It was so suddenly that Jerome bumped into her leg. She looked at Lorch, then turned back to the barker's stall.

"Princess, please," said Lorch. She stopped, turned, and looked at him, letting him have his say. "The game is rigged, Princess. Not obviously, but there is something amiss with it."

"The barker could do it. That means it is possible. I'm sorry." And she turned away and walked back to the stall.

A skinny woman handed a stuffed aloe toy to her young son, who took it like it was a rare thing of beauty. Eloise, Lorch, and Jerome stood patiently, watching four more people fail at the game. None got more than two balls through the hoop. When she stepped forward, the barker grinned. "Ah, Mistress Vera. So we are getting married, are we?" he joked.

"I would like to try again."

"Of course, pretty one. You never know your luck."

Eloise looked at Lorch. With great reluctance, he produced another five coins, which Eloise knew represented an oversized proportion of their remaining resources. He handed them to her and she reached to pass them to the barker, then pulled back. Adding a small simper to her voice, she said, "Goodness, Master Aloe, could you please show me again that it can be done?"

"Of course, sugar cheeks. Anything for my fiancé." This time, instead of a juggler's cascade, he used his hands and feet like a hockey sacking grunter, bouncing them on knees and elbows and adding the traditional grunts. Then, one by one, he flicked his foot and shot them clean through. "As I said, Mistress Vera, it appears it can be done."

So Eloise handed over the coins. As before, people gathered to watch.

The barker grandiosely motioned for her to join him behind the line. Eloise gestured toward his feet. "I shall stand where you are standing, Good Master Aloe."

"Oooh. Do you think the spot makes a difference, then? You can try to fill my footsteps, but I doubt your feet are big enough."

Eloise shrugged a feigned nonchalance. "It seems to have been luck for you. Perhaps it will be lucky for me."

"Well, Mademoiselle Luck is a fickle mistress. We shall see if she points her finger at you."

With an open-palm swoop of his hands, he motioned for her to choose her balls from the basket. Eloise shook her head. "I would use the same ones you used. There are three still on the ground over there, plus the one you picked up and put on the barrel, and the one in your hand."

"Oh, now she thinks she's clever," he said to the watchers, but there was a shift in his tone. Some of the mirth edged over into a sharpness.

"If we are affianced, Master Aloe, as you've suggested, then I'm sure it is a small ask for the one to whom you are betrothed." Eloise smiled the least sincere smile she'd ever managed, but it seemed to work on the crowd.

The barker hesitated long enough that a man carrying an aloe-costumed child called, "Let Vera have them, Aloe."

"Well, of course, my sweet Vera," he said. He tossed her the three from the ground, flicked her the one from the barrel, and handed her the one he had been holding.

Jerome frantically tugged Eloise's tunic, then mimed something, frustrated at not being able to speak.

"Really?" said Eloise. "I thought something amiss." To the barker, she took the tone of a wronged sweetheart. "Master Aloe, you disappoint me. Switching the last ball like that. How can we wed if I cannot trust you? As I said, for my five coins, and really, it is 15 now, I would use the ones you used."

"Ah, sweet Vera. Your rat friend is a sharp one. It is possible I gave you the wrong one." The barker produced another six seemingly identical balls from his coat and splayed them out between his fingers in front of Jerome. "Perhaps you can help us all remember which it was?"

"Rat?" objected Jerome, then clasped paws over his mouth at his error.

"So, you, too must be from the Western Lands and All That Allegedly Matters," chivvied the barker. "Well, welcome to a more sensible part of the world. Now, do you think you can point to the ball you'd like my fiancé to use?"

Jerome fumed and took his time examining each. Then he jabbed his finger at one to indicate his decision. With exaggerated slowness, keeping all the balls fully in sight, the barker stepped toward Eloise. "Will you swap the one you're holding for your rat's choice?"

She didn't bother to comment, flicking the last ball he'd given her back into the basket and plucking out Jerome's ball. "Shall I start, Master Aloe?"

"Of course, my beloved."

"Good luck, Vera," called a woman. "Çalaht's blessing on your throwing."

Eloise turned and smiled genuinely. "Thank you, Goodwoman Vera."

Then she blocked out the world.

There was her, the ball, and the hoop. No annoying Southie barker. No worried Lorch or indignant Jerome. No watching crowd. Just her, the ball, and the hoop. She felt the weight of the ball, which listed slightly to the left in her hand, so that had to be considered. There was a slight, intermittent breeze she'd have to allow for. She readied herself, then flung it.

It sailed straight through. The crowd applauded.

Without waiting to reassess, she threw the second and the third. Both found their mark without so much as a whisper of contact with the hoop itself. More cheers.

As she readied the fourth ball, the barker tried to distract her with patter. Something about the joys of their forthcoming marriage. But Eloise was beyond his teasing and taunts. The fourth ball followed its predecessors.

More cheers. Four in a row was more than any of them had seen before. The chameleon even seemed to have a small ray of hope kindled in him.

There was a wind spike, and the barker, flat out in patter, surreptitiously jostled the stand supporting the hoop so it swayed. But none of it mattered. Eloise was lost to the ordinary. She didn't know how to consciously draw on whatever weak magic she might possess—there was never any tingling or whooshing or buzzing or sounds. But she needed it now. So Eloise imagined the weak magic as light that flowed in through the top of her head and out through her extremities. She took five steps back, and then against all logic, spun into her hammer-throwing circles and released the ball at the perfect moment. It sailed through the hoop and slapped the canvas behind it.

The crowd exploded in whoops, but the barker was unmoved. "Ah, sweet Vera. You stepped over the line that time with yer purdy, loopy throwing." Lorch was ready to step up and defend Eloise's throw, but there was no need. A chant went up. "Give her the prize! Give her the prize! Give her the prize!" The barker knew there was no way he could breach such a public response. So with no grace or politeness at all, he pointed to the chameleon and said, "You. Go with the wench."

The chameleon didn't waste a second. He flung his fake mustache and monocle at the man, held clasped claws up in triumph, and ran over to Eloise, bowing with genuine thanks.

The barker began disassembling his stall. With no more top prize, there was no need to continue. But before he could gather the balls, Eloise stopped him. "Sir. You have forgotten something."

"You've taken enough from me, wench," he snarled.

"The contract. I did not win the chameleon. I won the contract. Please sign it over."

Caught out again, he reached under the counter, producing the scroll. Eloise took it, unwrapped the silver thread, made sure it was the correct document, handed it back, and asked the crowd, "Would any of you good people have a quill for my former fiancé to use?"

An elderly woman three rows back called, "Please use mine, Mistress Vera."

The crowd parted to let her through, and she pulled quill and ink from a hemp waist pouch. She handed it to the barker, who gruffly snatched it, wrote a sentence on the document and signed it. Eloise took the scroll, read it, then showed the scroll to the chameleon. "Is that his correct name, Master Cäääsëëëy?" The chameleon nodded. Eloise scrolled the document and retied the silver thread. Then, to the barker, she said, "Thank you. May you find a more honest living."

The barker jabbed a finger at her, looking ready to hurl invective, but Lorch moved between them, dismissing the man with a firm, "G'day to you, good sir."

Eloise bowed to the crowd, said, "Thank you, good people," and walked away from the stall and any further hint of aloe vera celebration. She felt the barker's burning glare on the back of her neck, but did not care. Lorch, Jerome, and Cäääsëëëy caught up and formed a triangle around her as she moved through the crowd. The protective formation surprised her, but it certainly felt good to have them with her.

52

DEBT

Alejandro agreed to carry Cäääsëëëy, and they rode on toward
the Sclerotic Wold through the rest of the afternoon and into
the evening. Cäääsëëëy was grateful to be away from the
barker, but remained silent. Eloise guessed it was the shock. Or
perhaps simply habit. But there wasn't the slightest hint that he was
someone prone to witticisms or soliloquies.

They found a clearing, and Eloise braced herself for another night of
rough sleeping, thanks to her having spent so much to free the
chameleon. Far from getting used to them, the nights outside were
getting harder. Her riding improved with time in the saddle, and her
muscles no longer howled at the end of each day. Although she was
tired, she did not sink into the oblivion of exhaustion, which meant
she was awake to the itches of her habits. The drizzle didn't help, but
at least her blankets were clean enough that she could tolerate them
on her.

Then there was her hair. Odmilla's journeyman's braid had not been
designed to stay in for so long, and long, curling clusters had worked
themselves loose. Eloise feared undoing the thing and making it worse.
She feared not undoing it and having a hair disaster tangle itself into

sentience, complete with an obstreperous resistance to combs. She'd have to deal with it soon, but continued to put it off.

Eloise recognized her mind racing for what it was and took out Odmilla's prayer beads, seeking comfort in their use and distraction.

Well after midnight, she heard an unfamiliar sound. It took Eloise a while to puzzle out exactly what it was.

Whimpers.

Specifically, chameleon whimpers.

She sat up, saw Jerome struggling to stay alert on his watch, and offered to take over.

"Thank you," yawned the chipmunk, sliding over to his own blankets, practically asleep before he had even nestled in.

She let the tiny sobs continue for a while, then went over to where the chameleon sat under a hawthorn. "Excuse me. May I join you?"

He nodded, trying to collect himself.

Eloise sat and leaned back into the comforting embrace of the tree. "I don't feel I've properly introduced myself. My name is Eloise." She offered him a hand to shake.

"Eloise? Like the Westie queen?" The chameleon shook his head absently, still absorbed in his own thoughts. "Don't let her find out that's your name. Over there, you can't be named 'Eloise' unless you're her daughter."

"I know."

"I hear she's frightful when she's angry."

"Yes. She can be."

In the silence that followed, the realization seeped in slowly. "Oh," he said. "Oh, my." His face flushed a bright red, either in mortification or as a result of being a chameleon. He stood up, bowed low and, formally, and still facing the ground, said, "Princess Eloise Hydra

Gumball III, I have no idea why you are in The South, nor how you crossed my path, but you have committed the single greatest act of kindness I have ever experienced. I, Cäääsëëëy Liïïss, am in your debt." He took her hand and kissed it, saying, "We chameleons pay our debts."

"Please, no," said Eloise. She leaned forward to bow to him formally. "Cäääsëëëy Liïïss, I release you from your contract of indentured service. You are free to go at any time and to any place that suits you," she said.

"Thank you, Princess Eloise. I accept your termination of contract," he replied. "However, that does not erase the debt. It has to do with the fact that you found me in the, uh, state you did."

"It's OK. And really. You're free to go."

"Princess, have you studied much Çalahtist literature?"

"To be honest, most of it is not to my taste. Too many gap-toothed smiles and stories about hanging from doorknobs."

"The Çalahtists have a concept called 'reciprocity.' Do you know it?"

It rang a bell. "I think I've heard it referred to as 'right relations.'"

"That is correct, Princess. I, myself, am also not a great fan of Çalahtism. As you said, all that gap-toothed smiling gets on one's nerves. But reciprocity guides my life."

"Oh?"

"Reciprocity has to do with the balance of things, the exchanges between people, be they human or non-human, as well as between people and anything else you might find in the realms, be they trees, stones, or soil. Like others who embrace reciprocity, I seek to stay in balance with all things. Value received must be balanced by value given. And I'm not talking in coins. I'm talking in the sum total of everything."

Suitably distracted by conversation, Eloise slipped the prayer beads back into her pocket and hunched her cape closer to her. "Reciprocity. One could do worse than live to that principle."

"It is why I put up with being, as you put it, a slave. I sought to restore balance for my family."

"But can you restore balance on behalf of someone else?"

"The Çalahtists seem to think so. I've not yet convinced myself either way."

"Then it is noble to try."

"Perhaps. Or perhaps it was the only right thing to do." Embarrassingly, Cäääsëëëy suddenly prostrated himself in front of her and said, "Princess Eloise Hydra Gumball III, I am in your debt for the great service you rendered me and my family. I would appreciate the chance to stay with you to repay that debt. Please. To restore balance."

She was moved by the chameleon's earnestness. "I would be honored," she said. "But know this. If reciprocity is about the balance of all people and all things, and if you find your reciprocity with someone or something else, that will be fine with me."

"Thank you, Princess."

And so they sat next to each other in silence, peering at stars through the branches of the hawthorn, until sleep finally came.

❦ 53 ❦

NAME GOES HERE

A
t first light, Jerome found Eloise asleep at the foot of the
hawthorn, and covered her with a blanket so she could rest a
while longer. The chameleon was gone. Odd, but perhaps
understandable. Why should he stick around? Jerome went to help
Lorch pack up.

An hour later, over a breakfast of crackerbread and their remaining
kiwi fruit preserves, Eloise told the others of her agreement with
Cäääsëëëy. The discussion was made more awkward by the chameleon's
absence. The others did not argue, but the unspoken additional strain
on their resources was clear enough.

Cäääsëëëy reappeared shortly before they were ready to ride off for the
day. No explanation. No excuses. But he carried a satchel made of
tightly woven willow twigs and wore an intricately patterned kilt of
felted cotton fluff. How he had found the materials and put them
together in so little time was a mystery, but he resumed his silence and
it seemed rude to break it by asking questions.

The "Sclerotic Wold" referred to both the large town that was the
birthplace of Çalaht and site of Queen Onomatopoeia's castle, and the
endless, rolling moors that surrounded them. Constant rain, inter-

spersed with epic mists and the occasional hail battering kept the region green, but the wold was also prone to winds that legends said carried off wicked children and their evil ways.

And it was such a wind that welcomed them with their first steps onto the moors—a relentless, driving blast that after just an hour made one understand the Southie saying, "A day in the Wold is a month in the cold." It was exhausting work to be in weather like that, and conversation ground to a halt as their focus narrowed to getting from here to there. Even Alejandro's endless stream of songs extolling the beauty of Andalusian mares was reduced to a background hum.

Once again, Eloise was grateful she'd not prevailed in her anti-saddle argument, as it gave her something to hold onto when the winds hammered. Days before, Hector had suggested that her riding was improved enough that she no longer needed it, and Jerome had hinted they might sell it to bring them some coin. But Eloise felt sentimental about it now. It was a tie to home. Plus, she did not like the idea of leaving it somewhere it would not be appreciated for its fine craftsmanship, not even for a few coins. Hector had allowed her to ride bareback for a while to get better at it, and Alejandro had carried the saddle then. But she was glad she had it now, and would even have said so, if asked.

But she was glad no one did.

They fought their way through the day, and finally made it to a hamlet called Name Goes Here, known, they soon learned, for the indolence of the village founders, who could never be bothered to name the place, and so their placeholder stuck. At least the Name Goes Here Something Something Arms served warm meals and gave them a break from being blown about.

Plus, there was supposed to be entertainment. Visible from where Lorch, Eloise, and Jerome sat (Cäääsëëëy stayed with the horses) was a chalked slate that spruiked "The Musicalistic Stylings of Jaminity Delgado Blister." Jerome's jaw dropped when he saw it.

"What?" asked Eloise.

Jerome swooned, whispering, "The Jammer, El. The Jammer is playing here! Tonight!"

"You might have to remind me who that is."

"Oh, come on! Really? I bet you know strong weights of his songs. 'Left on the Sacrificial Altar of My Heart?'"

"No."

"'Lean Into My Lean-To?'"

"Sorry."

"Well, I know you know the big one. 'Three Bags of Groats For My Sweetheart.'"

Eloise put down her spoon. "You're kidding."

"I kid not. The immortal Jaminity 'The Jammer' Delgado Blister wrote 'Three Bags of Groats For My Sweetheart.'"

"I'm going to have to kill him."

"Apologies, Princess, but that won't be necessary," said Lorch.

"No?"

"No. Because I'm going to kill him first. I have been listening to Champion Abernatheen de Chipmunk hum, mumble, sing, chant, and recite parts of that infernal song since we left the warm halls of Castle de Brague. Usually the lyrics are right, but sometimes he mangles them." Lorch placed his spoon carefully next to his bowl. "It might be fair to say that of all the songs in all the realms, I now truly hate that one the most."

"Fair point. Also, the poor man in the song seems dim. He's going to buy her a cask, a mask, and a flask so he can bask in her damask?" Eloise snorted. "No wonder she's unimpressed with the groats."

"Or the way the song rhymes 'chortle' with 'splortle,'" said Lorch. "That's not even a word. The song is a joke."

"You two are cultural ignoramuses," whispered Jerome. "The song is a classic, a heartfelt cry for understanding and a reprieve from longing."

"Actually, your friends are right. The song is a joke." The maudlin voice came from the table behind theirs. Eloise turned to see a man sopping up soup with crackerbread. He wore what once would have been a natty outfit, but which was now road weary. His face displayed enough beard stubble to show he preferred being clean shaven, but couldn't always manage it. He had a full set of fine white teeth, which he used to chew a chunk of crackerbread while they watched him. Once he'd swallowed, he added, "As for your offers to end my steps upon this plane of realms, well, there are days, even months, when I think that doing so would be a blessing to all involved."

"You— You're the Jammer," spluttered Jerome in the least whispery whisper possible. "I love you! I mean, I love your songs!"

"Oh, please don't call me that. It's demeaning, and no one who truly appreciates my work, or knows me more than a little, calls me that to my face. But yes, I am Jaminity Delgado Blister, at your service, or so Protocol indicates I should say." All this was delivered without interrupting his workmanlike consumption of his meal.

"I'm sorry, Master Blister," said Eloise. "I apologize for the harshness of my words. They were meant in jest, but truly, they were inappropriate, whether jest or not."

"I, too, apologize, good sir," said Lorch, mortified. "We have journeyed long, and certain behaviors, more than certain songs, have made it longer. Please join us for a haggleberry tea as a small apology."

Eloise looked at Lorch, surprised. It was more words than he normally said to anyone in public, and an uncharacteristic deployment of coin. It showed how embarrassed he was. When Blister agreed, Jerome practically fainted in delight, scampering to the side to make room for another place. Blister picked up his bowl and took a seat, clearly used to being invited to people's tables. He immediately went back to work on his dinner.

"So, Master Blister—" started Eloise.

"Please, call me 'Jaminity,'" he said. "You seem like decent people—even your overly enthusiastic chipmunk friend here. Plus, jealousy at the Bards' Guild meant the title of master was never granted."

"I know, I know," said Jerome, a little louder than he should have. "It was a scandal."

"'Travesty' is the word I use. But 'scandal' also covers it." He swallowed another mouthful. "So, the big fellow here called you 'Princess'? Term of endearment, or actual title?" Only a glint in his eye betrayed true interest in the answer. The question was more than practiced small talk, but only a little.

"Well, actually..." started Eloise. They had, by tacit agreement, chosen to hide her status as much as possible.

"Real princess," said Jerome, his voice a barely contained stage whisper. Then with, a casualness that fooled no one, he added, "I'm her champion."

"Really?" said Blister. Then to Eloise, "What's wrong with this bloke?" He pointed a spoon at Lorch, then without waiting for a reply added, "To each their own." If Jerome had hoped his bit of bragging might impress the singer, he was disappointed. The man had probably met too much royalty through his years to be impressed.

"So, Good Sir Blister..."

"Jaminity, please."

"So, Jaminity. Getting back to where we started. Why is the song a joke?"

The serving wench brought his tea, which he accepted with a flirtatious smile that lasted exactly as long as her attention was on him. "Well, for starters, I wrote it as a joke. And the first time I performed it, it was as a favor to a friend." He threw a generous heap of stevia into his tea, and Jerome hid his horror behind a fit of coughing.

"It was early in my career, and I traveled with another would-be bard. My companion had been recently tossed out as an apprentice—a justifiable act, as he was a layabout, his master should have turfed him a year before. But he was a friend, so he and I were commiserating in liquid form. Sometime into our fifth round of commiseration, one of us hit on the idea we would compete to see who could write the worst song in all the realms. We called for quills and hemp paper, and by the time my seventh commiseration was consumed, I'd quilled a ditty called 'Three Bags of Groats For My Sweetheart.' There was a great deal of hilarity between us as I read it out, but when I went to burn the thing, my friend snatched it from my hand and tucked it into his breeks. More hilarity was fueled by more commiseration, and by the time we stumbled onto our pallets for the night, the song was lost forever."

Eloise couldn't understand why he was not more successful than his dress and location indicated. She was riveted—he was a through-and-through raconteur.

He blew across his tea, but it was still too hot, so he set the cup down and continued. "The next day, my friend announced that he was going home for good, giving up the life of a would-be bard in favor of helping with his father's turnip farm. But he requested one last show, and asked me to be part of it. That night, we found an inn half the size of this one, whipped out our lutes and alternated songs, one his, one mine. The innkeeper knew the tragedy of giving up one's dreams, so supplied a certain quantity of commiseration on the house, which we consumed as the night went on. The crowd grew more boisterous, and we rose to the occasion with ballads and bawdiness, jigs and jiggery-pokery. At the end of the evening my friend declared we would play exactly one more song each. He went first, playing a stunning rendition of 'Fish Became a Fishwife,' which I can vouch was the best I'd ever heard from him. A little less layabout and a little more fishwife and my friend could have been one of the best. The crowd exploded in applause and bought the two of us yet more commiseration."

He sipped, then sipped again. "Needs more sweet," said Jaminity, dropping in another heavy pinch of stevia. "Anyway, by then we were truly well-commiserated, and my friend leaned over to ask if he could request the last song of the night. As it was his final show, I agreed. He stood and declaimed that his best friend, his bosom mate, Jammer Blister—that being the first time anyone had ever called me 'Jammer'—had a wonderful new song, quilled just the night before. Then he reached into his breeks, pulled out my half-legible scratching from the night before, and said, 'Now, for the first time ever, I give you 'Three Bags of Groats for my Sweetheart.' The inn crowd, fully primed by everything we'd done so far, were expecting genius, not some wretched tune where I'd rhymed 'chortle' and 'splortle.' But I had a bard's soul, if not a bard's title, and I determined to sell that song like it was a blessing from Çalaht herself. It didn't matter I had no tune for it. I plucked my lute, and—as if Çalaht were listening—I was graced with a melody that even today, I have to admit is as catchy as anything ever written."

He paused, a faraway look settling onto his face, back in that nameless inn, altered by the fluid of commiseration and once again enjoying his moment of performance magic. Moved by the memory, he opened his mouth, and a voice as strong and pure as Eloise had ever heard, sang out the first line of the song.

There's a lady who knows, all that glitters is groats.

"And sell it, I did. So much so, that I was asked to play it again immediately. Which I did. And the next night. Which I did. And every night since. And that is also part of the joke, you see." Blister broke off a chunk of crackerbread and dunked it in his tea. Jerome sucked in air through his teeth like he'd been punched, but Blister was too wrapped up in his tale to notice.

"That song I wrote as a joke, that I performed as a favor to my friend, well, it has defined me. Its popularity is what got the Bards' Guild so offside—jealousy, pure and simple—and is the reason I'm still to this day not a bard. The joke is that I have sung it too many times to count. I have written, as our friend here seems to know, many other songs that are much more worthy of praise than that bit of doggerel set to a beat. But it has assumed a singular place in the realms. Others have sung it more than me, which benefits me not at all, as I do not share in their fees or rewards. Lyndia Thrind herself, I'm told, uses it as an encore. That song is a monster. It has taken on a life of its own, and the life it has taken is mine. If I *don't* sing it in a show, the people want their money back. And believe you me, I come by little enough of that to be returning any.

"Since I cannot command a bard's rates, I still, to this day, travel on foot, enjoying the bracing breezes of the Sclerotic Wold, or the weather of whatever place I happen to be, and literally sing for my supper for the bumpkins, buffoons, and the occasional boffin." It was only now he let some of the bitterness bottled inside slip out. "That song is, indeed, the joke of my life, and if you should care to take mine for the creation of it, well, Çalaht's blessings on the knife you plunge into my heart."

Silence engulfed them. A deep silence, born of travail and a life skewered by fate and roasted over the flames of what might have been. It blanketed those who listened, enveloping them in a palpable sadness.

"That. Was. An. Amazing. Story!" Jerome's enthusiasm for his hero blurted forth unbidden, shattering the pensive mood. "I can't wait to tell it to my mother, who also loves your work, by the way. And I—"

People were already shushing Jerome when Blister held up a finger to still what he recognized as a coming torrent. "Thank you, my friend," he said. "Your love of my work is a balm. But I suggest you observe custom, lest we find ourselves unwelcome here."

Jerome nodded an "of course."

"Well, my new friends, I must sing for the fine meal I just consumed." He stood, bowing to them. "Perhaps we can continue this conversation on my break." And without waiting for their reply, he strode across the room toward a lute that stood waiting, found his stool on a narrow platform nearby, and tuned the instrument.

Like the bard he should have been, Jaminity Delgado Blister sang, joked, told stories, painted word pictures from history, and shared wisdom with a room that started almost empty but ended up crammed full. It lasted hours and was as good as anything Eloise had ever seen at Court. Jerome sat rapt, absorbing every word and nuance. It was cute to see him so smitten. Eloise put aside her discomfort at proximity to so many people, with their coughs, sniffles, and sneezes, and shared the joy of entertainment at its finest. Even "Three Bags of Groats for My Sweetheart," which closed out the evening, was delivered with a verve and energy that made it seem as fresh as ever. She expected to have it stuck in her head for a week, but at least she'd have Blister's voice in her head, and not Jerome's pale imitation.

Blister came back to their table during his breaks, and in the snatches of conversation, they learned he was also heading to the Sclerotic Wold, which is why he found himself in Name Goes Here. He hoped to find a way to perform in the castle, if not for the queen herself. "I've played there before, but it has been a while," he said. "It was in a phase where I absolutely refused to play That Song. Rule One of bardic practice is you have to give them what they need, but also what they want. I spent five years refusing to do the latter, and my last performance for Her Majesty Onomatopoeia was during that time. She saw fit to ban me from the castle. I'm hoping to undo the damage."

"Perhaps we can help," said Eloise. "Do you ride?"

"Yes, whenever I can."

"I'll have to ask, but we have a seat you can use, if you don't mind sharing it with a chameleon. We can make your trip to the castle a little faster, and perhaps a little more comfortable."

His look of relief told Eloise everything she needed to know.

"After we break fast, then," she said.

❧ 54 ❧

WINDWARD WALL

Alejandro and Jaminity were immediate best friends. They shared a love of song and a flair for the dramatic. The eight travelers relished the unusually sunny, calm day, and covered the remaining strong lengths to the heart of the Sclerotic Wold in good time, accompanied by duets between Alejandro and Jaminity. They harmonized perfectly. That Song was not sung, nor were any love letters to Andalusian mares, but they had enough tunes in common to keep themselves and the others entertained the whole way, right up to when Alejandro needed to be quiet to cross through the gates into the town of the Sclerotic Wold. They even cajoled Cäääsëëëy into joining them for a chorus now and then, breaking his habit of silence, with a shy voice that was unused to any strain.

In between, Eloise let Lorch fill Jaminity and Cäääsëëëy in on their trip so far. She noted that he kept to bare facts, but even unembellished, she could see that it intrigued them. Cäääsëëëy, breaking silence, asked about the route they'd taken, and the decisions that led them to choose the roads and trails they did. Jaminity homed in on the deception, digging into the clues and trying to work out definitively if Turpy was a longwalker.

On a short break for lunch, Jaminity asked a question that was obvious in hindsight, but which had escaped the others. "What will you do when you get to the Sclerotic Wold?"

One did not simply knock on the front door of a queen's castle unannounced and expect to be taken to her. Royal visits were normally preceded by correspondence and diplomatic preparations. Plus, there was the small matter of identity. Eloise had never met Onomatopoeia, so could not expect the Southie Queen to recognize her, nor did she have official papers to present as evidence. For all the queen would know, Eloise was just someone off the road in bad need of a week-long bath and skilled attention to her hair.

To answer Jaminity, Eloise said, "I don't know. We'll figure something out."

They reached the town walls of the Sclerotic Wold toward dusk. The walls were a feat of engineering boldness. Their designers had one main goal: keep the Çalaht-blasted winds from assaulting the castle. So they planned high, sloping walls at a carefully calculated distance around the castle. These walls would be tall enough and gradual enough to scoop up the incoming winds, heave them above the castle, and let them land on the far side, just beyond the far wall. It was an audacious, expensive, and daring design.

The queen at the time, Onomatopoeia's great-great grandmother, Queen Palindrome Banister Lúüùderming IV, had approved the plans and their funding, declaring, "We shall deploy coin from near and far. Let us break these horrible winds!" That the wall would run roughshod through some of the poorest areas surrounding the castle was of no concern. The wall was "The Most Important Project of Our Times," and so construction began. The poor were shoved out of the way, left to live on one side or the other, but inevitably in the massive wall's near-constant shadows. Over a decade of toil and privation, the Windward Wall, as it was named, rose up to nestle the castle and surrounds in comfort and calm.

And really, it should have worked.

And it would have.

Except for the small matter of a decimal point.

One of the planners dropped a decimal in his calculations. Easy enough to do, and if the people involved weren't so dogmatic in their desire for the wall to be built exactly as specified, they might have picked it up in time to do something about it.

But they didn't.

The result was an order-of-magnitude error in wall location and height, which meant that instead of lifting the winds and passing them to the other side, the walls lifted them up and dropped them directly in the middle of the circle—right on the castle. Queen Palindrome's residence became the focus of föhn, the midpoint of mistrals, the site of siroccos, the endpoint of eddies, the destination of diablos.

It was horrible, and there was no escape.

Plus, there was nothing the queen could do about it. She had practically bankrupted her realm to build the bloody thing—there was nothing left in the kitty to rework it or even tear it down.

And so they lived with it. Likely, that was why the Southie queens tended to be grouchy.

Of course, the poor also had to live with the Windward Wall, but there was a difference. The indigent of the Sclerotic Wold suddenly had a comfortable place to be, nestled at the foot of a massive wall that provided them lovely protection from the elements. It made their collective lives immensely better, and they thanked their queens for it.

That, too, tended to make the queens cranky.

By the time Eloise and her companions reached the Windward Wall, they had formulated a plan. First, they would find a friend of Jaminity's who owned a shop in town, and see if they could stay with her. Then, somehow, Eloise would try to present herself to the queen with none of the diplomatic rigamarole that normally preceded such visits. She'd enquire of the queen if Doncaster had been received by her recently and, if so, if Johanna was with him. In that case, they'd continue following his trail.

And if not?

They would head back north toward the Half Kingdom and try to find her there.

✥ 55 ✥

AUCTION

They passed through the Windward Wall at a fully staffed checkpoint around mid-afternoon. They were not individually scrutinized, as they had been at the Adequate Wall, but the guard asked plenty of questions, made notes, and inspected their sparse baggage. Once inside, they found a bustling town full of earnest people going about what looked like important business—but then, everything in The South appeared important. If a queendom reflects the tone set by its monarch, then Queen Onomatopoeia must be the most no-nonsense, controlling person in all the realms.

Jaminity's friend's shop was in the oldest part of town, near the greatest density of Çalahtist devotional houses. He led them through streets that became less planned and narrower the closer they got to the heart of the old section. The three horses eventually had to go single file to pick their way past shops, inns, multi-storied homes, and a surprisingly large number of governance buildings—or maybe an unsurprisingly large number, given the amount of bureaucratic over-sight they'd already encountered. Jaminity led them through the tightening maze like he'd been that way a hundred times, and eventually they found themselves in a hexagonal plaza dominated by dozens of the largest Çalahtist devotional houses Eloise had ever seen—massive stone buildings that rose to the sky in arching tribute to the gap-toothed one. "Why so many, so close?" asked Eloise.

"A remnant of more extreme times," said Jaminity. "The different strands of Çalahtism didn't always tolerate diversity of devotion. Neo-Çalahtic Purists wouldn't be seen dead with Methodological Reformationists. Progressive Literal Parapatetics would rather have had their artificially gapped teeth filled in with plaster than say a devotion next to a New Interpretive Salvationist. Modernist Universal Defenders of Faith took umbrage if Ecclesiastic Ecstatics even looked at them. And everyone hated the Pietistic Sisterhood, which was understandable, given their tendency toward extreme tattooing and meeting any disagreements in scholarly debate with axes.

"Back when Çalahtism was shaking out, everyone jostled for the best spots along the Plaza of Her Agonizingly Difficult and Much Longer Than Anyone Might Have Expected Birth and built the most dominating structures they could conceive, hoping to attract followers, repel those who disagreed, and crowd out the weak. Their intolerances and prejudices are writ large in the stone architecture we see here today."

"So, where is your friend's shop?"

Jaminity pointed. "Over there, where that crowd is."

The shop, Something Sacred This Way Comes, was the lower floor of a two-story building crammed between a huge Orthodox Anachronists devotional house and a domineering one for the Delirium Liturgical sect (commonly called the Happy Clappers). The shop specialized in devotional supplies of all kinds, and with so many houses of worship nearby, must have done a massive trade.

Jerome tugged Eloise's sleeve, indicated the shop above, then rubbed his stomach. Above Something Sacred This Way Comes was Leaven, the most famous bakery in all the realms. Leaven had been in business almost as long as the Gumballs had been on the throne, similarly handed down along family lines. Their pumpernickel loaves defied logic, tasting of eloquence and braggadocios certainty. Their kaiserin rolls had a majesty that marched across your taste buds. Their veggie pasties were poetry in a pastry. And if you knew who to ask and on which secret days, you could get a sourdough cobb that could induce a state of bliss not far off what the Happy Clappers achieved using prattleweed. Eloise had heard rumors back home that if Chef ever took any time off, she spent it apprenticing at Leaven. It was that good.

Or so it was said. Eloise had never had any of Leaven's bread because it was impossible to transport a loaf as far as Castle de Brague without it turning into a weapons-grade stony oblong. She looked forward to seeing if the bakery's reputation was matched in reality.

In front of the two shops was the most amused group of onlookers Eloise had yet seen in The South. A short man with a bald head and a waist-length beard stood on a fruit crate behind a small lectern, and even then, he could only just see over it. He held a ball peen hammer, and the eyes of the crowd were on him and two people directly in front of him. On the left, arms crossed and face set in expressionless determination, was a woman who towered over everyone by at least two heads. Her dress, a sober black cotton wrap, was embroidered with generic Çalahtist symbols in taupe thread. She wore her gray hair braided and bunned, and her only concession to make-up was a discreet eyeliner.

On the right was a man as short as the woman was tall, and as round as she was thin. He wore a baker's apron and hat, and the traditional blue-and-white striped baker's breeks. His nervousness was betrayed by sweat dripping from his stringy, thinning ginger hair, and the way his hands fluttered and his leg jigged. That someone with so much agitated movement could be so rotund seemed impossible.

"Oh, I think I know what's going on," said Jaminity. "This should be fun to watch." He led them to crowd in as close as possible so they could observe whatever it was.

The man with the extensive beard was an auctioneer, hence the ball peen hammer, used instead of a gavel. He shuffled documents and recited formalities to set up the sale. The property under the hammer was a flight of steps—specifically, the steps that led from the ground floor next to Something Sacred This Way Comes up to Leaven. Those steps had been a source of friction for decades.

The baker's great-great-grandmother, who ran Leaven, was prone to a wager, and known for coming out on the better side of her bets. She was also a devout Numerological Calculationist, a Çalahtist sect known for assigning values to words in the *Scrolls of Çalaht*, then using them to predict sacred occurrences. The man who owned the shop where Something Sacred This Way Comes stood was a bubbly Eastern Lands olive merchant. He was also a Relaxed Revelationist, whose entire dogma consisted of, "Eh, we'll see about that." The two of them had a deep friendship spiced with vociferous religious disagreement.

One year, the Leaven owner and her fellow Numerological Calculationists became convinced that scripture pointed to the end of the world on a certain date a few months away. She was so fixated on it she told everyone who would listen to "prepare their affairs and say their prayers." Her olive-selling friend refused to buy into it, saying, as befitted his faith, "Eh, we'll see."

This infuriated her. How could he be so cavalier about the onrushing calamity that dominated her life? She erupted into a flurry of righteous argumentation, determined to win him over for the good of his own soul.

But he remained true to his sect. "Eh, we'll see."

No amount of cajoling, inveighing, conniving, or badgering would move him to take steps that would see his soul go to stand at Çalaht's side. So finally she could think of nothing else to do but wager against him.

Her friend thought this a profoundly stupid idea, so when she asked what they could bet, he named the most idiotic and inconvenient thing he could think of: the steps up to her shop. If she won, well, the world would have ended and he would have been unprepared to stand with Çalaht. And if she lost, he would get the title to the steps and could charge rent for their use.

The bet was absurd. But she shook on it.

Unsurprisingly, the alleged end of the world came and went. The Numerological Calculationists wiped metaphorical egg off their faces and went on with their lives, continuing to look for clues to the future in the numbers they crunched, the steps to the bakery changed hands, and the baker and her descendants had been paying rent ever since.

But now, the owner's family line had petered out, and the flight of steps was up for sale. The baker wanted to buy it back and end the absurdity. But Jaminity's friend wanted it too. She was, like the original olive vendor, a Relaxed Revelationist, and felt that lessons learned ought not be forgotten. Owning the steps would help ensure that Relaxed Revelationist dogma remained in people's minds. Plus, it amused her that the baker might remain vexed by his great-great-grandmother's foolishness.

Formalities covered, the auctioneer began his repetitious, rhythmic bid calling. "I'm looking for an opening bid, an opening bid, who'll give me an opening bid?"

"Ten thousand," said the woman.

The crowd gasped, then laughed. It was an absurdly high price. You could buy a decent small house for that. The baker looked shocked, then indignant, then resolute.

"I got ten, how about fifteen, who'll give me fifteen thousand..." The patter went on until the baker said, "Eleven."

"Twelve," said the woman.

The auctioneer chanted his way to 15, then 20, then 22, where it stalled with the baker ahead. Sweat poured from him. "I've got 22, now who'll give me 23, 23? I'm looking for 23." The auctioneer looked at the woman, who looked back, blank-faced. "Madame, it is over to you. Will you give me 23, now 23? No? Going, going..."

"Thirty thousand," she interrupted.

Another gasp from the crowd. The flight of steps was fetching more coin than many would see in two decades. For the baker, that was it. His posture collapsed, and he resigned himself to continuing to live with the absurd situation. The auctioneer knew it was over, but continued for form's sake. "I got 30, 30 is what I got. Now 32, who'll give me 32, I'm looking for 32." He paused and looked at the baker one last time, who shook his head. The bearded auctioneer wrapped up with, "Going... Going... Gone!"

Then he slammed the ball peen hammer down on the lectern once, pointed it at the woman, and said, "And she's buying a stairway to Leaven."

MADAME RIGHTEOUS

Jaminity's friend was named Súüùsáään Jóöònéëès, but everyone called her Madame Righteous, including Jaminity. He gave his friend a hug in the stairwell she had just purchased, and it was immediately clear how deep their friendship went. For one, they dropped into a kind of shorthand commonly seen among couples, construction planners, and spies. It was also clear that Jaminity allowed her to call him "Jammer," but with a soft "j" and the "er" at the end as "ay," so it came out "zhahmay." Another coupleism.

The kiss, too, was a giveaway.

Jaminity introduced them and Súüùsáään invited them into her shop after telling Hector where the horses might find a stable nearby. She apologized that she couldn't accommodate them herself. Cäääsëëëy silently went with Hector, Alejandro, and the Nameless One, leaving Eloise, Jerome, and Lorch with Jaminity and Súüùsáään.

Something Sacred This Way Comes was a Çalahtist's paradise. It was filled with texts, texts about texts, commentaries, commentaries about the commentaries, commentaries on the texts about texts, and even profane writings for those who preferred to face their blasphemies head-on. Then there was all the hardware of Çalahtist devotional practice: pipes, hookahs, braziers, scales, thuribles and other censers, rosaries—truly anything someone might want to support a prayer methodology. In a secured part of the shop was the prattleweed itself, brought in from the few places it was cultivated, then categorized, rated, and made available in weak weights and fractions of weak weights.

On the walls hung Çalahtist tapestries depicting key moments in the Divine One's life, including a particularly gruesome piece covering her formative childhood hanging-from-a-doorknob-wearing-jester-shoes tribulation.

Súüùsáäàn found Eloise staring at it. "Horrific, no?"

"Yes, a very realistic rendering," said Eloise.

"Actually, I have to disagree. The artist has taken several liberties."

"Oh?"

"For one, the shoes should be red. Given we still have them stored in a vouched-for reliquarium, we know they were not green, as shown here. Second, the gap in her teeth is exaggerated. She looks like she is missing a whole tooth, which is wrong. Also, see how the artist has emphasized the elongation of the thumbs? Records show they dislocated, but they did not stretch like they were putty."

"There are two schools of thought on that," said Eloise. "So you are a Thumbs Dislocationist, and not a Thumbs Elongationist?"

"The scrolls are clear on it, to my reading, anyway. Still, you find a lot of poetic license in Çalahtism. But..." Súüùsáäàn waved a hand to indicate distaste. "I can barely stand to have the thing on my wall."

That surprised Eloise. "Why keep it, then?"

"A gift from a client. They like to think I appreciate the extra steps they take to schmooze and flatter me so that I might keep their special devotional needs supplied. I would, of course, do it anyway. It's simply business."

A somber, gray-robed assistant came up to her. "All is ready, Madame."

"Thank you," said Súüùsáäàn. "You'll mind things for a while?"

"Of course, Madame."

Súüùsáäàn led them through the back of the shop and into her home, a lavish apartment with artwork covering every inch of the walls, woven rugs brought in from the Western Lands and All That Really Matters, and furniture that would feel perfectly at home in the Legs Not Arms. A glass case displayed a range of rare Eastern Lands jarred olives, which she showed with great pride. Apparently the last olive merchant who had the space had passed away suddenly, and the cache of prized olives lay forgotten in the cellar until Súüùsáäàn took over the shop and unearthed them.

The servant's comment "All is ready" referred to a generous afternoon tea, laid out on formal china and served by a bespectacled orangutan in formal attire who had the most beautiful manners and grace Eloise had ever seen in one dedicated to service. "Thank you, Áäàlfred," said Súüùsáäàn as haggleberry tea, leek tarts, and savory biscuits were served, along with a plate of fruit placed on a low table in the middle.

Eloise looked around while Áäàlfred served and realized something wasn't quite right. It took a moment to figure it out, and then it hit her: there were no religious symbols, accoutrements, or images of any kind. Someone who dropped in there with no idea of who the owner was would never have guessed anything about her inner life, except that she had a penchant for romantic fictional scrolls, good taste in Repressionist School artwork, and the means to acquire both in volume.

Jerome saw Eloise looking around and picked up on what she had noticed. "I thought she was 'Madame Righteous.' Where's all the religious stuff?" he asked in a low whisper.

Súüùsáäàn replied. "First, Master Jerome, feel free to speak at full voice here. I give little truck to the prejudices against non-humans that many of my fellow Southies have. As for the whole 'Madame Righteous' persona, well, it works well in there." She gestured toward the shop. "And out there." She waved to indicate the world at large. "But in here, it is understood to be more ironic."

"I see," said Jerome. "And thank you."

Over their tea, Jaminity gave Súüùsáään a fuller picture of who the others were and why they were there. "Well, my dear, you've picked up interesting company," she said, touching his arm. "But if Doncaster has been here, it was done in extreme stealth. My network has said nothing. And from what I know of him, he likes a bit of a splash. I'll ask around, but my guess is that you've been led astray, as you suspect. In the meantime, two things. First, please be my guests here as long as you would like."

"Thank you, Madame Righteous," said Eloise. "That is most kind."

"Second, assume your presence will be known to all. Your progress from the border has likely been tracked. They may not think you are who you say because of the lack of papers and the way you have been traveling, but don't assume anonymity. I no longer have much of an in with Her Maj Ono, because her quarter-wit brother opened a devotional supply shop on the edge of town, and she feels obligated to send royal custom his way. But I do have a piece of advice. I suggest you try to formally present yourself to the queen. For a royal of your stature to come and go unannounced would be unseemly, official delegation or not."

"I'll see what I can do to get an audience," said Eloise.

Áäälfred showed Eloise to a private room where a hot bath awaited her, as well as another orangutan, who introduced herself as Áäälfred's daughter Áäälice. She had an hour or two before she needed to emerge for the evening, so grabbed the chance to soak away the grime of travel. Áäälice convinced Eloise to let her help with her hair, so for the first time since she had left Castle de Brague, it was untied, washed to remove road debris, washed again for the dirt, and washed a third time just because it felt good. And then, over an entire hour,

Áäàlice combed and oiled it into submission. The result was an elegant knot that Eloise was sure would hold as well and as long as Odmilla's journeyman's braid, but which she herself could never reproduce.

Áäàlice chatted amiably about life with Madame Righteous and in the Sclerotic Wold. She thought Her Maj Ono was grumpy but fair, and a little stuffy when it came to Çalahtism. At least she had become a fellow of the New Çalahtic Fellowship like her brother. It was difficult on everyone when she was in the Pious First Zealous Devotion, because "So the queen, so the queendom," and thank Çalaht she wasn't a Happy Clapper anymore. Áäàlice wound back to more personal chat, confiding that she had a young suitor who her father did not yet know about, and that he had asked her to a dance, which meant it was all about to come to a head. For Eloise, lost to perpetual worry, it was a relief to let her mind wander with the girl's frivolity.

Áäàlice helped Eloise into her just-in-case dress, and took her travel clothing to launder and mend, leaving the cloak for Eloise, as the evening was expected to be cool. Not that Eloise would have let the cloak out of her sight.

TWIN SOULS OF DIFFERENT SPECIES

T he evening started with dinner at an inn called the Gordian Naught. The food was ordinary fare, but it was soon clear why the venue had been chosen: Madame Righteous organized for Jaminity to perform, and the place was packed—a home crowd who knew and loved him. They hung on every musical phrase and sang along with every tune. He even did That Song to start off. It was wonderful to be there, seeing the performer in his element, and a relief to let go the constant worry about Johanna, if just for a little while. Even Cäääsëëëÿ, who joined Eloise, Jerome, Lorch, and Madame Righteous, seemed to smile, and if Eloise wasn't mistaken, he even hummed along a few times.

But Jaminity had something extra planned. As the candles burned low and yawns began to exert themselves, he unexpectedly stopped in the middle of his last set, picked up his chair and carried it and his lute over to a window, which he opened grandly, revealing nothing.

He turned to his audience and held wide his arms. "Ladies and gentlemen, human and non-human alike. We are friends, are we not? We do not share the narrow concerns of some of our fellows, do we? This is a private space, yes?"

Eloise wasn't sure where this was leading, but noticed the crowd murmured assent.

"I have traveled long and wide, and have had the chance to perform with many talented artists, some who you know and most you do not. Rarely, someone crosses my path who makes me stop and think 'Hmm. That's something.'" He reached for a sip of water, letting the pause linger. "Well, my friends, you and I are in for a treat, because we have a 'That's Something' here with us tonight, and I can't wait to introduce you to him. More to the point, I can't wait to join voices with him. Ladies and gentlemen, I give you, for the first time on stage, Alejandro Diego Ferdinando Felipe Esteban Iglesias Desoto de Lugo!"

Alejandro pranced up to the window and put his head through. He wore a jaunty, wide-brimmed hat of velour, which he tossed into the crowd (strategically aimed at Eloise, who caught it). The audience clapped and stomped their approval. "Dammas y caballeros! It gives me great pleasure to be here tonight. I—" He gave his usual, dramatic pause, but held it longer than normal, which showed just how thrilled he was to be sharing the stage. "I, Alejandro Diego Ferdinando Felipe Esteban Iglesias Desoto de Lugo shall provide you entertainment tonight with my new friend Jaminity Delgado Blister." Like Madame Righteous, he pronounced it with a soft "j," giving the name a slightly more exotic flavor.

As performers, they were made for each other. Sometimes Jaminity took the lead and Alejandro sang harmony, and sometimes it was the other way around. But their manner and banter blended as well as their voices, and they worked their way through "Last Carriage to Clarksville," "Take Me to the River Thurmond (And Drop Me in the Water)," "Rice Malt Magnolia," and a Southie favorite, "Come On Éëèm̃léëèéëèn." The crowd would not let them go, demanding encore after encore. When they finally finished with "When Doves Laugh" and "Mamas Don't Let Your Babies Grow Up to Be Jesters," it was well beyond late and Eloise was filled with the joy of having witnessed something unexpected and special, twin souls born of different species coming together to create beauty. It was a wonder to see and hear.

A perfect evening.

❧ 58 ❧

FOR SPEAKING IN PUBLIC

The evening air was damp, as expected, and the winds blew the moisture through even the most determined clothing. But Eloise could ignore it, still filled by the warmth of the evening at the Gordian Naught as she, Jerome, Lorch, and Cäääsëëëy walked the several blocks back to Something Sacred This Way Comes. Jaminity, Alejandro, and Madame Righteous were still at the inn talking to thrilled fans and giving Alejandro the chance to bask in the successful performance. They'd meet up at breakfast to work out a strategy for seeing the queen.

In the streets radiating away from the Plaza of Her Agonizingly Difficult and Much Longer Than Anyone Might Have Expected Birth, devotional houses for the most obscure Çalahtist sects were still, even these days, cramming themselves into every available cranny, as the nooks had already been filled, and were completely out of reach of anyone without an unreasonable hoard of coin. As for the larger non-nook, non-cranny options, they had been conquered centuries before, and anything within a razordisc throw of the plaza itself was murderously difficult to get. Not that sects didn't sometimes try.

There was a kind of ladder of acceptability that sects could climb, moving from cranny to nook to larger, but distant space, to one closer to the plaza. It all depended on how many people were attracted to what they offered, and how much those believers were willing to cough up. Every few decades, one of the older, established sects would crumble under the weight of skew-whiff doctrines and outmoded beliefs and declare both financial and religious bankruptcy. Their assets would be devoured by more opportunistic, nimble, broadly appealing groups, and one would take their spot in the cluster of devotion that ringed the plaza. The more fringe the belief system, the further away from Çalaht's birthplace they were located. It was hard, centuries-long work to move anywhere near one of the spots on the plaza itself.

Eloise found herself curious about how the sects differentiated, and stopped to read the noticeboards outside some of the houses. Each had a ten-point Summary of Practice that was displayed, as required by law, in a prominent location within five lengths of the front door. Some sects prided themselves on the literal interpretation of the *Scrolls of Çalaht*, or on rejecting specific scrolls as heresy. Others emphasized particular qualities, such as fellowship, equality, openness to ideas, cherishing difference, promoting peace, singing in harmony, or a preoccupation with food. Some focused on extreme devotional practices, like one that engaged in radical prattleweed use to induce constant glossolalia (as opposed to the occasional speaking in tongues that more mainstream sects encouraged). Eloise wasn't sure how someone who was always mumbling gibberish could function well in society. She figured they relied on gestures a lot.

It was Eloise's curiosity about practice and beliefs that got them surrounded by Happy Clappers.

The building was dingy and low-storied, the outside barely lit, which was unsurprising, given how late it was. The associated noticeboard was bright, with candles shielded from the wind casting a warm, inviting glow. Eloise stepped over to it to indulge her curiosity, and the others followed. A florid, barely legible hand-scrawled placard declared that the devotional house belonged to the First and Last Chance No

Really We Mean It House of Delirium Liturgical Correctness, and its Summary of Practice proclaimed the worst, most intolerant, inflexible, stuffy, and strictly-humans-only bunkum that Eloise had ever sullied her eyes with.

The clap took them by surprise—it was single, sharp, and in perfect unison. Eloise spun around to find that they were trapped against the wall by a semicircle of bodies five deep. That was why the noticeboard was so well lit—to lure unsuspecting people in and blind them to the people spilling out from both sides of the building in complete silence.

Lorch and Jerome instinctively jumped in front of Eloise, bumping into each other as they did. Under different circumstances it might have been funny, but this was far from it.

The four dozen people started a slow clap, maybe once every ten seconds. Their faces were obscured by hoods and the dark of night. The slow claps bounced in muffled echoes through the foggy air, and there was menace in their manner, which Eloise found distinctly at odds with the friendly tone of Çalaht's teachings, dislocated thumbs notwithstanding.

She stepped back in front of Lorch and Jerome, said a curt, "G'midnight" to them and went to leave.

No one moved. She would have to shove her way through, an unappetizing prospect, not just because she'd have to touch some of them to do so.

The clapping sped up slightly, still slow, but the energy of it raised a notch.

"Please, good people," she said, raising her voice. "We would go past, please."

No response.

"If this is an attempt to convert, rest assured, my soul is well and truly catered for."

"Her soul is catered for. Did you hear that?" A woman's voice. Low, mocking, and as pleasant as a horseshoe nail scraping glass. "Your soul is catered for. Like a nice picnic? Or a fancy dinner? Now isn't that just grand."

"I have no argument with you over the teachings of the Divine One," said Eloise. "We would be on our way."

"On your way, you'd be, eh?" The woman stepped from the side of the crowd. "It is not so simple. Let me ask you a question." She sauntered forward like she had all the time in the world, accompanied by the rhythmic claps. "Have you relinquished this well-catered soul of yours to Çalaht?"

"Yes, in my own way, I think I have." Eloise was a head-and-a-half shorter than the woman, and drew herself up to full height to avoid being cowed by her (a phrase offensive to bovines of all kinds). The truth was, Eloise went through the motions of religion as Court and some obscure bits of Protocol required, but did not find it much of a comfort, and preferred to ignore it.

The woman raised a finger and pointed it at her. Lorch tensed, which made Jerome do the same, but Eloise waved them down. The finger was jabbed in Eloise's direction. "There you'd be wrong."

"Wrong?"

"Wrong. Dead wrong. Eternally wrong." She joined in the clapping and led it to speed up just a little. Then she threw her arms wide. "There is only one way, catered-soul girl. When we say, 'First and Last Chance,' we mean it. I saw you reading our divine Summary of Practice. It is the only way to stand at Çalaht's side. The rest of them..." She slowly drew a circle with an upturned palm, implying all the other devotional houses. "The rest of them are demonstrably, provably, irretrievably, and sinfully wrong. As are you."

"Well, thank you for those kind and generous thoughts. But now, please step aside, as we'll be on our way." Eloise pitched her voice somewhere between unconcerned and annoyed. She really didn't want this to turn into a confrontation if she could avoid it.

The clapping sped up, and the group also took a couple of steps, closing in on them. Eloise could feel Lorch weighing his options, working out vulnerabilities, thinking through how much damage might need to be done to get out of this.

"Well, now, Catered Soul. We'd like to invite you and your friend here," she said, pointing to Lorch, "to come inside and join us in preparing yourselves properly to stand with Çalaht." Apparently Cäääsëëëy and Jerome did not exist.

"That's most kind of you," said Eloise. "But it will have to be another time."

The clapping sped up again. It was getting on Eloise's nerves. Why they were called happy clappers was a mystery—there was no joy in this exercise.

That's when Jerome stepped forward, putting himself between Eloise and the woman. "I have a theological question for you, Madame, if I may." The woman was clearly surprised, but chose to ignore Jerome. She opened her mouth to say something else to Eloise, but Jerome interrupted. "Do the Delirium Liturgists believe in the stretched thumbs doctrine or the dislocated thumbs doctrine for that particular tribulation? I'm a Thumbs Dislocationist, myself, but I was wondering what you believe."

The woman couldn't help herself. "You are showing your ignorance, rodent. Delirium Liturgists are always Thumbs Elongationists. Except for the heretics. Now shut your mouth..."

"I don't get that," Jerome continued, yelling to make his voice heard over the claps. Eloise realized he was trying to bamboozle the woman. "Have you ever had anyone pull your finger? It doesn't stretch. Not really. I mean, a little. But if you were hanging from a doorknob like she was, the nature of your fingers doesn't suddenly change. They'd pop out of their joints. Thumbs Elongationism is—and I say this with great respect—flat-out stupid."

There was a gasp, and the clapping faltered. They were not used to being insulted by chipmunks. "How dare you!" The woman bent over to address him directly. "She was divine! That her thumbs could stretch is a given. One such as she could have done anything!"

"Except, you know, get herself off the doorknob. If she was so holy and miraculous, why didn't she just float off the doorknob?"

There were shouts of "Heretic!" and "Blasphemer!" The woman, spittle gathering at the corners of her mouth, looked like she wanted to kick him. "How dare you question the Divine One. One such as she has abilities that surpass our imaginations."

Down the street, the night watch noticed there was a kerfuffle and turned toward it.

"Oh, I have a pretty good imagination," smirked Jerome. "So you're telling me that, instead of having her thumbs either stretched, which is nonsense, or dislocated, which is the truth, she could have, say, turned herself into a chamber pot, fallen to the ground, shattered, put herself back together, turned back into a gap-toothed woman, and walked out the door?"

"Why you—"

"If she has such abilities as surpass our imaginations, as you so eloquently phrased it, why not adopt my chamber-pot escape plan?"

"There is no chamber-pot escape in the *Scrolls of Çalaht.*"

"All I'm saying is there could have been. She could have escaped. Instead, she allowed herself to endure the most mind-numbingly dumb tribulation that the authors of the scrolls could think of."

"She wrote the scrolls herself!"

"What, from the grave? No wonder the quillmanship was so bad. No, my moronically clapping friend, the scrolls date to 150 years after she graced the realms with her presence, which you would know if you read even the most cursory analyses done on the hemp parchments and plant inks used. Oh, you know what? Maybe the Escape of the Chamber Pot is one of the missing scrolls."

"We have all the scrolls!" The woman looked like she was ready to thump Jerome, but he was crowding forward toward her. Not liking his proximity, she stepped back. Jerome was trying to open up an escape route.

"You think you have the scrolls," said Jerome, stepping forward again. "But then, you're a Thumbs Elongationist, so your facility for critical inquiry and questioning of texts is impeded by your inability to string together a question that involves words of more than two syllables. Allow me to ask another question." Step, step, step, moving the woman back through the semi-circle of hooded onlookers, some of whom tried to get the clapping going again.

"Let me ask, doesn't your missing Scroll of the Escape of the Chamber Pot throw into question every one of your other beliefs? That must rock you to the core, to know that one of the key foundational bits of information about the life of the Divine One is nowhere to be seen. It must hurt to have everything crack open like that."

The woman stepped forward, halting her retreat. "I have no idea what you are saying, but to claim there is a missing Scroll of the Escape of the Chamber Pot is deeply offensive, and should be punishable by..."

She didn't get to finish her sentence. Eloise saw the night watch arrive at the edge of the gathering that was fast becoming a disturbance. There were two men and a woman wearing dark brown tunics, darker brown breeks, and even darker expressions. There was no "G'evening to you. What seems to be the matter?" as Eloise might have expected. They simply pushed through the Happy Clappers, who opened for them like they'd rehearsed it a dozen times before. One of the night watchmen grabbed Jerome and shoved him into an official-looking brown sack. He held it up for the night watchwoman, who stepped over to it. Speaking to the bag, she said, "In the name of Her Majesty Queen Onomatopoeia, we arrest you for the crime of using the Queen's Tongue in public."

"What?" Eloise was incredulous. "He was trying to get these Delirium Liturgists to back away. They were menacing us."

"That's not a valid reason for him to speak in public."

"You can't put him in a sack!" Eloise couldn't believe the indignity.

"Yes, we can," said the man holding the sack. "And I suggest you don't interfere."

"Give him back!" Eloise snatched at the bag and grabbed an edge. She tugged it, trying to get it away from him. From the corner of her eye, Eloise glimpsed the Happy Clapper woman, arms folded across her chest, looking smug. Why smug? What did she know?

She knew what the night watchwoman was about to do, which was to blindside Eloise and tackle her onto the cobblestone road. Eloise's head clopped a stone, and a small cut opened above her temple.

Reflexively, Lorch pulled the woman off Eloise and threw her aside. But before he could check if Eloise was OK, he, too, was tackled. Happy Clappers scattered as more night watchmen poured toward them. The last thing Eloise heard before they put a sack over her head was Jerome's squeal of indignation.

✣ 59 ✣

THE SNIGGERS OF CHIGGERS

Eloise's cell was a ground-level room about four lengths by three lengths—smaller than her parents' closet by half. Growing up, it had sometimes been a comfort to crawl in there and snuggle in among the clothing. But there was nothing cozy about a Sclerotic Wold jail cell. At least she was alone and could deal with her feelings of panic in solitude.

Except she wasn't.

In one corner of the cell lay a trussed-up stoat with a bandage around his muzzle that meant he was able to breathe, but could not open his mouth. He'd been faced toward the wall, and it looked and smelled like he'd been there a while. Eloise wasn't sure whether to help him or avoid him like the ague. For the time being, she chose the latter.

But the stoat wasn't the only sound in the room. Someone—no, some-ones, plural—were making a quiet, high-pitched noise. She couldn't quite place it.

There had been no attempt to let her explain. They didn't ask her who she was, put her through any legal process, or shown any sign of advocacy. They just shoved her in here, took the sack off her head, and slammed the door.

The cell had a raised stone platform that would have suited as a bed if she'd been the size of a pomeranian. It was covered with loose straw, which Eloise sincerely doubted would add any comfort. Besides, it smelled like the stoat might have been there before her. One corner had a bucket. She didn't even want to think about that.

The whispered sound continued. She had the feeling she was being watched. Not just watched, but judged. No, mocked.

Someone was mocking her with barely audible sniggering.

Chiggers! Not just chiggers—jail chiggers.

Jail chiggers had a reputation, and these were living up to it.

They were used by the penal authorities as a subtle form of Enhanced Discomfort. Their job was to mock, ridicule, and harangue newly arrived inmates to help break them down and make them more pliable to the system. Or, if they were innocent, grateful to be free again. It was also in their mandate to physically "interact" with the imprisoned using "natural means," leaving them welted and scratching.

Eloise leaned down so her face was almost touching the straw, trying to see them. But you didn't expect to see jail chiggers, which was part of what made them so maddening.

Eloise opted for diplomacy. "Blessings of the day to you," she said, as a faint light tinged the cell's walls. "I'm Eloise. Would you care to introduce yourselves?"

Laughter. Faint, barely audible derision.

This would not be fun.

Six hours later, she had a much clearer sense of just how not fun it would be. Itchy swellings covered the exposed sections of her body and were appearing in more covered spots. She knew the proper thing to do was to not scratch, but that was nigh on impossible. No amount of reasoned discourse, foul language (or what passed as such for her), or trying to ignore the chiggers worked. What made it worse was her own imaginings combined with the inability to address her habits, the urge of which in this confined, dismal place was driving her spare. She'd worked and reworked the prayer beads. She had counted the stones in the wall in a vertical order, then a horizontal one, until she got the same number in both directions. She'd found the few bits of straw she could bear to touch and arranged them in sets according to various patterns. Even, odd, even, odd. Then according to the count of her prayer beads. Then by dates of significant events in her life. Then in a cross-hatch pattern that got bigger by a multiple of the previous cross in the pattern.

It was a distraction, but not nearly enough.

She assumed Lorch was not far away, enduring his own confinement. But he trained for hardship and deprivation, so was probably as stoic as ever. Jerome was more likely to be looking like the stoat—shell-shocked and as close to panic as she was. Whether his jail chiggers were getting to him like they were getting to her depended on how good his hearing was.

Had Cäääsëëëy gotten away, or was he snatched up as well? He had said nothing, so maybe when the night watch arrived, he'd beaten a quiet retreat. If so, had he found his way back to the others to let them know what happened? Or had he decided expedience was the better part of valor and slunk away, never to be seen again? Maybe it wasn't worth burning away one's life to help someone you didn't know all that well, reciprocity or no reciprocity. If he had spoken to the others, were they trying to help her get out, or were they too familiar with the futility of the Southie system of punishment?

The jail chiggers wheedled and taunted. They predicted, as far as she could hear, that she would be there for decades. As the hours stretched, she began to think them right. So much for inheriting the throne. Or coming of age. Or finding a king to take her family name. She would lose her mind a short number of blocks from where Çalaht had emerged into the world.

Order. That's what she needed to create. More order. They'd frisked her to make sure she had nothing too dangerous on her, but they had left her with her travel cape, knowing its warmth would be needed when the winds of the Sclerotic Wold slammed their way through the holes and cracks of the jail. As the afternoon sun showed the first hints of dusk, Eloise decided to repack the cloak to see if she could make it more efficient, or just tidier. And to make it more of a challenge, she decided to do it with her eyes closed. Identify and move the objects by feel. That would give her hands something to do other than scratch. Oh, Çalaht dragging a dray, the itching!

The first object was easy—the prayer beads. She liked where they were in a pocket near her right hand, so left them there, within easy reach. Next, a forgotten fragment of dried apple, which she immediately ate as slowly as possible, and her copies of the *Scrolls of Çalaht* and the *Livre de Protocol*. Those last two needed to be higher in the cloak, as they jounced against her when she walked. She felt her way up the cloak's inside, searching for one of the more out-of-the-way pockets. She found a good candidate and reached in to feel what might be in there.

There was something. No, two things. Odd. She didn't remember packing anything there.

Eloise opened her eyes as she remembered what they were. They were the two envelopes her parents had given her when she left, all those weeks ago. In the press of departure and the admonitions for secrecy, she'd stowed them in the out-of-reach pocket and promptly forgotten them. The cloak had protected them against the elements, against being slept on, and against discovery.

Until now.

That was it. Eloise broke down in sobs, much to the amusement of the chiggers. Even the stoat seemed to notice, giving a small, exasperated moan. This unexpected closeness to her parents, these unremembered tokens of affection, brought the weight of her journey collapsing in on her. All the disappointments and discomforts, failing to get anywhere close to bringing home her sister, the gnawing itch of her unfulfilled habits, and all the loyalty, kindness, and support of those who accompanied her—all this was repaid by her sitting in a chigger-ridden jail cell that Çalaht herself would have trouble blessing. Everyone was right. She was constitutionally unsuited to this. If she'd learned anything it was that she really was better off cosseted and tended to behind the walls of Castle de Brague.

She held nothing back, tears plummeting, nose fauceting, chest heaving. After a while, even the chiggers gave her some privacy.

How pathetic. To melt down so badly that even jail chiggers felt sorry for you.

By the end, she was empty, spent emotionally and exhausted physically. At least it was an improvement over focusing on itching.

The envelopes. She'd better look at them while there was still light.

The first one was unlabelled. She carefully broke the wax seal, and inside found a folded piece of hemp parchment, with "Ëëëlöööïïïsëëë" written on the outside fold. It was the northernification of her name, her father's nickname for her. Tears welled again. It'd been years since he'd called her that. He must have been feeling soppy when he wrote it. She unfolded it and turned it over. There were just two words at the top of the page, written in his hand. "Gööööööd Fööörtüüünëëë." That was it. "Good fortune?" she mumbled. It didn't make sense. She squinted in the failing light to see if there was anything else on it.

The other envelope was also blank on the outside and contained folded hemp parchment. A single letter "E" was written on the outside fold in her mother's formal, overwrought quill. She always said she signed official documents with an ornate flourish to make them harder to forge and to give historians something to enjoy. The "E" was distinctly bereft of sop, but that was Two, wasn't it? Sitting in that jail cell, Eloise truly doubted she'd ever be "Three." She unfolded the page and turned it over. Like the one from her father, it had just two words: "Goode Fortuna." Nothing else. "Good fortune?" she mumbled again.

What had they been thinking? And that both should do it, each separate from each other?

The jail door slammed open, and Eloise scrambled to return the letters to their secluded spot. An ocelot in jail fatigues wheeled a pot on a cart. From its garlicky smell, it seemed there was some sort of soup in it. "Bowl."

"I'm sorry," said Eloise. "I don't have a bowl."

"Better get someone to bring you one." He raised his voice, addressing the stoat. "Bowl?"

The stoat shook his head, a tiny movement.

"Right," said the ocelot. He slammed the door closed.

"Wait!" yelled Eloise, pounding on the door. "What about food?"

The closed door muffled the ocelot's reply. "You need a bowl."

❧ 60 ❧

SPELLING

T he chiggers really got to work that night. Any mercy they might have shown when she was crying was well and truly gone. Eloise was hungry, scratching constantly, and drawing blood when she did.

And she was confused. What in the name of Çalaht's grizzled, gray, gap-toothed mien did the pieces of parchment mean? She tried to sleep sitting against the wall, and when that didn't work, convinced herself that the stone platform might be an acceptable option. It wasn't.

As morning light finally crept into the cell, Eloise brought out the parchments again.

No. There was definitely nothing else written on them. "Good fortune," she thought. "What a joke."

She tried smelling them, touching them all over, She even tasted each, and was immediately so hungry that she had to restrain herself from wadding one up and eating it. At least there would be a small amount of nutritional value.

She looked at the one from her father. Why "good fortune"? She concentrated and thought hard: "Good fortune." No new insights.

She tried holding the page up to the light. No change.

She tried reading it out loud. "Good fortune."

Nichts.

She looked at her mother's. Waved it around. Held it to the light. Read it out loud. Traced the letters with her fingers.

Nothing.

Back to her father's. Rubbed it. Crinkled it. Read it out loud: "Good fortune."

Nope.

This was a waste of time.

In complete frustration, she said out loud, "Why give me this? Why write..." She dropped into a mockery of his northern accent, emphasizing the overlong vowels. "Whÿ wrïtë 'Göööööd Fööörtüüünëëë'?"

A light buzzing filled her ears for half a second, there was the mildest hint of a tingle down her spine, and then the parchment disintegrated into dust.

A spell! Her father's note was a weak magic spell. Of course. He always said how much he'd liked spelling when he was younger; he had even represented his realm at an inter-realm spelling bee, coming in second place.

But things had changed since then. Spell magic had weakened so much that they didn't even teach it anymore. That's why it had taken Eloise so long to figure it out. Plus, spelling was complicated, and easy to get wrong. Whether you used a spelling checker or went through the spelling yourself, it was too easy to end up with a spelling mistake that would render the whole thing useless or give an unpredictable result. And even if you got it right, the effects were miniscule.

Still, it was cute that her dad had tried.

That her mother had tried was even cuter. As far as Eloise knew, her mother had no talent for spelling at all.

Solving the puzzle of the parchment lightened Eloise's mood, and she could think beyond the itch of her skin and the pang of her anxiety for the first time since the jail door had slammed behind her. And for the moment, the jail chiggers were leaving her alone, thank goodness. She stood up and, despite the smell and unsavory leak of fluids, took the few short steps over to the trussed stoat. "Excuse me. I apologize for not asking sooner. Is there something I can do to help you? Would you like me to undo your restraints?"

The stoat did not respond immediately, but flicked his eyes left and right, like he was assessing whether this was a good idea. Finally he nodded furtively.

Eloise knelt down and picked at the knot that secured the bandage around his muzzle. It had been tied by someone who knew their business, but she finally loosened it and slid it off. The stoat licked his lips and whispered in a rural Southie voice strangely like Odmilla's, "Thankth tho much, Mithtreth. Jutht undo the knot on the ropeth, but leave them ath they are. And hurry. The next thift of jail chiggerth will be here in a few moment."

The knot was complicated and tight, but she got it loose. The stoat didn't move at all. He said, "Thlide the bandage back on my thnout, and for the love of Thalaht, leave me alone, for your own thake." Eloise didn't understand that at all, but did as he requested. With the bandage back in place, he nodded a thank you and went back to staring at the wall.

Eloise resumed her spot across the cell. Five minutes later, the chigger whispers started up again, and she was scratching at new welts.

The food ocelot came and went, and since she still had no bowl, she still went hungry. Eloise couldn't believe she'd only been in the cell a little more than a day. Or was it two days? It was starting to seem like the only life she'd ever known. She couldn't imagine how people spent years in places like this.

Mid-morning, the jail door creaked open and a guard's voice announced, "The Speaker for the Indigent." Then to whoever was there, "There you go mu'um." In walked a mole. She wore a formal tunic, long hair (for a mole), which pointed in every direction, and a distracted air. She carried a satchel with scrolls poking out of it and an absurdly thick monocle that dangled from a chain. The mole almost bumped into Eloise, but she stopped, put the monocle in place and squinted through it, looking her up and down. "Human," she finally said, as if solving a great mystery. She turned toward the stoat. Much to Eloise's surprise, he made a massive show of struggling against his bonds.

"Hello, Éëèdgar," said the mole. "Any progress?"

The stoat shook his head and grunted "nuh-huh," but continued to wrestle frantically against the ropes. It was the most active he'd been since Eloise arrived.

"You're running out of time, you know," said the mole. She set down the satchel, rifled the scrolls, and pulled one out to unfurl. Putting her monocled eye as close to it as she could, she read through the writing. "Two more days." The monocle dropped off her face as she re-rolled the scroll.

The stoat made a sound that was close to "I know," then increased his dramatic struggle.

"Well, not much I can do until you do something or the clock runs out. Shall I check back tomorrow?" The mole's manner was polite and professional, with a certain motherliness that conveyed genuine concern over what was apparently one in a long string of hopeless cases.

The stoat did not answer. He flopped, rolled, and struggled, trying to free himself. Sweat mixed with whatever other fluids were already there, taking the smell up a notch.

"Keep heart," the mole told to him. She turned toward the door and was about to knock on it to call the guard, when the stoat gave a triumphant cry through his bandaged nose. He stood, letting the ropes slide off and puddle at his feet. The mole stopped, genuinely surprised. The stoat made a big show of having difficulty pulling off the loosed bandage, which he finally dropped to the ground. He fell to his knees, raised both paws skyward, and said, "Praithe be Thalaht! I'm free."

The mole walked over, put the monocle to her eye, and scrutinized the panting stoat. "Well, yes. So it seems. How unexpected." She seemed genuinely pleased. She straightened and said, in a voice aimed at the entire cell, "I would speak with the Duty Chigger." She leaned down, waiting. There was a moment's silence, then the tiniest fleck of nothing bounded to stand by her ear. "Has there been any impropriety?" she asked the speck.

The chigger shouted back, and Eloise could make out the response, "We've only just come on shift. He wasn't struggling before."

The mole turned to Eloise. "Human. Did you interfere with this prisoner's restraints?"

Eloise looked at the mole, then past her to the stoat, who gave the tiniest shake of the head. "No, ma'am. Of course not."

"Well, a most pleasing turn of events," said the mole. She called to the door. "Guard!"

The door creaked open again. "Yes, mu'um?"

"Take Éëèdgar here to the magistrate's chamber. And for goodness sakes, clean him up first this time."

"Yes, mu'um."

"Éëèdgar, it appears we might just get you released," said the mole. "Please don't curse at the magistrate this time."

"No, Madame Thpeaker for the Indigent," replied the stoat. "I'm reformed." Eloise wasn't sure how sincere he was, but was glad he wouldn't have to lie in his own wetness any longer.

"Deeds will speak louder than those words, Éëèdgar," said the mole. "Now go with the guard, and I'll catch up with you at the magistrate's door. I've got to find the Night Duty Chigger before we plead for mercy on your behalf."

The stoat limped toward the door, legs uncertain after being bound for so long. The guard grabbed him by the scruff, and Ééèdgar winked a thank you at Eloise.

"So," said the mole, turning her monocle toward Eloise, then letting it drop. "We may as well talk. My name is Júüùniper Peephole Burrow-duster," she said. "Speaker for the Indigent."

"Please to meet you. I'm Eloise."

"Like the Westie queen?" The mole whistled her incredulity. "Don't let her find out that's your name. She'll rip your lungs out." The mole chuckled, replacing her monocle and immediately dropping it again.

"So I've been told."

"Have you seen the magistrate?"

"No."

"Are you indigent?"

"Actually, I'm not sure," said Eloise.

"Well, do you have any coin?"

"Not at the moment, no."

"Congratulations. You're indigent." The mole addressed the cell again. "As Speaker for the Indigent, I request confidentiality with this prisoner. Can the Duty Chigger please take your shift from the cell?"

Within moments, the cell was free of chigger sniggers.

"You're lucky it is me, and not one of the others," said the mole. "And you're lucky you haven't been to the magistrate yet. Perhaps we can speed things along; I will insist it be me who speaks for you." The mole shuffled her satchel in front of her, pulled out a quill, ink, and parchment, patted the satchel flat, and sat behind it like it was a desk, ready to take notes. "Now, let's start with why a nice girl with a dangerous Westie name is getting chiggered in a dump like this."

So Eloise told her the basics, and in response to Júüùniper's questions, expanded the story until most of the tale was laid out.

"So you have no official papers." confirmed Júüùniper.

"No, unfortunately not."

"Well, whatever happens, it won't be dull," chuckled Júüùniper. "That will be a nice change for me, anyway. I can't wait to bring this one before the magistrate and see what old Nostril Flare has to say about it. I wonder if there's a way to prove you are who you say you are."

"And my champion, Jerome? My guard, Lorch?"

"I'll do what I can to find them. Odds are good your champion—a chipmunk, you say? Really?—is roped and muzzled like Éëèdgar was. Standard practice, I'm afraid. The human is probably being chiggered in another cell somewhere."

"Thank you for that." Eloise paused, curiosity piqued. "May I ask a question?"

"Of course."

"How is it you are allowed?"

"What? You mean to speak in public? To represent people even though I'm not human?" The mole snorted a suppressed laugh. "Somebody has to represent the impoverished and non-human, and none of the humans can be bothered. So I have a special dispensation. But it can only be in my official capacity. Otherwise, silence." The mole flipped open her satchel, shuffled scrolls aside, and pulled something out. "You'll need this."

"A bowl! Oh, thank you!"

"Don't get too excited. You haven't had any of what is passed off as food here yet."

"It can't be worse than starving."

"You'll find it a close second." The mole fumbled in her satchel again, fishing out (an expression offensive to sea-based non-humans) a small, sealed gallipot. She handed it to Eloise.

"What's this?"

"Wart cream from the Half Kingdom," said Júüùniper. "I'm not allowed to give you any anti-itch salve. Mandatory Enhanced Discomfort and all that. But you might find yourself with a sudden need to treat welts, sorry, warts, in which case, this might be useful. Don't tell anyone where it came from."

"Thank you, Madame Speaker for the Indigent," said Eloise. "You are truly kind."

The mole looked at Eloise with eyes that saw and didn't see. "Hmmm... You might actually be who you say you are."

With that, she called for the guard and trundled out of the cell.

✣ 61 ✣

LIVRE DE PROTOCOL

Besides the scratching, hunger, gnawing panic again, and immersion in a situation where her compulsions had few outlets, the hardest part of being in the cell was boredom. Eloise could count, and she did. She counted stones, cracks, and straws. Counted breaths, how long she could hold her breath, welts, and how long she could hold off scratching them. Counted the prayer beads. Counted with the prayer beads. But eventually, counting lost its entertainment value. Desperate for diversion, Eloise pulled out her travel copy of the *Livre de Protocol*. She'd used an old, huge, two-handled version when she had attended Protocols and Procedures in the Bibliotheca de Records and Regrets, and the text was not known for scintillating plot lines. "Dull as dirt" covered it. But compared to numbing boredom, the *Livre de Protocol* was a ripping yarn.

Eloise turned to the beginning, a preface called, "Herewith, The Protocols," as dry an introduction to as dry a set of subjects as one could ever hope to read. It included the rather bold claim (or maybe it was just a hope) that the *Livre de Protocol* "shall apply to all realms in all times." She spent a while with the table of contents, which promised sections on everything about court life: the hierarchy of servants and nobles; manners; choosing flower pots for particular occasions; the proper distance to stand from different levels of royalty; how to address a monarch in formal and informal settings (turns out it's the same); and a list of celebrations, feasts, fasts, and other ceremonial goings-on with rules for who does what and when. There were three full chapters on small talk, three on large talk, three on remaining silent, and three on appropriate mumbling. There were protocols about Protocol, a tedious, exceptionally complicated description about the steps required to change an item of protocol, and rules governing what to do if you needed to retire a copy of the *Livre* (it has to be buried during a new moon at the bottom of a hole exactly one length by one length by one length).

Eloise flicked through it. She didn't really want to read about the hemp parchment you use for the introduction cards of nobles whose holdings are less than 1000 square strong lengths, the six different things you can say when someone sneezes during a formal speech, or the proper way to tell a queen she has spinach stuck in her teeth. A random page turn brought her to a chapter called "Audiences, Requesting and Rebuffing." It was a lengthy set of pages written in a deliberately difficult style, which Eloise suspected was a way to be simultaneously informative and obscure. It set out how different levels of nobles went about gaining an audience with different levels of nobles, from someone with no lands at all but still keeping their title trying to meet with someone in the same situation, all the way up to a ruling queen trying to see a ruling king or queen. Protocol prescribed different measures according to the land you had, the title you had, how long you'd held both, and how much notice you were trying to give. And it was different again if it was a family member, not you, who had the title and land. So if you were a third cousin thrice removed from a noble with 50 square lengths of land that had only recently been granted, and you were just trying to pop in for a cup of haggle-berry tea, you had certain options (they were certainly not rights), but not many. The same could be said of a sitting monarch trying to see another sitting monarch—there were certain options, but not a lot, especially at short notice.

This was all matched by an equal mishmash of Protocol on the other side of the transaction, for the person granting or refusing the audience. It was relatively easy if both sides wanted to meet. Where it got hair-splittingly complicated was when the answer to what was essentially, "Hey, can we talk?" was inclined to be "Nup." Protocol couldn't force anyone to do anything, but it was definitely leverage that could be applied.

Eloise spent several hours wading through long paragraphs written in small, dense letters, trying to figure out where she fell into this confusion of Protocol stew. She was a direct offspring of a sitting monarch, but arriving with no notice, no retinue, and no documentation. Actually, she did have a bit of a retinue, but a significant percentage, and the most important of them, were also enjoying the hospitality of Her Majesty's night watch. The sticking point, unsurprisingly, was identity. She'd never met Queen Onomatopoeia, so couldn't rely on that. Eloise had no idea who she might know here in the Sclerotic Wold who had sufficient standing and familiarity with both her and the queen that Protocol would allow them to vouch for her reliably. Presumably there was someone. But who? And how to get in touch with them?

The gap between sitting in here, with jail chiggers providing their Enhanced Discomfort for her benefit, and curtsying, washed and groomed before an unfamiliar queen seemed unbridgeable.

The food ocelot showed up again. "Bowl."

Eloise handed it to him and he half-filled it with the gray potage he wheeled from cell to cell. From the first close-up whiff, Eloise understood exactly what Júüùniper meant about eating coming a close second to starving. It was a vile, disgusting, inedible gruel. No, worse. It would have taken "vile, disgusting, inedible gruel" as a compliment. The slop's mother would have proudly pinned "vile, disgusting, inedible gruel" to her pantry door for anyone who came to her kitchen to see.

If it had been bland, Eloise could probably have handled it. But it was the opposite. The nondescript, thick mush was apparently where jalapeños went to die, going to their cauldron grave in the company of cassava root and mold, and seasoned with ash. Her first spoonful made her gag. Her second made her retch. Her third? There was no third. Perhaps cold vile, disgusting, inedible gruel would be more palatable than lukewarm vile, disgusting inedible gruel.

But she doubted it.

She went back to the *Livre de Protocol*, searching the endless text for an angle that would get her out of this Çalaht-forsaken hellhole and in front of the queen.

Around dusk, the Guard once again announced, "The Speaker for the Indigent," and let Júüüniper Peephole Burrowduster into the cell, fumbling away at her monocle. "Well, dear, the wheels on the cart of progress turn slowly, I'm afraid," said the mole. "But they do turn, and for you, they seem to be turning faster than for most. You are, my dear, the beneficiary of another's misfortune. Normally it would take me a week or two to get you into Magistrate Íîmmerhart Curcurbit-Tóöòn-sils' chamber, even for a first look. But he had an opening in his schedule."

"Oh?"

"Yes, one of my other clients, who was supposed to be sentenced tomorrow morning, engaged in a rather terminal bout of impact-induced, aerial-based sudden-velocity-stopping encounters with the boundaries of his confinement."

Eloise frowned. "I'm not sure what that means."

The mole looked at her. "Sorry, terms of the trade. It was a numbat, and he jumped off the platform into the jail wall over and over until his skull cracked open."

"Oh. That's horrible."

"Horrible, indeed. But not your concern. The upshot is that you're going to see Old Nostril Flare at his earliest convenience, which is likely to be mid-morning tomorrow. A small miracle."

"What do I need to do?"

"Tell the truth. Avoid speaking at all when you can, and for goodness' sake, only speak when you are spoken to. Try not to scratch. And if you see his nostrils flare, consider taking back whatever you just said."

62

OLD NOSTRIL FLARE

Old Nostril Flare was not old at all. He had five years on Eloise at most, with a boyish face, hair like a sunrise, and a ridiculously bad attempt at a mustache. Perhaps he'd grow one when he was older, but for now, it looked like scraggly russet moss parked on his face. However, he was a magistrate already, even if he only heard indigent cases dragged in by the night watchmen. That was, without doubt, impressive.

Eloise had been given a chance to rinse off a bit of grime and smear on some wart cream, which did provide relief, even if it left a purple tinge on her skin. That made her wonder just what the salve was made of, but the wart cream recipe, said to contain eleven or so different herbs and spices, was famously one of the Half Kingdom's most closely guarded secrets.

The magistrate waved Eloise and Júüùniper in from the doorway without looking up from his scroll.

"G'mid-morning to you, Magistrate Curcurbit-Tóöònsils," said the mole, approaching his desk.

"Whether or not the morning is good remains to be seen, Speaker for the Indigent," he replied automatically, eyes still down, quill poised, attention far away. When he finally looked up at Eloise, his eyes widened. "Speaker for the Indigent, you seem to have found yourself a slightly higher quality reprobate than normal."

"Magistrate, we must allow for the possibility that this one is not a reprobate at all."

"You know, you say that about all of them."

"Yes, but this time there might be some basis in fact, instead of hope."

Magistrate Curcurbit-Tóöònsils leaned back in his chair, steepled his index fingers, and tapped them on his chin, which Eloise now saw sported a stupendously unsuccessful goatee (a term goats found offensive, but which was named for them anyway). "I'm listening, Madame Speaker for the Indigent."

Júüùniper laid out Eloise's story, starting with the arrest, and adding backstory as needed. But it was all done in such an unfamiliar way, using language highly specific to their profession, that it reminded Eloise of the *Livre de Protocol*, and the way it simultaneously informed and obscured.

Eventually, the magistrate said, "I don't see how we deviate from standard practice here."

The mole gasped. "Surely not!"

"What wriggle room do I have?"

"You are the magistrate. You can exercise discretion."

"She disobeyed the direct warning of the night watch. Her companion spoke in public. Her other companion physically assaulted more than one night watch officer. What am I to do with that?"

"They are not from here, so don't know our ways."

"Ignorance of the law, and all that," retorted the magistrate. "That is why we give out information at the Adequate Wall."

"I would also state that the behavior of the Delirium Liturgists was a mitigating factor. You know what they can be like."

Nostril flare. "My parents are Delirium Liturgists."

"I mean no disrespect to the sect that until not that long ago was the preferred form of worship of our queen," hurried the mole. "But consider. There she and her companions were, late at night, minding their own business, when suddenly they were surrounded and verbally accosted," said the mole. "If the chipmunk and the other are who she says they are, then they were executing their duty of care toward her."

There was another nostril flare from the magistrate, but he said nothing.

The mole saw it. "Perhaps 'duty of care' is not the right phrase. But they would have been particularly motivated to protect her, especially when the night watchwoman engaged in a physical restraint against my indigent."

The magistrate snorted. "The conduct of the others is not at issue here, whether we're discussing her associates, the Delirium Liturgists, or the night watch. Your reprobate impeded the normal order of business being conducted by the night watch, she did not encourage her companion to stop speaking in public, and she contributed to the situation by not taking the Delirium Liturgists up on their offer of ministrations to her soul."

"Oh, for the love of... She should submit to the Happy Clappers?" spluttered the mole. "You may as well say she should let a random Pietistic Sister give her a tattoo. An unwelcome offer to minister to her soul is an unwelcome offer, no matter how sincere it might be."

"I'll grant that point, but the rest stands."

Eloise stood there listening to them discuss her like she was a carpet being haggled over in a market. This was her life they were talking about! And it didn't seem to be going her way. She decided on boldness and bluff.

"Excuse me," said Eloise. "May I please interrupt?"

The mole looked shocked, and the magistrate smiled, bemused. "Speak, if you must, young reprobate."

"My name is Eloise Hydra Gumball III, Future Ruler and Heir to the Western Lands and All That Really Matters. Under Chapter 298, Section 17, Sub-section 821, Clause 37a of the *Livre de Protocol*, I hereby assert my birth privilege and request an audience with Her Majesty Queen Onomatopoeia Handrail Lúüùderming, attended by my retinue. I would be most grateful if you could please convey my request to Her Majesty."

The mole's monocle clattered on the stone floor as she doubled over in laughter.

Magistrate Curcurbit-Tóöònsils' nostrils flared wide enough to insert a large radish, but Eloise was disinclined to take anything back. He stood, stepped to an overloaded bookshelf, crisply plucked out a thick, well-worn copy of the *Livre de Protocol*, and a thicker, less-used copy of the Commentaries, tossed them on his desk, sat down, and flipped pages.

Eloise stood there and tried not to scratch.

❧ 63 ❧

CONVEYING THE REPROBATE

The guards accompanying Eloise and Lorch walked in total silence from the night watch jail toward the Sclerotic Wold's castle—not that there was much chance to chat, since it took everything she had to walk through the buffeting winds which got worse with each step. Eloise wished one of the gusts would catch her up and carry her back to Castle de Brague. That would solve one set of problems, even if it created others.

She assumed Jerome was in the brown bag the guards carried, but couldn't be sure. There was no movement or sound from it.

Eloise hadn't really thought that her ambit claim would get very far, especially when she saw the guffaws with which Júüùniper responded. But Magistrate Curcurbit-Tööònsils spent an entire hour saying nothing while he read, re-read, cross-referenced and pondered the part of the *Livre de Protocol* she'd cited, along with passages from the Commentaries. Eloise sat on a short wooden stool by the wall, and the Speaker for the Indigent, having recovered her composure and checked her monocle for damage, eased into the chair opposite the magistrate's desk, set her face back to neutral, and waited.

The wart cream eased the itching, but not completely. Eloise remembered Júüüniper's advice that she not scratch, so tried to give herself comfort by imagining the relief scratching might provide. She also thought a show of piety might not go astray, so took out her prayer beads and used them to count the books, scrolls, and papers that formed an orderly clutter on the magistrate's shelves and tables, using motions and mouthing that could easily have been misinterpreted as prayer.

Not that a prayer to Çalaht was a bad idea, given the circumstances.

Finally, the magistrate humphed, closed the books, and slid them across his desk, away from him. He stared at Eloise, who did her best to look as innocent as one could with jail chigger welts all over one's face. As he stared, he once again tapped his steepled fingers against his failed facial hair. When the Speaker for the Indigent looked like she might say something, he stopped her with a raised hand, and continued his thinking.

Ten minutes of this felt like three days, but Eloise could sense the careful consideration taking place. She just wasn't sure if it was a good thing or not.

He broke the silence with one word: "Yes."

"I beg your pardon?" said the Speaker for the Indigent.

"Yes, I shall convey your reprobate's request to the queen's handlers."

"Really?" said the mole. "How extraordinary."

"I disagree," said the magistrate. "Oh, maybe in the sense it is not an ordinary request for this chamber to entertain. However, Protocol is Protocol, and it would not do me any good to deny someone their due if Protocol is being correctly invoked. It is not my problem to prove she is who she says. That remains your reprobate's concern. I shall, however, convey her request and discharge any obligation I might have."

Eloise raised her hand, asking permission to speak.

"Yes, young reprobate?"

"Thank you."

That was how Eloise came to be walking through the midday sun and gale-force breeze toward Queen Onomatopoeia's home, in the company of a dozen guards, Lorch, and the presumed bag of Jerome. It was not exactly an honor guard—the magistrate's last words were, "Please convey the reprobate to the castle"—but it beat being in her jail cell. That she had started thinking of it as "her" cell was enough to tell her she needed to do whatever she could to stay out of it.

Lorch said nothing, but that was his way. From the look he gave her, she could see he was both relieved and concerned, and was doing what he could to be ready to aid her. She could also see he'd endured a similar Enhanced Discomfort regimen, but had scratched less. Still, his face was replete with red welts, and she hoped she did not look too much worse than he did.

The castle walls ahead looked different to the ones at home. Castle de Brague was built using a white limestone found locally, with red limestone from the Eastern Lands and black limestone from the Central Ranges used in decorative patterns on the outside. Moving that much stone that far was an ostentatious show of wealth that Gwendolyn the Irritable herself had approved, and which subsequent generations enjoyed, even if they thought it a folly.

The castle at the Sclerotic Wold was also limestone, but had a strange blue tinge that made the building look cold, even on the hottest summer day. Where Castle de Brague was a hodgepodge of styles and tastes, here it looked like a single design had been executed and respected. There was a uniformity to the windows and rooftops, a regularity to the spacing of towers and turrets. It didn't look like much had been done since the Windward Wall had drained the realm's coin reserve, which meant all alterations made to deal with the winds looked slapdash and temporary, even if they had been there for decades.

To Eloise's surprise, about halfway between the jail and the castle, there was a small commotion behind her. Suddenly, her guards were being followed by Hector carrying Cäääsëëëy, the Nameless One, and Alejandro carrying Jaminity. Relief surged in Eloise's heart. Her friends (and they *were* her friends, friends like she had never had before) knew enough about the situation to know when she was being conveyed. They kept a careful distance so they didn't spook the guards, but they formed up like an accompanying honor guard.

The guards at the gate refused to let the others through, but that didn't matter. Their point had been made. Eloise, Lorch, and the guards carrying Jerome walked through the wind tunnel that was the gate to the castle. Eloise felt lighter than she had since she'd been taken into custody.

Stepping through the castle gateway offered no relief from the wind—quite the opposite, in fact. Eddies and whirligigs greeted them, picking up, swirling, and tossing away anything they could grab. The streets were unusually devoid of activity, but it was obvious why. No one would choose to conduct business outside if it could be done inside instead. You might have to put up with getting blasted by sand, dust, and grit to move from one place to another, but you got out of it as soon as you could.

Eloise wondered if the winds were seasonal, like they were at home, but didn't feel like her escorts would be willing to assuage her curiosity.

She was led around the back to a service entrance, and entered the castle proper behind a cartload of turnips and in front of a delivery of mustard pots. They might take her to meet the queen, but there was no ceremony to it at all.

Fair enough.

They winnowed through back halls and side passages toward the heart of the castle, finally emerging through a wooden door into a decorated hallway.

Eventually, a guard opened the door into an unremarkable waiting room. They put the sack on the floor, made sure Eloise and Lorch were seated, and then closed the door.

The wait for Queen Onomatopoeia Handrail Lúüùderming began.

Eloise had wondered if the Speaker for the Indigent might be there to represent her. But no, this was on her.

She still had no idea what she might say or do that could convince anyone she was who she said, but the dice had been thrown, and now it remained to see which sides came up.

The minutes stretched, coagulating slowly into hours. There was not a horological cuckoo in earshot, but Eloise followed a shadow cast through a small, drafty window. Clearly no one was in a hurry. Perhaps it was a tactic to see how she reacted. Perhaps someone was listening, hoping to hear something incriminating. Eloise and Lorch sat in silence, and the bag did not move.

While Eloise waited, she practiced calm, imagining counting her breaths with the prayer beads. She also wondered what Onomatopoeia was really like. Was Her Maj Ono as fierce as people made her out to be?

It seemed unlikely.

❧ 64 ❧

HER MAJ ONO

When the door finally opened, it was not the queen who entered, but a harried functionary who looked to be ticking off items from a list. The wheat-haired, plainly-clothed woman had the manner of one bustling to finish three times the number of tasks one could ever hope to do in a day, but who would achieve what she could anyway before taking up a similar burden tomorrow. "Which one of you is supposedly Eloise?" she said, still scratching her scroll with a quill.

Eloise stood, cleared her throat, and began a rehearsed speech. "G'afternoon. My name is Eloise Hydra Gum—"

"No time for that," said the woman. She pointed at Eloise. "You. Follow." She pointed at Lorch. "You. Pick up the sack and follow behind. I advise you both to hold your tongues. And for goodness' sake, crack open the bag and make sure whatever is in there hasn't rotted or suffocated."

That possibility hadn't occurred to Eloise, but a quick glance revealed Jerome breathing, alert, muzzled, and seething. Eloise gave him a small squeeze on the shoulder, but that was all she had time for.

The functionary led them out the door, down a hall, across a windswept corridor, and through another hall, turning left at a passageway that finally looked royal, and then to an open throne room.

Through the doorway, Eloise saw the queen sitting at a desk to the side, head down, quill up, vigorously marking through passages on a scroll. Standing a respectful distance away, waiting, was a second woman, wearing a head magistrate's robes.

The functionary led them in past two guards, then pointed to a seat by the door for Lorch and a fixed stone bench facing the empty throne for Eloise.

Eloise took her seat, surprised by how much cold came from it, adding to the chill of the inevitable winds that swirled dust, dirt, and the occasional leaf around the room. She could not see much of the queen from where she sat, just a purple robe with the hood pulled over her head, presumably for warmth. Eloise calmed herself, sat still, faced forward, and did what she was presumably expected to do—wait.

The queen set down her quill and parchment and looked at the head magistrate. "You're telling me the stoat got loose from his bonds."

"Yes, Your Majesty," said the head magistrate. "That's what I'm told."

"And he did not have help."

"The duty jail chigger said no help was observed."

"Well, this is unusual."

"Yes, Your Majesty, it is."

The queen tapped the feathered end of her quill on her desk. "Should we truss him up again and see if he can do it a second time? That would help us ensure no cleverness occurred."

"If I may, Your Majesty. You are, of course, entitled to order that. But it would seem he simply succeeded, against the odds."

"Has the reprobate shown remorse? Did he mouth off at the magistrate again?"

"Yes, ma'am. And no, ma'am. In that order, ma'am."

Queen Onomatopoeia picked up the quill, scratched something on the scroll, and handed it to the head magistrate. "Do as you see fit."

"Yes, ma'am. I'll make sure the queen's justice is served."

"See that you do."

The head magistrate left, and the queen returned to her paperwork, showing no sense of hurry. She picked up, read, and finished one document, then took the next from under the weight that held the unfurled scrolls against the breeze. One she signed, the next she glanced at briefly then dropped to the floor. She got irritable with another (so much so that she wadded it up and set it on fire using a shielded candle, holding the page till it singed her fingers), laughed at the next, and slipped another into her robe after a brief glance. If it was a performance, it was a dull one. If it was designed to put Eloise off guard, she'd seen her mother do this kind of thing to too many people to give it much thought.

Eventually, the queen set down her quill, smoothed the front of her robe, and stood. Eloise and Lorch stood as well, and the two guards came to attention. Onomatopoeia walked to the throne, used a clean cloth to wipe off a layer of dirt from the seat and back, sat, crossed her legs, closed her eyes, and dropped into a late afternoon nap. Within moments, she was snoring lightly.

Now this wasn't something Eloise had seen her mother do. She'd have to suggest her mother add it to her repertoire. It was a clear message of unconcern. In fact, it was insulting without resulting to words. It showed you did not value the other person's time, were not threatened by them, and didn't really care what they thought of you.

Clever.

So Eloise sat there, unwilling to move in case the queen woke up and she missed her chance to speak.

Onomatopoeia was a slight woman, twenty years older than her mother. The purple robe covered most of her olive skin, and the small drip of sleep spittle could not take away the fact that she had been a striking beauty a few decades before. In Protocols and Procedures, Eloise had been forced to memorize a lot of seemingly useless, now-forgotten details about other monarchies. While she sat on the cold, increasingly uncomfortable bench, she tried to dredge up what she could. She knew the Southie queen had a daughter who people rarely saw, but who would one day inherit, and a husband who'd died not long after her daughter was born. It was said she had a penchant for ginger snaps and curries, sometimes mixed together. Eloise wondered what similar things people would one day say about her. That she twitched a lot? That she preferred blue ink to black? That there were doilies and dollies on her vanity? Onomatopoeia's reputation for crustiness went without saying, but Eloise also seemed to remember that even her chosen envoys were brusque and brooked no nonsense.

The diffused sunlight in the room crawled along the wall, and Eloise fought boredom and her own drowsiness while the wait dragged from a first hour into a second.

Eventually, the queen gave a sharp snort and blinked awake. She looked around, figured out where she was, saw Lorch in the back, furrowed her eyebrows, then focused on Eloise, giving an irritated shake of the head. Eloise stood when the queen did, and watched her go to a table spaced the same distance away from the throne as her desk, but on the other side. A servant brought a tray with a hot meal on it. The queen sat down, her back to Eloise, and supped. This was another one she'd have to let her mother know about.

If Eloise was who she said she was, Queen Onomatopoeia was breaching Protocol left, right, and center. Obviously, that was the point. It was a statement of power, and Eloise had no choice but to keep her composure and let it play out.

From what she could see and smell, the queen had been served horse-radish soup. Horseradish and garlic with pumpernickel bread and gherkins on the side. Sour and bitter food for a sour and bitter disposition.

Eloise's stomach could not help but react as Queen Ono finished the dish, wiped it with her bread, then asked for more and repeated the entire process. Eloise was not a huge fan of horseradish soup but it had been a long day of waiting and sitting, with nothing to eat.

Another deliberate move.

By the time Onomatopoeia finished eating, the throne room needed its first candles . Back still turned, she dabbed the corners of her mouth, and let rip a belch of such scale and enthusiasm that for the first time, Eloise was genuinely taken aback.

She made another mental note.

More candles were being lit when the queen finally stood and sauntered back to her throne. She sat, and Eloise did the same. Eloise was afraid her dinner would be followed by another nap, but Onomatopoeia fixed her with unblinking eyes and stared.

Eloise stared back, head tilted down to avoid appearing confrontational, but locking eyes.

Eventually, the queen waved a dismissive hand and said, "Go ahead, whoever you are. Have your say."

Eloise stood again. At the back of the room, Lorch reflexively did the same, and the guards at the door stiffened, ready to react. "My name is Eloise Hydra Gumball III, daughter of Queen Eloise Hydra Gumball II of the Western Lands and All That Really Matters. I find myself in Her Majesty's realm somewhat unexpectedly, and present myself to Her Majesty as Protocol suggests, with respect and the greetings from my mother she would convey if she knew I was here." Eloise curtsied, then kneeled, as Protocol decreed.

There was a long pause. Then Onomatopoeia said, "That's it?"

"I beg your pardon, Your Majesty?"

"I asked, is that it? That's all you wish to say?"

Eloise wasn't sure where this was heading. "For the moment, I merely wish to pay respects. Does Her Majesty wish me to address any topic in particular?"

Onomatopoeia humphed and pulled out the scroll she'd slid into her robe while she was working. She scrabbled it open, read it, and set it down on the table next to her. "No pleas for clemency? No apologies for trespassing? No explanation for the lack of notice and proper preparation? No guilt for disturbing the queen's peace at a lawful public assembly? No complaints about your treatment? No mention of the undocumented nature of your movements? No offers of flattery? No sugary words designed to get me to release the uselessness in that bag? No indignation for your welts? No descriptions of your favorite impressions of this fair realm? No blessings to my health? No reasons why, if you are who you say you are, you did not come before me immediately? No thoughts on the weather?"

Eloise wasn't sure what to make of all that. "Your Majesty, if invited to do so, I am happy to answer any question you may put, to the extent I am able and allowed."

Another long pause. Queen Onomatopoeia shifted in her throne, a much less ostentatious seat than Eloise had at home and, from the look of it, less comfortable. She once again looked at the scroll. "Who is Abernatheen? My briefing appears vague on that point."

"My champion, Your Majesty. Jerome Abernatheen de Chipmunk. He's in that bag. If you would like, I could present him to you."

"No need. Apparently, he's been running around his cell non-stop for a few days emitting the most horrific squeals and disturbing the other law-breakers. I am told it was a relief to all, both incarcerated and incarcerating, that he was finally subdued, restrained, and muzzled. I'm sure the rest is doing him good."

"Yes, Your Majesty." So, a massive panic attack from Jerome. Unsurprising, perhaps, but not pleasant for him. She didn't know what damage might have been done, and feared the worst.

The queen stood, and stepped forward, eyes boring into Eloise like they were drilling for truth. Eloise knew to remain kneeling, as she'd not been invited to move yet. "You have the speech of one steeped in the Western Lands Court, but that does not make you a princess," said the queen. "Nor would it be the first time someone tried to pass themselves off as royalty within these wind-blown halls. If you are who you say you are, and I don't think that's the case, you would not have bumbled your way so incompetently from the Adequate Wall to here. You would not have taken so long to present yourself. And you would have respected the rules of the realm—*my* rules in *my* realm—and prevented your alleged companion from speaking in public. If you had any smarts at all, you would not have chosen a creature so unequivocally unsuitable in a role so important as champion, which leads me to conclude it is fakery or stupidity, neither of which give me confidence in your presentation."

Eloise said nothing, as there were no questions posed. She wasn't sure what she had expected to achieve in an audience with the queen, but she hadn't thought it would go this badly. So she simply said, "Yes, Your Majesty."

"Yes? Yes what?" said Onomatopoeia. "Yes you're incompetent? Yes you've promoted rule-breaking? Yes you are lying?"

"No, Your Majesty."

"You contradict me?"

"No, Your Majesty. I mean, yes Your Majesty." The prospect of going back to the chiggered cell squeezed at Eloise's throat. How could she make the queen believe her? How could she prove she was who she said she was?

A side door opened, and a squat servant carrying a bundle of sticks clattered in, dropping a few between the door and the fireplace, where a fire was laid. She looked behind her and mumbled at the sticks, "I'll be back for you in a moment. Don't go anywhere." She chuckled at her joke and pulled a flint and striker from the apron of her kitchen wench's uniform. Her failed attempts to strike a spark from a flint clinked loudly in the tense silence that now held the room.

Eloise blinked tears. "Your Majesty, I..."

"No," interrupted the queen. "I believe I've wasted enough time on this to satisfy Protocol."

There was a chortle from the fireplace where the servant had started the fire. "You'll keep Her Majesty nice and warm, you will," the servant told the fire. "Thank you for lighting." She went to pick up the dropped sticks.

Onomatopoeia crumpled the scroll, walked the few steps to the fireplace, and threw it on the just-catching fire. "You shall be conveyed to your cell and remain until proper processes resolve your transgressions."

Eloise gasped. "No! You can't! Please don't send me back there."

Her voice caught the servant's attention. "Oh, bless me with Çalaht's stretched thumbs!" she said. "Look who's here!" The queen watched, surprised, as the servant came over to Eloise and curtsied.

"I'm sorry, I..." started Eloise.

"Oh, yer Princessness. It's me. Hoarfrost de Blotter. We met at the Ceremonies of the Stone."

"Ah, Goodwoman de Blotter," said Eloise. "I, um, I'm not sure..."

"Oh, yer remember. I caught good luck from yer when yer bobbled the Stone of the Ancestors from yer mouth."

"There were a lot of—"

"And it was indeed a good omen," burbled Hoarfrost. "After I left yer castle, I found the warmest pair of socks I've ever had in my life, and ever since, me chilblains have been so much better. Such good luck, and all because of yer, Princess!"

"I'm pleased to hear—" said Eloise.

"And, best of all, when I got back from the Western Lands and All That Really Matters, me sister found me a place here at the castle. No more crofting those infernal windbeans for me. I hated growing them, and I hated eating them. Now, I get to help out Her Majesty here." She curtsied in Onomatopoeia's direction as a form of punctuation.

"That is lucky, indeed," said Eloise. "And I do remember you, Goodwoman de Blotter. You had a small bit of paperbark to help you remember the words, and there was an acorn that went astray."

"That was me, yer Princessness!" Her delight at Eloise remembering her lit her up. "I was feeling so skittsy to be in yer great presence. Yer and yer lovely sister were so kind to be understanding to the likes of me." Hoarfrost de Blotter turned to Queen Onomatopoeia, "Yer Majesty, it must be wonderful to have her Princessness Eloise visiting yer so unexpectedly. Can I bring yer both some haggleberry tea? And if'n I'm not mistaken, there's an almond, raisin, and kale cake just come from the oven. I could fetch some along with."

Onomatopoeia looked at the former croftwoman, then Eloise. "Princess Eloise Hydra Gumball III, would haggleberry tea be to taste?"

"Yes, thank you Queen Onomatopoeia Handrail Lúüüderming. That would be wonderful."

They watched Hoarfrost de Blotter bustle out the door, calling ahead for tea and cake.

"Will you join me in my dining room?" asked the queen.

"Thank you. I would be most grateful," said Eloise. "May I be so bold as to ask something?"

"Proceed."

"Do you think it would be too much to ask for you to have my champion unbagged and unmuzzled?"

"Normally, I would not. Certainly not so soon. Do you think he's learned his lesson?"

"I'm sure your methods have made a lasting impression."

"I shall hold you accountable for his behavior."

"Yes, Your Majesty."

"I do this as a favor to you. Nothing more."

"Yes, Your Majesty."

She led Eloise out of her throne room and toward a formal dining hall. "Now, tell me, how fare your mother and father?"

❧ 65 ❧

COUNTERINTUITIVE

Her Majesty Queen Onomatopoeia Handrail Lúüùderming was not as crusty as Eloise had first thought. Once they got past their initial awkwardness, Her Maj Ono turned out to be good, if somewhat formal, company. She invited Eloise, Jerome, and Lorch to stay at the castle in specially prepared draft-proof rooms, and made stables available for the others, although Jaminity stayed with Madam Righteous, Alejandro remained in the stable close to her shop, and Cäääsëëëy seemed to move silently between the two.

The queen also assigned Hoarfrost de Blotter to be Eloise's personal attendant, which sent the servant into a paroxysm of delighted, rural-accented chatter that lasted the entire time she helped Eloise bathe, scrub, scrape, trim, brush, comb, and clothe her way to a semblance of Court acceptability. Hoarfrost was unused to the role of handmaid, so it was all somewhat awkward, as Eloise had to tell her what to do step by step, and the servant was clumsy with excited nervousness. It made Eloise appreciate the automatic, effortless efficiency that Odmilla brought to her tasks.

Jerome was restored to the treatment normally afforded champions, even if he maintained a silent, huffy, even hurt demeanor. When he was first freed, Eloise had hugged him, and made sure nothing was broken and that no stray jail chiggers stayed in his fur. But she'd not had much time to speak privately with him, and was concerned for his mental health. However, he perked up visibly, as Eloise guessed he might, when he learned that the singer Lyndia Thrind was supposed to arrive in a day or two for a special royal performance.

And Johanna and Doncaster? Nothing. The trip to The South was a fiction perpetuated for their benefit. Eloise and the others had wasted weeks on a wild goose chase (a phrase offensive to both wild and settled geese). There was no way to characterize it other than as a disappointment and a frustration.

"So, are there any other options?" Eloise had called an impromptu meeting with Jerome, Lorch, Hector, the Nameless One, and Cäääsëëëy in the private stable the horses used, figuring they could canvas the other two when they saw them the next day. Eloise was not the only one who'd taken advantage of the chance to remove all traces of their journey from her body. Hector glowed like the supremely perfect being he was, with a trimmed mane and tail, and his coat restored to full gloss. Except now Eloise was not in awe of him, having felt his every movement for days at a time. She trusted him, knew his moods and preferences, and could even point out his favorite grasses.

The Nameless One, too, looked like he'd had the attentions of a groom, and Lorch was also shaved and bathed properly for the first time in weeks.

"I see no other choices, Princess," said Hector. "We head back to the Western Lands and All That Really Matters or we take the Northern Road toward the Half Kingdom."

"Neither has great appeal," said Eloise. "One means going home without Johanna. The other means dragging across realms into another uncertainty. Lorch, how long do you think a journey to the Half Kingdom would take?"

Lorch rubbed his chin. "It would be weeks, but not months, if we continue to travel lightly. Resources would remain one of our biggest issues, so we'd have to sleep mostly rough. But we've managed so far, more or less. I'm sure we can work it out."

"There's the matter of weather," said Jerome. "We've been fortunate, so far, despite getting soaked a few times. But we'd be going north as the seasons change toward Yule."

The five of them quietly contemplated weeks on the road with the days turning noticeably shorter and colder.

"There is another way." Cäääsëëëÿ's whispered voice was heard so infrequently, it startled when he said something. "East."

"East? How would going east help us?" asked Eloise. "Would that not be completely out of our way?"

"Yes, it would," agreed Cäääsëëëÿ.

"What kind of plan is that?" asked Jerome. "It's completely backward. We'd be going the wrong way."

"You should be used to that by now."

Eloise looked at Cäääsëëëÿ, surprised. "Why, Cäääsëëëÿ Liïiss. Did you just utter a witticism?"

The chameleon reddened. As always, it was hard to know if it was genuine embarrassment or affectation. "Yes, Princess, I believe I did."

"What a pleasant surprise. But Jerome is right. Heading east seems counterintuitive."

"I traveled with the barker for a long, long time. Not all of his activities were as honest and straightforward as fleecing marks at fairs. Some activities involved moving certain less-traded goods with little detection. Let's just say I learned a little about getting from one place to another." It was the most Eloise had heard him speak since they sat under the hawthorn tree. "My suggestion is we go overland to Port Port, then find passage on a not-necessarily-registered trade vessel across the Gööödeling Sea, land at Haze Town, below where the Purple Haze meets the water, then work westward toward the castle at Stained Rock."

Lorch reached into a saddlebag by the Nameless One's stall, pulled out a map, and unfurled it onto a table. "How much time could be saved?"

Cäääsëëëy shrugged. "It depends."

"On?"

"On everything. On how the haggleberry harvest has been, and whether that has amped up or dampened demand. On what manner of devotion Her Majesty embraces at the moment, and their ethical stance on gray markets. On how cold it has been and for how long. On how much power the Wheelwrights Guild can exert at the moment. On the contraband to legal goods ratio. On..."

"I get it, I get it," said Eloise. "Best guess? Or high, medium, and low guesses?"

Cäääsëëëy climbed onto the table and studied the map. He thumped his tail absently in thought while also changing his skin hues to match the map's colors. Finally, he puffed his throat, a gesture Eloise associated with decision. "Everything perfect? It takes a week. Everything lousy (a phrase offensive to lice, I know)? A month. Best guess? Ten days."

Lorch traced his finger along the route Cäääsëëëy suggested. "I have not traveled in these parts of the realms," he said. "I could not guide us."

"I can guide," whispered Cäääsëëëy. "I have been that way a dozen times during my indenture." He looked at Eloise. "It would be my hope you would allow me to do so, should you choose this option."

Eloise also traced the proposed path with a finger, then tapped the map with a knuckle. "I shall think on it. Lorch, could you please put together thoughts on requirements for resources?"

"Yes, Princess."

"In the meantime, Her Majesty Onomatopoeia has 'invited' me to a devotional observance tonight. It was phrased as optional, but had the tone of requirement."

Jerome smirked. "Do you know which brand of devotion you're up for?"

"Not yet. But we know she's not a Happy Clapper anymore, so we can be grateful for small mercies." The others murmured agreement. "I just hope it doesn't involve public bathing, singing solos, or formal memorized recitations of the *Scrolls of Çalaht*. I can probably handle anything else for an hour or two."

✣ 66 ✣

PURE EXPRESSIONISM

Eloise awoke with a blinding headache in an unfamiliar room with the curtains drawn tight against all light. Her mouth was dry and tasted like she'd loaned her tongue to a habanero appreciation club, her skin felt prickly and sensitive, and there was a faint gonging in her ears. Through the dim light, she could see there was a mug of something next to the bed—no, not bed, couch —where she'd slept. Her muscles felt like a dray had driven over her, circled around, slammed over her again, stopped, had someone turn her over, and then driven over her a couple more times for good measure.

Eloise had no idea why.

She picked up the mug to see if its contents were drinkable. The viscous fluid smelled vaguely of mint, pepper, and wood-tar creosote. And it smelled brown. She didn't know how it smelled like a color, but there it was. She put it down without tasting it.

The door creaked open like an avalanche of boulders, admitting the barest light and the hint of Jerome's shadow. It was like having her eyes skewered. "El? Are you awake?" he whispered.

"Too much light!" she moaned, pulling a blanket over her head. "What happened?"

"You're kidding, right?" He eased in, closing the door.

"No, I'm not. Why do I feel like a washerwoman has slammed me against rocks like an old towel?"

"What's the last thing you remember?"

Eloise cast her mind backward. There was the impromptu meeting with the others. There was getting ready for dinner, and dinner itself. She particularly remembered a delicious spicy black and white bean soup. Oh, yes, there was accompanying Onomatopoeia to her current devotional house. At that point things blurred out. "We went to a devotional service."

Jerome climbed the table and sat next to the mug. "You should probably drink this sooner rather than later. I understand that age does not improve the flavor."

"Really? I have to drink that?"

"No. I'm led to believe you're going to want to drink it."

Eloise slowly sat up, a feat that required tremendous will and strength. She lifted the mug to her lips, making the tiniest sip possible. It was like drinking evil itself. "You'd better tell me what happened."

❧

"I'M TRYING OUT A NEW SECT," SAID QUEEN ONOMATOPOEIA AS SHE, Eloise, Lorch, and Jerome walked toward the devotional house. The wind had lessened to a stiff gusting, making conversation possible. "It's called Pure and Open Expression of Çalaht's Will."

"I've heard of them, but not much more," said Eloise. "At home, they go by 'Pure Expressionism'."

"That's them. It is one of the oldest forms of devotion, but secretive. They guard their doors heavily. Even I had to be invited to join them."

"That's why we're walking instead of taking your carriage?"

"Yes. They believe that one should always approach the divine on foot." The queen pressed her hat against her head and let a sharp squall come and go. She continued, used to that kind of interruption. "All participants are sworn to complete silence about their goings on. It is said they enforced that oath with a zeal that would make a Pietistic Sister jealous."

"Ouch."

"Ouch, indeed. I've only recently become curious about their form of practice. It did not take me too much effort to gain an invitation to their devotional house. Tonight is my first experience of their worship. I hope you'll enjoy it."

"I'm sure it will be memorable. And thank you for allowing Jerome and Lorch to come."

Onomatopoeia waved that off.

They reached a nondescript building located respectably close to the Plaza of Her Agonizingly Difficult and Much Longer Than Anyone Might Have Expected Birth. The Pure Expressionist devotional house sat nestled between two much grander sects, the Regressive Non-Interpretive Stationary Ossifiers, whose house looked like a converted theater, and the Harkening Back to Better Times When People Respected the Old Ways—Revisionist Order, which looked like it prayed in an oversized wedding cake. The Pure Expressionists favored understatement and wood. Their ten-point Summary of Practice was written in a neat hand on simple hemp parchment and posted near the simple maple front door in a tasteful teak frame.

The assistant house minder who blocked the door greeted them with a warm "Blessings of the evening" but did not let them in, even though the queen stood before him. Onomatopoeia pulled out an oversized commemorative coin and handed it to him. One side was struck with a distended thumb and the other showed an engraved gap-toothed smile with rays of light shining through the teeth. The assistant house minder examined both sides, nodded, and handed it back to her, but did not move aside.

The queen added, "My companions and I ask permission to sing her gap-toothed praises with you tonight."

That phrase must have been a second part of the key. "Please be welcome," he said, making way.

Inside, the devotional house favored the same warm, simple style as the exterior, and it reminded Eloise of the rich, dark decor of the Legs Not Arms. It was deep, with several dozen rows of pews. The house minder bowed to the queen and took Onomatopoeia and Eloise to places of honor in the front. Eloise nodded that it was fine for Lorch and Jerome to stay behind at the back. She did not want a spectacle of Jerome being there.

When they reached the front, Onomatopoeia motioned to a spot on the pew. "Please sit to my left."

Eloise recognized this for the small nod of favor it was. "Thank you. That is very kind." Before she sat, she looked to the back, where Lorch and Jerome watched her from far away. She waved, Jerome waved back, and she sat.

The devotion started normally enough, with a hymn, "Dangle Thee Not By Thy Thumbs." Eloise didn't know the song, so she didn't join in. Next was a call to devotion from the rector in call-and-response form, which Eloise manage to fake. The rector then handed over to the Ecclesiastic to begin the devotion proper with another hymn, "Çalaht, I Hoist Upward My Protest Placard For Thee," which Eloise knew, but pretended she didn't so she could avoid singing.

Then came a lovely practice that Eloise had not seen before. "Who among you is new to our devotional house," asked the Ecclesiastic somewhat rhetorically. "I ask all the new faces, please rise from your seats and make your presence known."

Standing up in front of this unknown group was the last thing Eloise wanted to do, but she followed the queen's lead and stood, along with

Lorch and an elderly woman in the back row. Jerome, not being human, was not included. That irked Eloise, but now was not the time.

"Please introduce yourselves," said the Ecclesiastic. He nodded to Eloise to go first.

"My name is Eloise." There was a titter of response, presumably because everyone knew her mother's edict against people using her name.

"My name is Onomatopoeia," said the queen. Eloise noticed she used no title or the royal "we." Interesting.

After Lorch and the old woman had said their names, the congregation broke its formality, and the members came over and shook hands with the visitors. "Welcome to you," each said, and everyone seemed to mean it. It was the warmest welcome Eloise had ever received in any devotional house. It was charming, disarming, and made her feel emotional. Touching all of those unfamiliar people also made her want to gag, but she put that aside and enjoyed the moment of human connection.

"Please be seated," said the Ecclesiastic. "Let us honor the Divine One." The devotion then returned to things Eloise was familiar with. There were more hymns (which she avoided singing), readings from the *Scrolls of Çalaht*, a homily (topic: loving kindness), and (unusually, but not unprecedented) a spirited discussion of the homily, complete with someone who disagreed with the Ecclesiastic, and whose point of view was included respectfully in the discussion.

Next, the Ecclesiastic asked everyone to stand, and said, "It is time to sing her gap-toothed praises." The house minder uncovered an ornate silver tray with four clay bowls on it, which looked like they had been made by a child. He held the tray aloft, and without being asked, the room broke into a spirited version of "O, Çalaht (Don't You Cry for Me)." Slowly and ceremoniously, the house minder stepped down from the pulpit, lowered the tray, and walked until he stood in front of Eloise. The four clay bowls were filled with plant material—one dried leaves, one seeds, one dried flowers, and one shredded bits of bark.

Oh, prattleweed. Of course. Southies were famous for their use of prattleweed in devotional practice (so long as you were human), a practice that Eloise, having been raised in the Western Lands, found amusing, even naughty. She'd never been anywhere where it was used so openly, and felt quietly scandalized.

The house minder stood before her, smiling encouragingly, waiting for Eloise to do something. The standing congregation sang away, filling the room with an enthusiasm missing from the devotions she normally attended. Eloise was unsure what she should do, having never been in the situation before. The plant was part of the devotional, but what was expected of her? What did people do to be part of the service? Would it be rude to refuse? What did Protocol say to do in this kind of situation?

Eloise looked at Onomatopoeia, who shrugged an encouraging, "Why not?"

Eloise examined the unfamiliar contents of the bowls. The leaves were leathery and divided into halves along the mid-vein. The flowers were prettiest, with faded bits of pink and purple. The bark was shreds of brown and looked stringy and tough. The seeds were the tiniest little black specks.

The house minder, needing to get to the rest of the room, gave the tray a little lift—a polite, non-verbal, "Please make up your mind."

Impulsively, Eloise decided on the seeds, being smallest. She reached to the bowl, took a pinch, put them in her mouth, and swallowed. The house minder's eyebrows shot up in surprise, but he recovered himself immediately, gave a small dip of a bow, and said, "Thank Çalaht."

Eloise replied with a similar, "Thank Çalaht" as the house minder moved to stand before Onomatopoeia. Eloise saw the queen look at her with an expression of confused amusement. She gave an "Oh, well" shrug, faced the house minder, took a half leaf, placed it on her tongue, and lisped across it, "Thank Çalaht."

❧ 67 ❧

SINGING HER GAP-TOOTHED
PRAISES

E loise didn't feel anything from the seeds. Nothing at all. She wondered what all the fuss was about.

Other worshippers came forward to sing a song of praise for the congregation. A stately matron went first, regaling the room with "How Great Thou Ought To Be." Next, a prim man who looked like he could be the brother of Magistrate Curcurbit-Tóöònsils, ridiculously bad mustache and all, belted out an uninhibited "Rock of Mages." A couple held hands as they did a very moving, "Why Couldst Thou Not Have Been Born Somewhere Nicer (Than the Sclerotic Wold)?"

Eloise noticed a small tingling in the back of her neck halfway through "Sufficient Grace," a hymn from the Half Kingdom that her father used to sing as a lullaby. Eloise looked down at her palms. They also tingled. Right in the center, where Çalaht's mangled thumbs might have been laid when they were bandaged. She flexed her hands, but the feeling persisted. Odd.

She touched her palm to her face and realized there was perspiration on her upper lip. No time to think about that. "Sufficient Grace" made her think of her father, and she felt herself tearing up. Eloise dug out a handkerchief and dabbed her eyes.

356

The devotional house became a swirl of activity and emotion. Person after person, song after song. Eloise felt the tingling turn into a kind of buzzing that reached throughout her body. Finally, it subsided, but left her heart open wide to the joy of Çalaht. Devotion filled her being.

She imagined what she would look like if she could see herself from the outside. Probably no different. She was close to certain no one could tell that anything was going on for her. That idea made her happy, and she remained oblivious to the fact that her pupils were like carriage wheels, her teeth were clenched, her arms were clutched around her sides, and she rocked back and forth slightly in her pew, sporting a grin like one pardoned from the noose by a magistrate and feeling all warm, gooey, and chattery inside.

Suddenly, a chipmunk appeared at the foot of her pew. "Hey there, little fella," she whispered. "Why are you so worried-looking, sport?"

The chipmunk shook his head and drew a question mark in the air.

"You know what?" Eloise whispered. "I'd love to talk with you some time about the choice of colors for that there stained-glass window. That would be fascinating, elucidating, interesting. Looks like the artist had something against the woman it depicts, though. Look what the artist did to her thumbs. Sad."

The chipmunk—he looked a bit familiar—put a finger across his lips, trying to shush her, then waved a hand to indicate the room.

Eloise ignored that and kept whispering to him. "How come all these hymns are in minor keys? Aren't hymns supposed to be uplifting, joyous, inspiring? Glad I don't have to sing one. I'd hate that. Care to discuss the proper sealant to use when caulking up stained-glass windows? I have a deep fascination, curiosity, questioning about window caulking. Do you?"

The chipmunk made a talking motion with his paw, then used the other paw to clamp it shut. "That's OK, sport. You don't have to worry about singing," she whispered to him. "The singing bit is optional. I'd rather pluck out both my eyes and swap their sockets than get up there and sing like that."

Queen Onomatopoeia Handrail Lúüüderming reached over and tugged Eloise's sleeve. "You should sing her gap-toothed praises for us."

The prattleweed seeds and the suggestibility they caused took it from there.

The old woman from the back of the room was croaking out "Çalaht Is Rather Fond of Me, This I Know," but Eloise couldn't contain herself. She jumped up and charged toward the side of the room where the Ecclesiastic stood, directing traffic to and from the pulpit. He looked at Eloise, beaming his own prattled grin, and asked, "Are you feeling the power of Çalaht within you?"

"I am!" cried Eloise.

"Would you like to sing her gap-toothed praises?"

"Yes! I would!" Then, without waiting for his response or permission, she cut in front of the line and took the center of the pulpit as the old woman hobbled off. The congregants, knowing it was rare to see a royal of Eloise's standing offer to sing a devotion, braced themselves to be moved with the force of her spirit pouring forth the pure and open expression of Çalaht's will.

"I've never sung on my own in public like this," Eloise started, suddenly nervous.

"Sing it, sister, sing it!" called a woman from the back.

"OK. I will," she said.

But what song? What song did she know that reached down from her bones and expressed who she was, and this feeling, this glorious sensation, in song?

Eloise opened her mouth, and out it came. "Ladeeeeeeees and gentlemen—and all points in between! I'd like to sing a favorite for you. If you please? In A minor... 'There's a lady who knows all that glitters is groats...'"

"You're kidding me," said Eloise, mortified. "I sang 'Three Bags of Groats for My Sweetheart'?" She downed the mug, creosote taste and all, as a kind of penance. It did not have much effect on her headache, her sensitive skin, or the gonging in her ears, but it helped her mouth stop tasting of habanero afterburn.

Eloise thought it would be hard to keep the muddy drink down, but it had a surprisingly restorative effect.

"Yes, you did. With all the style and panache of a rip saw cutting into an ironwood log. I found it funny, but the Pure Expressionists didn't seem to care for your particular expression of Çalaht's will."

"No, please, no."

"What was particularly amusing, ignoring your complete inability to carry a tune, was your perfect mimicry of Gouache Snotearrow McCcoonnch, starting with 'Ladeeeeeeees and gentlemen—and all points in between!' Word for word perfect, you were."

"Stop. Just stop. Do you think anyone will notice if I never emerge from this room again?"

"It'll be OK, I think. Her Majesty found it endearing and amusing. It probably didn't hurt that she was well and truly prattled herself. Also, she's queen, so people cut her slack. This is her antechamber you're in. She wanted you watched over while you slept it off."

"I have to face her today? How am I going to do that?"

"There's more."

"What? No."

"Her Maj Ono encouraged you to sing another devotional hymn, and you obliged her."

"What did I sing?"

"'The Baleful Sorrows of Jedd the Sea Urchin.' Also in perfect imitation of Doncaster's jester. It was uncanny, except for the voice." Jerome's amusement finally bubbled out in a giggle.

"Are you laughing at my expense, Champion Jerome Abernatheen de Chipmunk?"

"It is true I am laughing, Princess Eloise Hydra Gumball III. Whether it is at your expense, well... OK, it is. I haven't laughed so hard in years."

The door opened another crack. It was Lorch. "Princess Eloise, may I enter please?"

"I suppose you must, Guard Lacksneck."

Lorch slipped into the room and kneeled next to the couch. "You are recovering, Princess."

"Yes, Lorch. Thank you. Do you also wish to chide me for my foolishness?"

"I'm sure Champion Abernatheen de Chipmunk has done that adequately."

"I beg to differ," said Jerome. "The chiding is still to come. We've barely gotten past the joy of revealing to the princess the extent of her, um, deeds."

"May I please ask a question, Princess?" Lorch wore his blank face, which told her just how concerned he was. "Just how much prattle-weed seed did you have?"

"A pinch. A small pinch."

"A pinch! Çalaht carrying dung baskets!" Eloise had never heard the guard take the Divine One's name in vain. "You're not supposed to have more than a seed. One single seed! And that's only for people who have a tolerance built up. We're lucky we didn't find you sitting on the steeple of the devotional house chatting with the weather vane."

"Oh."

"Oh, indeed. I shall fetch you another mug of the restorative. You'll need it. Champion Abernatheen de Chipmunk, if she looks like she might sing again, please do the entire castle the kindness of distracting her with something shiny."

"Yes, Guard Lacksneck. I shall."

He left Eloise to her mortification and Jerome thinking up chiding strategies.

✣ 68 ✣

AID FOR THE LITTLE SONGBIRD

Eloise found the queen at her desk in the throne room, humming That Song, so knew her performance of the evening before had not been forgotten.

Onomatopoeia looked up, and impishly asked, "How's our little song-bird today?"

"If it pleases Her Majesty, I would kindly request permission to curl up into a ball and expire."

"First time with prattleweed?" The queen put down her quill and slid her scroll away.

"There might be evidence to that effect," moaned Eloise.

"When you took the pinch of seeds, I thought that you must be an old hand at this. But somewhere into the second verse of your song, I suspected the opposite was the case."

"Your Majesty, I would like to formally apologize for my, uh, multiple lapses in both judgment and behavior last night."

"Oh, tish tosh."

"No. Please. I don't think I could have come up with a less appropriate song if I'd tried. I'm told the congregants did not take to it kindly."

"That's overstating things," said Onomatopoeia. "We had a rather lively debate about it afterward at the reception. Taken as a metaphor, it is a perfect ode to the desire for devotional unity with the Divine One. The singer's failed attempts to woo his sweetheart can represent our failed earthly attempts to find union with her through secular striving or rote sacrament. But in the end, she does take the three bags of groats, attesting to our ability to stand at Her side."

"The songwriter had no such thoughts in his head when he wrote it."

"True. My briefing scrolls tell me you have acquaintance with Jaminity Delgado Blister."

"Yes."

"Well, if you see him again, tell him I am open to an appropriate apology and an atoning performance."

"I'll convey that to him. I think he will be grateful," said Eloise. "Where was I when you were discussing the devotional merits of 'Three Bags of Groats For My Sweetheart?'"

"Slumped in a chair, mumbling," said the queen. "Who, might I ask, is Mr. Töööffëëënööösëë Biggensly?"

Eloise felt renewed embarrassment flood her checks. "That was my second-favorite stuffed toy when I was a toddler, after Bo Bo, my stuffed gila monster."

"Apparently you had an urgent appointment with him. You kept trying to leave to keep it. That's why you were on my sofa. You seemed happy that you could make that meeting with him once you settled there."

"This just keeps getting better and better."

"Don't worry, we've all done it at least once," said Onomatopoeia. "Now, I have a question for you, little songbird. Do you still plan to travel east then catch a ride with smugglers and other such miscreants to the Half Kingdom?"

"What? How——?"

"I had the stables bugged. The insects in there report regularly."

"Oh."

"You know, I cannot condone your interaction with people who have such disregard for the rule of law," said the queen. "Officially, I must condemn such actions and take steps to prevent you from engaging in law-breaking."

"Of course, Your Majesty." Eloise did her best to hide her disappointment.

Onomatopoeia softened. "Oh, don't fret, little songbird. Unofficially, please let me know what you need for your journey, and I'll have it provided. I might be able to suggest a, um, contact or two for you. I shall parlay with your guard."

"Thank you," said Eloise, surprised. "That is very kind. I am most grateful."

"Now, what shall I tell your parents?"

"My parents?"

"Come now. It's not like I can have the Future Ruler and Heir visit me unexpectedly and not send word to them. Likely, their sources here have already scribbled missives, which are slowly making their way on foot or in saddlebags. But I could deploy a bird and get to them first."

"A bird? You have a bird messenger?"

Messenger birds disappeared with the signing of the Great Avian Accord, which had been in effect across the realms for centuries.

At one time, bird messengers criss-crossed the skies, carrying love notes and espionage, court decrees and gossip, contracts and declarations of war. It was an exciting and profitable time to be a bird.

The Messengers Guild became one of the strongest forces in the realms. They exerted a monopolistic control over messaging, preventing rivals and freelancers alike from competing, often through means that would have gotten anyone else a long drop constrained by a short rope. But not the messengers. They literally got away with Enhanced Deterrence.

The Messengers Guild had two guiding watchwords: "Gosh darn it, we get your message delivered," and "Don't shoot the messenger."

The system worked for a long time. Until it didn't.

The whole business collapsed under its own success. As the value of the information carried went up, so, too, did the value of preventing the same. There rose up a class of interceptors dedicated to bringing messengers down from the skies, taking the information, and then making sure that messenger never flew again—if they happened to still be alive at the end of the process. At first, interceptors worked in small targeted missions, but as their power grew, they formed the Interceptors Guild, which led to the ongoing, systematic slaughter of members of the Messengers Guild. The Interceptors were so successful that birds turned up dead faster than the Guild could recruit.

But something else also became clear. The more successful the Interceptors were, the harder it became for them to succeed again. But by then, the whole situation had spiraled out of control. Faced with literal extinction, the Messengers Guild signed what turned out to be the death certificate of their business: the Great Avian Accord. Under the accord, message-flying ended for all time, and the Messengers and Interceptors merged into a single guild (the MI Guild), headed by a board of half a dozen elected officials (the MI6) charged with enforcing the accord. They were spectacularly successful, and had remained so to the present day. Particularly feared was an elite guard of specially trained agents empowered to use lethal force where necessary. Because victims would fearfully say, "Oh, oh" when confronted by these numbered, unnamed agents, they became known as the Oh Oh squadron. Some entered popular lore, especially Oh Oh Seven, whose daring exploits in the service of the MI6 were told by bards all over the land.

The upshot was that now all messages went overland, and painfully, deliberately slowly, and birds took on much safer jobs, like explosives transportation and sword juggling.

Which was why Eloise was so surprised to hear Queen Onomatopoeia say she had a bird who would take a message.

"Yes. He's incredibly stealthy. Not even I know what he looks like. I know he's successful, because my messages get through at such speed. He's expensive and valuable, and I don't waste him on frivolities. So you'd best make whatever you say to your parents good."

Eloise had never used a messenger bird before, and as far as she knew, her parents hadn't either. That Queen Onomatopoeia was willing to deploy one on her behalf showed how serious she felt the situation was. Eloise had thought of sending messages home, but kept concluding that she'd get back before a slowly hauled note ever arrived. If she was honest with herself, she also avoided it because she had nothing positive to say, and didn't want to disappoint her parents. But now, there was no avoiding it.

"The truth," said Eloise. "Please tell them the truth. That I followed false clues here, and now I'm heading to the Half Kingdom to complete my mission. Tell them I will succeed, whatever it takes. And if you have room, please tell them I love them."

"The truth has its place. I'll do as you ask," said the queen. "Now, one last thing."

"Yes?"

"When you get back to Brague and life returns to normal, please consider vocal coaching for your singing voice. A queen must some-times sing in public, and your people will appreciate it if listening to you is not a penance."

"I was that bad?"

"Let's just say Lyndia Thrind need not worry herself overly about competition from you." The queen squeezed Eloise's shoulder fondly. "Now, if the bugs were right, you're planning on leaving tomorrow. So best get preparing. I'll see you tonight for dinner and Lyndia's performance."

❧ 69 ❧

LYNDIA THRIND

To Eloise's surprise, Queen Onomatopoeia turned the evening into a formal dinner in her honor.

Lorch had spent the day working with the queen's quartermaster, preparing for their journey's continuation, but he'd insisted that Eloise rest and recover. She did not take much convincing. Feeling revived by additional sleep, a haggleberry tea, and a few moon and stars biscuits, she checked on him. She found him at the quartermaster's store, quill in hand, making notes on a piece of hemp parchment that lay on a barrel.

"G'afternoon, Lorch."

He startled slightly and looked up. "Ah, Princess. You slept?" He moved to stand in front of the barrel, which obscured her view of his work.

"Yes, thank you. Everything OK here?" She tilted her head to try and see what he'd been doing.

"Yes, Princess." He picked up the parchment, but did not show it to her. "Just going over provisions. All under control."

"May I see?"

"Of course, Princess, but I don't think my scratchings will mean much to you. Some of this and some of that. I can go over it later with you once I've worked it all out." He set the ink pot on the parchment. "Is there anything in particular you need?"

Why wouldn't Lorch want her to see his shopping list? "No. That's OK. Let me know if you need me for anything."

"Yes, Princess. I will."

Odd, thought Eloise. But then, maybe she was acting a little odd, too. Whatever. If it was important, he'd talk to her about it soon enough.

The banquet hall was even more drafty than the rest of the castle, being large, open, and full of windows. The meal was simple, tasty, and beautifully presented. Eloise particularly liked the pesto soup with gnocchi, beans, and goldbeet. The decorations honored Eloise in their colors, and before they ate, Queen Onomatopoeia formally addressed Eloise to welcome and farewell her at the same time. It was a Protocol-perfect performance.

Eloise had been the center of ceremonial events before, like the Thorning Ceremony, and even Jerome's Naming Ceremony, but never like this, never as the guest of honor sitting next to a monarch who wasn't her mother. Queen Onomatopoeia's fulsome words spoke of renewed and closer ties between their two realms, wished her parents long and happy lives, and invited Eloise to return for another visit, but perhaps with a little more notice next time (this was delivered with a warmth that made it humor, and not a dig). Eloise stood, as she had seen her mother do, and allowed words of genuine thanks to flow, voicing her appreciation for the hospitality and grace. She gave particular acknowledgement to Hoarfrost de Blotter, who dropped a stack of plates when she heard her name mentioned so publicly, and avoided any reference to getting to know the workings of The South's penal system, although there was still plenty of residual itch from her Enhanced Discomfort experience.

And then it was time for entertainment. The first performer was Jaminity. Earlier that day, he'd offered his personal apology to the queen, and she'd invited him to perform that night. It was a very different performance to the one Eloise had seen at the Gordian Naught. His presentation was more formal, and the choice of songs more floral. It suited the hall and the audience perfectly.

But, Eloise noted, he didn't sing That Song.

When Jaminity finished, it was time for The Stupendous One, as Jerome called her. He also referred to her as She, The Fabulous, Our Lady of the Wonderful, and The Voice That Launched a Thousand Drays. He'd spent the day getting increasingly excited to see Lyndia Thrind "Actually *in person*, El, *in person!*." In the privacy of her room, Eloise listened through her prattleweed hangover as Jerome's cheerful chatter returned for the first time since he'd been released from his bag. Of course, he knew all of Thrind's musical plays by heart, and could tell you that the daring "Rant" came after "All That Minuets," that "Backgammon" was much more interesting in its musicality than the much more popular "South Side Tale," and that "Oh! Brague!" (a Westie favorite) had played more times than the lesser "42nd Dirt Pathway," "Fur," and "Ocelots" combined (although Jerome had a soft spot in his heart for that last one).

He'd read the scores and seen as many shows as he could, which was a lot, as Brague had a thriving cultural scene. But to see Lyndia Thrind herself? That was special. Given she was closing in on four-score years, she no longer traveled, so this was likely to be the one time he ever got to hear her live. It wasn't surprising that his enthusiasm overcame his trauma.

"Do you think she'll sing 'On the Goat Trail Where You Live'? Or 'Climb Every Hillock'? Maybe 'Oh, What a Reasonably Pleasant Morning' or 'There's No Business Like Bard Business'? There are so many possibilities," said Jerome. "How could I possibly guess what she'll do? For that matter, how does she Herself choose?"

"I'm sure you won't be disappointed."

He wasn't.

Lyndia Thrind burst through the banquet hall door to a cascade of harp, trumpet, and drum, all sparkling robes, iridescent teeth, strong-length-wide smile, and hair piled so high that her attendant must have needed a step ladder to do it up. Lyndia didn't look her nearly 80 years, and Eloise wondered if there was a weak magic for beauty at work. Çalaht peeling purple potatoes, so much showmanship packed into one smaller-than-average person.

"Thank you, thank you, thank you, my darlings," she said in a voice that could have been heard over a Half Kingdom bombard. "Would you darlings mind if I sing a song or two?" The crowd cheered, and the visual spectacle of her entrance was immediately forgotten with the first notes of "Send in the Jesters." Her voice was like a whippoorwill had fallen into a bucket of rice syrup, then been dried off, glazed, sugared and lovingly dolloped with a swirl of chocolate mousse. It was pure. It was precious. It was perfect.

The performance progressed from "Don't Cry for Me, Stained Rock" and "Luck Be a Duck" to "I've Grown Accustomed to Her Pelt" and "Everything's Coming Up Haggleberries." Eloise could see Jerome mouthing along with every lyric, transfixed. "My mother would have loved this," he whispered during a break. "Eluminoscity, I know it bends Protocol if I'm not behind you, but would you mind terribly if I took a seat closer to the stage for her last set? I could sit next to Lorch."

Eloise smiled. "Of course. Come back when she's done."

"You're the best, El. The best!" Jerome scampered away, tail swishing in barely contained joy.

His decision to move closer brought a moment he'd never forget. Lyndia began singing "The I'm Fond of You Song," and like Gouache did with "Jester Went A-Courtin'," she chose an audience member to be the object of her song's desire. Lyndia picked Jerome.

She approached him as she sang, belting out the words of love. Jerome looked like he was ready to stand at Çalaht's side with happiness.

When she finished, she kissed him on the cheek, patted him gently on the shoulder, and got the crowd to give him a round of applause.

Now *that* was something to tell his mother about.

She finished her set, but the audience would not let her go. "Thank you, darlings. I have one more if you'd like." Lyndia waved to quiet the cheers and whistles, then said, "I'd like to bring someone up to help me with this one. Ladies and gentlemen, welcome back to the stage Jaminity Delgado Blister!" Jaminity swept in from the side carrying his lute. He knelt in front of Lyndia like she was a queen, and kissed her hand. The diva spontaneously grabbed a gladiolus from the flower arrangement on stage and with it, tapped one of his shoulders, then the other. "I dub thee Sir Blister of Quill, scribe of the most beautiful songs. Arise, Sir Blister!" The crowd ate it up.

Jaminity sat on a high stool, positioned his lute, and plucked some of the most familiar notes in all the realms. Lyndia began singing.

"There's a lady who knows all that glitters is groats..."

The arrangement was slow, contemplative, and gave Lyndia plenty of room to work the tune for all it was worth. Jaminity joined in, adding subtle, sweet harmonies, and the song wove a spell over the room. But before the final verse, Lyndia stopped singing, leaving Jaminity filling the space with a looping set of lute notes. Lyndia looked like she was trying to figure something out. "You know what, Jaminity?"

"What's that, Madame Thrind?"

"I think we could do better than this."

"How, Madame Thrind? How could we do better than this?"

"Maybe if we add another voice?"

"That could work," agreed Jaminity. He stopped plucking his lute and began clapping, motioning the audience to join in, then beginning a chant. "We need another voice! We need another voice! We need another voice!"

The banquet hall door slammed open, and in charged Alejandro, his magnificent white mane flying as he galloped around the perimeter of the room once, twice, three times. That he could do so without hurting anyone or even knocking over a glass was a feat of grace. As cheers rose, he slowed to a trot and moved between the tables to the stage. Like Jaminity, he, too, bowed at the feet of Lyndia Thrind, then stood, and turned to the audience.

Lyndia faced the queen. "I must ask for a special dispensation. Does Her Majesty consent to this non-human's participation?"

Eloise looked at the queen. She'd pursed her lips, not happy about being put on the spot. Her position on non-human use of the queen's tongue was clear from the moment one went through the Adequate Wall. One might as well have asked if they could serve spit soup for dessert.

Queen Onomatopoeia stood, and the crowd drew a collective breath. They were hers to please or disappoint, and there was no telling which way it would go. She looked at Eloise and raised an eyebrow. That simple gesture seemed to say, "Watch and learn how a queen works." Eloise fully expected the queen to impose her will, enforce her edicts, and order all three arrested.

"This comes dangerously close to transgression. This should have gone through my office," she said. She let a silence hang. "However, in honor of my visitor, Princess Eloise, I grant an exemption. This one night. This performance only. Make good use of it."

Everyone applauded, and several people called out, "To the queen!" The attention turned back to the stage. Al took a step forward and puffed out his chest. "I..." He paused dramatically. "I, Alejandro Diego Ferdinando Felipe Esteban Iglesias Desoto de Lugo..." He paused again, even longer this time, letting the moment hang. "I am another voice!"

The crowd erupted, cheers filling the room.

Jaminity helped Lyndia up onto Alejandro's back, then grabbed his lute and resumed the notes of the song. The three of them sang the last verse, where the singer convinces his sweetheart to trade the groats for true love's first kiss. The three-part harmony blended like they'd been singing together for decades, the notes weaving together with Jaminity on the bottom, Alejandro in the middle, and Lyndia on top, her voice dancing and twirling.

They finished That Song, bowed to the explosion of applause, and then, with Jaminity at his side, Alejandro strutted out of the room, carrying a waving Lyndia Thrind with him and ending the concert.

Queen Onomatopoeia leaned over to Eloise and said, "Now *that's* how you sing 'Three Bags of Groats for My Sweetheart.'"

GOING ON THE ROAD

Eloise, Jerome, and Lorch found Jaminity, Lyndia, and Alejandro in the courtyard, laughing. "Spectacular! Simply spectacular!" Lyndia was saying. "I haven't had so much fun in decades!"

"Señora Leendia, thank you for providing me such a splendid opportunity." Alejandro said this as softly as he could manage, the courtyard being considered a public space.

"Well, Al, darling, you were splendid yourself. I've never met anyone who could make an entrance like that. You knocked them out of their stockings, for sure."

"And that I could sing, out loud, my full voice in public here in The South without immediately being thrown for weeks into jail? Why, that is a miracle unto itself."

"Darling, the old girl still has some sway," said Lyndia. "It doesn't hurt to hold up a mirror and show people how stupid their prejudices can be."

Alejandro glowed, both from the compliment and the general rush of performing.

It suited him.

He pranced over to Eloise and the others, joy crackling from every hair. "Oh, Señorita Princesa! You have given me a most wonderful gift."

"I've given you a gift? You were the one who sang so beautifully."

"Ah, but Señorita Princesa, if you had not allowed me to accompany you on this magnificent adventure, then I, Alejandro Diego Ferdinando Felipe Esteban Iglesias Desoto de Lugo, would not have met this wonderful man, my new best friend, Zhaminity Delgado Blister, nor this incredible living legend, Leendia Thrind. Nor would I have had the chance to sing with not one, but both of them. In public, in The South! For these gifts, Señorita Princesa, I will be forever in your debt."

"Then some good has come from this undertaking," she replied. "I'm happy for you."

"And now, Señorita Princesa, I must beg of you to grant me a request."

"Oh?"

"I would ask that you allow me to remain behind when you leave tomorrow morning."

"No. Really?" Eloise's shoulders drooped. "You don't want to continue with us? We'll still need you when we find Johanna." She pressed a hand to her face, trying to hold back the feelings.

"Señorita Princesa, the truth is that I am the spare wheel on the carriage that is your grand expedition. But thanks to you, a new world of possibilities stretches out like a golden pathway before me. My new best friend Zhaminity has invited me to go on the road and perform with him. I shall be his transportation and his harmonies, his partner and posse, his *caballero* and *compain*. Plus, with your agreement, I would like to wipe clean the slate that tallies my very reasonable rates to you, and we shall call it all balanced and even."

"That's..." Eloise swallowed. "That's very kind, Al." She looked at Lorch. "You knew?"

"I suspected, and had to ask so I could secure the proper provisions."

"Which is why you didn't want me to see your list."

"That's right, Princess. My apologies."

Jaminity and Lyndia joined them, and Eloise blinked back tears. She put a hand on the horse's neck. "Alejandro..." Her voice cracked, and she coughed to clear her throat. "Alejandro Diego Ferdinando Felipe Esteban Iglesias Desoto de Lugo, I thank you for your faithful and enthusiastic service, and I release you from all obligations, save one."

"Yes, Señorita Princesa? What obligation will I have the honor of carrying with me?"

"That from time to time, I would be grateful if you and Jaminity would endeavor to travel through Brague, and grace me and my family with the beauty of your song and the radiance of your wit."

Alejandro smiled his toothy horse-smile. "That, Señorita Princesa, is an obligation I will be most delighted to fulfill."

The group spent the rest of the evening in Alejandro's private stable, joined by Madame Righteous, who sat with her head on Jaminity's shoulder, his arm around her. They told stories, ate a meal provided by the queen's kitchen, laughed, and enjoyed the warmth of friendship. Alejandro had traveled with them for just a few weeks, but Eloise felt like she'd known him so much longer. Their journey would change without his singing and banter, which had really come into its own once Jaminity joined them. The rapport between the two of them was instantaneous, and this outcome, in retrospect, inevitable.

Too soon, it was time to say farewell. Eloise embraced each of them, gave them a formal Western Lands kiss, wished them Çalahtspeed, and wiped away her tears as they walked the blustery streets of the Sclerotic Wold back to the castle, and sleep.

THE MOST PRECIOUS OBJECT
IN ALL THE REALMS

Despite the late night, Eloise and the others were up and readying themselves at first light. Gone was the constant feeling they needed to hurry so they might catch up with Johanna and Doncaster. It was replaced by the knowledge that there was a long journey and a specific destination. They had many strong lengths to cover.

Eloise and Jerome finished a breakfast of oat and millet porridge served in her room, then came out to the queen's stables to see how close they were to leaving. Very close. Hector and the Nameless One were laden and ready.

But something was different about the way Hector was organized.

"Where's my saddle?" asked Eloise.

"Princess Eloise, I have reconsidered our loads while we have been in one place for a few days," said Lorch. "The weight and carry effort represented by your saddle is better deployed for more useful resources. I've arranged for your saddle's return to Castle de Brague."

"Really?" said Eloise. "Thank you for your confidence."

"I am adjusting to the evolving realities, Princess Eloise. One change is that you no longer need the saddle. According to Hector, you have developed quite a good riding seat. And Champion Abernatheen de Chipmunk has apparently become much better at not clawing Equine Designate de Pferd's neck at every bump. I am confident he will be able to continue this even without the saddle."

Jerome scowled at Hector. "Every bump? Really?"

Hector gave a small shake, the equine equivalent of a shrug.

Ten minutes later, they emerged into the windswept main courtyard to find Queen Onomatopoeia stepping through a doorway on the other side, ready to farewell them. Eloise walked over and stood before her, and at an unexpected wave from the queen, the others followed. They lined up behind Eloise, who began to kneel. "Queen Ono—"

"Hold on. I'm not quite ready for that," said the queen. Eloise straightened and watched Onomatopoeia walk over to Lorch. "Boring travels to you." He bowed in response, and said, "Thank you, Your Majesty." Then she stood in front of Hector, Jerome, and the Nameless One. She did not say "Boring travels to you," but she nodded to them regally. It was the first time Eloise had seen her engage any non-human openly and directly, and she was sure it was a concession for her benefit. Like Lorch, the three bowed, but unlike Lorch, they also kept silent.

The queen walked back to Eloise. "I would like to say thank you for the diversion of your visit. I hereby formally invite you to return sometime."

"Thank you, Your Majesty," said Eloise. "And if my mother knew I was here, I'm sure she would ask me to reciprocate. On her behalf, and on my own, if I may be so bold, I would like to formally invite you to visit my family at Castle de Brague to see our queendom."

"I appreciate the invitation," said the queen. "And I'm sure your mother will be most surprised to hear you've done that. She might even be more surprised to know I'll consider it."

"Again, thank you, Your Majesty."

"Now, I have a small something for you." She drew out a small, beautifully wrapped parcel from a pocket. "A reminder, if you will, of your time here in the Sclerotic Wold, and the ties we have fostered between us."

"Shall I open it?" asked Eloise.

At the queen's nod, Eloise carefully untied the ribbon and unwrapped three delicately embroidered bags. One had the Western Lands crest on it, the second the crest of The South, and the third had the two crests, cleverly interwoven. Clearly they were made at the queen's specification. The contents of the bags were lightweight, and felt granular. And then it clicked. "Groats," said Eloise, smiling through chagrin. "You've given me three bags of groats."

"It was your most human moment in all the time we spent together," said the queen. "For those of us responsible for others, it does us well to remember our humanity."

"Thank you, Your Majesty," said Eloise. And she meant it. But then she had to scramble to think what she could gift in return, as Protocol suggested. It could not be too serious, as Onomatopoeia's gift was jocular, nor too grand, as the queen's gift was small and personal. On impulse, she reached into a pocket of her cape and pulled out the lavender hair ribbon that Odmilla had originally tied into her journeyman's braid. "This ribbon was fashioned here in The South, brought to Court by a merchant, and somehow ended up with me. In traveling with me from the Western Lands and All That Really Matters back to its place of origin, it is now a symbol of the ties between our two realms, and the hope that I might someday return to see you again," said Eloise.

"Very nice," said the queen, taking the ribbon. Eloise began to kneel, but Onomatopoeia stopped her, and unexpectedly gave her a Western Lands kiss, then pulled her into a hug. "I shall miss the company of my little songbird." She let go, and smiled. "Boring travels to you."

"Thank you," said Eloise, somewhat shocked by the sudden warmth and familiarity. "Be well—"

Eloise's words were cut short by the door bursting open. Out spluttered Hoarfrost de Blotter. "Excuse me, mu'um. Excuse me." She dropped an autonomic curtsy toward the queen. "Çalaht snorting sycamore seeds, I thought I was too late to say goodbye to Her Princessness. But I see yer still here." Breaking seven kinds of decorum and countless items of Protocol, the croftwoman broke into tears, dropped to her knees, and hugged Eloise around the legs. Lorch looked like he was about to snatch her away, but Eloise waved him off. Through her crying, Hoarfrost whimpered, "Yer've been so kind to the likes of meself, Princess. I'm sorry. I know I shouldn't hug yer, or even look at yer so much, but yer've opened me heart with yer patience and friendliness. I had to say thank yer, in case I maybe never laid me eyes on yer again."

"That's very kind of you, Goodwoman de Blotter," said Eloise. "Very kind. Now, can I ask you to do something for me?"

"Anything, Princess. Anything." Eloise could feel the first hints of tears soaking into her breeks.

"Would you be so kind as to stand up?"

"Of course, Princess. I can stand up. Fer sure."

There was a pause.

"Would you be OK to do that now?" Eloise unconsciously added just enough of The Tone to cut through the croftwoman's sobs.

"Of course, Princess. Of course." Hoarfrost de Blotter dabbed her eyes with the edge of Eloise's cape, then stood, sobs receding, but only just.

"I have something for you, Goodwoman de Blotter." Eloise didn't know what she would give her, but a gift seemed like a good diversion. Buying time, she felt the outline of the various things in her cape. Nothing there. "Oh, it might be in my pannier." She walked to the saddlebag, flipped it open, and immediately saw it. The chintzy, cheap-as-grass aloe leaf bag she'd won on her first attempt to free Cäääsëëëy from the barker. Mustering all the solemnity she could, she returned to Hoarfrost holding the scraps of sewn cloth in front of her like it was her mother's crown. "Goodwoman Hoarfrost de Blotter, I would be most grateful if you would accept this small token of my gratitude toward you. Please."

The croftwoman's eyes widened to barrel lids. "Really, Princess? For me?" Hands trembling, she took the bag like it was the most precious object in all the realms. And in that moment, it was. "Thank you, Princess! Thank you! I will never put this down," she sniffled. Then her reciprocal obligation under Protocol dawned on her. She looked pained that she didn't have anything. Then her face became determined, and she shot one hand into her top apron pocket, then her lower apron pocket, and then her right dress pocket. A look of relief came over her face when she found the object she sought. "Princess, if'n it pleases yer, would yer please accept this here token gift from meself?" She reached out a kitchen-muscled arm and handed Eloise a small oblong.

An acorn.

"Why thank you, Goodwoman de Blotter."

"Do you recognize it?"

"The acorn? Should I?"

"Of course, Yer Princessness," laughed Hoarfrost. "It's the acorn that went a'skitterin' away during the Ceremonies of the Stone. See here..." She pointed at the top of the acorn. "It's still wearing its wee little acorn hat. It's said that be good luck."

Eloise cupped the acorn between her hands and bowed to the servant. "Thank you, Goodwoman de Blotter, for this gift. It will remind me of your care, attention, and unparalleled enthusiasm."

The smile that beamed from the croftwoman's face could have stilled the winds. Hoarfrost looked at her queen. "Did yer hear that mu'um? She likes it!" Then she gasped, a new thought having bubbled up. She gently waved the aloe leaf bag. "I have to show t'others this!" With that, she dropped a massive oscillation of awkward curtsies, one for each of the travelers and two for her queen, and then rushed back inside, her yells of "Look everyone, look!" preceding her.

"You were most gracious," said the queen. "Others would not have seen beyond her peasant past."

"She is open-hearted and kind," said Eloise. "I think the realms need more of that."

Queen Onomatopoeia gave the smallest of nods. "Princess Eloise Hydra Gumball III, Future Ruler and Heir to the Western Lands and All That Really Matters, we wish you boring travels."

"Thank you, Queen Onomatopoeia Handrail Lúüùderming," replied Eloise. "Until we next meet."

❧ 72 ❧

EASTWARD HO!

"It is a blessed relief," said Eloise, a gust slamming into her and almost knocking her off the saddleless Hector. They left the confinement of the Windward Wall and the hammering Sclerotic Wold winds mercifully dropped from intolerable to insufferable.

The roadway toward the east was demoted from road to trail almost as soon as the castle fell from view, and within an hour had embarrassed itself down to track. By the time the sun settled down, it would have been generous to call it a path. Still, it was marked well enough, and Cäääsëëëy knew the way. They rode in silence, hunched against the wind, and Eloise concentrated on adjusting to life without a saddle.

Settlements dotted the landscape with ancient Southie names like Hill Hill and Village Village. The going was even more difficult at night, so they found a modest inn at Flat Flats and called it a day. Eloise asked Lorch if they'd better not conserve coin and sleep rough, but he assured her that the quartermaster, at the queen's instruction, had provided both coin and materiel. Inn Inn, run by an elderly couple who looked like they had never been further than Paddock Paddock, was clean in a way that displayed pride, and the supper they cooked was filling and contained nothing suspicious.

Midway through the next day, the wold landscape gave way to hills, which led into the Fake Mountains, so named because they were so beautiful they seemed fake to all who saw them from a distance. Up close, however, they were less charming. The cliff faces and soaring peaks, so appealing from a distance, were a complete pain to traverse, and the ever-present clouds, with their magical display of lightning, were deadly when one was too close.

As a pelting rain set in, Cäääsëëëy carefully threaded into a treacherous mountain crossing, avoiding most of the lethal risks a traveler through the Fake Mountains had to face. The mountain pass gave Eloise plenty of opportunity to decide if she was acrophobic (not particularly), dendrophobic (nope, trees didn't bother her), cremnophobic (somewhat, given the proximity of the cliffs), and astraphobic (that close to lightning? Down to the core.).

Cäääsëëëy promised them shelter in a cave he knew, and they eventually found its mouth. But it took blundering around in the rain and dark for way too long, and by the time they saw that the last occupants hadn't restocked the firewood store, it was too wet and too late to hunt for dry wood. The result was a long, chilly night of rough sleeping.

As they settled in, Eloise patted the ground, inviting Jerome to come sit by her. He settled on a corner of her blanket.

"So, are you OK?" she asked him in a soft voice.

"Of course. I'm fine."

"Are you sure?"

"Of course I'm sure. Why?"

"You're not acting like you. You're quieter. Drawn in. I haven't heard you humming about groats, and I think you're behind on your Hector-teasing quota."

He didn't react to her jest.

Eloise drew her cloak closer around her shoulders. "So, what happened to you? What did they do to you in jail?"

Jerome shrugged, but said nothing.

"It can't have been easy. At least I wasn't put in a sack, although I had one over my head for a while. It wasn't easy for me, and you had it worse."

"I guess."

"So, talk."

"El, I really don't want to go back there. Not even in my mind."

"Come on, Jerissimo. Talking about it might—"

"El, please. I want to put it behind me and move on."

"But, you can't just—"

"Please, Princess Eloise, please. I really don't want to talk about it."

She realized from his tone that she'd probed as far as he would let her, for now at least, so she left him alone.

The morning saw an even heavier rain develop, and Cäääsëëëy suggested waiting it out, as the next section would not be helped by slipperiness. So they ate, and they rested, but the habit of non-human silence had taken hold during their time in The South, and conversation was sparse. If Jaminity and Alejandro had been there, they would have filled the waiting time with songs, but the best Eloise could manage was to have That Infernal Song rattling around in her head. Eloise used her prayer beads to try to count the song out of her consciousness, but she ended up ticking off the beads to the song's rhythms. Maddening.

They stayed for a second night. Lorch ventured out during the day to scavenge wood, and miraculously found enough that was dry to strike a fire. It lifted the mood, and the dance of flame on the cave wall provided Eloise welcome distraction, but the group remained silent.

Morning brought an ease to the weather, and they headed out as soon as they could. Cäääsëëëy quietly suggested that Lorch and Eloise walk, and it was soon clear why. Compared to the trail they now faced, the previous days had been a biscuit walk. Not having the horses accommodate the load and awkwardness of a human made it a little easier. It took constant vigilance to keep correct footing, and there was only once or twice that Eloise thought she would die.

Plus, there was the matter of depth perception. With two eyes facing forward, the humans could easily perceive depth, which made placing their feet on the narrow ledges relatively straightforward. But the others, and the horses in particular, had eyes on the sides of their heads—wonderful for peripheral vision, but terrible if you were trying to gauge if the water you were about to step into was a tenth of a weak length deep or 20 strong lengths. (Cäääsëëëy, with his chameleon eyes bulging out and swiveling, could have it both ways.)

Still, Cäääsëëëy was happy with the rate of progress, and said they'd reach Port Port the next day.

PORT PORT

I t was midday when they finally made their way out of the Fake Mountains and descended a trail into the seaside village.

If ever there was a place that deserved its name, it was Port Port. Port Port was the portiest port in all the realms and deserved every nuance of its porty reputation. From the reek of putrid seawater to the seafarers with body parts replaced with wood and metal, from the inns spilling over with drunks, grime, stale food, and all forms of liquid consolation to the buzz of trade flowing on and off the ships, Port Port was a sea town cliché made manifest.

Eloise, Lorch, Jerome, and Cäääsëëëy stepped through the doorway of a tavern called the Schooner. It was unclear if the name was a reference to a ship or to the glasses used by its inebriants. Clove pipes and badly ventilated cooking fires belched smoke into the room. The reek of sweat and oregano mingled nauseatingly with rotted cabbage and what smelled like mop water, if the mop had been used in a place like this and never cleaned.

"What was his name again?" asked Jerome.

"Stúüübing. Captain Stúüübing of the *Barco del Amor*." said Lorch.

"Do we know what he looks like?" asked Eloise.

"Her Majesty Queen Onomatopoeia described him as 'tall, dark, and handsome,' and assured me we would find him in this fine establishment if he was in port."

Eloise looked over the people in the room. It was clear the prejudices and restrictions that held sway in the rest of The South were blatantly ignored here in the Schooner. Dozens of species sat elbow to elbow, swapping stories, slurping swill, and slugging down consolation as fast as it could be drawn from the tap. The din was as overwhelming as the stench, but nowhere did she see anyone who could be described as "tall, dark, and handsome."

"See any candidates?" she asked Lorch.

"No, Princess. But I'll take a closer look." With Cäääsëëëy following, Lorch waded into the mass of bodies. Eloise had no intention of pressing in among the throng, so stayed at the doorway with Jerome. His whiskers twitched, a sure sign that he thought as much of the place as she did. "So, if Stúüùbing isn't here...?"

"Lorch had a list from Her Maj Ono, but Cäääsëëëy crossed off all the names bar three, and on two of those he drew a frowning face, which I presume is not a ringing endorsement."

"Right."

They waited in the doorway, watching Lorch bob around the room, occasionally leaning over to ask someone a question, but inevitably getting a shrug or a head shake.

"Pardon me, dear lady. Might I pass?" The cultured voice came from behind her. Eloise turned to find that she was blocking the way of the largest alpaca she'd ever seen. He was dressed for the sea, but his choice of clothing was so ambiguous, it might have admitted him to either a queen's war vessel or a pirate's flagship. His fleece was a dark charcoal gray, except for a jaunty white tuft that sprang out from under his jet black, flat-brimmed sombrero. One cheek was puffed out, hinting at a pinch of something spittable tucked into his jaw. A spyglass dangled from a lanyard around his neck.

He was magnificent.

Also, he was tall and dark.

"Captain Stúüùbing, I presume?" asked Eloise.

"At your service, dear lady. I am known as Stúüùbing, although I have recently shed 'captain' for 'commodore.'" He smiled wryly. "It's all nonsense, anyway."

"Commodore? Then you are in Her Majesty's service?" asked Jerome.

"Not exactly, good sir."

"Do you fly a pirate's flag?" asked Eloise.

"Also, not exactly, dear lady. But, if I did, I might be circumspect about saying so."

"Fair enough. Could my friends and I invite you to share luncheon with us? There is a matter we hoped to discuss."

Stúüùbing gave a small flick of his head, which tossed the sombrero off so it could settle halfway down his long neck. The movement was as unconsciously graceful as anything Hector did. Eloise reckoned the two of them would get on like a hovel on fire.

"But if you wish to eat, there are better options than the Schooner, " Stúüùbing suggested.

Jerome retrieved Lorch and Cäääsëëëy, and they followed Stúüùbing away from the wharf, down a side street, and through an unmarked door. The unnamed, hidden inn was run by alpacas, and its fawn-colored proprietress greeted Stúüùbing warmly. "Méëèrrïïll, how lovely to see you, darling." She air-kissed his cheeks and led them to seats at the rear. Stúüùbing stopped long enough to deposit his chaw in a cuspidor before settling on cushions by their table.

Over a spicy borscht accompanied by a non-consolation cranberry cider, Lorch spelled out their needs to Commodore Stúüùbing without exactly saying who they were. Stúüübing looked uncomfortable to learn that his name had been supplied by Onomatopoeia, clearly worried that the whole thing could be an entrapment. But Lorch handed him an envelope from the queen, containing a letter with a single word: "Even."

Reading it, Stúüübing grimaced, but immediately stood up, bowed, and flicked his sombrero to a jaunty angle on his head. "I am at your service, dear lady."

They peppered him with questions, which he answered calmly and competently. Yes, he would take them to the harbor at Haze Town. Yes, it should not take more than two or three days at sea, weather allowing. Yes, he could leave on the next tide. Yes, he would accept coin for the passage, but only at a fair market rate and not at a rate that would normally reflect such a disruption to his existing plans. Yes, the *Barco del Amor* was suitable for horses. No, the rules of The South were not applied on board. Yes, Eloise could have her own berth. Yes, the orientation of its bed was lengthwise with the ship, not crosswise. Yes, the ship would also carry trade goods. No, he would not comment on the status of the ship's registration. Yes, the borscht was delicious. No, he would not have any more, but a dessert of lime custard could be recommended. Yes, they should order the haggleberry tea. Yes, there was a risk of the ship floundering off course (a phrase offensive to certain fish). Yes, it had happened before and would happen again, but the routes were well known, so the risk was minimal. No, they were not likely to be smashed into by marauding beluga whales, as the Sea Lanes Agreement seemed to be holding, despite disgruntlement among certain groups of cetaceans. Yes, he would see them on his ship in approximately five hours, which would allow them time to settle in before casting off.

That left Eloise and the others those few hours to stock up on provisions, enjoy the remaining sparse charms of Port Port, and find the dinghy that would row them out to the *Barco del Amor*.

🦂 74 🦂

BARCO DEL AMOR

The trip on the *Barco del Amor* was a new anguish for Eloise. She'd heard of seasickness, but to experience it so urgently and so soon after leaving the calm waters of the harbor at Port Port took her by surprise. She'd expected to maybe feel a little queasy, but was sure it would be nothing ginger couldn't fix.

Wrong.

Eloise's nausea grabbed her full force by the guts, emptying her of borscht, custard, and cider almost immediately and leaving her to dry retch over and over. "Çalaht sorting slimy socks," she moaned. "Nausea *and* vertigo." Her instinct was to take to her cabin, crawl into bed, close her eyes, and try to sleep or tough it out. But that turned out to be exactly the wrong thing to do.

Lorch and the Nameless One immediately made themselves available as crew so they'd have something to help pass the time, and from simple habit. They'd sailed other seas on enough campaigns that they were genuinely useful, and moved about the ship with grace. Jerome, who'd told Lorch he'd look after Eloise was, if it was possible, worse than her. The two of them spent several long, uncomfortable hours practicing their heaving skills.

Eventually, Lorch looked in on them, found their collective misery, and hauled both out of the berth and into the fresh air. He found an out-of-the-way spot on deck, faced them forward, and pointed at the horizon. "Look into the distance, and try to ignore what's nearby. That should help."

It did. A little. But by dawn, Eloise's stomach muscles were sore from overuse, and Jerome looked like he was considering flinging himself overboard. Both were reduced to monosyllabic grunting when asked questions.

Hector was no better. He looked as green as a magnificent black horse could.

"Can horses regurgitate?" asked Eloise.

"No, Princess, as much as one might wish one could."

Commodore Stúúùbing was everywhere, the ship's master and heart. His sombrero and spyglass constantly popped up from some new direction, his padded feet glided across the deck and up and down ramps that led to the ship's innards. There was a still firmness to his manner with his crew, his words punctuated by short, sharp expectorations over the rail toward the sea. Occasionally, he would come over to enquire after Eloise and the others, but he knew there was not a lot he could do. "I would invite you to sup with me," he said at one point. "But truth be told, there is not much point until your stomach settles. Perhaps that will happen before we land." He politely left them to their suffering.

At the end of the first full day at sea, the weather worsened. Thunderheads had been biding their time, stalking them from a distance. Suddenly, they raced forward, lashing the *Barco del Amor* with a freezing rain that sent Eloise and Jerome racing to her berth so they could continue to suffer out of the weather.

Stúúùbing was exhilarated, heading toward mania. As Eloise ran past him to get below deck, he called to her, voice half-demented. "Dear lady! Can you feel that wind blow? Woo hoo!" While Eloise spent the storm clutching a bucket and moaning, the commodore trotted back and forth, ensuring the cargo and crew were safe and secure. Each flash of lightning was mirrored by a flash in his eyes. The harder the rain and wind buffeted the ship, the more manic his laugh became, and the more frequently he spat at the elements in disdain. He constantly harassed his navigator for location updates, monitoring how far astray the winds took them—wildly, it turned out—and more than once took over the steering to correct course. One minute he was ensuring Hector and the Nameless One, who could not grip, were not sliding overboard, the next he was grappling a rope with his teeth to help his crew reef a sail. Stúüübing fighting a tempest was very much at home.

The raging rain and wind lasted hours, and the denouement was slow. Eventually, the seas calmed enough for Eloise to fall asleep for the first time since she boarded, even if it was more stupor than slumber.

When she woke, it was to an eerie calm that was such a startling contrast to the weather of a few hours before that it left her disoriented. She emerged weakly into a sunny day where the ship sat becalmed. The few exhausted crew on deck dragged themselves perfunctorily from task to task.

Eloise found Stúüübing standing at the rail, looking far into the distance through a spyglass mounted on a stand so he would not have to hold it with a two-toed foot. "G'mid-morning, dear lady," he said, not interrupting his observations. "You are better?"

"Yes, thank you, Commodore Stúüübing. I have left my bucket behind. For now."

Eloise peered in the direction he was looking. There was nothing special, as far as she could tell. Stúüübing stepped back and nodded to his spyglass. "Have a look."

She put her right eye to the cylinder and squinted shut her left. She moved it around, but only found water. Nothing on it or below it.

"Look for where the water meets the sky," said the alpaca.

Eloise slowly moved the spyglass up and down until she found and held the horizon.

There. She'd never seen it before, but knew exactly what it was. The sight of it set her teeth on edge, even if she did not understand why. A lavender line of fog several strong lengths away stretched across the ocean and rose toward the heavens. "The Purple Haze."

"Exactly, although on the water, one calls it the Devil's Veil."

"It doesn't look like much," Eloise said, hiding the unexpected revulsion it elicited.

"Not from here, no."

"And close up?"

"By the gap in Çalaht's teeth, may I never find out, dear lady. And I wish the same for you. The Devil's Veil will embrace you and never let you go. Twice in my life, I have seen a ship cross into it. Twice. Once deliberately, because the captain was a madman, and once accidentally, during a typhoon. What is so profound is how completely those ships disappeared. The ships plus the souls on board. Gone. Totally. I know not if those souls writhe in torment or live in peace. I just know no one and nothing ever emerges from behind the Devil's Veil."

Eloise stood back from the spyglass. "Are we in danger?"

"No, dear lady. Not anymore." Stúüübing spat overboard as an exclamation point. "There was a time, though, when the wind was pushing us, that it took all of my will not to break down and prepare myself to stand with Çalaht. But fate smiles on us today, and we can gaze on the horror of the Devil's Veil from a safe enough distance." He stepped forward and resumed looking through the spyglass. "Please rest, dear lady, then try to have a bite of crackerbread. And water. You and your small friend must put fluids back into your bodies. The winds will resume this afternoon, and I shall sail the *Barco del Amor* hard for Haze Town to arrive as the next tide allows. With Çalaht's help, you will sleep on land late tonight."

"Thank you, Commodore Stúüübing. For everything."

"You may thank me once I have safely delivered you and your friends, dear lady. Or, should that be 'Princess?'"

"Ah. How did you figure that out?"

"There were many clues. Your speech. Your accent. Your clothing. How you hold yourself. The way your people defer to you, care for you, and without even thinking, position themselves to protect you. The fact that you delivered that envelope with its contents. Its author would not do such a thing for just anyone. All of that, plus your guard called you 'Princess.' That was perhaps the biggest giveaway."

"I see. Well, again, thank you. And here on your ship and in front of your crew, 'dear lady' is fine."

"Thank you, too, dear lady."

❧ 75 ❧

HAZE TOWN

I f Port Port was a dump, Haze Town was a cesspool. It was like someone listed everything that was good and bad about Port Port, erased the "good" column, multiplied the bad by seven, then rounded up. The stench, the dirt, the dilapidation, and the wooden legs and hooks for hands were everywhere. There just wasn't any counterbalance. Haze Town also lacked the buzzing activity of Port Port—the ships were fewer, the people slower, the trade sparser. Most of the ships leaving Port Port went in some other direction than Haze Town.

Behind the town and blocking out half the sky was Foggy Mountain, a big brute of a long-dormant volcano. Cutting across it was the Purple Haze, which loomed about a strong length away, a baleful curtain of fog and menace.

The Haze Town harbor was deep enough that Stúüübing docked the *Barco del Amor* rather than use dinghies. Thank goodness, because rowing the two horses out to the ship and getting them up was cumbersome, not very dignified, and involved nets and pulleys. Here, Hector and the Nameless One could leave the ship down a gangway, though they'd want to make sure they avoided the many missing and broken planks that were becoming hard to see in the fading light. "We're lucky," said Stúüübing to Eloise once the ship was tied off. "This wharf is in relatively good shape. Half of them here are so bad I'd rather wait for another ship to leave than risk using one."

Stúüübing disembarked (a term dogs found offensive, but only if uneducated), padding down the gangway and stepping lightly across the wharf, his sombrero at its usual jaunty angle and his spyglass bouncing on its lanyard. "Step where I've stepped," he called back to the others. "It would be best if we did not have to fetch you from the water, which is filth itself and would leave you with an ague about which bards could write an epic ballad." Eloise didn't need more warning than that and made her way to the shore by stepping on the exact spots where Stúüübing's padded feet had gone.

"So, Princess Eloise Hydra Gumball III, welcome to Haze Town, such as it is," said Stúüübing, sweeping his neck to encompass the entire dismal village. It was the first time he'd spoken her full name. "It is an honor to have been of service to you."

"Thank you, Commodore Méëërríïll Stúüübing," replied Eloise. "Your help has been invaluable."

"Thank you, Princess."

"If you find the winds bring you to Brague, I hope you'll visit."

He paused, slightly longer than he should have, like he was weighing up unseen and incalculable consequences, then smiled. It was the second biggest smile she'd seen on him (the biggest being the deranged one during the storm). "Dear lady, I shall."

Eloise gave him a formal Western Lands kiss, and he kissed her hand. She made her way up the road, but ten steps on, glanced back to see him one last time. He nodded at her, the motion being both an acknowledgement and a way to resettle his sombrero at a more mysterious angle.

Cäääsëëëy led them past the Foggy Inn and the Hazy Taverna, not to be confused with the Föööggy Inn and the Häääzy Taverna, all four of which looked so desperately awful that Eloise kept crossing the road to avoid them. Stúüùbing recommended a couple of other places, both run by Southies. The Inn Fóòòggy was supposedly "pretty tolerable, if bland," and if it was full, then the Taverna Háäàzy was "acceptable."

After walking for half an hour in the failing light, they found what used to be the Inn Fóòòggy, but was now a burned-out husk. Only a sign on a pole proclaimed it as a place that had once accommodated lodgers. "Right," said Cäääsëëëy. "Probably not quite what we're looking for." With no further comment, he led them through side roads and increasingly badly lit alleys. Fortunately, the Taverna Háäàzy was still there, and there were definitely people inside. Unfortunately, a scrawled sign hammered to the front declared it was "Temporarily Closed Due to the Detection of Various Poxes Within." Those inside were trapped there by boards across windows and doors. Eloise did not want to imagine what they might be suffering in there, nor did she care to find out.

"Also not quite what we seek," said Cäääsëëëy. He turned and led them back toward the less-savory possibilities they'd already passed.

Their progress was interrupted by a small, barefoot boy who ran out from a side alley on the right, and slid to a stop in front of them. At the same moment, a goat kid in a torn tunic rushed out from the opposite side, also impeding their way. Lorch and Jerome stepped in front of Eloise, in case this was an ambush.

"Excuse me, good people," said the boy and kid at the same time. They looked at each other, annoyed, then back at the travelers. "Are you looking for—" They both stopped again.

"They're mine," said the goat. "They are on my side of the street."

"They're mine." The child puffed out his underfed chest. "I got here first."

"Oi, biscuit off, you Wilbur," said the goat. "They're mine. You had the last one. That old biddy."

"You biscuit off. The biddy bolted bye-bye because you blemished my blarney." The boy shoved the goat for emphasis. "And don't call me a Wilbur, you Agnes."

"Agnes! You called me an Agnes!" The goat reared up on two back legs, tilted his head, and aimed his horn buds right at the other child's abdomen. Half a second later, the two were wrestling in the middle of the dirt road, the scuffle peppered with "You Wilbur!" and "You Agnes!"

Eloise and the others stepped around them, and the youngsters realized their marks were about to walk away. "Wait, wait, wait!" said the goat kid.

The boy released his headlock on the goat, and the two scampered in front of them again.

"Excuse me, good people," started the goat again. "Are you—"

"Don't listen to an Agnes like him," interrupted the boy. "I'm—"

"You Wilbur! You called me an Agnes again!" The return to wrestling stopped any further conversation.

Once again, Eloise and the others went to walk around them. This time, the pair did not stop their scuffle, but moved enough that they continued to be in the way.

Eloise cleared her throat. "That. Will. Do." Her use of The Tone stopped them at once. She pointed to the boy. "You. Say your piece."

"Excusememisstresswouldyoubelookingforaplacetostay?Mymumand-granhavearoomthatscleanandtidy. Icantakeyouthererightnow. Anditwillnotcosttoomuchcoin. Ipromiseyou'llbesleepinglikeababy." The rehearsed words spilled out like an upturned bucket.

When he paused for a breath, Eloise held up a finger to stop any more, and pointed at the goat. "You."

"Excuse Me Mistress. Would You Be Looking For A Place To Stay?" The goat kid's attempt at clear enunciation slowed his delivery way down.

Eloise stopped him with the finger again. "How far?"

"Just around the corner, Mistress." He pointed with a foreleg to the left.

"And yours?" Eloise asked the child.

He pointed in the opposite direction. "Around the corner and down a ways."

At a nod, Lorch and Cäääsëëëy left with the boy to check out his offering, and Hector and Jerome trotted off with the kid to do the same. Eloise and the Nameless One ducked beneath a shop awning to wait, their position giving them a clear view of both side streets.

They stood there in silence, quiet and comfortable. After a while, it occurred to Eloise that it was the first moment she'd had alone with the Nameless One since their journey began. He was always with Lorch or Hector. Eloise turned to him, straightening to a formal posture. "Might I say something?"

The horse cocked his head slightly, a sign of both curiosity and permission.

"I want to say thank you. Thank you, Nameless One, for being with us. And more, thank you for taking such good care of Guard Lacksneck. Your partnership is a joy and a treasure."

The Nameless One straightened as well and bowed a formal reply.

Eloise had nothing to add and relaxed back against the wall. The horse also adjusted, so he was beside her at a proper distance. The two watched the late dusk become night, and the town's dull colors becoming even duller.

Enveloped in darkness, Eloise heard the Nameless One make a rasping sound. She glanced toward him, then back to the night.

He made it again.

Then the Nameless One did something Eloise thought him incapable of.

He spoke.

His voice was low and rough. He formed words slowly, clearly out of practice. It was like listening to stones yodel.

"I." He stopped.

"Yes?"

"I." He stopped again and made another rasp. "I have a name." His cadence was even slower and more deliberate than the goat kid's.

"I see." Eloise waited. The Nameless One said nothing else, so Eloise added, "Would you like me to hear it?"

The horse nodded. "My name." He paused again. "My name is." Another long pause, full of possibility. "My name is Patchouli."

"Oh." Eloise was grateful for the dark, as it meant she only had to keep her voice neutral, and not her face.

"Patchouli Bee-swill Nectarbucket."

"Oh. Oh, my."

There was another silence.

"Patchouli is a fine name," said Eloise.

"Maybe if you grow haggleberries. Or prattleweed. Not if you are a warrior." The words came a little easier for him now.

"Fair enough."

"My parents were fond of prattleweed. Very fond."

"That might explain a thing or two."

"Yes, Princess. It would. Nectarbucket isn't even a family name. They made it up."

The sounds of the night seemed loud, compared to the quiet of the girl and the horse.

"Princess?"

"Yes?"

"Guard Lacksneck knows, but I'd rather you didn't tell the others."

"Of course not." Eloise faced him. "You have my word. You remain the Nameless One."

"I wanted you to know."

"Thank you for telling me."

"This has been the finest journey of my life."

"Mine, too, everything considered. And that is in part because you are along for it."

"You are kind, Princess."

"And you are brave, capable, and true."

They lapsed back into stillness, and moments later, the others returned from two directions at once.

Both places turned out to be acceptable, so they split up. Eloise, Jerome, and Lorch stayed at the goat kid's home, as the rooms were fairly large and immaculately cleaned, smelling nothing of goat, while the boy's place had better paddocks for the horses. Cäääsëëëy again chose a stable over a house.

As soon as she politely could, Eloise fell onto the straw-stuffed mattress of the rope-sprung bed. She thought how wonderful it was to be on land again, and she drifted off to sleep with thoughts of patchouli flowers and Patchouli the horse in her head.

76

AND STRONG LENGTHS TO GO
BEFORE I SLEEP

Before dawn, Eloise had broken fast, Lorch settled their room and board, and Jerome finished his pre-ride stretches. He'd also called Eloise a "Wilbur" twice and Lorch an "Agnes" three times.

"You know that's going to get tiresome," said Eloise.

"Oh, don't be such an Agnes, Elotastic."

"Get it out of your system, Jeriatric. But watch out with Hector, or you might end up in a punch bowl again."

"He's such a Wilbur."

It was good to hear Jerome in a lighter mood. Eloise wondered what might have changed, or if it was just a matter of time.

They set off from Haze Town with Cäääsëëëy riding in front of Lorch. "That way," he said, pointing to a trail marked "Not this way."

"Are you sure?" asked Eloise.

"I'm sure."

A few dozen lengths on, there was a second sign: "Don't Go This Way. Really, We Mean It." Eloise let that one pass without comment.

Fifty lengths later, a third sign read, "What, Can't You Read? Go BACK!", followed almost immediately by one that said, "OK, Now You're Just Being Obstinate. Don't Say You Weren't Warned."

"Cäääsëëëy?" asked Eloise.

Lorch and the Nameless One stopped. "There must be a reason for these signs, Cäääsëëëy Lïïïss," said Lorch.

"Princess, Guard Lacksneck, these signs are for the stupid and the careless. Foggy Mountain is a problem for the lowest common denominator and the middling. But we are careful, sure-footed, and in a hurry. This approach will save us four days. I ask that you trust me with this."

Then he waited, having said his piece.

"I trust him," said Hector. "And I am sure-footed."

The others nodded their agreement.

"Lead on, Cäääsëëëy," said Eloise.

It was soon clear why barely any trade came this way from Stained Rock, and why all the warning signs were there. When the Purple Haze sliced across Foggy Mountain, the route that had once let commerce flow fell behind it. This remaining path was passable, but if you were heavily burdened or had a cart or carriage, it was a shortcut to a quick demise at the bottom of Please Don't Make Me Go There Gorge. It made the demanding crossing through the Fake Mountains seem like a frolic in a sculpture garden. Breathtaking drops snuck up on the unsuspecting, and the switchbacks seemed to cling to the narrowest of hopes. In places where the ground was brittle, loose stones tumbled into the maw of the gorge, barely audible when they hit the bottom. If the falling rocks were large enough, they echoed around Foggy Mountain like a slow staccato warning from Çalaht herself.

Walking in single file, the group progressed along the ill-used trail. Each length walked was an accomplishment. Eloise found it exhausting.

Not Cäääsëëëy. He was like Commodore Stúüübing facing down the tempest. The chameleon got more animated the further they went. He bounded on and off the Nameless One to scout their trail, and seemed to greet every rock slip, every broken shelf, every unstable boulder like an old friend. His body, built for living in trees, was perfectly suited to this task. His feet, with two toes forward and two facing back, could grip and move with a certainty none of the others felt. Cäääsëëëy looked like he was having the best day of his life.

Eloise was not. With little more to do than make sure she did not plummet to her death, her anxieties reasserted themselves. The discomforts and irritations of her habits, which she'd been able to push down or distract herself from since being in prison, began talking to her all at once. She noticed how dirty she was, how her sweat soaked her tunic and made it sticky, and the movement of the objects in her travel cape against her body. The prayer beads might have helped, but she needed both hands to clamber, and she didn't want to risk losing them. Counting footsteps didn't work because it brought focus to the danger she faced.

Breaths. She could count breaths.

Eloise counted her inhales and exhales, matching them to the pace of her heart—six beats in, six beats hold, six beats out. It helped.

Somewhat.

They paused for a late lunch at a spot where the path flared onto an open shelf wide enough for the horses to rest without fear of tumbling. The difficult walking did one good thing: it exhausted Jerome enough that he stopped calling everyone Agnes and Wilbur. Eloise would take her mercies where she could find them. They ate quietly, looking out over the gorge. "So much beauty in such a hostile place," said Eloise.

"It's only hostile to our desires, Princess," said Cäääsëëëÿ. "If we were not bent on crossing it, and were content to look and enjoy, then there would be no hostility."

Eloise took a bite of raspberry leather, which Lorch had somehow located in Haze Town. She chewed, contemplating Cäääsëëëÿ's thoughts on intent and how it shapes one's view of the world. How many times had she framed a situation, or characterized a place or person, based on the filter of her own intent?

Probably all the time.

ALL THAT DAY, CASEY SAID HE WAS HAPPY WITH THEIR PROGRESS. But then suddenly, he wasn't. It was late afternoon, and they had traveled ten or twelve of the hardest strong lengths Eloise ever experienced, Cäääsëëëÿ pulled them up. "Hold on," he said, his voice the whisper they'd first heard in The South. "This is not right."

"What's the matter?"

"I'm not sure yet. But something is wrong."

The path disappeared. Not just the path, but an entire section of the land. "Look, from there to there." He pointed across a section that was a quarter strong length across.

"What is it?" asked Eloise.

"A breakdown. The mountain has broken away. This part of the Foggy Mountain's face is gone, fallen into the Please Don't Make Me Go There Gorge. And freshly so, from the way it looks."

They stood, taking in the majesty of the destruction.

"So," said Jerome finally. "What do we do about this Foggy Mountain breakdown?"

"What choice do we have?" said Lorch. "We have to find a way through."

"I suppose we could go back, but that holds little appeal," added Hector. "A day to travel back, plus the extra four days needed for the other road? No, thank you."

Eloise craned her neck (a phrase offensive to certain long-necked birds) to see the extent of the impasse. "Surely there must be a way forward that does not involve another visit to the hole that is Haze Town."

"I could make it," said Jerome. He wiggled his claws. "These were made for this kind of thing."

Cääsëëëy also held up a foot. "I, too, would find a way across. The problem is our differing abilities to grip."

"You are right that gripping is not high on the typical equine skillset," said Hector. "Endurance, speed, exceptionally good manners, precise movement—yes. But not gripping."

Lorch shrugged off the bag he carried. "I suggest we use the remaining light to scout our possibilities. Princess, I ask that you prepare this place for the night's rough sleeping."

"I could help scout, too."

"No doubt. But this Foggy Mountain breakdown moved fast and suddenly," said Lorch. "Who knows how unsteady the land near it might be."

"And?"

Lorch put on his "I'd rather not say" face.

"Guard Lacksneck?"

"Relative value, Princess."

"Pardon?"

He sighed. "Princess Eloise, it is simple. If I do not return from this trip, there will be those in the queendom who will miss me, especially at Lower Glenth. But that will hardly leave a dent in the realms. But if you do not return, the effects will ripple out and directly or indirectly touch everyone."

"Guard Lorch Lacksneck, I do not consider my life more valuable than yours."

"That is kind of you, Princess." He looked like he was eating a lemon. "But wrong-headed. You are not the one who can make that calculation. Our relative values are for others to ascribe. This journey has been full of risks I have been unhappy about, but we have found our way through. If I can decrease the risk to you in this situation, then I would like to. No, make that, I will do so."

Eloise looked at him, his serious face blank and steely. "Right then. What would everyone like for supper? Crackerbread and tuber soup?"

"It's potato soup, you Wilbur," said Jerome.

"I'll get it started."

77

RUNNING DOWN THE MIDDLE

It was Jerome who found the way through. He, Lorch, and Cäääsëëëy split up and went in different directions for the rest of that day, but each came back with nothing. At dawn, they did the same, leaving Eloise and the horses to sit and rest. Mid-morning came and went, as did noon, but early in the afternoon, Jerome came scampering back. "El! El! I think I've got something. Come have a look."

He led her off the trail and into the trees that dominated Foggy Mountain. They climbed for most of an hour until he led her into a clearing that had an outlook. They climbed a boulder, and Jerome pointed toward the east. "Tell me what you see down there. The green thing."

"It's a shrubbery."

"And next to that?"

"Um, it's another shrubbery, only slightly higher."

"Yes, and running down the middle?"

"A path? A path!"

"Exactly, El. A path. A path heading in the right direction—and one a horse could go on."

"You, Jeremiad, are the biscuit."

They walked back to where Eloise had been waiting and found the others. Within hours, they'd worked out a way for the horses to reach the path. It was cut off from the trail by a rock slide, a steep climb, and the largest patch of rash ivy Eloise had ever seen, but they made it.

They picked their way forward until darkness and then kept going for extra measure so they'd be that bit further along. Eventually, they settled for the night.

"Settled" was overselling it. Eloise couldn't find a comfortable position no matter how she lay on her blankets. Her thoughts were everywhere, and when she dozed, a low buzz, like a debate team of wasps, invaded her dreams.

The first words she heard the next morning were from Jerome. "Sweet Çalaht licking limp lima beans."

Eloise jumped up to see what was wrong.

It was the Purple Haze, at most half a strong length ahead of them, and very, very close to the path they followed.

Jerome looked like his soul had taken a little stroll and had just come back. "If we'd kept going last night, even just a little while..."

"We could have run straight into it," finished Lorch.

"That would have been a suboptimal outcome," said Eloise.

"A suboptimal outcome? Really?" Jerome stamped the ground. "Princess Eloise Hydra Gumball III, Future Ruler and Heir to the Western Lands and All That Really Matters, I am committed to this task of retrieving Princess Johanna, but like El Lorcho here, I am even more determined to return you home safe and sound. We could have blundered into the fog last night, and it would have been because of our own carelessness. So perhaps from now on, we can be just a little more cautious, and avoid that kind of potentially 'suboptimal' result."

"Jerome!" He never spoke to her that way.

"Don't you 'Jerome' me, El. I'm serious. We had no business continuing on that late, and it was hubris to have done so."

It was the most serious she'd ever seen him. "Yes, Champion Abernatheen de Chipmunk, that caution is well observed. Thank you for your concern. We shall adjust accordingly."

Jerome turned to roll up his bedding, muttering, "'Suboptimal.' Sheesh."

"Please don't call me 'El Lorcho,'" said Lorch, but not loud enough for Jerome to hear.

They packed, ate, and got going as fast as possible, because storm clouds and the cold of the season both threatened. Their trail veered away from the Purple Haze and then wove back and forth, sometimes nearing the fog as close as 200 lengths, but normally keeping a decent distance. Mostly, it was just hard slog moving forward under Cäääsëëëy's guidance. By the next afternoon, after a night dusted with frost and the first hints of snow in the air, they made it off Foggy Mountain and onto a long expanse of grassy plains. It had been a long time since they'd seen so much open land. Picking through the Fake Mountains, the voyage on the *Barco del Amor*, and finally this tiptoeing over Foggy Mountain had all been slow and tedious.

Hector and the Nameless One shared a knowing look, then Hector said, "Princess, how are you feeling today?"

"Fine, I guess."

"And you are riding comfortably?"

"Yes. Why?"

"I suggest you settle in low and snug. You too, Champion Abernatheen de Chipmunk."

"Why?"

Without further warning, the two horses launched into a full gallop, whooping and racing each other for the far horizon. Eloise's riding instincts kicked in, and she hunkered down and let Hector go. His powerful body pounded across the prairie lands, sometimes ahead of the Nameless One, sometimes behind. The two horses were fit, had spent too long pent up by circumstance, and were enjoying the simple pleasure of speed and distance.

Eloise focused on Hector's movement. Every stride of his gallop included a suspended moment when all four feet were off the ground. His trot was one-two, one-two, one-two. His canter more a waltz—one-two-three, one-two-three, one-two-three. But this? The gallop was one-two-three-four—air, one-two-three-four—air. Unless dragons magically appeared and offered her a ride, Eloise knew this was as close to the rush and wind of flying as she would ever get. These moments on Hector's back, with Jerome holding on for dear life and Cäääsëëëy doing the same with Lorch and the Nameless One (she mustn't think of him as Patchouli), were a treasure to remember.

⚜ 78 ⚜

FOR SHE ONCE WAS...

Eventually, the path became a trail, which became a road—one Cäääsëëëy recognized as leading to Stained Rock. Similarly, sparse settlements became clusters of homes you could call hamlets, which gave way to villages, and then towns. The horses pushed themselves the whole way, clawing back some of the time lost on Foggy Mountain.

After another night in the rough, complete with a hard frost, and a morning's hard riding, finally, there it was. They crested a rise and could see Stained Rock, its castle sitting atop the highest point.

"I welcome you to the heart of the Half Kingdom," said Cäääsëëëy.

"You can see why they called it Stained Rock," said Jerome.

The town was named for a huge rock which acted as the castle's foundation and was visible from strong lengths away. It wasn't so much a rock as a stony finger that jutted above the ground. The stone included large amounts of iron, which gave it a rusted red hue, like someone had thrown a massive cup of cherry cider at it, leaving a stain washerwomen might have nightmares about.

They might also have nightmares about the Purple Haze, which cut across the land and from this point of view looked like a purple curtain behind the castle. "That's awfully close," said Eloise. "Can you imagine living so near it?"

"It gives me the creeps," said Hector. "I keep thinking I will get used to it, but every time it comes into view, I want to look the other way."

"You, too," said Eloise. "I thought it was just me. Well, let's get down there."

"Princess Eloise, if I may have a moment first." Cäääsëëëy climbed down the Nameless One's leg and walked away from the others to wait for her in the shade of a liquidambar.

Eloise swung a leg over and slid off Hector, following. "Yes?"

Cäääsëëëy knelt and lowered his head. "Princess, I ask permission to take leave of you and the others."

Whatever she had thought he might say, this was not it. Eloise felt a lump swell in her throat, and unexpected tears threatened. "Oh, Cäääsëëëy. Will you not continue with us? We..." She swallowed. "We will miss you. *I* will miss you."

He bowed once more, then assumed a more natural stance. "Princess, the gift of freedom you gave me is something I can never repay. We agreed that you would allow me to bring you to Stained Rock, and while it does not balance the scales, there is some degree of reciprocity now."

"Yes. There is." She coughed and dabbed the corner of her eye with the heel of her hand.

Cäääsëëëy's skin turned a deep pink, and his voice quivered. "It has been a long time since I have seen my family, my friends, and perhaps one who might be waiting for me. I hope she still waits, but I fear she does not. It aches me to find out, for she once was my one true love."

"Of course, Cäääsëëëy. Of course," said Eloise. She took a deep breath, giving her emotions a chance to settle. "I had no idea. As far as I am concerned, reciprocity has been met. Do not feel you are under obligation anymore."

Cäääsëëëy shook his head. "The scales are far from balanced, Princess, but I appreciate your trying to say so."

The chameleon went back to the others and began his goodbyes. Eloise saw a particular, silent something pass between Cäääsëëëy and the Nameless One (not Patchouli!), and then the horse reached down and gave him a small, affectionate nudge with his nose.

Eloise was last, and to the chameleon's surprise, she got down on hands and knees and gave him a formal Western Lands kiss. The chameleon turned a shade of crimson Eloise had never seen before. "Boring travels to you, Cäääsëëëy Lïïïss."

"Thank you, Princess Eloise. Boring travels to you."

And with that, the chameleon headed into the nearest scrub and was gone.

Their group suddenly had a chameleon-sized hole in it, which Eloise felt no one else could ever fill.

79

THE FOGGING

There were several gates into Stained Rock, and Cäääsëëëÿ had suggested they try one closest to the castle to avoid some of the delays the main gate might present. They followed a road around to the eastern side of Stained Rock and made their way toward the smallest of the town's gates.

For days, Eloise had been struck by the manner of the people in the villages they'd been through. They went about their lives, and there was plenty of evidence that farms, shops, guild workers, and petty officials all plied their trades. But there was a lassitude to it, a certain dullness. The great wound the realm had suffered centuries before echoed still in day-to-day life.

She'd expected things to improve as they got closer to Stained Rock. Surely proximity to the royal seat and all the activity that brought would give the people more pep. But if anything, the mood was turned down another notch. The guards who checked them at the city gates were disinterested, simply waving them through. The panhandlers and accommodation hustlers who immediately accosted them on the other side of the town wall were half-hearted. So, too, was the innkeeper at the Rusted and Runcible, where they landed. Such a contrast to the eager bustle at Brague.

In The South, they'd said, "So the queen, so the queendom." If so, what did this say about Doncaster and his kingdom?

"Let's get to the castle," said Eloise. "If Johanna is there, I want to know if she's OK."

"Will that work, Princess?" asked Lorch. "Can we attempt the castle this close to dusk and unannounced?"

Eloise swallowed back her impatience. "You're probably right—it's too late to see Uncle Doncaster today," said Eloise. "Let's get a sense of Stained Rock for the rest of the afternoon, and then present ourselves to him first thing in the morning, rested and refreshed."

The Rusted and Runcible was lower to middling at best, but at least it had space (and a reasonable brown bread and roast kohlrabi lunch). Stained Rock was packed full because it hosted the equivalent of a local fair—the annual Wart Cream Extravaganza-o-rama®.

"You're not excited, Jerome?" asked Eloise. "I'm sure it'll be fun. They'll have wart cream everywhere—in shop windows, at the Miss or Mister Wart Cream Pageant, and in the Wart Cream Parade. There probably won't be wart cream fritters or wart cream and sarsaparilla cordial, but there's certain to be wart cream tossing, wart cream juggling, wart cream stacking, largest pot of wart cream, purplest wart cream, slimiest, greasiest, and oiliest wart creams, best use of wart cream for decorating, and feats of strength involving weights and strong weights of wart cream."

"You can josh me all you want, Princess Eloise," sniffed Jerome. "But there's nothing to get worked up about when it comes to the Wart Cream Extravaganza-o-rama®. Maybe a few decades ago it would have been worth attending. These days, it's known among festival enthusiasts as a tacky, commercialized sell-fest, and not a celebration of something wonderful in the world, like, say, grapefruit or aloe vera."

"So, no hankering after an invitation to the Wart Cream Gala?"

"None."

After lunch, Eloise, Jerome, and Lorch left Hector and the Nameless One (still not Patchouli!) to rest at the Rusted and Runcible, and pushed their way into the streets to have a look at the town. There was no way to avoid the Wart Cream Extravaganza-o-rama®. The powerful Wart Creamers Guild made sure of that. Handbills for its events were posted everywhere, the streets were decorated in a wart cream theme, and Stained Rock was awash in the purple hue of the stuff. Unfortunately, it felt perfunctory, a bit false. There wasn't the genuine celebration and joy of the other festivals.

They walked the streets of Stained Rock, gravitating toward the castle and its gates, which also brought them nearer to the looming Purple Haze.

"Look." Eloise pointed to a steep hill right next to the castle wall. A cluster of people gathered at the top.

"Shall we check out what the locals are doing?" asked Jerome. "Some warty silliness, I'm sure."

"Yes, let's," said Eloise.

The three of them made their way up the hill, which had an exceptional view of the nearby Purple Haze.

They soon wished they hadn't.

Three dozen people, including several dogs, stood atop the hill looking stricken. The center of attention was a brute of a man bound at the wrists and gagged, and next to him, a scruffy, three-legged, one-eye spaniel, similarly bound and muzzled. They were surrounded by a serious contingent of guards keeping them in place. There was also an official wearing the cloak of a guild that Eloise did not recognize, that was the exact same shade as the Purple Haze. Her face was obscured by a hood, and she read from a scroll. As they neared, her voice became audible above the light buzzing in Eloise's ears. "And lastly, because you have been convicted for these various and sundry crimes against the Crown and against his people..."

Lorch leaned over to Eloise. "Princess, we should leave."

"...you have been brought here to this place. And so at the command and authorization of His Majesty King Doncaster Worsted..."

"Why?"

"...Halva de Chëëëkflïïïnt, I hereby officially proclaim these things to be true, and commend..."

Lorch pointed to the woman. "She wears the robe of the Foggers' Guild. This..." He swallowed. "This is a fogging."

"...your body and soul to the uncertainty of the fog. Good luck and Çalaht be with you." The fogger rolled up her scroll and slipped it through a collar around the spaniel's neck. The canine snarled back through his muzzled snout.

There was a hush, and then the fogger pointed at the dog, swept her arm toward the fog, and said, "Proceed."

The spaniel mustered all the dignity he could, and despite his front legs being hobbled and having only one back one, he walked down the steep slope and disappeared into the Purple Haze.

Silence.

No screams, no cries, no laughter, nothing. The spaniel simply disappeared into the lavender mist. The only sound was a sad, low howl from one of the dogs in attendance.

"By Çalaht's distended digits, that's—" whispered Jerome, but Eloise hushed him.

The fogger let the silence linger, then pulled a second scroll from her sleeve. The brute with tied wrists whimpered as she read. "Jääämëëës Thööömäääs Shääänkääär Giïït, known widely by various aliases, including 'Jack the Tripper,' 'Three Card Montgomery,' 'Loan Shark Jim' (a nickname offensive to some of our aquatic brethren, I'll mention), 'Slim Jim,' 'Slim-ish Jim,' 'Really Not So Slim Anymore Jim,' 'Boy You Have Let Yourself Go Jim,' 'I Hardly Recognized You At All Jim,' 'Have You Seen Someone About That Rash Jim,' and 'Çalaht's

Gift to Numbats,' you are hereby called to account for the following crimes and misdemeanors." The fogger paused and looked over the top of the scroll at the man. "Do you want me to read the list? I can, and officially I'm supposed to, you know. But it'll take a while. I mean, look at it." She showed him how long the scroll was. "Your call, mate."

The gagged man, embarrassed, shook his head.

The fogger returned to the scroll, skimming. "Armed and dangerous, yada-yada, grievous harm, yada-yada, two strong weights of emu sludge, yada-yada, a candle, a whisk, some grease and a lute..." She looked at him again with a pinched expression. "Really, how could you?"

He shrugged contrition.

She returned to her skimming. "Extortive tactics, yada-yada..." She flipped the scroll over. "Excessive forms of persuasion, yada-yada, public display of—now that's just disgusting—yada-yada... Ah, here we go." She looked at him again. "Ready."

The hulk shook his head again.

"Sorry. Time's a'wasting." The fogger resumed her official tone. "Because you have been convicted of these various and sundry crimes against the Crown and against his people, you have been brought to this place. And so at the command and authorization of His Majesty King Doncaster Worsted Halva de Chëëëkflïïïnt, I hereby officially proclaim these things to be true, and commend your body and soul to the uncertainty of the fog. Good luck and Çalaht be with you." She rolled up the scroll and tucked it into his shirt, then with a sweep of her arm, invited him to walk into the fog. "Proceed."

Unlike the spaniel, he stood there, petrified.

The moment stretched.

"Go ahead," encouraged the fogger. "It's not that hard. Just, you know, in you walk."

The man shook his head again.

The fogger sighed at this inconvenience and turned to one of the guards. "Geoffrey, we have a stander."

"Yes, ma'am," said the guard.

The guard slowly walked over to Have You Seen Someone About That Rash Jim and put a reassuring arm around the quaking man's shoulder. "Bit nervous, are you, mate?"

Jim nodded.

"Yeah, I'm sure you are. There's all that uncertainty about the fog, no?"

Jim nodded again.

"Look, mate, I understand. I really do. But you don't want to keep folks waiting, do you?"

Jim nodded, then shook, then nodded again. He wasn't sure what the right answer was.

"Well, you know what it says about this in the *Scrolls of Çalaht*, don't you, mate?"

Jim relaxed and looked at the guard, puzzled. He gave another shake of his head.

"Nothing, mate, nothing at all." The guard shoved with all his strength, sending the prisoner rolling down the steep decline of Fogging Hill. Terrified, gagged screams filled the air.

Then Have You Seen Someone About That Rash Jim disappeared into the Purple Haze.

His screams cut off.

Silence.

Complete, deafening silence.

The fogger pulled the hood from over her head, and Eloise could see the "all in a day's work, mission accomplished" look on her face. The people watching lined up and gave her coins. Apparently, the families of those who got fogged paid for the fogger's services.

Eloise turned and ran, hurtling down the hill, away from the Purple Haze.

She stopped at the bottom of Fogging Hill, gulping for air. Jerome and Lorch were there in a moment. "That's twisted," she gasped. "Barbarous."

"Which part, El?" asked Jerome, pulling up beside her. "Shoving someone into the Purple Haze or charging them for the privilege?"

Eloise felt as queasy as she had on the *Barco del Amor*, and wasn't sure if she'd keep down the roasted kohlrabi. "All of it. It's just wrong."

Lorch gently took her elbow and guided her toward a nearby public inn. "Let us find you a sip of water, Princess Eloise. It will help."

The inn had a garden in the back, and the three of them found a seat under a massive fir tree. Eloise slumped onto the bench and leaned back against the tree's trunk. She held back tears, along with the contents of her stomach. But why? She didn't know the people who'd been fogged, nor the people in attendance. Those who'd been fogged had a list of crimes they'd been convicted of. And like the guard who shoved Jim said, there was all that uncertainty about the fog.

But it felt wrong. Wrong down to the marrow.

For no reason she could fathom, Eloise felt she had to do something about it. She didn't know what, why, or how. She just knew she should.

She promised herself she would if there was ever a chance.

80

NOT ON THE LIST

B y the next morning, Eloise had shaken off her ill feeling from the fogging. Spruced up, she and the others headed for the castle.

"So, we're just going to knock on the door and say hello?" asked Jerome.

"Do you have a better idea?" Eloise stepped through the door Lorch held open for her, which was, unsurprisingly, both rusted and runcible.

"Not yet."

The five of them worked their way to the castle gate, passing all manner of wart creaminess. The wart creamification of Stained Rock was truly immersive, from the sample pots all around and the oversized labels bedecking the walls to papier mâché representations of the legendary discoverer of the secret wart cream recipe, Jööösïïïäääh Scüüürgëëë. There were pretty boys and prettier girls strutting around wearing wart cream and not much else, and the young and beautiful Wart Creamettes performing precision wart cream interpretive dance.

Jerome huffed at the crassness of it all.

The castle gates were, unsurprisingly, closed. Three guards looked up from a dice game as Eloise approached. One of them, the smallest, most cheerful guard Eloise had ever seen, stepped away from the barrel they were using as a gaming table, and nodded to her. His cheeks were dabbed with ornamental blobs of wart cream in honor of the festivities. "Happy Wart Cream Extravaganza-o-rama® Day to you, Mistress. What can I do for you, lovey?"

"And a happy Wart Cream Extravaganza-o-rama® Day to you, too, good sir," said Eloise. "It's a good one this year, isn't it?"

"The best in a while, I reckon. But then, I love them all." He pointed to the wart cream on his cheeks as evidence.

"Me too, me too," smiled Eloise. "So, I'd like to see King Doncaster, if I may."

"Sure thing, lovey. What time is your appointment, and can I please see your royal invitation?"

"Oh, an appointment. Hmmm. Well, I don't actually quite have one yet."

"Well, lovey, then you're probably out of luck. With the Wart Cream Extravaganza-o-rama® on, security is tight."

Jerome stepped forward. "You don't have a list or something?"

"Actually, my potentially good friend, we do have a list." The diminutive guard turned to the others, who'd stopped their game because it was the small guard's turn with the dice. "Lääärry, can you please bring me the List of Allowed Entrants?"

Lääärry seemed put out at having to actually stand up and retrieve a scroll from a desk, but he did so. "Here you go, Möööëëë."

Möööëëë unfurled a rather long scroll. "What's your name, lovey?"

"Eloise. Eloise Hydra Gumball III."

The guard looked at her. "Really?"

"Yes, really."

"Well, your parents were brave. Better not let the Westie queen find out, or she'll slice open your guts and have your spleen in a sealed jar and added to her collection before you can say, 'Gee, I guess my parents shouldn't have done that.'" He chuckled at his own joke. "But, no business of mine." The guard carefully scanned the list, mumbling the odd name as he went. "Nope. Sorry. No Eloise of any sort on the list. Sorry, lovey."

"Um, there aren't any other lists, are there?" asked Eloise.

"Actually, we do have other lists." He turned to the others. "Cüüürly, Lääärry, please bring me the other lists."

Clearly put out by having to move once again, the two other guards went to the desk, gathered more scrolls, and brought them to Möööëëë. He unrolled them one at a time, looking for her name. It wasn't on the List of Trades Persons, the List of Persons Who Trade, the List of Authorized Entertainers, the List of Entertaining Authorizers, nor the List of Attendees of the Wart Cream Gala. At that last one, Möööëëë gave a rueful sigh. "I'd give my eye teeth to attend the Wart Cream Gala, but it's only for the king and the other hoity-toity ones. It's invite-only, and if you think getting a royal appointment is hard, getting a Wart Cream Gala invite makes it look like a biscuit bake-off. I bet it would be easier to get a seat at Çalaht's thumb hanging than an invitation to the Wart Cream Gala." He went back to checking all his lists, not finding her on the List of People Who Know Embarrassing Things About Certain Other People, the List of People Allowed In For No Particular Reason, nor the List of People Responsible for Lists. "Sorry, lovey."

Jerome pointed to one last scroll on their desk. "It looks like you may have missed one."

Möööëëë turned and looked. "So I have, so I have." He walked over to the desk, giving the two other guards a simultaneous swat on the back of their heads as he went past. He snatched it up. With an unnecessary, exaggerated flourish, he unfurled it. "Oh, look. Here you are. Eloise Hydra Gumball III."

"Really? Wonderful." said Eloise. "What list is that?"

Mööööëë squinted at the top of the list, reading its title. "List of People to Arrest on Sight. There you go, lovey. Looks like I'm supposed to arrest you now I've seen you. Do you mind staying there a minute?" He turned to the others. "Come on boys, we have an arresting to do."

Eloise felt her stomach tighten. Lorch stepped closer in protection, and Jerome did the same, his hackles rising. But Mööööëë's attention was on Lääärry and Cüüürly, who grumbled their way up from their stools in exaggerated slow motion. "Do we have to?" grizzled Lääärry. "I hate all that paperwork."

"Now, now Lääärry, we talked about this at your semi-annual performance review, didn't we?"

"Yes," groused Lääärry,

"And what did we say?"

"No eating onions on the job."

"I meant the other thing."

"Pants and undies are 'always' clothes, not 'sometimes' clothes when dressing for work."

"Well, there was that, but I meant the other, other thing."

"Don't use explosives for condiments? Wash at least once a month whether or not I think I need to? When singing 'Three Bags of Groats For My Sweetheart,' wear a bucket?"

"You're doing well to remember all that, but I meant the other, other, other thing."

"Don't complain in front of the customers."

"Very good, Lääärry."

"Sorry, boss." Lääärry hung his head. "That wasn't complaining, was it?"

"Don't you think your comments about paperwork could fairly be characterized as complaining?"

"Yes, boss. Sorry, boss."

Meanwhile, Cüüürly tried to hide his snickering.

All this gave Eloise plenty of time to feel her panic rising. Could they sneak away? Probably not. Should they bolt, or would that be admitting guilt? Could they fight their way out of this? Lorch could probably handle the three guards, but if anyone raised an alarm, others would surely come after them. Eloise knew she had to try something. Anything. The idea of sitting in jail again brought her close to fainting. "Excuse me?" she said.

Möööëëë stopped providing feedback to his subordinate. "Yes, lovey?"

"On what grounds?"

"Pardon?"

"On what grounds is this poor Eloise person supposed to be arrested?" asked Eloise.

Möööëëë checked the scroll again. "It says 'Suspicion of Being Suspicious.' Now there's a rare one. You don't see that often. Here, look."

He showed her the scroll. There was her name, letter perfect, and beautifully written, along with "Arrest on sight, by authorization of King Doncaster." But the signature wasn't her uncle's. It was initialed with "TSM."

"Um, sorry. It was 'Möööëëë,' was it?"

"Yes, lovey."

"I think there's been a small mistake. That's not me."

"No?" He looked befuddled. "Didn't you say your name was Eloise Hydra Gumball III? It says that right here, doesn't it? Can't be too many of those in the world, can there, now? Especially not with the Westie queen being so vicious about it, and all."

"Well, yes, it says that. But that's not how I spell my name."

"No?"

Eloise shook her head, looking slightly embarrassed at the misunderstanding. "I use the proper northern spelling. So for me, it is 'Ëëëlöööïïïsëëë Hÿÿÿdräää Güüümbäääll ÏÏÏ.' You wouldn't believe how often this happens." She laughed to make a joke of it. "It's an easy enough mistake to make, I guess, especially if one is not attuned to our vowels. But nope, that's some other Eloise Hydra Gumball III skulking about somewhere waiting to be arrested on Suspicion of Being Suspicious."

Mööööëë turned to the others. "Stand down, boys." Having hardly stood up, it was no big effort for them to slump back onto their stools. The small guard rerolled the arrest list. "Well then, my apologies, lovey. I'm sorry you can't come in but I'm glad we don't have to go through all that arresting paperwork. You enjoy the rest of the Wart Cream Extravaganza-o-rama®."

"Thank you. You are one of the kindest, and most effective guards I've ever met."

Mööööëë smiled at the compliment. "Just doing my job, lovey."

"Well, we'll be off. And once again, happy Wart Cream Extravaganza-o-rama® Day to you all."

"And to you, lovey."

Eloise turned, and forced herself to walk, not run, back down the road.

♜ 81 ♞

IT'LL WORK OUT

"Arrest on sight,'" said Jerome. "I don't think I've ever associated with someone who is supposed to be arrested on sight. Congratulations, Elumination, you have provided me with yet another new experience."

"My pleasure, as always."

The five travelers gathered for a strategy meeting in the paddock behind the Rusted and Runcible. Lunch was spread on a temporary table, and despite the nearness of the cold season, it was pleasant to be in the open. Various wart-creamy sounds wafted toward them from the surrounding town.

"Including my name on an 'arrest on sight' list isn't exactly putting out the welcome mat," said Eloise.

"I wonder if we were on the list as well," said Hector. "I almost hope so. That would be as close to infamous as I'm likely to ever get."

"Sorry," said Eloise. "It didn't seem prudent to linger on it."

"And you said your name had the initials 'TSM' as the authorization," said Lorch. "Since when does a jester wield such authority?"

"It didn't look like he had such sway when they were in Brague," said Jerome. "He must have come up in the world somehow."

"The jester could do things like put me on the list behind the king's back. But that seems a very dangerous game." Eloise plucked an olive from a dish and nibbled it. It had a different, flatter taste than the Eastern Lands olives she was used to. "So, what are we going to do if showing one's face gets one arrested?"

"Send an emissary?" suggested Lorch.

"Go in costume?" said Jerome. "Or dress in black and sneak in at night?"

"That might get me inside the wall. But what good will that do if I can't get to Johanna or Doncaster?" Eloise put her olive pit in a dish and nudged it with her index finger so it formed an isosceles triangle with two other pits. "Let's say I get into the castle. What am I supposed to do, skulk around hoping I run into one of them? The castle's a big place, and I'd be having to hide or bluff my way through. Neither seems very effective."

The Nameless One (not Patchouli!) pawed the ground to get attention. Lorch looked at him. "Yes?"

The horse pointed at a handbill posted at the back of the inn. It was for the Wart Cream Gala.

"You think she should go to the gala?"

The horse nodded.

Jerome drummed the table with his claws. "I don't know how we'd pull that off. Lorch, you heard the guard. It's by invitation only, and those are rare."

"True, but if you *could* get in, you know for sure you'd be in the same room as King Doncaster and, if she's here in Stained Rock as his guest, Princess Johanna as well," said Lorch. "The guard said it was for the king and the hoity-toity. I'm sure Johanna qualifies as hoity-toity."

"Perhaps the hoitiest-toitiest of all, save the king himself," agreed Jerome. "And you're right, we don't even know if Princess Johanna is in Stained Rock." Jerome also took an olive, but for him it was closer to a full meal than a snack.

They all sat there, eating flat-tasting olives and thinking.

"I've got it," said Eloise. "I think I can get us into the Wart Cream Gala."

"How?" asked Jerome. "It starts in, what, three hours? Good luck with that."

"I'm not sure how. But I'm sure it'll work out for us." Eloise stood. "I will need to get ready and make sure I look like I belong there."

"I'll organize for someone to help you, Princess," said Lorch.

"If they can do something with my hair, that would be good."

"Yes, Princess."

"And Lorch, Jerome, you two will need to clean up as well, since you will be my retinue."

"Yes, Princess," they said together.

Eloise stood. "We'll meet here at dusk and make our way."

82

GOODE FORTUNA

Lööölää, the hedgehog Lorch hired to attend Eloise, normally worked as a showgirl. She had a patient manner, a mischievous smile, and fingers as deft as a pickpocket's. Eloise let her draw a bath and scrub away her road dirt. She even let Lööölää unbraid and wash out her hair, but only after a lengthy interview to convince her the hedgehog knew a thing or two about making hair look fancy. During the subsequent hour of comb tugging, Lööölää kept her smile, even if now and then she let slip certain northern-inflected words young ladies of culture were not supposed to know. At the end, Eloise's curls were subdued into a shape and presentation that could be called fancy.

"Very nice," said Eloise, looking in a hand mirror, and she meant it.

Lööölää helped Eloise put on her just-in-case dress, having hung it over a steaming pot of water to remove some of the wrinkles then dried it by the fire. She also scurried off to find a shawl to match the dress and raise its fanciness quotient. A few baubles in Eloise's hair and a wipe down of her travel cape so it looked like an accessory and not a sleeping roll, and Eloise was ready to face the cool night air.

There was one more thing to do. She thanked Löööläää and let her go, then closed the door and curtains. Eloise knew exactly which pocket in her cloak to go to, and, with a breath to settle herself, pulled out the envelope from her mother. She opened it, removed the hemp parchment, looked once again at her mother's ornate "E", and unfolded it so she could see the words written on the other side. Using an inflection as close to her mother's way of speaking as she could muster, Eloise held up the parchment and said "Goode Fortuna."

Just like her father's spell, a light buzzing filled her ears for half a second, but the tingle down her spine had a different quality—more feminine somehow. Not so what happened next. Instead of the parchment disintegrating into dust, it flashed into flame and was gone.

"Spelling is weird," Eloise said to the air where the parchment had been.

Eloise gathered herself, wrapped Löööläää's shawl around her shoulders, threw her travel cape on top, and headed down to meet the others.

Lorch and Jerome met her at the front door, and Jerome whistled his appreciation. "Looking sharp, Princess Knock 'Em Over. Looking sharp."

"Thank you, Champion Abernatheen de Chipmunk."

Lorch also nodded his approval.

They walked up the now-familiar street toward the castle gate.

"So what's the plan, Elucidate?" asked Jerome.

"I still do not know."

"So we're winging it."

"Birds and insects find that phrase offensive, but yes, we're winging it."

They joined the throng heading toward the castle. Expensive carriages clattered up the road, and there was ample tonnage of elegance, frills, and lavishness being transported toward the gala on foot.

The bottleneck was at the castle gate, still manned by Mööööëë, Cüüürly, and Läääarry. They'd changed into more formal uniforms and were joined by a handful of additional guards. Mööööëë, still in charge, was as cheerful as ever, and had a "Happy Wart Cream Extravaganza-o-rama® Day to you" for one and all, plus a "lovey" if you were female. People clustered to have their names and invitations checked, but with so many people, it took a while. Particularly slow was the current person at the front of the line, an ancient, venerable-looking tortoise dressed in a cravat and a formal coat. He had trouble getting his invitation from his coat pocket, but it would be rude to do it for him without his asking for help. So everyone waited.

Eloise joined the line, with Jerome and Lorch behind her. "Princess Arrest on Sight, I fear this is a bad idea," said Jerome.

Eloise shrugged and looked around to see if anyone or anything was the opportunity she needed. All around her were dandies and dolls, fops in socks, and as much glittery frippery as you'd find anywhere. She was glad she'd made the effort to get her hair gussied up, and hoped she'd fit in with the crowd.

A page boy ran up from behind them, skidding to a halt when he saw Eloise. No, not her, but the finely dressed warthog standing in front of her, who carried a beautifully carved cane and wore clothes that were some of the finest Eloise had ever seen. She wondered if perhaps he was a royal of some sort. The page handed him a note, and the warthog tipped him an entire coin as a thank you. The page smiled like he had been given the sun itself and scurried away.

The warthog read the note, then gave a grunt of despair. "Great Çalaht's grit-filled girdle. This is the worst." He humphed and ate the note.

"Good sir, are you in need of help?" asked Eloise. "Is something the matter?"

He turned around so he could see her. "Apologies for my language, young lady. It's just I've been given some displeasing news." He jabbed his cane at a paving stone in emphasis. "My companion for this evening's event appears to have fallen to the influences of an ill-timed ague. She assures me she will be fine soon enough, but her attendance would..." He pointed to his stomach to indicate the note. "Would be 'spectacular, but not in any of the ways one would want people to remember one by.' Such a delightful person. She'll be most disappointed not to attend."

"I'm sorry she's unwell."

"Yes, yes, me too. But for my own, selfish reasons, as well."

"Pardon?"

"Well, it isn't proper for me to arrive alone. If nothing else, the gap in the seating chart would be noticed and commented on. The lips of the gossip heralds would flap, flap, flap with 'Oh, he was on his own,' and 'My, my, jilted again,' and 'It must be those tusks.' You know what the gossip heralds are like."

"Indeed, I do," said Eloise. They had gossip heralds in Brague, of course, but they seemed to respect her mother too much to be overly scurrilous. Those in the Half Kingdom were known for their looseness with facts and their willingness to embellish. The bards, of course, hated them, being the true carriers of knowledge, but the gossip heralds carved out a niche of eager listeners, and became entrenched in Court life. "Heralds are one thing, but gossip heralds are a whole category of misery unto themselves."

"That, my dear, is a perfect characterization." He chuckled. "And they love talking about me. I can normally ignore it, but being on my own tonight would cause distress for others. That's what bothers me. Oh, well."

"Actually, I'm in a similar predicament. I was supposed to meet my sister here, but it seems she's already gone through. That wouldn't be a problem, except she was in charge of the invitations."

"Well, young lady, that should not matter. Your name will be on the list."

Eloise gave a rueful shake of the head. "Sadly, I fear not. I was her last-minute 'plus one' when her gentleman caller sent word that, like your companion, he was stricken with a dramatic and embarrassingly forceful ague. I wouldn't mind, but…" Eloise let her voice trail off, and willed some tears into her eyes.

"There, there, young lady." The warthog found a handkerchief in his pocket and gave it to her. Eloise smiled a grateful thank you and delicately dabbed her eye. "You were saying?" he prompted.

"It's just that, ever since I was a little girl, I've wanted to attend the Wart Cream Gala. My mother used to tell stories about how wonderful it was—she'd been a serving wench there when she was younger—but my father was a lowly worker in an obscure wart creamery. So we were neither hoity nor toity, and an invitation would never be headed our way. Going to the gala was a far-away dream, but then my sister managed a friendship with someone beyond her station. And when he fell to the ague, she invited me. It was a dream come true! But I was late to arrive, because I was attending our dear grandmother, who was having a false teeth crisis. By the time I made it here, it was clear I should not have bothered to get my hair done or sell some of my dowry for this dress." Eloise hoped the story was not too thickly laid on. She pushed out a few more tears, so she could dab them away as a distraction.

"Now, now young lady. I might have a solution." The warthog straightened, bowed, and said, "Would you allow me to invite you as my plus-one this evening?"

"Really? You would have me go to the Wart Cream Gala with you? Why, I couldn't possibly impose."

"No, no! You'd do me a favor. Providing a little less slop for the gossip heralds would make my life that bit simpler."

"Why, good sir, that would be wonderful!" Eloise giggled in what she hoped was a fetching way. "You are kindness itself. And if I may say so without being too bold, your tusks are distinguished, and should not be the subject of comment by gossip heralds."

"Tish, tosh, young lady." But Eloise could tell the warthog was not averse to the flattery.

At that moment, it was their turn to check in with the guards. Mööööëë, looking hassled by the press of people trying to get through after the delay caused by the tortoise, was lost in looking at his list of attendee names, and therefore somewhat perfunctory with his "Happy Wart Cream Extravaganza-o-rama® Day" to them. When he looked up, he snapped to attention. "Good evening, sir," he said to the warthog. "Happy Wart Cream Extravaganza-o-rama® Day, sir!" Then he saw Eloise, and his eyes went wide. "And to you, lovey, er, Mistress Eloise. Happy Wart Cream Extravaganza-o-rama® Day to you once again."

"Thank you," said Eloise, giving him a small curtsy.

The warthog tried to hand Mööööëë his invitation, but the guard, still at attention, waved him off. "No need, sir. No need at all. Please go through."

"Very well then. Come along, young lady."

Lorch and Jerome followed, and Eloise's goode fortuna seemed to extend to them as well, for they walked past the guards and into the castle grounds behind her.

"Is your name really Ëëëlöööïïïsëëë?" asked the warthog.

"Well, I use the Westie pronunciation of 'Eloise,' but yes."

"It amazes me what risks people take with their children." The warthog chuckled. "Best be careful if you actually go there. If the Westie queen finds out, she'll have you dipped in wax and lit on fire if she needs a reading lamp. Or so I've heard."

"I've heard similar."

He chuckled again. "Anyway, my name is Búüùttons."

"A Southie name, then."

"You have an ear for dialect, young lady. Most people around here mistakenly say 'Büüüttöööns' or just 'Buttons,' both of which, if my mother—may she stand with Çalaht—ever heard, would make her ashes spin in their urn. Pardon the strained metaphor."

"Well, Mr Büüüttons, I am grateful to make your acquaintance."

"And I yours. Shall we make our way to the ceremonial hall?"

"Yes, let's."

Eloise and Büüüttons promenaded arm-in-arm through the rather plain, but adequately wart creamishly-decorated castle grounds, followed by Lorch and Jerome, who kept pace like they were the couple's retinue, Lorch behind the warthog and Jerome behind Eloise.

The castle's ceremonial hall thrummed with guests, the upper crust of Half Kingdom society and the best, the brightest, the most entrenched, and the most rusted-on that Doncaster's court offered.

Eloise hung on the warthog's right arm, and he balanced himself using his cane on the left. This enabled him to walk slowly and deliberately through the hall, greeting everyone by name and saying "Happy Wart Cream Extravaganza-o-rama® Day" about a thousand times. He introduced her as his "new best friend," which Eloise was OK with, and which she considered more appealing than alternatives like "date," "girlfriend," or "companion for the evening." As they moved through the crowd, Eloise noticed that their general direction was toward the front of the room. He must have scored himself some good seats if he was this close to the dais.

And then, at his request, she stepped up onto the dais itself, followed by Büüüttons, Lorch and Jerome.

Who was this person?

They walked around to the side of the table with seats. Eloise tried to take an inconspicuous one at the far end, but the warthog smiled a "No, no, no," and ushered her toward the middle of the main table, stopping her two seats away from the throne. He allowed Lorch to pull out her chair, and then his own, and they sat in the seats of greatest honor near the king and king's companion.

Eloise leaned toward the warthog and delicately whispered, "Mr Búüùttons, how is it we are seated so prominently?"

The warthog guffawed. "You truly have no idea who I am, do you?"

"No, sir. Please accept my apologies."

"Why, young lady, no apologies needed. It is refreshing not to be recognized. My name is Wáäälter Áäàloysius Búüùttons, and I'm head of the Wart Creamers' Guild. This..." He swept a foreleg around to encompass the entire hall. "This is my party."

83

INTRODUCING THE NEXT
QUEEN

A ny further conversation was strangled to a halt by the ear-
splitting sounds of not one, not two, but two dozen bombards
letting fly with an intestine-loosening rendition of "Çalaht
Save Our Currently Reigning (Fill in the Appropriate King or Queen)
and Let's Hope (Fill in the Appropriate Gender Pronoun) Lasts a Bit
Longer Than The Last One." It was slightly less pleasant than having
your eardrums scraped clean using a corroded shish kebab skewer, but
slightly more likely to cause them to bleed. The crowd stood at once,
and in swept King Doncaster Worsted Halva de Chëëëkfliïïnt, looking
well, if distracted, and resplendent in a fine black robe, embroidered in
blacker thread.

And there she was.

On Doncaster's arm, allowing herself to be escorted to the center seats
on the dais, was Johanna Umgotteswillen Gumball, dressed in the
finest wart-cream-purple dress Eloise had ever seen, and looking as
happy as one could with so many bombards inciting so many
headaches. Eloise's eyes spilled over with tears, and not just from the
"music." Johanna was safe. She was safe. She was alive. And she was
here. Thank Çalaht. There had been so many weeks of travel over so

many strong lengths, so many hardships, never for sure knowing if she'd ever see her sister again. And now she was walking straight toward her.

She and Doncaster were too busy waving to the crowd to see her yet, so Eloise dried her eyes with the warthog's handkerchief as the bombards finally wheezed across the last notes of the song.

Búüùttons leaned in so she could hear him. "Truth be told, I get teary myself when I see His Highness. Especially when brought in with the stirring strains of 'Çalaht Save Our Currently Reigning (Fill in the Appropriate King or Queen) and Let's Hope (Fill in the Appropriate Gender Pronoun) Lasts a Bit Longer Than The Last One.'" He dabbed an eye with a sleeve.

Eloise nodded agreement.

Johanna glided to her spot next to Eloise, her attention still on the wider room. There was a stifled squeal from Jerome as Turpentine Snotearrow McCcoonnch emerged from behind Doncaster and pulled out Johanna's chair for her. He slid it in as she sat down, and only then did he see Eloise. "You!" he choked out. "What are you doing here?"

"Good evening, Turpy. Lovely to see you again."

Hate shone from his eyes, and had the circumstances been less public, Eloise would have feared for her safety, Lorch or no Lorch.

Eloise sat with Lorch's help, and only then did Johanna look around to see who her right-hand dinner companion was. "El! How delightful, how lovely, how enchanting to see you. Not to mention surprising, unexpected, and unforeseen."

"Hi, Jo. Lovely to be here." She went to give her sister a hug, but Johanna had already turned away. She patted Doncaster on the arm. "Look, Uncle D, look who's here, who's in attendance, who is in this place next to me."

Doncaster looked at Eloise. He seemed to have trouble focusing on her, or at a minimum, reconciling her presence there with the other things he thought he knew about the cosmos. "Niece. Daughter of my brother." He seemed stuck for another synonym, so said, "niece" again. "How unanticipated, how unpredicted, how astonishing to see you here."

They were prattled.

He then saw Búüùttons. "Buttons, you old bastard, you aged illegitimate son, you decrepit mongrel." He gave the boar a massive handshake. "Good to see, lay eyes on, view you again."

Búüùttons stood, then knelt before his king. "Your Highness. Happy Wart Cream Extravaganza-o-rama® Day to you. And to you, Princess Johanna."

"Thank you. And to you, good sir," she answered.

With that, both seemed to lose interest in Búüùttons and Eloise. They turned to speak with the man sitting to Doncaster's left—Theoplonkilis, the king's foppish wart cream trade representative.

This was worse than Eloise had feared. No surprise that she barely registered on Doncaster. But Johanna? How prattled must she be to be so distant and disconnected from her sister? Or maybe Eloise's twin really didn't give two figs about her, and the prattleweed merely gave it a chance to express itself. Yeah, that'd be about right. Non-fig-giving was exactly how Johanna had been ever since the Thorning Ceremony. She was the one who'd withdrawn. She was the one who'd stopped using the sign language they'd made up. What was her problem? Eloise appeared unannounced from across two realms, and a single "delightful" was all Johanna had in her. Prattleweed or no prattleweed, this is not how...

Búüùttons interrupted the downward spiral of Eloise's thoughts. "Young lady," he said in a low voice. "Is it possible you have not been entirely forthcoming with me?"

Eloise tried to look demure. "In our so-far very short acquaintance, some salient details have not yet been conveyed, and others might have been accompanied by a small degree of embellishment."

He didn't stand, but he did a passable formal bow from his chair, and quietly said, "Princess Eloise Hydra Gumball III, I am most honored to make your acquaintance." He kissed her hand.

"Thank you, Guild Master Wáäàlter Áäàloysius Búüùttons. And I am genuinely delighted that you took pity on a young woman you did not know and invited her to this gala. There is a tale here that someday I hope to tell you, even if I can't do so tonight."

"I hope to hear it one day."

She gave him a Western Lands kiss, which was a little tricky with his tusks, and their friendship was sealed.

Through dinner, Eloise tried to engage Johanna in conversation, but her twin was too excited (and too under the influence) to string many coherent thoughts together. Perhaps these were not ideal circumstances for discussing Eloise's mission of bringing Johanna home. Maybe the next day might be better.

"Jo, Uncle Doncaster, can I ask you something?"

"Sure, El. Certainly. Assuredly. Absolutely. You bet. As always," said Johanna.

"Could I come visit you tomorrow?"

With that, Turpy leaned in and said something to Doncaster. Doncaster looked at him, surprised, then shrugged agreement. He looked at Eloise. "No." Then he went back to his grilled watermelon round seasoned with a walnut gremolata.

"I beg your pardon?" said Eloise.

Doncaster paused his fork. "I said, 'no.' As in nope, nuh-uh, negative. Was that not clear?"

"May I ask why not?"

Doncaster looked at her, confused, then over at Turpy, who stepped forward and whispered to him. Doncaster nodded, and said, "It is not convenient."

"When might it be convenient, Uncle Doncaster?" It was like talking to a board.

Another whisper from Turpy, and Doncaster replied, "Never. We're very busy right now."

Johanna, who'd been following this conversation by turning her head left and right toward each speaker, now looked at Eloise. "Sorry, El. Looks like it won't work out, be successful, happen."

"Right," said Eloise. She looked at her own watermelon steak, not sure what to do next. She glanced at Jerome, who stood, sweating, only a length or two from both of Doncaster's jesters (Gouache was slumped on a stool a little further away). Her champion looked like he might lose his composure at any second. Lorch stood at attention, taking in the room and assessing it for any threats. Neither of them would be much use here.

"Uncle Doncaster," said Eloise.

"Oh. You're still there," he said, cheeks puffed with half-chewed watermelon. "What is it this time?"

"My name is Eloise Hydra Gumball III, Future Ruler and Heir to the Western Lands and All That Really Matters. Under Chapter 298, Section 17, Sub-section 821, Clause 37a of the *Livre de Protocol*, I hereby assert my birth privilege and request an audience with His Majesty King Doncaster Worsted Halva de Chëëëkflïïïnt, attended by my retinue."

To her right, she heard Búüüttons drop his fork.

Johanna squinted, like she was trying to remember something. "You know what, Uncle D? She's right, correct, on the coin. Chapter 298, Section 17, Sub-section 821, Clause 37a covers this explicitly. You have to grant her an audience."

"Done, then," said Doncaster. Turpy leaned in and whispered. "Four weeks from tomorrow morning at ten o'clock." Turpy whispered again. "Make that eleven o'clock," said the king.

"King Doncaster, I believe you and Princess Johanna will receive me tomorrow," said Eloise. Jerome recognized her use of The Tone. "To-mor-row."

The prattleweed's influence of suggestibility plus her inadvertent use of The Tone did the trick. "OK. We'll see you tomorrow," said Doncaster. He took another bite of watermelon.

Turpy looked annoyed. He cued waiting trumpeters, who coughed up something close to a fanfare. The room quietened. The jester touched Doncaster on the shoulder and again whispered something in his ear. The king put down his fork, saying, "Yes, you're right."

"Uncle Doncaster has some important news to announce," Johanna whispered to Eloise. "I'm so excited!"

The king stood and readied himself to speak. "Ladies, gentlewomen, female subjects of the crown, and gentlemen, hombres, uh, male subjects of the crown. Thank you for coming this evening, and for being part of the Wart Cream Extravaganza-o-rama®'s special gala event. I'll leave all the more specific thanking to other people, including Guild Master Büüüttöööns to my right here. But I have one important piece of business, agenda item, um, thing, yeah, thing, that falls to me to do. I must introduce our new queen."

The room buzzed in excitement, and Eloise and Jerome looked at each other. Both mouthed "new queen?" Johanna wriggled in her chair, hardly able to remain seated.

"Jo, what's going on?" said Eloise.

Doncaster continued. "At this year's Wart Cream Gala, it is my greatest pleasure, my biggest delight, my largest enjoyment to introduce to you our new queen, Johanna Umgotteswillen Gumball!"

Applause broke out, as did a slightly better trumpet fanfare. Johanna stood up, taking the hand that Doncaster offered. There were cheers of, "To the queen! To the queen!"

Eloise, Jerome, and Lorch looked at each other, stunned.

Doncaster raised a hand, and the room quietened. He turned to Johanna. "Congratulations, Princess Johanna. I pronounce you this year's Wart Cream Queen!"

The cheers from the room were deafening, and even Búüùttons clopped a hoof on the table, adding to the din. Johanna allowed Doncaster to place a crown on her head in the shape of a pot of wart cream, then curtsied to the room, saying, "Thank you, thank you for this honor, accolade, recognition."

Eloise slumped back in her chair, relieved that it was only a Wart Cream Extravaganza-o-rama® thing. She, Jerome, and Lorch shared a quick "Well, that was scary" look.

Doncaster and Johanna allowed the applause to continue, then sat down as it faded. Jerome flinched again as Turpy moved to whisper something. "Right, right, of course," Doncaster replied.

The king stood and tapped his glass perfunctorily for attention again. To the not-yet-quiet room, he added, "Oh yes. Johanna has also agreed to marry me. So, she'll be that queen too." Then he sat down, winked at Johanna, and went back to eating his watermelon.

There was a moment of silence while what he had said sank in. Once again, "To the queen!" was called out in the room, but it was oddly anti-climactic after the huge fanfare of her being named Wart Cream Queen. That, and the fact that an uncle had just announced he was to marry a direct blood niece, which was, as Jerome would later put it, "Disgusting."

Eloise gently squeezed Johanna's elbow. "Is this for real?"

"Yes! Isn't it wonderful, fantastic, tremendous, phenomenal?" She patted the wart cream crown. "I'm a queen now!"

✵ 84 ✵

DOWNER DOWN

"That's disgusting," said Jerome.

"You're putting it mildly," said Hector. "It must break seven kinds of Protocol. Also, it's most definitely disgusting."

Eloise paced the small room, unable to get that moment out of her head—the way Johanna had patted the crown. Her twin seemed oblivious to the implications, both political and personal, of being named Doncaster's betrothed. "How can she allow this? What would possess her to agree? Do you think she even knows what she's doing?"

Lorch put down his cup. "In a word, no. I don't think she does."

"What are we going to do? We have to do something!" More pacing.

Doncaster had not extended the castle's hospitality to Eloise, so after a full and what would have been enjoyable night (had it not been for the shock announcement) of speeches, music (including a version of That Song, recast so it was about wart cream and not groats), and dancing (Búüùttons was surprisingly light on his feet), Eloise bid her "new best friend" good night, and tried to wave to Johanna, who did not see her from across the room. Then she, Lorch, and Jerome had made their way back to the Rusted and Runcible. They ordered a late round of haggleberry tea, which Eloise hoped might settle her, and filled Hector and the Nameless One in on the night's developments.

"So it is as we suspected all along," said Hector. "Prattleweed."

"Yes," said Lorch. He sipped his tea with relish. Having listened to Jerome bang on and on about haggleberry tea for weeks, it turned out Lorch had paid attention, refining his discernment and palate. The cup brewed by the Rusted and Runcible was particularly to his taste, and even Jerome found little to complain about. If Eloise wasn't careful, the two of them would trade phrases like "fruity, sanguine aftertaste," "insolent nuttiness," "audacious insouciance," "tasting the terroir," and "bracingly impertinent."

Eloise stopped pacing long enough to sip her tea, and decided that "insolent nuttiness" actually would be an apt description, but that saying so would hopelessly derail the conversation. "What are the implications, then? If Johanna is heavily prattled, what does that mean for bringing her home?"

"Wouldn't she be pliable?" asked Hector. "Wouldn't she simply accede to a request that she come with us?"

Lorch shook his head. "It is more complicated than that. She still has a strong free will, so won't act in a way that she sees as being against her self-interest. Plus, if one makes suggestions that are too contrary to the ones she is operating under, they'll cause distress and resistance, not compliance."

"You seem to know a lot about this," said Jerome.

Lorch went quiet, filling the space by sipping his tea.

"Lorch? Are you OK?" asked Eloise.

The guard once again put on his I'd-rather-not-say expression and sipped more tea. Then he made a decision and put the cup back on its saucer. "Princess Eloise, I must reveal to you my shame."

"Your shame?"

"Well, not my shame. But the shame of my family." He stood. "If you might sit, Princess?" He paced the same track she had, hands clenched behind his back. "I come from a family of prattlers. Serious, heavy duty, completely committed prattleweed users. Some were religious. Some were not. But, except for me and my uncles and aunts who have served at Court, prattleweed was like salt—it went into everything. It made them all useless. I'm sorry to say it so harshly, but it's the truth. I have seen firsthand what extensive, long-term prattleweed use can do to the mind and the body. It corrodes both."

"I'm sorry," said Eloise. "I had no idea your family was troubled this way."

"Those of us who broke free of our history have been honored to serve the queendom and tend not to speak of our family's woes. But there are many of my blood at Lower Glenth who waste away over decades." He paused a moment and made it clear he spoke to all of them. "I do not tell you this for pity. I tell you this to explain why you need to trust me on deciding how we deal with Princess Johanna. Physically and emotionally, it's unlikely she's in permanent danger. Yet. But decisions are being made that will affect her future, and she is not making them from a position of clarity. That is the real risk she faces."

Lorch stopped pacing, reached inside his tunic, and extracted a hemp pouch. From this bag, he withdrew a folded parchment, like one might get at an apothecary. Slowly, he opened the parchment to show a matted bundle of white fibers.

"What is it?" asked Eloise.

"It's the fluffy seed head of the sober flower, but with the seeds removed."

"I've not heard of that plant," said Eloise.

"I'm not surprised, Princess. It is rare in the Western Lands and All That Really Matters. Cropping has changed the places where it once thrived, so it no longer grows there. Have you ever seen prattleweed in the wild?"

"No, I haven't."

"Again, I'm not surprised. These days, the plant is deliberately grown on farms and crofters' plots." A small breeze wafted in from a crack in the window and tickled the white fibers into movement. Lorch quickly, but carefully, cupped the parchment in his large hands so he did not lose any. "If you ever find a wild patch of prattleweed, you will find the sober flower growing nearby. The plants are, in the wild at least, like an old married couple—always companionably together. The sober flower blooms a tight little blossom made up of bright blue florets. If these are allowed to continue growing, they turn into a fluffy, branched seed head, similar to what you see with dandelions. If you gather the seed heads, then separate the fluff from the seeds, you get this." He hefted the parchment. "The prattlers call it 'downer down.' It has a very effective sobering influence. These days, it is rare, it is expensive, and it is very difficult to prepare properly."

"May I see it again?" asked Eloise. She and the others moved closer, careful not to jostle Lorch or disturb the fluff. "Where did you get it?"

"From Madame Righteous. Did you notice how none of her shop assistants at Something Sacred This Way Comes were prattled?"

"Only now you mention it. They all seemed most capable and clear-headed."

"I suspected she requires them to not just abstain, but to use downer down to render any accidental exposure to prattleweed harmless. Since we suspected prattleweed, I diverted some of our resources to purchasing this, just in case."

"I see." Eloise leaned down to look more closely. "How is this used?"

"Do you remember how Commodore Stúüübing was never seen without a chaw of something in his cheek? It is administered that way. A wad of it is placed between cheek and gum and allowed to reside there. It takes a few minutes for the downer down to have effect, so it normally requires the person to cooperate. Sometimes that is the hardest hurdle. Plus, there is the taste."

"What does it taste like?" asked Jerome.

"If you or I had any, it would be like chewing a slightly fruity cinnamon stick. But there's some interaction with the prattleweed, and to a prattler, it tastes like a soldier's week-old socks dipped in jalapeño juice. It is like the prattleweed tries to protect itself from the downer down."

"Do the prattlers ever leave it in there so it can have an effect?" asked Eloise.

"The strength of the flavor increases the longer it is in the cheek. They have to tolerate it long enough for clarity to hit."

Lorch folded the parchment again, put it back in the hemp bag, and handed it to Eloise. "My suggestion is simple, but not necessarily easy. You, Princess, have to get Princess Johanna on her own, get her to put that in her mouth and keep it there for the five minutes it will take for her to regain her senses."

"No problem," said Eloise. "Johanna has always loved jalapeño-dipped soldier sock."

❧ 85 ❧

AUDIENCE

Eloise said a cheery "Blessings of the day" to Möööëëë, Cüüürly, and Lääärry as she breezed through the castle gates to get to her audience with Doncaster and Johanna on time. Unlike the previous night, she and Jerome rode Hector, and Lorch came on the Nameless One. Eloise wasn't sure exactly what to expect when she arrived—certainly not the formal fanfare that Doncaster received at Castle de Brague—but there ought to be something, so she wanted to look as impressive as possible.

Except there wasn't anything. Nothing at all. Not a welcoming party, not a secretary with a scroll and a formal hello, not a page to lead them where they needed to go.

"Rude," said Jerome.

"Yes," agreed Eloise. "If nothing else, it is a clear message about how important this is to him."

"We'll stand over there and wait," said Hector, indicating a sunny spot to the side.

Eloise hopped off him and knocked on the front door. Nothing.

"He did say four weeks from now, originally," said Jerome. "Perhaps that's what stuck in his head." He swished his tail, annoyed.

Lorch opened the door for her, and Eloise peeked inside. Still nothing. "Hello? Anyone there?"

A kelpie in a doorman's jacket lounged on a stool, whittling a piece of wood with his teeth. "Yes?"

"We're here to see the king?"

The kelpie glanced at a piece of hemp parchment on a table next to him, using the wood as a pointer. "Nope, still can't read. You'll have to wait until His Jesterness gets here."

"His Jesterness," said Eloise.

"His Jesterness Mr Turpentine Snotearrow McCcoonnch."

"I'm familiar. Why him?"

The dog sniffed. "Dunno. He'll be along for you."

So they waited.

And waited some more.

Finally, there came the sound of padded soles and a faint discordant jingle of sewn-on bells. "You're late," said a voice like irritable, broken glass. Turpy strode toward them, scowling. Jerome reflexively backed away. The jester wore the same harlequin of black and gray he had in Brague, and had his jester's scepter stuck in his belt and the black fool's hat of his office tucked under an arm. His head looked freshly shaved, but the baldness emphasized the unpleasant angles of his skull. "You were expected two hours ago."

"What?" said Eloise. "The king said ten o'clock, then changed it to eleven o'clock. We're early."

"He was waiting for you at nine o'clock."

"No one told me that."

"That is not the king's problem. Follow."

Eloise, Jerome, and Lorch fell in line behind Turpy, who walked like he was late to a funeral, taking rapid steps that forced Eloise to up her pace to an undignified jog. They finally reached a windowless, chairless waiting room lit by a pair of candles, and Turpy said, "Wait here. I'll let the king know you've finally deigned to arrive."

"That's not—" started Eloise, but Turpy left them without another word.

With no seats, she and the others were forced to wait standing.

"You're being set up to fail," said Jerome.

"And who's ever heard of a jester acting as personal secretary?" added Lorch. "Princess, we must tread carefully."

The wait was interminable and uncomfortable, standing in the cold, stuffy room.

Eventually, Turpy fetched Eloise, but insisted the others not come. He led her not to a throne room or formal receiving room, but to a room near the kitchen where Doncaster and Johanna were being served morning tea by Gouache. The hulking jester held out a jam pot for Johanna, who spooned a generous blob onto her plate, then gave back the spoon with a smile and a thank you. Johanna still wore the wart cream crown from the night before.

Doncaster glanced up at Eloise and frowned like someone put pepper in his orange juice. "You again. What do you want?"

Nettled, Eloise swallowed half a dozen sharp retorts and said, "King Doncaster, you were going to receive me."

"That was hours ago." Doncaster shoved a scone into his mouth. "I was told to be ready at nine, and I was. You couldn't be bothered to show up. Now you interrupt me here in the Scone Room. So, like I said, what do you want?"

Whatever Eloise had thought might happen, this was not it. She stumbled into the words she'd prepared. "King Doncaster Worsted Halva de Chёёёkflïïïnt, I bring you greetings from my mother, Queen Eloise

Hydra Gumball II, and from your brother, King Chafed Motley Gumball née de Chëëëkfliïïnt."

"Do they know you are here? You're not just bumbling, stumbling, parading around the countryside, and happened to bumble, stumble, parade your way to Stained Rock?"

Eloise wasn't sure how to respond to that. The truth was, they *had* been bumbling around the countryside, and likely he very well knew it. She ignored the comment. "May I compliment you on the success of the Wart Cream Extravaganza-o-rama®."

"Is there a point to this?" He slathered jam on another scone. "Can't you see I'm busy?"

Time for a direct approach. "King Doncaster Worsted Halva de Chëëëkfliïïnt and Princess Johanna Umgotteswillen Gumball, may I be the first of our family to congratulate you on your betrothal."

Doncaster raised a jammed scone in silent acknowledgement, and Johanna said, "Thanks, El. Can you tell mom and dad?"

"Uh, sure. You're not sending out a formal announcement?"

"We didn't think we'd bother, hassle, put up with all that," said Johanna. "People will find out when they find out, right Uncle D?"

Turpy whispered in his ear. Doncaster nodded. "Yes, we'll be married too soon for all that. So, yes, we're skipping the formal nonsense, hooey, silliness."

"When will you marry?" asked Eloise.

Turpy again provided Doncaster the answer. "Tomorrow, apparently," said the king. "The prelate is coming later today to set it all up. Sorry you won't be able to join us. Small, tiny, eensy ceremony and all that."

Eloise was aghast. "Oh, Johanna. That's wonderful! I'm so happy for you. It doesn't matter at all that by getting married before me, you're defying Protocol in countless ways. I'm thrilled for your happiness." How could she stop this?

Johanna swallowed her bite of scone. "Thanks, El. Turpy has explained, discussed, clarified everything. Protocol has been cleared with the king. We're good on that account."

"That's excellent!" said Eloise. "And I'm so looking forward to being your maid of honor."

"Oh, El. That's so sweet of you. But I had no idea you were coming to visit, to call upon, to see me. I've already asked someone else."

"Really?" Eloise feigned a hurt pout. "Who?"

She pointed at Turpy's brother. "Gouache. He's kindly agreed to be my maid of honor." Gouache blushed, but was clearly thrilled at his role in the wedding ceremony.

This wasn't weird. Not at all.

At Turpy's cue, Doncaster said, "So, if there's nothing else..."

Eloise would not be shown the door. Not yet. "Where will the ceremony be held?"

"In the garden I'm renovating, fixing up, redoing."

"Since I won't be there for the wedding, I'd love to see it," said Eloise. "Can you show me, Jo?"

Prattled or not, Johanna was proud of her gardening, and the inclination to chatter that the prattleweed engendered had her leaping up from her chair. "Come on, El." She grabbed Eloise by the hand like they were six years old and dragged her into the hallway and out a side door. Behind them, Eloise heard Turpy and Gouache thumping to follow them out of the Scone Room.

✺ 86 ✺

TRYING ON A DRESS

J ohanna and Eloise threaded through half-hearted gardens (Doncaster really did need help from someone like Johanna) until they reached an enclosed courtyard. Johanna opened a wrought-iron gate with a "Ta da!"

As soon as she stepped into it, Eloise had a sense of Johanna like never before. Her sister could only have been working in there a few weeks, but the difference compared to the rest of the grounds was stark. There was a vibrance to the plant life that was missing elsewhere. If this was what she could do in such a short time, Eloise wondered what Johanna's garden at home must be like.

"Jo, I need to talk to you," whispered Eloise. She could hear the jesters' footsteps close behind. "Is there somewhere private?"

"Hello, my darlings," said Johanna, ignoring Eloise. "Hello my garlic, my goldbeet, my petunias, and my sweet alyssum. How is everyone today?"

Johanna, prattled, was lost in the La La Realms of her garden and its plants. "El, do you have a favorite flower, bloom, blossom?"

"Daisies. Jo, really, I need to talk to you."

"Daisies? Really? I had no idea, didn't know, was clueless. Why daisies?"

"I don't know, Jo. They're simple. Unpretentious. I've got to talk to you about..."

Turpy came up behind them, followed by Gouache. "Princess, we have a lot to do today. The prelate will be here shortly. There really isn't time for this. Perhaps you can show Princess Eloise your garden next time she visits you."

"Lovely garden, Johanna. Really lovely. You were going to show me your wedding dress next."

"I was?"

"Sure. You just said you couldn't wait to show it to me."

"I did?"

Turpy scowled. "The dress isn't finished yet. You can't show her something that doesn't exist."

"Actually, it was finished just as the king and princess went into the Scone Room." Gouache, proudly acting as maid of honor, was pleased to contribute to the conversation. "It was put in her room."

"No one asked you," snarled Turpy.

"There you go," said Eloise, taking Johanna's hand again. "To your room, then." She led Johanna back through the wrought-iron gate, which she tried to close on the jesters, but there was no lock, so it merely clanged. The two jesters followed them out of the courtyard. Johanna took Eloise up a flight of stairs and down a long hall. The whole while, Eloise tried to work out how she might convince Johanna to put the downer down in her mouth and leave it there despite the taste. She'd reason with her sister, using logic and persuasion to convince her to cooperate. Or maybe she could somehow use Johanna's prattled state to trick her. But if the stuff tasted as vile as Lorch suggested, she'd have to come up with something persuasive.

They reached Johanna's room, where Turpy blocked the door. He must have used a short-cut.

"Pardon us," said Eloise, trying to go past.

"No."

"No?"

"No."

"The princess would like to show me her dress. Please allow us to pass."

"I said no."

"We're just going to try on her wedding dress." Eloise tried to open the door handle, but he barred the way. "What is the matter with you?"

Johanna jigged up and down a little, tugging Eloise's sleeve. "I wanna see my wedding dress, my bridal outfit, my nuptial coverings."

Turpy stood, flat-eyed and unperturbed. "I will not leave you alone with her."

"Well, come on in and join in our girl time," said Eloise.

"I shall."

"Oh, Turpy, that's funny, witty, amusing," said Johanna.

"I'm a jester," said Turpy. "I'm supposed to be funny." He looked Eloise directly in the eyes. "You will not be alone with her." Cold menace flavored every word.

"It's fine with me if you come in," said Eloise. "Presumably that means it's normal in the court of King Doncaster for his jester to watch the king's affianced undress and dress. Or are you thinking Princess Johanna will slip her wedding dress over what she's wearing to try it on? One way or the other, Princess Johanna will show me her wedding dress, especially since I won't be by her side for her wedding."

Turpy said nothing for several long seconds, thinking it through. Finally, he opened the door and stepped aside so the twins could go through. "I'll be out here waiting. You have 15 minutes, then I'm coming in."

"We'll need 25."

"Fine. But I'm here, and I'm listening."

Johanna drew Eloise into her room. Her things were everywhere. It was like her travel cases had experienced a spectacular and forceful stomach ague, and Johanna was waiting for Nesther, her handmaid, to tidy up. Which perhaps she was. The duck's skills were definitely needed.

"There it is!" Johanna stepped through the antechamber to the inner room, where a boofy, multi-petticoated, snow-white, layer-cakey dress lay on the bed. Eloise followed, closing the door to the inner room behind her. Johanna picked up the tooth-rottingly ornate dress and held it to her front. "It's beautiful! Gorgeous! Wonderful!" she squealed.

Suddenly, Eloise knew exactly what she needed to do. Time was ticking. There was no way she would talk Johanna into anything involving the downer down. There'd be no convincing or cooperation. There was no time for rational explaining in the 22 ½ minutes she had left.

Eloise did what she'd seen hockey sacking defensive girders do on the fields at home. She ran at Johanna from behind, threw her arms around her, and tackled her. They slammed onto the bed. Eloise immediately muffled her sister's mouth with a hand to stop her screaming, wrapped her legs around her to immobilize her, and searched for the parchment of downer down in her pocket. "Oh, it's beautiful!" exclaimed Eloise for Turpy's benefit. "Just exquisite. Let me see it on you."

Johanna was stunned for a moment or two, then squirmed and bucked, trying to loosen Eloise's grip. She was strong, and even slightly bigger, but Eloise was stronger, having muscled up over weeks of riding Hector, and following her routines of running and hammer throwing at home.

Eloise extracted a wad of the white fluff, balled it between her index finger and thumb, and tried to shove it into Johanna's mouth. Johanna's muffled screaming was likely audible to Turpy, so Eloise kept up her patter. "Here, let me help you with those buttons. Have you lost weight? You look fantastic."

Johanna, still struggling with all her might, clamped her teeth together against the downer down. This proved a mistake, since it meant Eloise could simply push the ball of fluff across Johanna's clenched teeth and into her cheek. Now it was a matter of keeping it there. "Wow, look at the quality of this stitching. Here, raise your arms and I'll slide it on. I wish Mother could see you. She'd be so happy."

Was that Gouache humming "Three Bags of Groats For My Sweetheart?" Eloise wanted to laugh at the incongruity, but figured any humming out there meant less noise could be heard from in here.

Johanna tried every move she could to shake off Eloise, including standing up and trying to run backward into the wall, which would have worked if she hadn't tripped over a pile of dresses she'd left lying around. The two girls ended up on the floor, Johanna fighting with everything she had, and Eloise doing what she could to hold on and not hurt her. The downer down must have heated up and started tasting of soldier sock, because Eloise saw Johanna's eyes widen in the floor-length mirror, and she shook her head in a renewed attempt to escape the grip over her mouth. Johanna bit Eloise's palm, and Eloise surprised her by letting go completely, grabbing a nearby nightdress, and clamping it down on her sister's mouth. She could bite all she wanted now. "Çalaht wearing woven weeds, Jo, that looks amazing! Turn around and let me see the cut of the back. Would you call that blouson or empire? Whatever you'd call it, it highlights your waistline beautifully." Meanwhile, Johanna tried to land elbow blows into Eloise's ribs, but couldn't get enough force to dislodge her.

Lorch said it would take a few minutes, but it seemed like hours. Hours of wrestling, scuffling, and keeping her from alerting Turpy.

Finally, Johanna went limp, like she'd blacked out or, Çalaht forbid, died. "Let me adjust that ribbon," said Eloise. "Now, let's see how it looks with your veil. No, no, no. Let me put it on you. I insist." Then she whispered to Johanna, "Jo, you there?" She nodded as much as she could in Eloise's grip. "If I let you go, will you scream?" Johanna shook her head. "Jo, I love you, and I'm so glad I found you. But you're in danger, and I have about four minutes to explain. Can you stay quiet while I do that?" Nod. "I'm going to let you go now." Nod.

Eloise loosened her grip and Johanna bolted away, rushing toward the door. Eloise panicked, and got ready to tackle her again, then realized Johanna wasn't going for the door. She was rushing for her chamber pot. Johanna spat out the downer down, then scraped out the remnants from her cheek with her fingers. She grabbed a pitcher of water and sluiced, spat, sluiced, spat until it was gone. "That. Was. Vile," she panted. "What was it?"

"What was that?" shouted Turpy through the door. "What's going on in there?"

How could Eloise convey as much as she needed to without the jester hearing every word? Without thinking about it, Eloise did something she hadn't done in three years—she used their private sign language. *Sorry. I really am. No time to explain that bit. How much do you know about what's going on?* she signed.

Johanna looked at Eloise like she didn't understand. Then she looked at her hands and clasped them together.

Turpy knocked on the door again. "I said, what's going on?"

"It's OK. I had an apple in here and took a bite. But it was off. That's all," called Johanna. Then, to Eloise's relief, she signed back. *What? What do you mean?*

Do you know you're at the castle at Stained Rock?

Yeah. Sure. I'm working on the gardens.

Do you know you've been under the influence of prattleweed?

Sorry, what?

Eloise rushed through a version of her story that left out everything that could be left out, but still got her sister on the same scroll. Johanna's face veered from mortified, to fascinated, to confused, to horrified, and back to mortified. Finally, Eloise signed, *So, yes, Uncle Doncaster is trying to make you queen.*

That doesn't make sense. I'm already queen. Johanna pointed to the wart cream pot crown.

No, he means his queen *queen. Hence the dress.*

Oh. Johanna held still for a moment, then wiped her face like she needed to clear away the prattleweed muzziness. *I'd like to be queen. I've always wanted to be queen. It's nice that he wants me to help rule. Why wouldn't I do that?*

Jo, come on.

You want to be queen. Well, so do I.

Really?

Really.

You don't see an issue there?

Another silence, a long one that took up way too much of the time Eloise had left. The sisters ignored Turpy's pounding at the outer door.

Oh, signed Johanna. *Heirs.*

Right, signed Eloise.

To be queen, I'd have to marry him. Marry marry *him. With everything that goes with that.*

Eloise nodded.

Johanna's face sank into horror. *That would be too disgusting! How could I possibly do it? Not with him. I... I couldn't.* She shuddered. *Ugh.*

Turpy pounded on the door of the antechamber, inside her room now. "Time's up," he growled.

"She's just getting out of the wedding dress now. It really looks fantastic. We'll be with you in a minute."

What can I do? Queen on offer or not, I can't marry Uncle D. I can't! signed Johanna frantically.

I know, I know. Look, we'll figure something out. But listen, you have to pretend to be prattled. They can't know you're not. You have to be prattled, but you also have to have a stomach ague or nerves or something, because you can't eat anything. That's how they're giving you the prattleweed.

Right. Act prattled. No food. Got it. Johanna spat one last time in the chamber pot.

Eloise took Johanna's hands in hers. "You have no idea how good it is to see you." Then she let go and signed, *The danger is real. From Uncle Doncaster and...* She pointed at the door. *From him. So, again...*

Act prattled. Don't eat, finished Johanna.

THE BRIDE, THE MAID OF HONOR AND THE FLOWER GIRL

Eloise and Johanna emerged from the room and walked past Turpy and Gouache. The sisters paid them no mind, chatting about taffeta, flattering crinolines, and the proper length for the train of a bridal gown, agreeing that five lengths was not too long if you had a couple of flower girls trailing along carrying it behind you. Eloise could feel Turpy's eyes on her, but did her best to ignore it. Johanna did a fair imitation of a prattler's babbling.

The two brothers continued to shadow them.

"Let's go find Uncle D and tell him the good news," Johanna said for their benefit.

"Right. Let's." Eloise had no idea what Johanna was talking about.

They found the king in his counting house, counting coins, looking at ledgers, and muttering about debits and credits not adding up, summing, reckoning. Turpy and Gouache were ten paces behind them. Doncaster looked up and, seeing Eloise, said, "So, you're still here, present, accounted for?"

"Great news, Uncle D," bubbled Johanna. "Eloise has agreed to be my flower girl."

"I thought we already had a flower girl, a petal lass, a blossom female," said Doncaster.

"That's correct," said Turpy. "Mrs Güüündëëërsööön."

"Oh, please, Uncle D. Please let Eloise be a flower girl, too. She and Mrs Güüündëëërsööön can both be flower girls. They'd look fantastic together."

"We're deliberately keeping the wedding party small," said Turpy, barely containing his annoyance. "The catering will be wrong."

"The catering is a problem," said Doncaster, as though it was his idea.

"I don't need to eat anything," said Eloise. "I'll just strew around some petals, watch the two of you say 'I do,' and be off home. No big deal."

"That's right," agreed Johanna. "No biggie."

"We really don't need two flower girls," said Doncaster. "I thought we'd agreed on all this." He looked at Turpy. "Didn't we agree on all this?"

"Yes, Sire." Turpy walked to stand behind Doncaster. "We did."

Johanna pulled out the big guns—huge eyes and batting eyelids.

Doncaster shrugged. "Oh, OK. She can stay and throw, toss, fling flowers around. I don't really care. Now, could you please leave me alone? I need finish this before the prelate arrives and asks questions about contributions, payments, donations to his Çalahtist devotional house."

"Sure thing, Uncle D. We'll skedaddle. How about a walk, El? Have you seen much of Stained Rock? We have time for a quick stroll before everything gets all complicated this afternoon. I need some air."

"Princess Johanna, we shall accompany you," said Turpy. "I can make sure you return in time for the prelate's visit."

"Thanks, Turpy!" Johanna hooked Eloise's arm in her own and strode out of the room calling out a quick, prattle-like, "See you soon, Uncle D" over her shoulder.

Johanna headed them toward the castle's front, the jesters following a dozen steps behind. It had only been a few hours, but it seemed like forever since Lorch opened that door for Eloise. Thinking of Lorch and Jerome, she wondered if there was any way to swing by and get them, but things were moving too fast. It was more important to leave the castle. She'd have to find them later. Somehow.

Johanna kept up a stream of chatter. She talked about plants and her thoughts on the castle's gardens, how she couldn't wait to be a real queen, and how maybe Eloise could come and visit her once or twice a year. Wouldn't that be fun? Someday they'd both be queens, although she didn't want anything to happen to their mother, so maybe she shouldn't wish for that to happen too soon.

They reached the castle gate. "Hi again, Möööëë, Lääärry, Cüüürly," said Eloise to the guards. "We're just going for a quick walk. Back before you know it."

"Nice day for it," said Möööëë. "Not too cold yet. Not like it will be in a few weeks."

"Exactly," said Johanna.

They crossed through the gates and into the streets of Stained Rock. "We need a private place so we can talk," whispered Johanna to Eloise. "Somewhere where we can keep an eye on those two, but where we can speak without being overheard."

"I have an idea. It's macabre, but it's close." Eloise turned Johanna toward Fogging Hill. She skipped to increase their speed, and Johanna did the same, pretending to laugh. The girls put a few more lengths between them and the jesters.

"Do we have to go up there?" asked Johanna. "It means going closer to the Purple Haze. I hate that thing."

"Everyone does. That's why there won't be people there. Unless there's a fogging going on, we'll have privacy."

"I guess," muttered Johanna. And then she stopped, turned to Eloise, and giggled for the jesters' benefit. "Race you!" Off the two of them went, running for the top of Fogging Hill.

Eloise got there first by several lengths. She stopped right where the fogger had stood, which gave her a clear view of Johanna coming up the last part of the hill, her dress hiked to her knees, and the two jesters standing at the bottom looking up at them. "Quick, Jo. Here."

Johanna stopped next to Eloise and bent over to catch her breath. "All that running you do has its place, I guess."

"We have to work out how to get you out of this. Here's what I think. We go back and act like everything is the same—you're marrying, it's happening tomorrow, you're totally prattled, and you're too nervous and excited to eat. So you don't."

"I can do that."

"Then tonight, Lorch, Jerome, and I will work out how to sneak you out of here."

"You have Lorch and Jerome here? Really?" said Johanna. "Where are they?"

"At the castle. We don't have time for that, Jo."

Johanna grabbed a stick and scratched in the dirt, drawing a mud map of the castle layout. "Here's the front door. My room is here. Here's the Scone Room. Here's the courtyard. Here's the counting house. You know those places. So, Uncle D's room is here. Kitchen. Throne Room. Ceremonial Hall. Maybe what we can do is slip out—"

She never finished her sentence. Johanna screamed as Gouache wrapped his massive arms around her and hauled her up so her feet dangled a length off the ground. Turpy clunked the back of Eloise's head with his jester's scepter. Eloise was dazed, but conscious, as Turpy grabbed her hair, dragged her upright, and pinned her to his chest holding his scepter across her throat. She tried to shake her head to clear it, but couldn't move. She kicked and clawed at his face, but he tightened the pressure on her neck, choking her. Eloise stopped struggling, knowing she couldn't afford to black out.

Johanna struggled, but she may as well not have bothered. Gouache was at least three times her size, and he ignored her flailing.

"Do it," said Turpy.

"I don't want to." said Gouache.

"Fog her," commanded Turpy.

Gouache's face dropped. "But if I fog her, I won't get to be maid of honor."

Eloise tried to yell, but Turpy added pressure to her neck. She grabbed his hand, trying to pull the scepter away.

"There won't be a wedding."

"No wedding?" Gouache's face crumpled in disappointment. "Why not?"

"Because, idiot, these two know what we're doing." Turpy pointed at Johanna. "That one isn't feeling the prattleweed anymore."

"How can you tell? She was still talking the whole time," said Gouache. He shifted Johanna so he held her by the waist with his left arm, and chewed a hangnail on his right thumb.

"That was all fakery," spat Turpy.

"Sounded real to me."

"There were no synonyms," yelled Turpy so he could be heard above Johanna's screams. "She stopped using synonyms when these two came out of her room."

"Synonyms?"

"Words that mean the same thing. She wasn't repeating herself. This one..." He choked Eloise a little more for emphasis. "She did something while they were trying on the dress."

"Oh."

"Now do it. Fog her. She's useless to us now she knows. I can't have her blabbing to the king."

"I guess." Gouache walked over to where the criminals had stood and shifted Johanna again, so he held her by the neck and waist of her dress. Two-handed, he swung her once, twice, like he was about to heave a sack of barley onto a dray. Then he stopped again and gently put Johanna's face into his tunic to muffle her screaming. "But she's nice to me, Turpy. I like her."

"I said fog her. Fog her now!"

"OK." Resigned, Gouache readied himself to swing Johanna again.

Panicked, Eloise grabbed Turpy's right thumb with both hands, pulling with all her might. Turpy grunted in pain, but held Eloise tighter, the scepter across her throat, forcing her to watch the fogging.

Gouache swung Johanna once.

He swung Johanna in another wind-up arc. A little higher, a little harder.

Eloise closed her eyes, focusing every weak weight of her strength on Turpy's thumb. She drew on all of her force and will, plus whatever weak magic she might have. She imagined his hand coming away from his scepter. In her mind, she saw herself throwing him by that thumb, throwing him like she was on the Flinging Field back home.

There was a sickening crack. The bones and tendons snapped, the thumb shattering in Eloise's fists, her weak magic for throwing responding to her intention. Turpy nearly fainted at the unexpected pain, and lost his grip.

Gouache swung Johanna a third time, still higher and harder. Her anguished cries were a background white noise of terror. Her legs kicked empty air.

The instant Eloise's feet touched the ground, she charged toward Johanna and the brute who was seconds away from fogging her. The distance was eight lengths at the most. Just eight long strides. Surely she could get there.

Gouache swung around in a full circle, not unlike a hammer thrower, using his entire weight to give Johanna's body as much momentum as he could.

As Eloise ran toward Gouache, she knew there was no way she could stop her sister's fogging. In the same moment, she knew there was no uncertainty in that fog, no matter what the foggers said in the patter of their rituals. "I commend your body and soul to the uncertainty of the fog" was a politeness, the perpetuation of a lie. The Purple Haze had felt like death to her from the first moment she'd seen it aboard the *Barco del Amor*. Back then, she hadn't been able to put that word on it, but she knew now that's exactly what the Purple Haze was—a curtain of death. That's why nothing ever came out. Johanna would be swallowed and killed by the fog, and there was nothing Eloise could do.

Grunting, Gouache finished the full turn, and released the girl at the top of his swing. Johanna Umgotteswillen Gumball, no-longer-prattled betrothed of King Doncaster Worsted Halva de Chëëëkfliïnt and future queen of the Half Kingdom, hurtled through the air toward the Purple Haze. At that instant, but a lifetime too late, Eloise slammed her full bodyweight into Johanna's executioner.

If Eloise had seen his face, she might have pitied the confusion that welled up in him—a confusion that didn't know what had hit him so unexpectedly, a confusion that sensed there was no way he could stop himself from overbalancing and falling, a confusion that continued as he and Eloise crashed down Fogging Hill in a crushing tangle of limbs, a confusion that didn't grasp he was being swallowed by the same fog that had just embraced Johanna. Eloise didn't see that look because her mind was filled with the horror that she was crashing toward her own death.

Gouache's expression had only one witness—his brother.

From above, Turpy watched as Johanna, then Eloise and Gouache, plunged forever into the fog. The silence of Fogging Hill was broken only by his cries. He screamed, partly from the pain of his mangled thumb, which now imitated one of Çalaht's (both elongated and dislocated). Mostly he screamed for his brother. His mind strained with the shock of sudden loss. As Turpentine Snotearrow McCcoonnch howled, something broke within.

Absent of a fully sound mind, Turpy walked back to the castle, shrieks and sobs marking his steps.

❦ 88 ❧

NO ONE SHOULD HAVE TO

Eloise slipped past the curtain of the Purple Haze, and the rest of the world ceased to exist.

The first thing she noticed inside the fog was the humming buzz. Eloise had sensed it before, but now it felt strong enough to rattle her teeth.

The second thing she noticed was that something was pressing her down, and whatever it was, it jerked in a palsied fit.

She pushed against the twitching mass and shoved it off.

It was Gouache.

It was Gouache dying.

The twitching was a grand mal seizure. Spittle flecked his mouth. His arms stretched and juddered in front of him, like they were reaching for a long-gone mother. His eyes darted left to right and back, his brain overloaded with the task of trying to keep him alive and failing. Even in the dim lavender-tinged luminescence of the fog, Eloise could see the paler hues stealing across his skin as death laid cold fingers on him.

She remembered being entangled with Gouache as they rolled down the hill. She remembered the crunch of landing against something hard. She must have blacked out after that, and awakened to find Gouache doing his death dance.

The third thing Eloise noticed was that she, herself, was not dead, nor did she seem to be dying. This took a few moments to sink in, because for a while, it competed with the fourth thing—the overwhelming presence of death all around her. The skeletal remains of centuries of foggings were piled everywhere. To her right, she could see what was left of the spaniel who'd been fogged just two days before. She identified him from the bound front feet and muzzle, the collar, the scroll, and the missing hind leg. But that was it. His flesh was stripped away.

Visibility in the fog was only a few lengths, but a little further away, Eloise could see what was left of Have You Seen Someone About That Rash Jim. Like the spaniel, he was just clothes, a scroll, and bone, his bound wrists held forward, reaching toward some unseen succor or terror. Eloise thought how, now that he was just a skeleton, rashes would not be such an issue, and then decided that kind of thinking might indicate she was in shock.

She stood, wondering why she was so calm about being around all of this. Normally her habits would have her running as fast and as far as she could from so much dust and decay. She put that down to shock as well.

Eloise looked back at Gouache, who was still spasming uncontrollably. No one should have to die this way. Not even her sister's killer.

Her sister!

Eloise scrambled, trying to see Johanna, but Gouache had got a high, long throw with her, and Eloise hadn't seen which way she went. A glance around revealed no sign of her. Gouache looked like his time was running out.

Without further thought, Eloise grabbed Gouache's arms and tried to pull him in the direction they'd come. Çalaht's pimply posterior, he was heavy! She moved him a little, but with the palsied fit, it was hard to hold onto him and haul him uphill at the same time.

She'd have to roll him.

Eloise got on the downhill side of Gouache and, using all her strength, shoved him from face up to face down. He was one body width closer to "out." She did it again, thinking that because he was stiff with the seizure, he was probably easier to move than if he'd been limp with unconsciousness. Or limp with death. Best not think about that. Flop. Flip. Flop. Face down, face up, face down, face up—rest, making sure he didn't slide back downhill, then back to the flipping. "Come on, you," she muttered at him as she turned him over again. "If you die before I get you out, I'm gonna report you to the Jesters' Guild for inappropriate use of humor. Although they'd probably see it as funny. But I won't." Talking like that was inane, but it was something to do while she shoved him toward what she hoped would be safety. It also distracted her from noticing how the dust of the fogged landscape stuck to her clothes, hands, and face, and painted Gouache's skin a similar gray to the color palette death was trying to use.

Exiting the fog was surprisingly sudden. With a final heave, the fog parted, and she rolled him into the sun, adding a last few flops to make sure he was a safe-ish distance away. The buzzing in her teeth stopped, receding back to the level of an argument between bees. A breeze tickled her cheek. She could hear a bird busking in the distance. As soon as he was out, Gouache's palsy lessened, then stopped. He remained unconscious, expression slack, but color returned to his face, and his eyes lost their manic oscillation.

The last thing Eloise wanted to do was go back into the fog. But Johanna was in there somewhere. Someone else could find Gouache and make sure he got whatever care he needed. Someone else could try to figure out how he got out of the Purple Haze. For now, she had to find her sister.

Eloise turned, and like the spaniel, like Have You Seen Someone About That Rash Jim, and (from the look of all the bones she'd seen), like thousands before her, she faced the uncertainty of the Purple Haze—although now it was less uncertain than before.

Eloise sprinted into the lavender fog, becoming the first person ever to go in there twice.

The mist swallowed her whole, and the rest of the world ceased to exist.

❧❧

The series continues with Eloise having gone back into the Purple Haze, and trying to find out if Johanna is alive. And what about Lorch, Jerome, Hector, and the Nameless One? ***Read The Star of Whatever to find out what happens next.***

❧❧

Want to read more about Eloise and Jerome? Six months before the start of *The Purple Haze*, they
played hooky from Court and headed out for a stolen adventure. It goes well. And then it really doesn't.
Claim your copy of The Wombanditos today to find out what happened!

❧❧

And if you're wondering just what exactly happened at their Thorning Ceremony that caused Eloise and Johanna to go from being as close as twins can be to as estranged, then you'll definitely want to check out the standalone novel, *The Thorning Ceremony*. I promise you, you'll never guess what caused the rift.

THANK YOU

Thank you for reading *The Purple Haze*. Reviews are crucial for helping other readers discover new books to enjoy. If you want to share your love for Eloise, Jerome, and all the gang, please leave a review. I'd really appreciate it.

Recommending my work to others is also a huge help. Feel free to give this book and the whole series a shout-out in your favourite book recommendation group to spread the word.

NEXT IN SERIES

AVAILABLE NOW

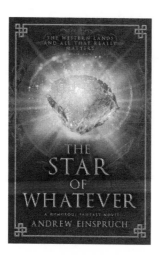

No one returns when they fall into the fog. Can she break its lethal haze and return to save her friend from death row?

If you like clever characters, subversive jokes, and spectacular exploits, then you'll love this vibrant step beyond the veil. Read *The Star of Whatever* today (and get it using the QR code below).

ACKNOWLEDGMENTS

It is a joy to get to say thank you to those who have helped me bring this book to the world.

Tamsin Dean Einspruch, our daughter, has from the word go been my first port of call for ideas, perspective, and thoughts on words. She is my first reader, and has been with this story every step of the way. She helped me talk through the story, and over and over helped me head the right direction. Thank you, sweetie.

Many, many thanks also to Cheryl Hannah, Janet Watson Kruse, and Olivia Martinez for their beta reads. Cheryl was the first person outside my family to read the manuscript, and her encouragement gave me the heart needed to keep going. Janet and Olivia both brought keen eyes to the words, and provided very different perspectives to what they read. Valuable and valued input all.

Thank you to my editor, Vanessa Lanaway, and my proofreader, Abigail Nathan. Sharp eyes and red pens, both. Y'all rock. It's that simple.

Thank you to Maria Spada for the fantastic cover.

A huge, massive thank you to my bride, Billie Dean, who reads and gives incredible input on everything I write, who has encouraged me forever, and who believed in my creative soul much, much earlier than I ever did. I love you and I thank you. L^3.

And finally, thank you to you, whoever you are, for picking up this book and having a read. I appreciate it very much, and I'll see you in The Star of Whatever.

ABOUT THE AUTHOR

Andrew Einspruch is fond of the wordy, the nerdy, and the funny, which means that if you arranged for him to have lunch with Weird Al Yankovic, Tom Lehrer, William Gibson, and any of the Monty Python guys, he'd be your friend forever. Visit his web site for a complete list of his books at andreweinspruch.com.

Andrew is an ex-pat Texan living in Australia, and is the co-founder of the not-for-profit charity the Deep Peace Trust, which fosters deep peace and non-violence for all species. With his wife and daughter, he runs the Trust's farm animal and wild horse sanctuary. (You can see why there's the odd animal or two in his books.)

If pressed, he'll deny he ever coded in COBOL for a bank.

If you haven't done so yet, use the QR code below to claim your copy of the standalone prequel, *The Wombanditos.*

Made in the USA
Monee, IL
15 April 2023

31929625R10284